THE BATTLE FOR THE HALO

The Battle for the Halo
Copyright © 2017 Shea Swain

Warning: The Battle for the Halo is for 18 years and older.

ISBN-13: 978-1976215421
ISBN-10:1976215420

Cover Designed: Sanja Balan of Sanja's Covers
Edited: Pam Howard
Proofreader: D. Swain
Format: Shea Swain

Other Books Written By:

Shea Swain

The Pulse of Provocative Romance

What Lilly Wants
previously known as Lascivious
An Erotic Novella

INVIDIOUS Betrayal
A Full-Length Paranormal-Sci Romance

ABSOLVE
A Short Romantic New Adult Drama

The Changing of the Seasons
Winter's Icy Heart
A Taste of Spring
Contemporary Romance

Chained to the Devil's Son
A Full-Length Dark Romance

The Binding of the Halo Series
Four Full-Length Paranormal Romance Series
The Binding of the Halo Book I
The Awakening of the Halo Book II
The Descent of the Halo III
The Battle for the Halo IIII
&
The Coesen-Origins

Heaven on Hell Island
A Contemporary Romance with Sci-fi undertones

Dedicated to my inspirations…
Sonserae
Daniel III
Cianne
Daniel IV

Prologue

The attractive anchorwoman did mouth exercises as she silently counted down from ten with the new guy who did the countdown to live. She beamed for the camera a second later when they both reached, one.

"Good morning viewers. This is your host, Stacy Crain," Stacy said from the plush cream sofa located on the newly remodeled interview stage. She looked to her co-host and smiled.

"I'm Russell Dumas."

"And this is Coesen News Today," they said in unison.

Russell brandished a dazzling white smile. It was stunning against his dark skin tone. "Today, we are diverting from our standard show because it's a very exciting time for us all."

"You are so right, Russ," Stacy confirmed then inhaled deeply. She fanned herself with one hand, placed the other over her breasts, and dramatically batted her eyelashes. "Grab a pen and a calendar people, and prepare to Save the Date."

Russell chuckled at his co-host's excitement. "Sovereign Cianne Bertram and Royal Whodai Tam have chosen a date for their mating ceremony."

"I'm so excited, Russ. It seemed only yesterday that rumors of Royal Whodai's involvement in a secret Tandot when he was just a boy were leaked to the public. For years, he managed to avoid questions from the press about the mystery bride whose hand he won."

Russell nodded in agreement.

"I, for one, am glad he will have his happily ever after," Stacy continued, but her smile suddenly transformed into a straight lipped grimace of concern. "All of our viewers are aware of the rollercoaster that our succeeding Sovereign has been through this past year, but let us recap.

"Whispers of the existence of our Halo has always circulated throughout our history," Russ picked up, "but CNT brought you an exclusive broadcast. We were told by our beloved departed Sovereign, Vivian Harper, that the Halo did indeed exist."

Both news anchors turned their heads to face the monitor as video footage from that recorded show, featuring Sovereign Vivian speaking to both anchors, replaced the station's logo on the wall of screens.

Vivian's hair was loosely curled and fell over her shoulders. The station's stylist decided it would give her an approachable look, something her tightly pulled back ponytail bun didn't accomplish. She was dressed in a delicate designer pale mint top, a gray jacket, and slacks to maintain a sense of professionalism. In the video, Vivian spoke of the reasons her grandchild was hidden from the Coesen people.

When the clip was done, the screen switched seamlessly back to the logo.

"I remember that day like it was yesterday, Stacy." Russell stared at the camera. "We received tons of responses after that broadcast, a good amount proclaiming the Halo's uncovering to be a hoax or propaganda, but in the following months the unbelievers were transformed into believers."

"Yes, they were, Russell. Soahn Harper provided not only photos of Cianne Baxter, but to everyone's surprise, she granted access to the beautiful princess in an unprecedented display of total disclosure."

7

Stacy's expression grew morose. "We rejoiced when Soahn Baxter married her high school sweetheart and the father of our very first set of Royal twins, Tristan Bertram."

"We mourned with her when we lost our esteemed Sovereign Harper," Russell said, then held his chin up then sighed, "and again after the tragic accident that claimed the life of our White Lion, Tristan."

Stacy shook her head. Then she offered her audience her most sincere look. "Like our new Sovereign, we must hold our heads up high and look to the bright days ahead."

"And it doesn't hurt to do so while looking a million bucks either. I will say it here, Sovereign Bertram is one of the most beautiful, yet gracious women I've ever had the pleasure of meeting."

"She truly is, Russ," Stacy said in agreement with a nod. She took a deep breath of reflection then said, "Well, let us make this union one of cheer."

Chapter One

Norway
The Present, May 6th
Missing over 11 months

Cipher launched from one rooftop to another, undeterred by the snow and ice that covered them and landed solidly on the balls of his feet. He gracefully slid just a few inches, and while still in motion he crouched down, pushed a button on the device in his ear, and pushed the hood of his white camouflage suit off his head.

"Should I engage?" Cipher asked in a low whisper.

"Are you sure he's still there?" Caleb questioned.

It was up to Cipher to find Tristan Bertram, the White Lion and rightful mate to the Halo. He could find anyone anywhere. Being a half-breed or Breed, it was expected that if he had any abilities at all, they would be greatly muted. Cipher's abilities were substantial in every way. He wielded a multitude of heightened senses and other gifts that overshadowed some of the strongest full-blooded Coesen.

Well, all but three. He suspected he wouldn't hold a candle to the Halo. Plus, Caleb Scott, who wasn't a Coesen, was a bit of an enigma. One minute, Cipher felt they were evenly matched, but then Caleb did something well beyond Cipher's capabilities.

He wondered if Caleb liked to keep him guessing.

Cipher also found it difficult to track Soahn Tristan Bertram. Every time he had a bead on him, the man disappeared before he was able to make contact. Cipher wasn't sure how Tristan kept one step ahead of him but he welcomed the challenge.

"I am certain." Cipher stealthily reached for the edge of the roof then pushed off with his feet, dangled, then dropped to the snow-covered ground four stories down with a soft crunch. He listened while Caleb spoke to someone on his end.

"We don't know how he's been able to detect you yet. It would probably be best if you put some distance between you and him or you'll be hunting him down again," Caleb instructed.

Yeah, I should steer clear, Cipher thought.

"Besides, the last time you encountered each other, you were trying to gut him with a blade," Caleb said.

Cipher thought back to when he first laid eyes on Tristan Bertram at Caleb's cabin. With no knowledge of Tristan's identity, Cipher's main objective was to keep Caleb safe. That day he felt Tristan was a threat to his objective and he reacted. To his surprise, Tristan not only dodged his attack but responded in turn, by throwing one of Cipher's knives back at him. It took all of Cipher's skill to avoid his own blade.

That happened months ago and now he was in this winter wonderland tracking his King.

"I have someone else in mind but I need you ready if he runs again," Caleb said, then disconnected.

I'll be ready.

Later that night

Zeta peered at the nondescript building. The only reasons she knew it was a pub was the sign above the door and the roar from the patrons that echoed into the white haze outside where she stood.

The Ice Cave, per the ice-covered sign, was a basic one-story structure at the edge of what the residents referred to as a town. Several other buildings littered the landscape but were just as basic. Most looked as if they doubled as businesses and homes.

Conversation in the native language stalled as Zeta pushed opened the heavy door. The patrons ogled her as she stood in the doorway and scanned her surroundings. It could be because of the lightweight wool coat and pink pom-pom hat she wore. Her attire wasn't the kind of gear the residents wore in this frigid climate but she wasn't like them.

Zeta scanned the curious faces, finding who she was searching for instantly. Of course, the man sat at the bar in the darkest corner, alone. She could tell by the way he ignored her entrance that this man wasn't like the locals either.

After closing the bone chilling cold out by shutting the door, Zeta stomped her snow-covered legs free of the caked-on white powder. The patrons, mostly men, seemed to settle back into their usual habits, dismissing her presence or purpose.

Zeta appreciated the privacy as she made her way to the large bar in the rear of the building. She settled near the loner, leaving only the space of a stool between them. The bartender, a husky man with large hands and thick curly hair, looked at her with a questioning glare.

"Anything that'll warm me up," she told him, speaking his language as a native would.

The bartender raised a brow as he gave her a good once over. He then frowned. Zeta recognized that look. She reached inside the breast of her coat and pulled out a thin wallet. She flipped it open as the Bartender leaned over the counter toward her. He peered at the well-crafted fake ID for a few seconds, looked at her again, then shrugged.

"Anything to eat?" he grunted.

Zeta shook her head. She watched the barkeep walk away then turned her attention to the sole reason she was in this place. As she regarded him, she realized he hadn't spoken a word or moved a muscle since her entrance.

It wasn't humanly possible to be that still.

As if on cue, the man coughed, shifted in his seat, then lifted his glass up to his thickly bearded face. She assumed he somehow managed to find his lips because she saw his throat moving.

Zeta offered him a silent greeting, a nod, but she couldn't tell if he saw her because of the dark glasses that framed his face. The beard and sunglasses covered so much of him that she still wasn't sure if this was Tristan.

The bearded man didn't acknowledge her greeting but he did silently drink the remainder of the dark liquid inside his mug. When he was done, he slowly pulled money from his pocket and placed it on the well-worn wooden bar.

Zeta watched him out the corners of her eyes. His hair was long, which made it difficult to see his face, and he wore loose fitting clothing that left everything to the imagination. Yet, she determined that he was the right height.

As the man lifted his jacket and swung it around his back, the bartender placed Zeta's drink in front of her. She nodded at the bartender then looked over at the bearded man. "I'm looking for a friend of mine who I think came through here," she said to him as he continued to wrap up. "I was wondering if you might know him."

The bearded man didn't so much as glance at her as he finished putting on his winter coverings.

"Jack don't do much talking." A man seated at a table behind her offered. He stood and made his way over to where she sat.

Jack, is it?

Zeta flicked the nosy stranger a glance. She noticed his appreciative glare when she initially walked inside the establishment. It was times like these that she wished she looked less pixie and more Amazonian.

The stranger, a sloppy-muscular man with a neater beard than her target and at least two feet taller than her, stepped up behind Jack. "Do ya, Jack?" He patted Jack's back hard enough to drive him forward. *It would take more than that to unbalance Tristan,* Zeta thought as she watched the bearded man, Jack, right himself. "Sam, you leave Jack be now. I don't want none of your shit tonight." The bartender's gaze fell on Zeta. "Leave the girl be too."

"Thanks," Zeta told the bartender, "but I don't think *Sam* is going to be any trouble tonight. Are you, Sam?" Zeta looked at him.

Sam flashed her a coy smile.

Jack moved around Sam without acknowledging her interest in him while Zeta's new husky admirer slid up between the stool she sat on and the one next to her. Her focus remained on Jack, and when she moved to get up a heavy hand pressed down on her shoulder. Zeta didn't hesitate or look at Sam when she grabbed hold of his hand and twisted it.

Sam shrieked as he tried to relieve the pain in his arm by turning in the direction of his twisted wrist. The move caused Zeta to apply more pressure, ultimately driving Sam to his knees. Every patron in the pub watched as he screamed out in agony. Every patron except Jack, because he was on his way toward the door.

Still watching Jack's back as he moved further away, Zeta raised her leg and placed her foot inches from Sam's nose. "Do we have a problem, Sam?" Zeta asked, peering at the door that Jack left through and slowly closed behind him.

The Bartender snickered when Sam only grimaced.

His failure to answer in a timely manner was a mistake. Zeta moved her foot so fast that no one in the bar saw what happened, but they did hear Sam screech. Sam's broken nose spouted blood that drizzled onto the old wooden floor.

Zeta turned her full attention to Sam. "Do we have a problem?"

"No problem," Sam panted out. When Zeta released his hand, Sam cursed as he fell against the side panel of the bar, rubbing his uninjured but sore arm.

Zeta moved as slow as she could manage to the door. She pulled on the door handle and stepped into the frigid night air.

Bearded Jack was gone.

She spun on her heels and pushed the bar door open and strolled back inside. Zeta walked up to the bar and placed a fifty-dollar bill next to the glass meant for her.

She turned to leave when the bartender cleared his throat. Zeta stopped and looked back over her shoulder, ignoring the patron's whispers about her.

"Your ID says you're from America," the bartender said in English. Zeta nodded. "I rarely get to practice my English. Anyway, uh…Jack, the fella who just left. That's not his name but it's what we call him cause he only drinks Jack Daniels," the bartender said, as he slid the bill off the bar and placed it in his pocket. "He hardly comes around here, and when he does it ain't for conversation. I sense he's a good fella, just had some bad luck." The bartender shrugged. "Guess we all had our share. He stays at Elmer's old cabin. If you head north toward the mountains, you'll eventually see it."

"Thank you."

The bartender looked down at Sam and chuckled. "No young lady, thank you." He laughed louder as she walked away.

The Next Afternoon
The cabin was exactly where the bartender said it would be. It didn't take long to locate it. After tapping the door a few times with no answer, she listened. Hearing nothing inside, she turned the knob. It was locked so she applied only a small amount of pressure to break in.

When she entered, Zeta noted the small dwelling was virtually empty of furnishings. A single bed sat against a windowless wall. A worn upholstered chair was in the center of the room with a small bookcase filled with books and magazines sitting next to it. The kitchen consisted of a small countertop with two cabinets, a wood burning stove, and a sink. An ancient icebox finished the decor. The bathroom door was ajar so she could see the empty tub and small toilet from the doorway.

There was no place for Bearded Jack to hide but she had to make sure that the cabin was empty because if he was Tristan, he was capable of hiding in plain sight and keeping quiet. After a fruitless search of the facilities, Zeta casually sifted through the few belongings this Jack owned but came up with nothing that would reveal his identity.

She tapped the device in her ear. "If it is him, he may have jumped already," Zeta reported.

"I'll be right there."

Zeta frowned as she repeated Caleb's response a few times in her head. *I am not waiting in this icy hell for him to charter a flight.* It would take days, days she could be hunting down Tristan.

"What? You want me to wait for you to get here or do you just want to get that tracker friend of yours to find him again?" When Caleb didn't respond, Zeta tapped her ear piece. "Hello. Caleb?"

Zeta cursed then walked over to the kitchen and opened the ice box.

Caleb saw Zeta standing by the stove as he listened to her speaking to him through the ear-com she wore. She didn't see or hear him. They never did if he didn't want them too. He was a ghost in every sense of the word—quiet, invisible, and without form as he drifted through the open doorway of the cabin without making a sound.

There were benefits to having a silent partner/parasitic entity inhabiting his body. Pythos was what Caleb called his tenant since they merged over a hundred and fifty years ago.

Soon after they bonded, Caleb was infused with a number of abilities that surpassed the power of the Coesen, a clandestine race of humans who also had abilities.

Kill her, then press her broken body against yours as her warmth fades, Pythos hissed.

Caleb ignored his parasite as he stared at the young Coesen called Zeta.

She is the enemy. Kill her.

A long-dormant flicker of hate glimmered inside Caleb. It wasn't a blaze or even a smolder but the fact that he felt Pythos' emotions unsettled him. *I don't have long*, he told himself as he made his invisible form solid and cleared his throat.

Zeta spun around, resembling a bumbling teen instead of the proficient killer she was. "What the heck?" she gasped.

"I said I'd be right here." Caleb busied himself with inspecting the empty cabin. He wasn't ready to let her in on the particulars of his abilities just yet.

Zeta stepped toward him, her mouth gaped open and her eyes wide. "How did you…?"

"Redeye," he quipped, as he lifted an empty fruit can. He placed the can back on the countertop then moved toward the door. "He's still here."

"I thought you said you couldn't sense him?"

He *should always* be able to sense the boy, especially with the new DNA cocktail injections Bannerman whipped up, which remaining stock Tristan stole months ago. It should be a matter of Caleb focusing on that part of *him* that flowed inside his son-in-law's body for a short time after each injection. Only, Caleb wasn't able to get a lock on Tristan often, and if he managed it didn't last long.

Tristan must have just injected himself with the serum.

"I have one, maybe two days of sensing him." Caleb walked out of the cabin into the blistering morning wearing only a long sleeve shirt and a pair of jeans. He slowly turned in every direction.

Zeta followed. "So where—"

Caleb held his hand up. Zeta narrowed her eyes at him but did stop talking.

"He's there," he told her as he pointed west.

Tristan stepped lightly over the newly fallen snow, leaving little evidence that he walked over it at all.

For the past few months, he lived like a hermit while drinking like a fish. Alcohol didn't have the effect on him it once had but it still numbed him enough. Though he needed to consume enough to put down an elephant.

Tristan hoisted his backpack over his shoulder as he continued to put distance between him and the small cabin he used for over seven weeks. The fact that it wasn't home, made leaving easy.

Hell, nothing would ever be home, he thought as the image of Cianne standing over a kneeling Whodai, flashed in his mind. The memory made him stop in his tracks.

Because he wasn't in motion, Tristan sank into the soft white snow. He took several deep breaths as he conjured thoughts of a time when he was happy, when she was happy with him.

Tristan sighed. It didn't take long for him to find those memories.

There was a time when he didn't have to try to be what Cianne needed him to be. The need to protect her, to love her, was instinctive from the very beginning. She was his life, his love, his calm. He offered her unconditional love, acceptance, and his strength. Yet, all he had now were his memories.

Remembering Cianne's beautiful eyes, the way they glowed with love for him, eased some of his heartache.

They're safer without me, he reminded himself.

Tristan bent at the knees then launched himself out of the small hole he sunk in and into the air. He moved forward in a fast-paced sprint on top of the snow. His steps were once again light, just grazing the top coat of the powdered flakes as harsh winds blew into him. Tristan kept his pace.

Do I want to be found, he asked himself?

Tristan first sensed a Coesen was near him last night while he sipped his alcohol. The irritating tingle, a warning that manifested just recently, cautioned him whenever a Coesen was near…but that ability didn't last long. It usually faded shortly after the injections and was just about spent now.

Last night he allowed his mind to play with the possibility that Cianne may have come for him. That feeling diminished the moment he felt the faint awareness that it was Zeta who walked into the pub. He didn't have to look up to know it was her. With her being in close proximity, Tristan recognized her unique scent and power that she emitted.

Because he didn't sense the tracker who shot at him months ago; and discounting Zeta's ability to keep up with him, Tristan allowed himself to relax last night and took his time, versus leaving right away. It was an error that he now regretted. He screwed up and it was evident when the swift movements nearby reached his ears.

He looked ahead and saw that somehow Zeta was in front of him.

Tristan slowed to a middling's pace, lifting his leg out of the high snow. If he moved any faster, Zeta will know it was him. He was certain she still wasn't sure.

He lowered his head and continued to walk along the snow-covered base of the mountain, knowing that he and Zeta will be face to face in a matter of minutes.

"Afternoon," Zeta said as she approached.

He noticed she wasn't dressed for the weather. Just like Zeta's, his body regulated his temperature according to his surroundings. He would be just as comfortable wearing a pair of swim trunks with no shirt right now, but only for several hours. Like any other living organism, hyperthermia will eventually set in. Being Coesen, or a hybrid like himself didn't mean he was indestructible.

Tristan didn't respond. But he did lift his gaze to take in Zeta's young beautiful face. Her eyes seemed more mature, her face more emotionless, and she seemed leaner than he remembered. But she was still the Zeta he loved like a sister and missed more than he wanted to admit.

Tristan wanted to pull her into his arms and hug her tight when she showed up at the pub last night. Yet, he played his role of a human hermit to the end.

"I'm not sure," Zeta whispered as they passed one another.

Not sure of what?

Tristan wanted to look back at her but didn't.

"What? You can't. What if it's not him?" The panic in Zeta's voice was unmistakable.

Tristan stopped in his tracks and turned around to face her but she wasn't looking at him. He followed her gaze to a large snow-covered mountain far to the right of him. He heard the snow shift before he saw the man at the top.

Not just any man. Caleb was perched at the very top of the mountain. Tristan watched as Caleb seemed to now float above the mountain.

Everything seemed to slow down around him. That was how it was for Tristan when his adrenaline kicked into overdrive. A hiss of warning sounded before the snow mound started to slide. The spray of snow that burst into the air was beautiful to witness.

That Caleb engineered an avalanche was unsettling. *An avalanche that is on a path that Zeta and I will soon be buried under if I don't act.*

Tristan assessed his options as large clumps of ice and powder barreled down the mountain toward them. A frozen lake was to his left and was not too far away. Only, he couldn't be sure if the icy lake was frozen hard enough to hold their weight. The water under the ice had to be cold enough to stop a man's heart.

He could continue his path across the base. Out-running the engineered destructive force would be hard but not impossible. He was fast, much faster than he was before, thanks to the monthly injections that held the poison in his body at bay.

Only, Zeta wouldn't be able to outrun it.

Tristan didn't notice that Zeta closed the space between them until she reached out her small hand and gripped his as she tilted her head up to look at him with sadness in her eyes. She most likely wanted to save *him*, the hermit Jack. In her eyes, Tristan also saw resignation. Zeta knew she couldn't outrun the avalanche, and even though she will most likely survive she knew she couldn't save *him*.

Caleb wants me to show myself, but why risk Zeta's safety?

Just as the thought formulated, the answer was clear. His father-in-law was one of the most no-nonsense beings on the planet, and to get what he wanted he had no problem throwing everyone in his path under a bus.

Not ready to let go of the façade just yet, Tristan turned back in the direction he was headed, pulling Zeta along with him. He sprinted across the base of the mountain at the speed a Middling would move, trying to beat the onslaught.

"We can't outrun it!" Zeta yelled. "We should head for the iced over water."

No, we won't make it at the rate we're running.

Zeta still seemed unsure of his identity because other than the way she was dressed, she didn't seem willing to reveal her own abilities. All the while, the promise of pain and possible death continued to tumble toward them, and it was moving fast.

"Shit!" Tristan cursed.

With no other choice, Tristan pivoted toward the shore. At the same time, he launched Zeta into the air, toward the lake. With the force and power he wielded, Zeta's little body propelled forward like a bullet. Her body arched in the air, resembling a pole vault jumper before she landed lightly on her feet then slid over the slick snow-covered water like an ice skater.

Tristan moved like the wind and was there by Zeta's side when she landed. He ignored the sounds of the ice cracking beneath them as he lifted her off her feet and cradled her in his arms as momentum pushed them along. He glided across the ice as small cracks webbed out around his feet.

"Water looks really cold," Zeta said, hugging his neck.

"Yeah," Tristan agreed. He looked to the shore but the avalanche was filling the closest areas of the shoreline with more snow and ice.

Tristan looked around as they slowed, trying to decide the best course of action as the ice continued to crack around them. When they stopped, he moved to a section of ice that seemed it would be a bigger break-away. The icy surface broke into pieces, leaving them on a small section.

"Caleb!" Zeta yelled out.

She sounded calm but the hitch in her voice told Tristan she was angry. He understood because their bodies' temperature regulation was about to be tested. Beneath them, the icy water crept over the slab of ice Tristan balanced them on.

Standing still would only cause them to sink quicker so Tristan decided on ice hopping. Just as he jumped to a larger slab of ice floating nearby, he felt a set of strong hands on his shoulders. He knew it was Caleb, but when he turned his head to look over his shoulder vivid colors flashed before his eyes. Then came the pain. It felt as if his body was being torn in two. He couldn't even cry out because all the air was ripped from his lungs.

Is this death?

The pain seemed to last forever but it eventually abated. Tristan felt queasy and had a raging headache but he *felt*. That meant death didn't claim him...yet.

Zeta? She wasn't in his arms.

Concerned for Zeta, Tristan opened his eyes but quickly closed them as dizziness, nausea, and the bright sun all seemed to punch him at the same time. He placed his hand on his head in an attempt to steady himself but instead of finding his center, he was even more confused. He had on gloves and a hat but he realized his hands and head were now bare as he covered his eyes with his arm.

With his eyes still closed, Tristan used his other hand to feel around the surface he rested on as he relied on his other senses. Unfortunately, his ears felt like they were stuffed with cotton so they were of no use. But his sense of touch was fine, and by the texture and scents around him, he deduced he was on grass.

Grass? He was on grass and all his gear was gone.

Tristan squinted his eyes partly open as he tried to sit up but he fell back. Lush green blurry grass was all he could make out.

After squinting for a few second more, he managed to open his eyes without feeling like he was in a spin cycle. Tristan pushed up on his elbows and took several deep breaths as he glared up at the blue sky.

What the hell did they give me?

His blurred vision prevented him from seeing clearly but his ears jolted to life. Thanks to Caleb's little upgrade, his ears were better than fine, so he listened to the sounds around him. The hum of far-off traffic, people, and nature were unmistakable but not useful.

Tristan tuned those annoyances out and focused on the closer sounds. The whisper of air rustling leaves on the trees and the ground was clear. The distinct beating of four relaxed hearts, one accelerated heart, and one almost dead calm heart was very close by. Each heartbeat was irregular enough for

Tristan to make out that at least four belonged to Coesen. One of those heartbeats must belong to Zeta.

…and what is that awful sound?

Tristan rolled to his knees then climbed to his feet. He wobbled then fell forward but extended his hands fast enough to keep from face planting in the grass. The ground was solid under his palms and that was what Tristan tried to engage as he closed his eyes and attempted to stand for the third time.

Once on his feet, Tristan opened his eyes again only to close and reopen them several times. He noted it was daylight as the faded images around him began to clear. He closed his eyes and shook his head again in an attempt to clear the last of the fogginess.

Am I dreaming?

Tristan looked around. A large white old-style mansion with navy blue shutters loomed in the near distance. It gave off an air of familiarity that confused him. Looking down, he found his bulky outerwear thrown about at his feet on the greenest green lawn he ever saw. He turned the other way and saw a small cottage designed and painted just like the main house a few hundred feet away. Lifting his head, he noted the position of the sun.

It looked to be morning, so that meant he was most likely on the east coast of the United States. The style of the mansion…renovated…suggested the South.

Where though?

A repeat of the horrible noises Tristan heard earlier pulled his attention away from the structure.

Two mysteries solved.

That God-awful noise was coming from Zeta. She was bent forward on her knees, hurling the contents of her stomach over a patch of the beautiful grass. Tristan's stomach lurched, but with a couple of deep breaths and few slow swallows, he was able to keep everything in. He moaned in relief as his body involuntarily shivered.

Dr. Bannerman stood over Zeta. He rubbed her back as he spoke encouraging words in a soothing tone. "He promises that you'll be fine in a few hours. Just try to relax a little," Bannerman told her.

Zeta nodded but continued to dry heave.

"How is he?"

That voice belonged to Langley. The lawyer sounded worried, an emotion Tristan didn't think him capable, but he looked calm. Tristan turned his attention to the other people who stood around. None of them noticed that he was on his feet yet.

Well...*one* of them noticed. He locked eyes with Caleb.

Son of a bitch.

"You asshole!" Zeta's outburst was directed at Caleb. "He, he, he brought us..." Zeta cried before her body jerked forward. She spewed the contents of her stomach again.

"He's fine," Caleb said calmly. He ignored Zeta as he stared at Tristan.

A second later a roar erupted from deep inside Tristan that caused everyone to focus on him. *They* didn't matter. Only getting his hands around Caleb's neck mattered. Tristan stalked forward, closing the distance between him and his target.

Caleb stood there looking as calm as ever.

Fury and revenge radiated off Tristan like waves of heat. It was no surprise that Langley and Perkins backed away from Caleb. But the one person Tristan didn't know stayed put. He stood beside Caleb with nothing resembling fear reflected in his body language.

As Tristan got closer to Caleb, he took a good look at the stranger who wore dark shades over his eyes. Another sense of familiarity hit Tristan and he knew then, without a doubt, this person was his persistent tracker.

"Where the hell am I?" Tristan growled as he continued toward his target.

Caleb looked at Tristan as if he was an anxious toddler instead of a pissed-off opponent. "We are at Maiden Hall," Caleb answered. He raised a brow then smirked.

The smug son of a bitch somehow got him to the states. *How?*

Tristan didn't know what pissed him off more, the fact that he was back in the United States or the fact that while his ire was at level...critical, Caleb appeared as stoic as a mannequin.

There were only a few feet between Tristan and Caleb but the Tracker stepped between them. With no intentions of stopping, Tristan balled his fist as he advanced, but the man's actions forced him to an abrupt stop. Confused, he looked down at the "tracker guy", who dropped down to one knee and lowered his head. It took a moment for Tristan to realize that the tracker was kneeling to show his loyalty.

The man's Native American heritage was evident with his high cheek bones, sculpted jaw, silky dark hair, and beautiful toffee skin tone. His eyes were covered with sun shades but he looked as if he was in his early to mid-twenties. He also bore the mark of the Arkean tribe.

Tristan thought that seeing the mark on a Breed was odd, but it was unimportant at the moment.

For a few seconds, Tristan stood there, at a loss of what to do next. Then he realized that nothing mattered anymore. He was no one's King and he didn't need anyone's allegiance. All he wanted was for Caleb to suffer for bringing him back. Being on the same continent as Cianne hurt. Hell, it was almost debilitating.

Determined to rip Caleb's head off, Tristan took another step, hoping the stranger would get out of his way. There was no love lost on Caleb from the Coesen, but if anyone had a notion to defend the bastard, Tristan was prepared to kick multiple ass.

Caleb must have read Tristan's intent because he placed his hand on the stranger's shoulder. Tristan took the action as a silent command for the stranger to let things unfold without interference.

Caleb even walked around the stranger to meet Tristan head on, avoiding every single attack Tristan threw at him, easily pushing away punches and avoiding kicks meant to maim.

Tristan almost celebrated when he eventually landed a blow to Caleb's jaw. The force of the blow sent Caleb flying into the air but he did some kind of twirling flip and managed to land on his feet, all the while looking no worse for wear.

"We do not have time for this, Tristan. If you continue with this aggression, I will have to put you on your ass," Caleb said, then sighed. He glanced at his feet as if he was simply bored or put out.

Tristan's speed ate up the distance between him and Caleb. Only, his mentor moved so fast, Tristan wasn't able to track him. Next thing Tristan knew, he was flat on his back looking up at Caleb who was standing over him. There was an ache in his left ankle but it was more annoying than painful.

Tristan rolled to get to his feet but before he could, Caleb's foot came down hard on his other ankle. The bone cracked under the pressure, causing Tristan to curse. He heard Zeta shriek and her footfalls running toward him. Tristan saw the stranger move forward as if he was going to do something but Langley blocked his way with his arm. Tristan swallowed the pain and tried to stand but Caleb used his foot to push him back to the ground.

"He's had enough!" Zeta cried, as she squatted beside him.

"I'm going to rip your head off," Tristan growled.

"And we worked so hard on that anger of yours," Caleb said, then grinned. It was an unsettling grin. He sighed then waved over Dr. Bannerman. "I've broken both ankles." Caleb looked down at him again. "Keep it up and I'll break your pelvis next."

"Fuck you!" Tristan spat out as Bannerman kneeled over him. He prepared himself as he watched Caleb raise his foot, aiming for his pelvis.

Zeta moved to protect him and though she was fast, Caleb was so much faster. She was kicked several feet away.

Caleb's foot rose again to fulfill his promise. He always kept to his word. He only paused when the doctor spoke.

"I would ask you to not do that," Bannerman said plainly.

Tristan watched the hovering foot while Caleb regarded the doctor. When Caleb looked back at him, Tristan stared daggers at his father-in-law, refusing to flinch. His pain was minute but knowing he already wouldn't be able to walk for a few hours was enough to knock a little steam out of him.

Caleb must have sensed that he had calmed because he slid his hand into his jean pockets and lowered his foot to the ground. He stared at Tristan for several seconds before he turned away and slowly walked toward the mansion.

"I can't believe you're alive," Perkins said as he crouched down beside Tristan.

Tristan didn't respond. He just watched Caleb walk away, wondering what that look meant.

Caleb didn't have any time for games. The fact that he was here in his ancestral home with these people spoke volumes. Tristan refused to see beyond his anger to realize that. Caleb felt like all his hard work was for nothing. Already irritated with this situation, he stared out of the large picture window.

He heard Perkins and Cipher enter the room, assisting Tristan who limped between them. Bannerman and Langley walked in behind them. Caleb glanced over his shoulder, and inwardly shook his head as the four men hovered around Tristan as he chose a sofa to sit on. Zeta, Tristan's biggest fan, wasn't with them so Caleb reached out with his senses. He felt her presence in one of the upstairs rooms so he let his attention fall on his other guests.

If he had been a laughing man, he would find humor in their unlikely group. A world-renowned doctor, Bannerman, was the ideal Coesen with his unrivaled skill and intelligence regarding all things medical. Perkins was a fallen Protector, who until a few months ago still gave his loyalties to the very people who shunned him. Langley was the Arkean family lawyer and trophy Child of Jai. Even after several generations Jai's descendants still garnered no respect from the Four Tribes.

...and then there was Cipher.

Cipher was still a mystery. He served in the U.S. military, and by the look of him, Cipher was a Breed who somehow escaped Coesen law. They generally killed off all Breeds at birth or soon after.

He almost forgot the lovely, petite Zeta. She was in love with the "would be" King and loved the "would be" Queen.

A foolhardy group if I ever saw one.

What fascinated Caleb the most was how all these people looked to Tristan as if waiting for long-awaited orders. All were seasoned Coesen with a particular ability and wisdom that set them apart, but each of them trusted his son-in-law for guidance.

Unbelievable.

There was something about blind allegiance that didn't sit well with Caleb. Following someone because of a title given at birth or due to a marriage was just...well, it was just strange.

Caleb sighed. He chose to sit on one of the sofas closest to him but furthest from his guests. Oddly enough, Cipher didn't sit with the others. Instead, the Breed strolled across the room and took the seat beside Caleb.

Bannerman waited for Tristan to settle before examining the boy's ankles. "They're almost healed," he scoffed as he gave Caleb a disapproving glance.

Caleb offered the doctor a devil-may-care grin.

Bannerman shook his head then said, "You don't understand. Protectors don't heal this fast."

"Then, why is he?" Langley asked, standing over them. "Is it because he's linked to the Sovereign?"

Tristan pushed up on his elbows and glared at Langley. "You mean, *am* I linked to Soahn Cianne?" When Langley turned away, Tristan looked to Bannerman. Both men suddenly seemed uncomfortable but neither offered a response.

"Cianne has taken the oath. She is now the Sovereign of the Four Tribes, though she still prefers to be addressed as Soahn." Zeta said as she walked into the room. She dropped a large brown bag next to Bannerman then took a seat on a chair that was closer to Tristan.

Tristan fell back on the sofa. He just stared up at the ceiling as he tried to make sense of what happened in his absence. Cianne was now Sovereign. It was a title she never wanted.

He covered his eyes with his arm. I should have been there to help her through it all.

"I have to break and reset them both," Bannerman told him.

Tristan raised his arm and lifted his head to glance at the doctor as he cut his jeans open to work undeterred. The doctor was instrumental in helping him through his Cycling when he was just a child, recently when he was shot, and once again when he was poisoned.

It was Bannerman who created the serum that kept Death's Door, a poison that had no known cure, at bay. Tristan literally trusted the man with his life so he shook his head dismissively at Dr. Bannerman as he turned to stare at Caleb who was seated across the room.

Caleb stared back.

Bannerman huffed. He looked over his shoulder. "A little help would be nice. His bones are very hard."

When the stranger sitting next to Caleb got to his feet without hesitation, Tristan raised a brow but kept staring at his father-in-law. It was for only a second that the guy's body blocked Tristan's view of Caleb but it effectively broke their staring contest.

Caleb seemed to have no interest in mending the bones he broke. He sat with his ankle crossed over his knee while he flipped through a magazine.

"Ready?" the stranger asked.

Tristan looked down at his foot that rested in the stranger's hands. He nodded then braced himself before he felt a slight tug, then a sharp pain. He didn't flinch or cry out as the searing pain trailed up his leg. In fact, no one in the room moved. They were all hardened souls and soldiers at heart.

Dr. Bannerman wrapped the newly broken ankle before giving the stranger the go ahead to break the other. Again, Tristan relaxed his mind and leveled his pain as his gaze fell on Caleb.

It was a smart move, Caleb seating himself so far from his reach. Though, Tristan knew it was entirely for his benefit. What happened outside was a clear reminder that if Caleb wanted him dead, he would be. Caleb swatted him down like a fly. His father-in-law was lethal and Tristan doubted he had an equal.

At one time, Tristan thought Cianne could contend with her father but now…

Once both ankles were wrapped, Tristan swung his feet down and sat up on the sofa and watched the stranger walk away. He always thought that Protectors moved, or rather glided, the way animals did—with polished elegance, due to long hours of training and/or other factors. But his guy embodied animal grace as he returned to his seat beside Caleb.

So, Caleb has a new friend.

Tristan remembered he couldn't care less.

As he rubbed his head, Tristan knew he shouldn't ask but he needed to know. "So, you all were able to talk her into taking over, huh?"

Langley sighed. "Cianne has accepted her role but no one in this room swayed her decision. We are rarely in her company these days." The lawyer sat upright like a soldier; he was unable to relax even when Vivian ordered him to.

It must be hard to be on your P's and Q's all the time, always cognizant of those who see you as inferior, never letting your guard down.

Tristan didn't care what others thought of him. Well, he cared what...

Don't think of her. Don't think of them.

"Why did you bring me here?" Tristan shifted, a movement that perhaps everyone noticed as if he was planning to stand. Especially Caleb, who raised his brow as if questioning a challenge.

Caleb placed the periodical he flipped through on the arm of his chair then focused all his attention on the man of the hour. "You move in aggression and you will suffer more than two broken ankles," he promised.

A triumphant laughter roared in Caleb's head.

Pythos made himself known more and more in the past few months, so much that Caleb didn't react anymore. Well, he didn't react much. His eyes did widen briefly but he relaxed immediately.

Caleb ignored Pythos' disembodied hiss of laughter as it slowly faded. Pythos offered no words but the threat was clear. Caleb had things to do, and for once, time was not on his side. He cared for Tristan but he indulged no one.

"And as for why you're here," Caleb said, "it's time for you to go home."

Tristan stood. He headed for the entryway as he said, "I'm not going home."

"How much serum do you have left?" Caleb asked quietly, almost whispering. Yet, the question had the effect he wanted.

Tristan stopped a few feet from the entryway, only he didn't turn around.

Caleb massaged his temple while images of a future he didn't want to come to pass played out in his head. "I estimate that you have another dose, or two." He hated pointless dramatics. "Do you want to die?"

Tristan shifted but didn't move forward.

"No? I don't think that's what you want, Tristan." Caleb stopped rubbing his temple. He placed his hand in his lap and let out a deep breath. "Even if it was what you wanted, you know I cannot allow it." He refused to allow it. His daughter's fate was linked to Tristan's.

Caleb could feel his daughter's soul darkening with each passing day. They were connected in ways Cianne didn't know. Well, they weren't connected to the extent they should be and that was why he couldn't get a good feel for her currently. What he did know was that Cianne was slowly losing her grip on reality. She was losing her grip on the part of herself that threatened to wreak unprejudiced havoc upon the world.

Caleb watched Tristan, who remained immobile just inside the room. "*It's time you go back to them,*" Caleb transferred to Tristan.

Just as he sent the mental message, maniacal laughter sounded off in his head again.

Chapter Two

Jamiah strode through the hallway toward the throne room with the confidence of a leader. He was tall, built for battle, and intelligent. Yet, for all his strengths he had one weakness. A weakness he was about to face.

He entered the grand room, holding his head high as his steps echoed off the walls. Jamiah came to a halt a few feet away from the woman he came to see. He bent to one knee and lowered his head.

"Please," Soahn Cianne said as she smiled down at him, "you don't have to bow."

Her soft tone drifted to him, carrying his first command. Jamiah inwardly smiled. The Sovereign was extremely beautiful and kind, and her eyes were mesmerizing. She could have been his to possess in all ways. He could have been seated by her side instead of Whodai.

Whodai's jaw ticked as he spoke, "Yes, Soahn Cianne, he does."

Jamiah inwardly sighed as he fought not to grind his teeth. When he heard that the Halo chose another to mate, he prayed to the heavens that it wasn't Whodai.

Wishful thinking.

"You may rise," Whodai smirked.

Jamiah disregarded Whodai and looked to his Sovereign and waited patiently.

"Please stand, Jamiah," Cianne said to him.

Jamiah stood. He placed his hands behind his back and focused his full attention on Cianne. It took virtually no effort at all to block Whodai out.

"How are you today, Sovereign?"

"I'm well," Cianne answered. "How are you?" She graced him with a partial smile.

Jamiah returned her smile with one of his own. "I am good. The young royals, how are they?" The question charmed a full smile from her this time and it was breathtaking.

"They are well, thank you for asking."

Jamiah nodded; delighted that he coaxed such a genuine reaction from her.

"So, *you* are the head of the Royal Guard now?" Whodai sneered.

"Handpicked by Cassius," Cianne added with pride.

Jamiah hid his smile as he kept his gaze on Cianne. Her silky hair was shorter than the waist length tresses he was informed she wore. It lay straight with a part in the middle and just long enough to curve under her jawline. Her face was perfectly symmetrical, a trait of pure beauty. He couldn't imagine anyone thinking this woman was nothing short of perfection though she looked very tired and maybe even a little pale.

"I'm sure you're just perfect for the job." She continued, "What can I do for you today?"

"Just your time, Soahn. There are some things that Cassius briefed me on, I would like to discuss with you." Jamiah stepped forward and boldly extended his hand then said, "In private."

Cianne only hesitated for a brief moment before standing to take his hand. Only, before Jamiah took hold of it, Whodai stood and took her offered hand.

"You can talk here," Whodai grunted.

There wasn't much Jamiah could do to Whodai. They were both Royals, wealthy, and first sons. If not for Whodai's mother, who held a chair on the Council of Four, they would be evenly matched. As it stood they weren't, but Jamiah knew the law, and right now those laws benefited him.

"Unfortunately, I cannot," Jamiah said with a shrug. He and lowered his eyelids in a mock apology. For the first time since entering the room, he looked at Whodai. "Law is law. I'm sure you are aware that as Head of the Guard, I cannot discuss business with anyone but our Sovereign, her mate, and my Elite Guard. Sovereign Bertram is not mated to you yet and you are not one of my Elite Guards." Jamiah smiled, displaying his dimples.

Jamiah thought the look on Whodai's face was priceless as Cianne pulled her hand free and offered it to him. He helped her down the three steps then released her hand.

Jamiah felt the urge to look over his shoulder and smirk at Whodai but he didn't. He won nothing during this encounter except Whodai's retribution for his subtle disrespect. The eyes never lied and Whodai's eyes spoke volumes.

As Jamiah followed Sovereign Cianne into a small chamber adjacent to the Throne room, he pushed memories of his and Whodai's past away. He decided to focus on Cianne. He saw glimpses of her over the past few months but was never so close to her as he was now. Despite the sadness reflected in her vibrant blue-green eyes, he saw intelligence and compassion.

When she sat, she said, "I can't say that I understand all the laws yet, but I will do my best." She motioned for him to sit. "Before we begin," she said with a grimace, "I want to know how bad this 'thing' is between Whodai and you."

"And here I thought we gave nothing away," Jamiah said. He sat down in the chair that was next to hers, easily transforming from easy-going to strictly business, and said, "It won't interfere with my duties."

Cianne knew this whole transition from middling to Sovereign wasn't going to be easy but she didn't expect it would be so confusing. "Alright," she shifted in the chair, closed her eyes, and rubbed her right temple, "…alright." She tried to focus on the present but her thoughts turned to Vivian.

Her maternal grandmother handled her role as Sovereign with knowledge, compassion, and grace. At her best, Cianne was capable of the compassion and maybe some grace but her knowledge of the Coesen was limited. The little she did know was fragmented due to her prior lack of interest.

In the state she was in, Cianne wasn't sure she could handle ordering lunch, let alone run a nation of supernatural beings. The headaches, nightmares, and lack of sleep were literally driving her crazy. The dreams were so real now, it was hard to determine whether she was asleep or awake most times.

"So how does this work?" she asked as she bit the inside of her mouth. The slight pain and the metallic tang of her blood were what it took to snap her out of her haze.

"Cassius says he briefed you on what I will be doing but I'll explain my role again. My job is to keep you informed of any and all situations that may affect peace and harmony among Coesen and any dealings we have with Middlings. I head both the Royal Guard and the Sentry Guard. Cassius was trusted with handling most issues on his own with only a mention to Sovereign Harper during an end of day briefing. I don't expect you to trust me on my own right away. I hope—"

Cianne held up her hand. "I trust Cassius with my life, Jamiah, and you are his choice so I trust you." She closed her eyes for a brief moment, then looked over at him again. She hoped she didn't look as tired as she felt. "To be honest, I don't really know much about your…our laws. As it stands, Whodai is better suited for your briefings than I am."

"I respectfully disagree." Jamiah frowned. "The fact that you would even admit that someone maybe better than you are, puts you ahead of the rest. It shows me you will do great. Your grandmother had faith in you and she was an amazing Sovereign. You will be as well. We all understand you are learning and everyone here will do what we can to help.

"My job is to make sure our people stay in line, and when they don't my team will crush any resistance as quickly and quietly as possible. I am your eyes and ears, your protection and enforcer. And, I answer only to you."

Cianne smiled. She and Jamiah were going to get along well. She just wished that he relaxed a bit more. "I hope everyone's faith isn't misplaced. So, tell me," she said, a bit more energized, "what do I need to know?"

Jamiah pulled a handheld device from his breast pocket. "First, let me fill you in on Koves Glenn, and the power surges that have been plaguing the community."

"Koves Glenn?"

Jamiah stared at her for a few moments then frowned. "Yes. The Glenn." He handed her the small tablet. "It is a gated community comprised of Coesen, their middling mates, and their Breed offspring. It was founded by Sovereign Harper as an experiment of sorts. In the Glenn, Coesen can live with their mates and raise their Breed without retribution. It's the only community of its type. To assure the safety of the Glenn residents, The Four implemented some extreme requirements for the people who agree to live there."

Cianne scrolled over what looked like a satellite view of a town. She pinched her fingers together then spread them. The image zoomed until she saw a huge gate the read The Glenn, and a security house.

"I had no idea..." Cianne swallowed. "So, you don't kill them?"

Jamiah shook his head. "No. The practice was outlawed when your grandmother was passed the crown. Of course, that information isn't widely known. We are a clandestine race among people who would fear us. Fear brings about war. The Four thought it best to leave the threat of death on the books to discourage that sort of relationship."

"I see." There was so much Vivian didn't tell her. Yet, Cianne couldn't fault her grandmother. If she had shown an inkling of interest, then maybe…

Jamiah sat forward. He touched the tablet several times, and when a grid appeared he leaned back. "The community is experiencing power surges that have caused blackouts in and around the community. I'd like to take a team to investigate."

"You need my approval?" Cianne asked.

He nodded. "I have special access but the Glenn is a well-guarded project where Sovereign Harper invested a great deal of time and care. She liked to be briefed on any and everything that affects its tranquility."

"I understand," Cianne said. "I'd like to be informed as well."

"Sure," Jamiah said. "Now. There's the issue of the Rootstones and the Glenn."

"Rootstone?"

Cianne scrolled through her memory of the briefings Cassius gave her—through the security projects, the risks, and Coesen law. She learned of Coesen outcasts called Dregans, who followed most laws but spoke out against the ruling houses. Those who cared nothing for the laws were called Sodregs. The Dardregs were Coesen who believed in the dark arts and were considered very dangerous because they altered their bodies or the bodies of others to gain more power.

She was also briefed by Cassius about the laws. That, human laws were to be followed but Coesen law took preference. Sentries, the police of the Coesen community, were located all around the world but were split by regions. Sentries and Royal Guards report to Lieutenants. Lieutenants report to their tribal heads and to the Commander of the guard, who reported to the Sovereign who ruled over them all.

In all of that newly acquired knowledge, Cianne knew the Rootstone was mentioned at some point. She sighed as she looked at Jamiah. "Can you refresh my memory. What exactly is the Rootstone?"

"The Rootstone is an object that acts as a mainframe that powers all Keystones. Keystones are similar to the Veilex stone, but instead of alerting you of enemies in your midst, it grants access to areas warded off to unauthorized people." Jamiah explained. "Sovereign Harper was looking over a proposal to unveil the Glenn. I'd like to propose that we update Koves Glenn's access to Keystone security before doing so."

"Unveiling," Cianne whispered, "Right, because I am out, so why hide them?" She nodded. "I'd have to review the plans for this unveiling and have a formal meeting with Cassius in attendance since he has more insight on the project than we do. I'd also like to understand these stones better."

"I'll contact Cassius and set something up with one of our engineers to meet with you," Jamiah motioned to the tablet.

Cianne handed it over to him. Assuming they were done, she moved to stand.

"There's one more thing, Sovereign," Jamiah said. "I would encourage you to reconsider your protection detail. I feel—"

Cianne shook her head. She held her hand up and said, "We have enough protection. Jacobi protects the kids. Four Guards are stationed at posts around the property, and Whodai is here most days. I can take care of myself so there is no need for more Guards."

"But, Sovereign Bertram—"

"Cianne," she said cutting him off again. "You can call me Cianne, but if you insist on being formal, then I prefer Soahn and not Bertram."

Jamiah gave her a sympathetic look then nodded. "Alright, Soahn Cianne, I implore you to allow me to assign more Guards to assure your safety."

Cianne's mind was made up on the matter. "I won't budge on this. Now, I suddenly feel a little tired."

With quiet resignation, Jamiah followed her to the foyer. His jaw tightened as he bowed his head before leaving her alone in the foyer of the massive mansion.

She looked to the throne room's entrance but decided to go to the nursery instead. She really was tired, and if she hurried she could catch a few winks in the glider that sat between the children's beds.

As she climbed the stairs, Cianne decided she liked Jamiah and knew why Cassius chose him to be his successor. Jamiah seemed dedicated, informed, and determined. She didn't see the two of them having the same relationship as Vivian and Cassius, though. He wasn't her Protector.

In the history of the Sovereigns, she was the first whose Protector wasn't head of the Royal Guard. No other Protector had been chosen for her by whatever source that did the choosing. She took solace that another Protector hadn't been chosen. That was another sign that Tristan may indeed still be alive.

Based on their personal observations and rumors, the Council felt that her abilities were rebooting from being bound for so long and that when they were at full power, another Protector would be chosen for her.

Cianne wanted *him* to be alive, but more doubt set in as each day passed. Even knowing that he may hate her for her decisions, she wished for his return.

She pushed the nursery door open, crossed the room, and slid down into the glider. Cianne closed her eyes but willed her thoughts away from Tristan. *Please*, she prayed, *I just want a drama-free nap.*

Chapter Three

Tristan walked the grounds until he found a path that led him to the picturesque lake behind the mansion. The property at Maiden Hall was vast but it wasn't big enough for Tristan to lose himself. No matter where he went, he felt eyes on him. They watched him constantly. To make sure he didn't leave or crack up, he guessed.

When he reached the small beach, he surveyed the settled water. The temperature was mild but Tristan still wrapped his arms around himself. He heard something hit the water and focused on the source of the sound. Tiny waves rippled out from the contact point but the water eventually settled before something else hit the water.

Tristan looked around the shore then swept his gaze upward. Stretched out on one of the thickest branches of a large tree, was Caleb. Tristan wondered if he would ever have the ability to sense Caleb but knew it depended on whether Caleb wanted to be detected.

Sighing, Tristan dropped his arms and slid his hands into his pockets. "I have enough eyes on me. I don't need to be followed too."

Caleb spread his arms out. "You forget son, this is my home. I'm not following you. I'm relaxing."

"Relaxing," Tristan repeated sarcastically. Then it hit him. This was Caleb's house and the tree was *the* tree. The very tree Caleb spoke of. The one Caleb used to sit in when he was a boy.

Tristan gazed out over the lake. This was the lake that Marda swam in. Everything Caleb told him came to life in that moment. As Tristan let his imagination take over, the modern splendor of Maiden Hall was replaced with the sights, sounds, and scents of Caleb's description of the 19th-century plantation it once was. Tristan knew Caleb's story was real. He lived each moment through Caleb's retelling, but to see Maiden Hall—to actually touch it—was unbelievable.

"There are people in west Africa who plant a tree when a child is born. As the child grows, so does the tree. When flowers bloom, the child knows it's time to marry, and when the child dies, it is believed that his or her spirit will live on in the tree." Caleb seemed to search the water then turned to Tristan. "Have you ever wondered where the spirit goes once it leaves the body?"

"No," Tristan shrugged, answering honestly.

"No? Not the hell fire and brimstone type, eh?" Caleb sighed then moved as if he was shifting his weight. Instead of getting more comfortable, he landed effortlessly on the sandy beach beside Tristan.

"No, and if you're looking for some kind of religious answer, you're asking the wrong person." Tristan turned his attention back to the water but he felt Caleb's eyes still on him.

"I'm not looking for answers, religious or otherwise. Just curious about what you believe. I see you've shed all the hair."

Tristan faced Caleb. He often found it hard to look at the man. Those green-blue eyes of his were like a Judas Kiss to Tristan. On one hand, he loathed peering into their depths. On the other, he loved the familiarity and comfort Caleb's eyes offered. Imagining those eyes, Cianne's eyes, pieced him back together more times than he could count.

As Tristan stared back at Caleb, he didn't see the hard, heartless warrior who walked through time. He saw controlled strength in Caleb's eyes. But yesterday, for a moment during the meeting in the sitting room, something spooked the hardened immortal. Tristan saw the moment it happened. It was so sudden that if he didn't know Caleb, he might have missed it.

Though, as he looked Caleb over now, he saw nothing to suggest the old geezer had an unsettling moment the day before. Though he was wary of what could possibly affect such a man, Tristan rejoiced that Caleb could be unsettled. It meant there was still some humanity left in him. For some reason, that thought was refreshing.

Tristan let his gaze fall to his feet and he rubbed the back of his neck to ease his mounting headache. "What do you want from me, Caleb? You kept me from her, from them, because you felt I wasn't…what?" he whispered, "…able to do what I needed to do if my family was threatened? I would have protected them with my life."

The truth was, without Caleb's training, he wouldn't have been able to keep them safe. But that didn't give Caleb the right to play God, and now his family belonged to someone else.

"Now you want me to go back to them after she chose to accept another as her mate." Tristan shook his head, still unable to wrap his head around how fast Cianne gave up on him. His anger built but he contained it. "She is better off without me," he mumbled.

"Cianne needs *you*. She loves *you*."

Tristan's laughter came out strained and filled with pain, "Yeah, once upon a time."

He had eleven months to think about his and Cianne's relationship. He had five months of wanting nothing but his family and six more months to question if what he and Cianne had was real. In those six months, he wondered why she didn't feel him inside of her like he felt her inside of him. In those six months, he accepted that she moved on and that Whodai, the arrogant asshole, finally had her all to himself. Even without the Protector/Coesen bond, he FELT her through all that.

Tristan turned his back to Caleb. Planning to walk away, he took a step before he felt a sudden and excruciating pain bleed through his body. He fell to his knees, clenched his teeth, and placed his hand over his heart where the searing pain was most intense. He heard faint footsteps approaching but his pain was so debilitating that he was unable to react, to defend himself. With watery eyes, he peered up at Caleb, who looked down at him with a blank, unholy expression.

"Well," Caleb said in a matter of fact tone, "there's no point in keeping your whining *woe is me* ass around. Is there? If you're not going to fight to get back what's rightfully yours, to be with the woman you love, then ripping out your heart and relieving you of your sad existence would be humane."

The intensity of Tristan's pain increased. Even as the sound of approaching footsteps caused Caleb to tilt his head toward the dark figure, he didn't let up. "Interfering this time will cost you your life, Cipher," Caleb warned.

Through the pain, Tristan was able to make out the dark figure behind Caleb. His ears rang but he was still able to hear.

"Forgive me for intruding once again on your training session. I just thought that I could be of use, somehow," Cipher said, bowing his head.

Caleb released his phantom hold on Tristan's heart, then lazily returned his gaze to Tristan, who gasped for breath. He said, "Reclaim your wife and children."

The pressure was gone but Tristan still felt an echo of the pain. Coughing, he hoarsely asked, "Or what?"

"Never was one for threats, so I won't bore you with them." Caleb shrugged. "Swallow your pride, Tristan. Being together is what you both need but if you require a noble quest, something to convince you that Cianne needs you..." Caleb said as he strolled away. "I'm sure your friends have just the thing to motivate the hero in you."

The stranger rushed forward to help Tristan to his feet.

Cipher...Tristan heard Caleb call him by name. Accepting the offered hand, Tristan allowed the stranger to take on most of his weight as they walked back to the mansion. By the time they reached the grand back patio stairs, Tristan felt almost whole again and was able to walk on his own.

"What is he talking about?" Tristan asked, referring to Caleb. He pushed himself hard to get up the stairs.

"I've heard only rumors," Cipher answered, keeping pace.

Tristan made his way through the house, following the sounds of low voices coming from the study. The conversation stopped when he entered. Perkins, Zeta, and Langley looked to him as he entered.

"Is Cianne in danger?" he asked.

Zeta spoke up first. "Not exactly."

"Not exactly," Tristan repeated. "Either she is or she isn't. Give me a straight damn answer."

Zeta flinched.

"It's complicated," Perkins added. He was seated beside Zeta on the sofa.

Langley inched forward, to the edge of the single chair where he sat, and placed his drink on the table. "We've been concerned about the decisions she's made in the last few months. She has isolated herself and the children inside Ark Mansion, refusing to see almost all visitors, other than your parents, who she allows inside only to see the kids. Zeta has been reassigned, and Cianne avoids Brian and Tranae. She sees me and Bannerman but our time with her is limited to business."

Perkins hung his head. "Bannerman says she barely sleeps. She spends most of her time with the twins and she relies on Whodai to counsel her regarding our nation."

Tristan counted on Cianne to surround herself with friends to get her through the hard times. He even knew that Whodai would swoop in and make his play for her. After all, the bastard won her hand, he would want her heart. The thought of his wife relying on...

She's no longer mine.

That Cianne was relying on anyone other than him, burned Tristan inside and out.

Tristan rolled his shoulders and neck as the reality of his thoughts slammed into him. Whodai was gunning for or may already have Cianne's love. He didn't like it but he was the one who walked away. It didn't matter that he left to keep her safe, to keep their children safe. So, he accepted that Whodai weaseled his way into her life and her heart, no matter how much it peeved him.

"Alienating herself is a defense mechanism. Relying on Whodai," Tristan said tersely, "is natural, considering she has been through so much and is so unfamiliar with Coesen law. I would have liked one of you to have filled that role but she's made her choice. You all are not looking at this from her point of view. Cianne is grieving. She feels responsible for all that's happened over the last couple of years. All the deaths, she's taken personal responsibility for. Cianne is keeping the people she cares about far away from her because in her mind that is the safest place for you all."

Zeta stood and paced the room a few times before turning to face everyone. "You know her better than all of us so I want to believe you are right, but there is more going on. I can feel it. Cianne's not just mourning. She's losing herself." Zeta grimaced. She crossed her arms over her chest. "I hate that I'm going to say this, but Caleb might be right. Losing you has done something to her."

The worried look on Zeta's face coupled with her fidgeting picked at Tristan's resolve. Nothing, aside from him finding out that Cianne's and the children's safety was in question would make him go to her. Seeing him would only cause Cianne more pain. He would save her from that heartache if he could.

"I need to think," Tristan said, giving them one last look before leaving the room. He chose the same bedroom he used the night before. Falling on the bed, he closed his eyes and prayed that he could keep Cianne out of his dreams tonight. Just long enough to think.

The Next Day
Tristan didn't think his old private school buddy would answer a call from an unknown number at all, but Raul always was a little too curious. He answered on the third ring.

"Who is this and where did you get my number?" Raul asked, in his rehearsed yet perfected Australian accent. "You have five seconds."

"Trident." Tristan dragged the name out so Raul would have no problem understanding him.

No one but Tristan knew the details of Raul's night with their professor's daughter. Raul and the far from innocent Heather were busy going over parts of their anatomy. Heather's father, back early from a convention, happened across the pair. Neither Raul nor Heather heard when the Professor, who loved Hindu folklore, ripped the trident off his wall and returned to his precious girl's bedroom where the night's lesson was well underway.

The Trishula or trident is mostly a huge blade, so Raul was pretty lucky he moved just as the Professor struck. Three permanent reminders marked Raul's right ass-cheek, but he credits his survival to the God Shiva, who is said to have used the Trishula to destroy the past, present, and future. Raul truly believed that Shiva whispered to him to move at that exact moment, thus granting him reprieve from his scandalous past, wiping away the taint of the present, and destroying the future path he was on, enabling him to create a new one.

Of course, Raul was back to breaking hearts and laws a few weeks later but he still believed that it was divine intervention that saved his life that night.

There was a loud gasp on Raul's end. "Asshole!" Raul yelled through the receiver. "I sent your family my condolences and a shit load of flowers. I shut down for five days, reviewing every detail of your accident. It didn't make any damn sense but when this official looking fuck, definitely from some branch of the military, broke into my damn flat and threatened my life and everyone I know if I didn't stop poking around your untimely death, I backed off. I don't know what the hell you've gotten yourself into but that fucking guy got past my safeguards, found me, and got into my flat without tripping a single tell. The guy meant business, Tristan."

Yeah, whoever it was who found Raul did mean business. Yet the fact that his friend shut all work down, losing unspeakable amounts of cash and/or favors, to investigate his sudden demise spoke volumes.

"Did he hurt you?" Tristan had to ask.

"Got the impression that he could hurt me real bad if he wanted to but he left after wiping everything I had on the accident and about you. Every photo, ledgers of our business dealings, and even school shit. Hell, everything I had that contained anything about you was destroyed."

All standard procedure for the Guard but Raul didn't need to know that. "I'll replace whatever was damaged. I am sorry, Raul," Tristan said, sighing, "but I wouldn't be calling on you again if I had someone else." The other line went silent other than Raul's easy breathing. Tristan was sure his friend would not help, but then Raul sighed.

"I'm the best. No one can do what I do. What do you need?" The sound of Raul's swift typing filled the line as Tristan spoke.

After explaining what he needed Tristan said, "Don't do this if it can be traced back to you."

Raul chuckled. "Yeah, I've since learned from my prior mistakes," he said sarcastically. "Believe me, no one will be able to tell it was a hack, let alone trace it."

"Thank you, Trident." Tristan smiled. "I assume the price—"

The clicking sounds of the keyboard sped up. "Went up, I'll go ahead and just move my fee from your hidden account. I assume you never closed it…because I just accessed it."

Tristan was two miles away from Ark mansion when he called Raul. Getting away from Maiden Hall wasn't too hard. Getting his father to arrange their family's private jet and getting to Canada was even easier. Now, just days after being brought back to the states, Tristan was hiding just outside the main wall of the mansion.

During Vivian's Fasen or funeral service, he became intimately familiar with the security and the grounds. That was a year ago. The security might have been upgraded.

Tristan heard the mass *whoosh* from houses blocks away as power all across the landscape shut down. "Raul, you're the best," Tristan whispered to himself. He had only two minutes to get into the mansion without being seen, heard, or captured on video. Surprisingly, that wasn't too difficult for him either. Tristan scaled the outer wall and was on the property in under fifty seconds. It would have been sooner but he took some time to get reacquainted with the all the cameras.

When he decided on the room he planned to enter, his heart rate jumped into overdrive. Tristan didn't waste time as he scaled the side of the mansion. When he reached the balcony, he climbed over the rail and peered at the large French doors with the dark windows. There were no knobs on the outside that he could use to open them. Someone from the inside would have to let him in.

"Just great," he mumbled. He would have to break the glass and shatter his plan of sneaking in and out.

All I need is to see…

Hell, he didn't know what he needed to see before he let Cianne know that he was alive. Maybe he just wanted to see her with Whodai. To somehow gauge what she felt for the Coesen. But more than that, Tristan needed to know that she was alright; to confirm that he sacrificed his heart for her happiness.

Tristan peered at the door, assessing the darkened glass panels. Of course, they were hooked up to some kind of alarm system. All he could hope for was that the generator didn't kicked in yet but he was sure it did by now.

Here goes.

Just as he raised his elbow to smash the glass, a soft click on the other side of the door halted his action. The distinctive sound of a sealed door opening was next, then both French doors slowly eased open.

Tristan smiled but it was due to his nerves. He knew who was on the other side of the slow-moving doors and he could barely restrain himself. He wanted to burst forward and push them open but he had to consider that his presence wouldn't be accepted.

Once the doors were fully opened, Tristan glanced around the room from where he stood. All the other doors in the room were closed. Two small beds sat together in the middle of the large room. Standing at the end of the tiny gray, lushly decorated bed, was Aidan. His round face was guarded. His green eyes were curious as they stared at him.

Movement on one of the beds drew Tristan's attention. Nadia, who seemed to have been asleep, now was awake. She pushed her tiny purple blanket aside as soon as her green eyes met his. Her face lit up like the sun, full of awareness.

She recognizes me. Tristan sighed.

Nadia got to her knees and started bouncing up and down on her bed. Her dark brown curls rose above her head then fell over her shoulders with each contact her feet made with her bed. Only, her excitement calmed after she turned her head and look at Aidan. His angel, who was somehow the spitting image of her brother and the perfect combination of him and Cianne, frowned as she stilled. Tristan looked at them both.

Wait, weren't both of their eyes blue like mine?

As soon as he thought it, Nadia's eyes flickered as if a light were behind them. When the light was gone, her eyes were blue. Tristan glanced over at Aidan. Just as his sister's eyes turned; his son's eyes were now blue.

"Did you change your eyes for me?" Tristan whispered. He took one careful step, then another, as he closed the distance between him and his children. When he was a few feet away from them, he dropped to his knees to see them both on their level.

Neither reacted to his question but Nadia did look at Aidan. Aidan's face was impassive but he eventually nodded.

"And you opened the door for me?" Tristan couldn't help smiling when Aidan nodded again. "So, you know…who I am?"

Aidan nodded a third time and Nadia bounced on the bed once more with her sunshine smile filling her face.

"I've missed you both so much." Tristan raised his hand to reach out to his son but pulled it back before touching him. He swallowed then sighed. "Can I touch you? Can I, have a hug?"

Again, Nadia looked at her brother.

It amazed Tristan how smart they were and that they clearly looked out for each other.

With a single nod from Aidan, Nadia dropped to her bottom, swung her feet off the bed, and slid down the side until her little feet almost hit the floor. Tristan didn't give her the time to finish getting to the floor. He pushed to his feet, flashed to her, and lifted her up in his arms so fast that the bedding on both beds billowed into the air and was left disheveled.

Even after Tristan cuddled and kissed a receptive Nadia, Aidan didn't move. Aidan looked like an average boy of one and a half years. His loosely curled hair was a little lighter than his sister's but shorter, just reaching his dark brows and just past his ears. He wasn't a pudgy toddler. Aidan was taller, leaner than a lot of the babies his age. But those intense, soulful, beautiful eyes, framed with long eyelashes, showed his intelligence.

"Will you allow me to hug you too, Aidan?" Tristan asked.

When Aidan took a step away from the bed toward him, Tristan sucked in a breath. He didn't let it out until he had both his children in his arms. Bent on one knee he finally allowed himself to breathe. "I love you both so much. I'm going to try and fix this as best I can. I promise I will never leave you for so long again," Tristan said as he held his children tightly against him.

Maybe too tight but neither of them complained.

He rocked them back and forth, never wanting to let them go again. It was Nadia stiffening and Aidan stepping away but not completely separating from the embrace, that alerted Tristan that something was wrong. He lifted his head from their soft curls, wondering what it was that spooked them.

"Daddy!" Aidan cried out.

The bedroom door swung open so hard that it banged into the wall with great force. Tristan reacted on instinct, pushing the twins behind him so he could face the threat.

The threat.

Threat?

His heart stalled as he stared into the most stunning pair of eyes on the most beautiful face he'd ever seen. "*Cianne*," he breathed. Her name slammed against his mind but it was only a whisper out of his mouth. She lost some weight and under her eyes was darker, but he doubted anything could really take from a beauty such as hers.

Cianne's, once long flowing silky, hair was much shorter and curved under her chin. Her gray nightgown clung to her curvy breasts, her waist, and hips. Tristan appreciated how the fabric caressed her form as it draped down her legs to lightly brush the tops of her feet.

Tristan traced the familiar lines of her face as she opened her lush peach tinted lips in a shocked O shape. They were lips he wanted so desperately to kiss. But those lips thinned out almost instantly, replacing her shock with confusion then anger.

"Get away from my children," Cianne hissed.

"Ci…"

Her name was all Tristan was able to get out before he felt every nerve in his body tingle then he was roughly yanked forward, past her, and thrown out of the children's room. His body slammed against a wall in the hallway as every molecule in him lit with pain.

"Please Ci, I'm sorry. I can explain."

Cianne's eyes wavered. She seemed confused and placed her hands on her head. But then she shook her head as if clearing it. Her expression looked both confused and pained.

"I won't let you harm us."

Grunting, Tristan said, "I could never hurt them…you. I. Love. You."

"Lies."

Cianne's pain-filled cry tore at his heart.

She moved a step closer, exiting the children's room. Her breaths came out labored and quick. "You are not him. He's," she gulped then caught her breath, "he's gone. You, will not hurt anyone else I love."

What?

Tristan's response was stalled by his confusion but a few seconds later he realized his silence was a dreadful error. His body was seized with a new assault of excruciating pain that hindered his ability to think, let alone form words.

"Daddy!" Aidan called out.

Through the horrible pain, Aidan's angelic voice calling out to him enabled Tristan to focus some. Incapable of speech and movement as his body was pinned to the hallway wall, Tristan focused his eyes on his children. Nadia was whimpering but her back was to him because Aidan had her facing him with his hands covering her ears, though he probably didn't need to physically cover them to keep her from hearing.

It struck Tristan in that moment, that Aidan was protecting his sister, but he was also watching his father's imminent death.

No!

Tristan knew the look on his son's face. He wouldn't allow his son to help. "*Aidan, shut your bedroom door. NOW*," Tristan transferred. He wasn't sure if he had the mental connection with the children like the link he used to share with Cianne, but he knew that the twins were part Caleb, and like Caleb, they may be able to communicate with anyone mentally.

The question of whether there was a link between him and the children or if they shared their grandfather's ability was never answered but the bedroom door slammed closed.

Relieved that his children would not see his end was comforting, but they would know that their mother was the one to deal death's blow and that was upsetting.

"*This isn't your mom's fault. She loves me but she's confused right now. Never blame her*." Tristan mentally sent to them both.

"*I can help you*," Aidan transferred.

The word "No" was almost a full thought when a distant sound distracted Tristan. *What the hell is that sound*? His interest in the noise faded as he tried to keep his eyes open.

"*Stay in your room*," he transferred, though he sounded weak. "*Stay in your room*."

Grateful their bedroom door didn't open again, Tristan let his blurring vision focus on Cianne just as what looked like a kitchen blade pierced his right arm. Another two knives, possibly steak knives, entered his left shoulder faster and harder than the first, causing his body to jerk on impact. The pain was minimal compared to what she was already doing to him.

The sound was...

Tristan laughed, allowing blood to drip from his mouth. That faint sound was metal slicing through the air. It was the only warning he received before a pair of scissors tore into his side, jolting him again.

Tristan grunted. He focused on Cianne now that the kids were safe. The crimson of her eyes glowed, but oddly enough, the rage seemed to be draining from her face.

He didn't expect his life to end like this, virtually crushed and prodded with kitchenware. Whenever he thought of death, which was almost never, he pictured himself dying while protecting his wife and children. Not like this.

Yet, even with Cianne squeezing the life from him, all he saw when he looked at her was love. Unrequited love for an unattainable beauty. A new and fresh love that fed the butterflies you never knew you had. The undying, unyielding, unconditional love that energized every cell in his body from the first moment he tasted her sweet lips.

When Tristan heard something larger than what already impaled him coming his way, he chuckled. He knew he had little time left so he needed to say something. "I'll always love you," Tristan grimaced. His eyes felt so heavy.

"Good to know."

Good to know? That was going to be the last thing he heard before he died. Tristan couldn't help but laugh at that.

Chapter Four
May 8th

Zeta didn't plan on sticking around Maiden Hall. She planned on leaving last night but when she heard footfalls rushing past the bedroom she was in, she knew something horrible happened.

She hated when she was right.

"How's he doing?" Zeta asked. She stood over Tristan as he lay immobile on the bed.

Bannerman rubbed his eyes. The man looked wiped out. "We can thank those Caleb cocktails he's been injecting himself with for the past year for saving his life, but his body seems to be adapting to them now. It doesn't help that the connection he and Cianne used to share was so fragile. Being apart during those vital bonding years when the connection should be solidifying was wasted during their younger years. He could be so much stronger. Possibly as strong as her."

"Tristan is stronger and faster than most seasoned Protectors," Zeta countered as she stared at Dr. Bannerman.

"Yes, but he could have been more so. Without their bond, and with the poison…his broken spirit, Tristan's recovery will be challenging."

Zeta gave Tristan one last glance then followed Bannerman out into the hallway. They walked silently to the kitchen. She acknowledged Perkins, who was pouring two mugs of coffee, with a nod.

"I could use some of that coffee," Bannerman said.

"Me too," Cipher added as he walked into the kitchen.

Zeta was still curious about Cipher, who bore the mark of the Arkean tribe. He seemed genuine and dedicated to Caleb, which oddly enough meant that he was on Cianne's and Tristan's side. But still, she was curious as to how was it that he lived, bore a birthmark, and more importantly, why was he helping?

"I still don't know how he got past me." Cipher murmured. His face projected a mix of regret and worry.

Why does he keep his eyes covered with those shades all the time?

"Don't take Tristan sneaking away as your personal failure. He isn't like most Coesen." Zeta lifted the coffee mug to her mouth but didn't take a sip. "As a matter of fact, he technically isn't a Coesen at all. But he is stubborn and excels at everything he does. If he wants out, he will find a way…eventually." She took a sip of her coffee, allowing the warmth to infuse her, feeling cold and a little helpless.

Cipher looked her way but she couldn't see his eyes. She wished she could see them. She guessed they were odd, or he was blind, or both.

Cipher nodded. He sat down and took the cup Perkins handed him. Bannerman sat too and accepted a cup of coffee from Perkins as well. Perkins filled his own cup and placed the carafe on the heatproof base located in the center of the table then he also sat down.

No one spoke for a long time. Each of them was lost in their own thoughts when movement to her side caught her off guard. On edge, Zeta jumped to her feet. She watched the cup slip from her hands and tip forward but the cup never hit the floor. Zeta balanced the cup from the tip of her outstretched fingers while the coffee floated above the mug and small drops suspended above the table.

Zeta glanced around the table, noticing that every one of them was at the ready. Cipher had a dagger in his hand, poised to throw. Perkins was up with his fist raised. But what surprised Zeta more was the gun that Dr. Bannerman was pointing at her.

Well, not exactly pointing at her. Bannerman was aiming in her general direction. The target was beside her.

Caleb appeared out of thin air and was seated in the chair beside the one Zeta was seated in seconds before.

"Jesus!" Perkins picked up his overturned chair then flopped down on it. "You never used that freaky pop-up ability before. Now you're popping up all the damn time."

Caleb lowered his slightly raised hand. The floating coffee slinked back into the cup Zeta held. Next, her chair rose from the floor and bumped into the back of her legs, urging her to sit. Shaking her head, Zeta sat.

"Adjust," Caleb said insipidly. He poured himself a cup of coffee.

Zeta stared at him as he lifted the black liquid to his mouth. She shivered at the thought of drinking coffee with no sugar or cream.

"It's been a full day. Has there been any chatter about Tristan's return?" Caleb asked.

Zeta frowned. Why didn't she think of that? She glanced around at the people settling around the large country table. Apparently, she was the only slow thinker in the room.

"Nothing," Bannerman spoke up first. "The kid's Guard, Jacobi, was out of town. I spoke with Langley, who will be arriving tomorrow. He doesn't know of Tristan's visit to Ark Manor. I've purposely contacted several companions who are usually in the know and they didn't mention Tristan at all."

Cipher placed an empty coffee mug on the table then reached for a pastry. "I've been snooping around, looking to hear that the mate and rightful King has returned, but..." He shook his head as he picked at the corners of the buttery crust.

"Same here," Perkins added, "No one knows Tristan is alive. There's one good thing working in our favor." Perkins paused then said, "Whoever is after him won't know either."

Zeta could kick herself. She forgot someone was after Tristan's head. Here she was thinking their only concern was smoothing things out with Cianne. "Why doesn't anyone know yet?"

"That's what *you're* going to find out," Caleb said. He stood with his cup in hand and walked out of the room.

◉

May 11th

Cianne heard his voice. It drifted through her unconscious mind in the darkness.

"I'll always love you."

The absence of light frightened many but here, Cianne felt relieved. It was better to see nothing than to experience the nightmares that tortured her. For months, she suffered. She nearly forgot what a peaceful night's sleep was. But in this darkness, only the sound of his soothing voice offered her the calming quiet that eluded her for so long. He had that effect on her, always did.

"I'll always love you."

Cianne was tired. Even inside her dreams, she was exhausted. As she lay in the absence of light, it was his voice that soothed her. Tristan sounded sincere, but he always did in her dreams. His voice never betrayed her. Not like his image did…when it transformed into Caleb and attacked her. He always attacked her.

Her eyes sprang open, only to be assaulted by the blinding sunlight streaming through her window. Moaning, Cianne buried her face in one of the pillows that didn't quite feel like hers. It occurred to her then that she was at Ark Manor.

Cianne sat up and pulled the sheets back. The gray silk nightgown she wore to bed clung to her damp skin. Shaking her head, she sighed as she fell back on her pillows. She slept. She actually slept. God, sleep was a curse these days but she slept peacefully last night. The last time she remembered sleeping so peacefully was when…

It was only when Tristan was near.

"I'll always love you," she whispered. Cianne shivered as she felt his love warm her from the inside out.

Tristan? He…

Cianne shoved to her feet and sprinted the short distance to the doors that led to her children's room. Her breath hitched as she came to a wobbly stop just as she reached their small beds. Both of them were asleep. Their serene faces were in total contrast to the confusing memory that echoed through her mind.

Another nightmare?

But as last night's scene played in her mind…

It seemed real.

Cianne looked around the pristine room trying to find evidence that she wasn't completely losing her mind. Nothing was out of place. But then nothing would be. She remembered that the altercation happened in the hallway. That was where the signs of a struggle would be.

Quietly, Cianne walked to the door leading to the hall and eased it open. Closing her eyes, she took a deep breath. Then she walked the several steps and placed her hand on the wall and absently traced her fingers over it.

There was no damage to the wall. No gashes from knives that she knew went clear through flesh. She opened her eyes. No blood. The wall was unblemished. Cianne's shoulder fell and she lowered her head. Her mind was crumbling.

"Oh," Ms. Eleanor gasped as she walked into view. "Soahn, I thought you were resting. Is there something I can get for you? One of those energy drinks perhaps?"

Cianne turned her gaze on the nanny then back to the wall. "No thank you, Eleanor. I'm fine."

"I'll prepare the children for you then. The Bertrams will be here around noon." Eleanor shifted then moved toward the children's room. The older women paused and turned back to look at Cianne. She pushed her glasses up her nose then smiled again, "Shall I tell them you will be joining them today for lunch…or dinner perhaps?"

Seeing Tristan's parents amplified her pain, her loneliness, and her guilt. She couldn't be around them without breaking down. Seeing them…

Wait.

Furrowing her brows, Cianne turned around and said, "It's only Wednesday."

"No Soahn, today is Friday," Eleanor informed her. She relaxed her hand that held the door knob then dropped it to her side when she turned to face Cianne. "You've been asleep for two full days."

That wasn't possible. Cianne shook her head. "Why didn't anyone wake me?"

Eleanor lowered her head but kept her eyes on Cianne. "We were told to never wake you if you are sleeping, Soahn."

"Who told you this?"

"Royal Whodai Tam, Soahn."

Why would he order this? Didn't he understand that her children needed her? Speechless, Cianne just gawked at the middle-aged woman. Did Whodai know how close to the edge she was?

Eleanor gave her a weak smile. "If you don't need anything, I'll just get the children ready for the day."

"Yes…alright," Cianne said, nodding absently. She turned back to the wall, brushing her fingers over the pristine finish. It seemed so real, so vivid. She let her hand fall from the wall to hang at her side.

Surely if Caleb actually breached Ark Manor, she would have been told. People would be scurrying about. Whodai would have been notified and would have returned to her side to get her and the children safe.

Satisfied that it was just a case of her leveling up her crazy and not a real attack, Cianne strolled back to her room. She resisted the urge to turn back to look at the wall. There was no use reliving the nightmare.

In her bathroom, Cianne turned on the shower, undressed, and stepped in. The water was cooler than she preferred but she didn't adjust it. She used it to soak her hair and body while ignoring the slight shivers that moved through her.

Cianne was running her hands through her hair, still adjusting to the new length when the image of Tristan slammed into her mind. She braced herself, using the shower wall to remain on her feet.

Tristan was whole, he was there. Cianne remembered staring into his penetrating blue eyes, saw them darken as they took her in. She recalled the way those eyes sparked with desire as they caressed her body, touching on every visible part of her intimately.

Did I see it wrong? Did I see what I wanted to see?

Whatever the case, Cianne resisted his pull; she felt the driving need to go to him, but it didn't feel right. She attacked him. He seemed surprised when she did.

He whispered my name.

Cianne leaned against the wall then collapsed into a pile of flesh on the shower floor. A low agonized squeal escaped from her clenched lips. The sounds of the water faded into the background because her frantic breathing and sobs drowned it out. She lay there with her face near the drain, with her knees pulled into her arms and touching her chest. Cianne's salty tears mixed with the water as realization slapped her in the face.

For the first time in her dreams, she attacked Tristan first.

It was just another dream.

After her cries were reduced to a soft whimper, Cianne found the strength to pull herself off the floor to wash. As much as she wanted to lie down and wilt away until there was nothing left of her, she couldn't.

Their children needed what little she had left to offer. Plus, somewhere in the recesses of her splintering mind, there remained a sliver of hope. Hope that she would never again express out loud.

"It was just a dream," she softly repeated until her throat burned.

Tristan rolled to his side and groaned as he woke. He immediately sat up and moved his hands over his body, searching for the damage that was inflicted. Only, there were no bandages or...pain.

Confused, he took in his surroundings.

Maiden Hall. Bedroom. Caleb.

Sighing, he fell back on the bed and threw his arm over his eyes. "Would it be too much to ask, to wake up and not see your face?" he snarled. He moved his arm and peeked out of one eye.

Caleb didn't turn from the window he stood in front of. "And here I thought you loved me," Caleb said, dryly.

'I'll always love you.'

The words Tristan thought were his last whirled around in his mind.

"Good to know".

It was Caleb's voice he heard as he blacked out.

Tristan sat up on the side of the bed and saw that he wore just a pair of pajama pants. He ran his hand over his bare chest, again realizing he had no injuries. He was saved again by the very man he hated. Well, not exactly hated...but still sort of hated.

"Fuck!" Tristan yelled. Everything was so screwed up and the man who kept saving his life was the one who started it all.

Tristan swung his gaze to the bedroom door as it swung open. Zeta rushed inside. Her eyes moved around the room before falling on him. Cipher stood in the doorway with his hand behind his back.

"We...," Zeta began but stopped as her eyes fell on Tristan's bare chest. Her eyes grew big and her cheeks flushed with color. Her eyes lifted and she glared at Caleb before she looked down. "I apologize for storming in." Her eyes were focused on her feet. "Are you alright, Soahn?"

Confused, Tristan just stared at her. He couldn't understand the formal tone she addressed him with. And what was with her calling him Soahn? "Zeta, what's wrong?"

"I just thought that you... I thought that you were in danger," Zeta told him without lifting her head. "I did not know that you were awake or that you were meeting with..." Her voice cracked, "I am sorry I did not knock before entering." She glanced at Caleb then backed out of the room before Tristan could respond.

Tristan's eyes narrowed as he turned his head to look at Caleb. "What the hell did you just say to her?" he demanded.

"Just that she has nothing to fear from me. Also, that if I pose that danger she fears of me, that neither she, you, nor anyone staying in *my* home would see me coming." Caleb sighed. "Definitely not in the time it took for you to scream the word 'fuck'."

Even though it grated on Tristan, he knew he was no match for Caleb. None of them were. Accepting that truth with a nod, Tristan asked, "What's with her calling me Soahn?'

"*Your* people," a hint of amusement lightened Caleb's normally uninterested tone, "discussed and decided that addressing you formally will remind you of your role and duty to them."

"Oh," Tristan said. He absently nodded as he rubbed the back of his neck. Tristan moved his hand up the back of his head, relishing the freedom of having a close cut again.

Caleb turned around. "Everyone is waiting to hear how your visit went. Bannerman came to care for you, but left and just returned to make sure you've healed properly. Let's not keep everyone guessing."

Tristan watched Caleb leave the room before he moved. He groaned as he stood. His muscles felt tight but it was nothing a hot shower couldn't cure.

After he showered and dressed, Tristan opened the door leading to the hallway. Outside his door, Caleb stood with his arms crossed over his chest.

Is the old man scared I'll take off again?

Tristan followed Caleb down the stairs and to the sitting room. It seemed that despite the size of the place, everyone preferred this room. Inside, Perkins and Langley sat on the sofa while Cipher sat near the small wet bar that was built into the wall. Zeta was behind the bar, reaching into the fridge.

When they noticed him and Caleb, the Coesen bowed to him. Tristan offered a slight bow of his own before he entered. He took a seat across from Perkins and Langley.

"Sorry I'm late," Bannerman said as he entered. He sat down his briefcase and took a seat next to Tristan.

Langley waved his hand. "We're just getting started."

"Before we do, I want to say that you all don't have to be so formal," Tristan said as he looked at each of them. "I've known Dr. Bannerman since I was a kid. Zeta and I have faced death together. Langley, you have stood by my side through personal and business endeavors. Perkins, you have watched my back on more than one occasion." He turned to Cipher. "I don't know you, but Caleb hasn't felt it necessary to take your head and everyone here seems to trust you, so I'll trust you." Tristan sighed. "What I'm trying to say is, I know my place and duty but you all are family. I would have you use my name."

Tristan waited until he got a nod of agreement from everyone. When he looked at Cipher, the man stood and walked over to him. Not knowing what he planned to do, Tristan stood.

Maybe I offered my trust a little too soon.

When Langley stood, Tristan frowned.

Removing the glasses that always covered his eyes, Cipher took to one knee as he spoke, "I am Cipher Shawn to the US Army."

Tristan stared into the oddest pair of eyes he ever saw. Both the irises and pupils were a stormy gray that seemed to be in a constant state of movement like they were actually smoking.

"But," Langley said, "his Coesen name is Cipher Shaw-Langley. He's my son," Langley placed his hand on Cipher's shoulder.

"As a Breed, I am unable to serve as your guard but I offer…" Cipher said, then looked to Caleb, who turned from the window to look at him, "…my loyalty and skills to you both."

Tristan was staring and though he knew it was rude, he couldn't help himself. Cipher's eyes were entrancing.

Get a grip.

Tristan shook his head then said, "No need to be formal. Currently, my seat beside the Sovereign is filled. But, your friendship is appreciated." Tristan extended his hand.

Cipher took it and allowed Tristan to help him to his feet.

Tristan sat back down while Cipher placed his shades back over his eyes then sat. Everyone in the room waited for Tristan to speak but he didn't know where to start. He wanted to shield himself from their hopeful eyes.

They seemed to believe in him when he didn't believe in himself. What should he say to that kind of misplaced faith? At one time, Tristan believed he was worthy; the only man who was capable of being everything the Halo needed. He actually had the audacity to assume he was the only man who could make her happy. Now, he wasn't so sure.

"There is only one man and you are that man," Caleb said.

Rolling his eyes, Tristan grunted, "Uh huh, clearly she didn't get the memo. And stay out of my head gramps."

"Clearly, your visit didn't go well?" Perkins' tone was one of concern.

When Tristan didn't answer, Perkins glanced around the room.

Zeta drank the last drop of water from her bottle with an audible swallow that drew everyone's attention. She tossed the empty bottle in the bin then took a seat beside Cipher, leaving a cushion empty between them. "It didn't," she said.

Tristan winced as the memory of last night replayed in his mind. He still wasn't sure how he was going to fix this thing between him and Cianne. She was mad enough to kill him, and he was worried she would have, but that thought was set aside because something about Perkins' presence was bothering Tristan.

"I thought you were driving to Florida to talk to Cassius about what he's discovered?" Tristan asked.

"I did," Perkins informed them, "but he was long gone. I should have left as soon as I got word he was in the area but I wanted…" Perkins looked down at his drink as he tilted the ice around in small circles. He shrugged. "I'll catch up to him eventually."

The safety and survival of Tristan, their ousted leader, was apparently a collective undertaking. Enough of an undertaking that these people aligned themselves with Caleb, their enemy. That, in and of itself, was an eye opener.

Tristan looked at each of his allies.

Perkins was driven by proven facts, and from the very beginning, he deduced that Caleb wasn't the one who killed Vivian. He was hunting down clues that would prove his gut feelings on the matter when the attempt on Tristan's life was carried out.

Langley was a shrewd lawyer who ran a rather prosperous law firm that offered their services to Coesen and Middlings alike. Getting to know Langley and befriending him was effortless due to the man's easy disposition and non-judgmental outlook. Tristan got the impression that if Cianne abdicated the throne, Langley would have distanced himself from all matters Coesen.

Tristan regarded Zeta. Her motives may be a bit personal. He was still salty about her role in dragging him back here, but he was sure that Zeta was only interested in seeing him and Cianne happy, and in her mind, that meant them being together.

Bannerman's involvement was both professional and duty bound. He was a Coesen through and through, but he was also a close confidant who has practically been with him through every major stage of his life, though only as his physician. Tristan cared for Bannerman and felt that the doctor cared for him, but it was a promise to a beautiful woman over a decade ago that moved the good doctor.

Tristan didn't remember meeting Cianne's mother, Kayla, when he was lying in that hospital bed when he was a boy, but he was sure that the lovely and beguiling woman could have garnered a promise from the Pope if she saw fit.

Tristan turned his head to look at Cipher. Cipher was Langley's son and that alone could explain his involvement, but Tristan wasn't sure it was the only reason.

And that left Caleb. His eyes took in his father-in-law. It was clear with whom Caleb's loyalties lay. Cianne's safety and happiness were his ultimate driving force. Add in a couple of grandchildren the old man probably never thought he would have, and Caleb would do whatever it took to see them all safe.

Just like Zeta, Caleb felt Cianne's happiness was linked to him. Again, Tristan wasn't so sure.

"My friend contacts me every Friday at eleven pm." Perkins glanced at his watch then said, "That gives me a few hours. Hopefully, there'll be some information on Cassius' movements. The old Captain may be more civilian than Protector now, but he's skilled."

It's Friday?

Tristan took a minute to soak in that tidbit of information. "Guess she was really pissed to knock me on my ass for two full days." Questioning eyes fell on him but Tristan didn't elaborate.

"Soahn Cianne almost succeeded in killing him when he went to Ark Manor," Zeta sighed.

The room erupted with gasps, shocked expressions, and overlapping questions.

"What happened?" Langley demanded over the raised voices of the others. The authority he wielded was apparent when everyone quieted. Langley stared at Cipher, who lowered his gaze.

Apparently, neither Caleb nor Bannerman shared the details with the others. Zeta seemed to regret her candid statement, shrinking into herself as everyone stared at Tristan. He surveyed the room, seeing faces with expressions mixed with horror and compassion.

Tristan turned his attention to Caleb, who was still staring out of the window. He always seemed uninterested in the conversation but Tristan knew he was committing every word to memory.

"I wasn't aware he left the mansion, sir," Cipher answered. His face reddened but he looked his father dead in the eyes.

Tristan looked his friends over again, noting their discomfort. Zeta seemed awkward. Perkins looked relieved for a moment, then sorrowful.

Did I miss something?

When Tristan turned his confused gaze on Langley, he saw that he peered at each of the others. The man's gaze was hard and uncompromising. Was Langley in charge?

Chapter Five

Caleb didn't need to look at Tristan to know the boy lowered his head and was moving his hand over his short hair. Caleb preferred his own hair longer, a sign of his old way of life in a simpler time. There were some things he liked about the 19th century, but admittedly those things were low in number.

"She didn't let me say a word," Tristan murmured. His voice was low as if he were talking to himself instead of the room of people. "She may never forgive me."

It was dark out but Caleb saw every leaf, every knot on the large trees that sat on his property. He loved those trees. Being home didn't spark the pain he thought he would be consumed with. At one point, he was afraid that his senses would be overwhelmed with objects and smells that would induce painful reminders of his parents, of Fredrick, of Jai, and of course his Marda. Yet, returning only brought back the beauty of everything he once loved, in glorious high definition.

Everywhere he looked, Caleb saw his loved ones moving about as they had once, long ago during happier times. He glanced over to a corner in the room. There, if he willed it, he could see his mother with her blond springy curls pulled up with pins in some grand design, as she sewed or sipped tea.

His thoughts brought the shadows of his past forward. His mother's green eyes sparkled as her ghostly image looked approvingly at him. His father waltzed into the room with his commanding presence, doing something he never did in front of him or his brother. His father kissed his mother on the lips. Though it was a chaste kiss, it would have never happened outside of his parent's bed chambers.

Caleb glanced back out of the window. A shadow moved in the darkness over the lawn. *Marda.* He sucked in a deep breath. Marda stood below his favorite tree looking at Samuel, who was sitting on the very branch Caleb still loved to sit on. Little Selene and her mother, Jai, sat on the beach laughing at William, who splashed water on his mother, Abigail, and his father, Fredrick Jr.

It was easy to picture them in this way, with them healthy, young, full of life, and together.

"Has there been any chatter about Tristan's return?" Langley asked.

Caleb looked over his shoulder, briefly taking in everyone's position in the room again. He focused on Langley, who seemed to have found his inner leader.

"None," Bannerman offered.

Caleb discussed this matter with Perkins, Bannerman, Zeta, and Cipher yesterday. He got Tristan out of Ark Manor without being seen but he wondered why didn't Cianne report the incident. The Coesen world should be teeming with the news that their White Lion was alive.

Langley sighed. "We need to find out why."

Zeta was going to Ark Manor. Caleb planned to tell Langley, but Tristan spoke up.

"She just attacked and I couldn't do a damn thing to stop her," Tristan whispered.

"That's not exactly true, now is it?" Caleb transferred to Tristan. *"You could have let Aidan and Nadia help, but you chose not to."*

"You son of a bitch!" Tristan yelled as his fist connected with Caleb's jaw.

The kid was getting faster. He moved from his seat to Caleb before any of his Coesen friends realized he moved. The force of the blow would have killed a Middling or floored a Coesen guard, but it only succeeded in throwing Caleb's head to the side and dislocating his jaw.

Though capable of avoiding Tristan's attack, Caleb knew the kid needed to connect.

"They're just kids, *your* grandchildren, but you would allow them to be in the middle of that misunderstanding!"

Opening his mouth wide, all Caleb had to do was move his jaw around to fix the minor injury. "They're more than just kids," he said. He pulled a handkerchief from his pocket and wiped the blood that gathered in the corner of his mouth. Caleb folded the cloth back up and placed it back into the breast pocket of his suit jacket.

Tristan punched him again.

Caleb was all for letting the boy vent, taking another blow to let whatever pent up issues Tristan had. But when Tristan raised his fist a third time…

"**ENOUGH**." With a raise of his hand, Caleb pushed Tristan back several feet. Cocking his head to the side, he glared at his son-in-law who looked back at him with hard narrowed eyes.

Everyone in the room felt the sudden threat. Caleb didn't base that observation on their reactions, but because he also felt the weight of energy he discharged.

Of course, they wanted to protect their would-be king.

Zeta stood but managed only one step toward Caleb before he froze her in place. Bannerman and Perkins got to their feet next, but with a slight wave of Caleb's hand, they too froze. Caleb didn't even have to look in their direction. Out of the corner of his eye, he saw Langley slowly stand while Cipher took small careful steps to get closer his father.

"Not going to defend your delusional King?" When neither man answered, Caleb raised his brow as he observed the pair. "You're not sure what to do. You have conflicting loyalties." Caleb said, focusing on Cipher. "Why is that, counselor?" he looked to Langley, "Why aren't you..."

Before Caleb could finish his question, a fire seemed to ignite inside him. His blood felt as if it was boiling in his veins. He grabbed his head with both hands as if he needed to stop it from exploding.

Kill them. Kill them all.

"Your eyes," Cipher whispered.

Caleb didn't hear Cipher. All he heard was Pythos yelling in his head as they fought each other for control.

KILL. THEM. NOW!

Tristan noticed immediately when the invisible hold on him waned. Pushing with all his strength, he took advantage. His body quaked with rage from his anger and the energy it took him to tear free.

Murder was on Tristan's mind when he flashed over to Caleb to end this. But as he focused on Caleb's ruthless eyes, he saw a flicker of fear. Everything changed in that instant. In those eyes, Tristan saw...

He saw death.

Without thinking of the shit storm he and the others faced, Tristan reached out and placed his hand on Caleb's forearm. His only comfort was that the crimson ring in Caleb's eyes wasn't fully spread throughout Caleb's irises, but it was slowly engulfing them. Blue-green was still the prominent color and that meant Caleb was still in charge, barely.

"If you can hear me in there, Caleb, you're losing it. Fight it or you're going to kill me and fail this mission you're on."

Tristan applied more pressure on Caleb's arm as he watched the red continue to grow.

It was as if time was standing still. Images of the carnage Caleb inflicted on the Coesen village filled Tristan's mind. The air in the room thickened, making it hard for Tristan to breathe. No one was going to survive this.

Tristan sighed…as the idea of death settled in him.

Then, Caleb blinked.

Caleb roared as he as he pulled away from Tristan. Furniture, tables, and the beautiful piano in the corner exploded. Everything in the room was in shambles.

Everything except for all of the people, Tristan realized as he turned to make sure everyone was unscathed. They all looked alright physically, and not one piece of debris seemed to have touched them.

Relieved, Tristan turned his attention back to Caleb. He was gone.

"What the hell just happened?" Bannerman turned in place looking at all the damage.

"We survived," Tristan said, then chuckled. There was nothing funny about what happened but he felt like laughing.

Zeta rushed to him. She began touching and scanning his body for injuries.

"Zeta," Tristan said, trying to get her attention. He said her name several times as she looked him over. She stopped her inspection only when he grabbed her shoulders and gave her a slight shake. With startled wide eyes, she stared up at him.

"I thought he was going to kill you," Zeta admitted as tears ran down her cheeks.

Tristan wiped her tears away as he shook his head. His tone was soft and gentle, reserved only for the women in his life. "Don't you ever come between Caleb and me, Zeta." He lifted her chin when she looked down. "Don't even allow the thought in your mind, because if he wants to he *can* hear it." He looked to each of them in the room. "I need you all to promise me that you will never stand against him."

"Whatever you say," Bannerman offered. He flopped down on what was left of the shredded sofa.

"Red means dead. We got it," Perkins surmised out loud, causing everyone to glare at him. "What?" he said, lifting a chair cushion off the floor and sitting it on what was left of the chair. He sat on the very edge as if concerned the frame would not hold his weight. "It's just my way of simplifying and remembering."

Tristan eased Zeta over to a stool and helped her sit. "Look everyone, I'll deal with Caleb. I know you're all here because you think that I can fix things with Cianne but if the result of my visit says anything, it's that getting her back isn't going to be easy. She would have killed me if Caleb hadn't stepped in."

"I can't believe she would raise a hand to you," Zeta said with disbelief.

He couldn't believe it himself but the knives that were dug out of his flesh was a telling slice of the truth. "Well, she did."

"There had to be a reason why. Attacking someone, especially you isn't normal behavior for her. She's been under an immense amount of stress, which could lead to serious issues if it goes unchecked and untreated." Bannerman's eyes had that far off look he got when he was running possible explanations through his mind. He shook his head. "If I could just examine her, talk to her, I may be able to find out what is happening in that head of hers."

Zeta groaned. "Yeah, but she refuses to allow you to."

Tristan looked over his shoulder to find Langley staring out the same window Caleb was looking out of earlier. In comparison to the disarray the room was in, Langley was immaculate in his designer suit, polished shoes, and tie.

Langley smoothed his hand over his tie. "You can't risk going back there if she wants to kill you."

"I'm going." Zeta cut in. "I leave tomorrow, early afternoon."

Langley walked over to Tristan. "So, it's settled? You're home?"

Tristan was ready to do the most selfish thing he would ever do in his life. He was going to do whatever he had to do to win Cianne back. "I'm home."

"Good," Langley said. "I have to attend to some business. I'll be in my room."

Tristan watched Langley leave, then looked around the trashed room again.

Where did Caleb go?

The next morning
Tristan leaned forward in his chair. He played with the edge of the napkin that his banana sat on as he listened to his friends discuss what happened yesterday in the sitting room.

"I just think you should give him time to cool off," Bannerman said as he sipped his coffee.

Tristan wanted to laugh. Caleb often appeared cool but Tristan knew what boiled under the surface. The man was never calm. He was just skilled at convincing everyone that he was.

On the other side of the table, Zeta pulled at the sleeve of her shirt.

"Something you want to say, Zeta?" Tristan asked.

Zeta opened her mouth then closed it. She seemed to struggle with herself but soon noticed that everyone's attention was on her. She opened her mouth again just as one of the servers entered the room with a tray containing coffee and juice. Zeta said nothing as the middle-aged gentleman placed a glass of orange juice and a cup of coffee in front of Tristan.

The staff, a few men and women, already knew what he liked. They were only on the premises for a few hours a day, but after having no one to care for him in months, Tristan appreciated their attention.

When the server left, Zeta spoke, "You must know how dangerous he is. You've read the Annals containing our history. We shouldn't be here." She looked around the room with wild eyes then focused on Tristan. "*You* shouldn't be here."

Tristan read the Annals, a detailed account of the history of the Coesen. He was able to accept that the Annals were the Coesen version of the truth. He listened to Caleb recount his life, *his* truth. Both sides did their part in creating the hate between the two, and though Tristan once hated the Devil he read about in the Coesen Annals, he found it difficult to hate the man he unwillingly grew to know. Caleb and the Devil the Coesen made him out to be was two different people.

"Not true," Tristan said, as he filled his plate with fluffy eggs, biscuits, and various meats. "This is exactly where I belong."

Langley and Cipher said nothing, giving him no indication of what they were thinking on the matter of Caleb. "We need him. So, I suggest you put aside whatever negative feelings you have toward him and focus on *your* reasons for being here."

Tristan didn't wait for their responses. All he wanted was Cianne and his children back. That these four were on board even though he screwed up was enough for him. He finished his meal as quickly as possible while maintaining the grace he was taught. As he excused himself, Tristan heard Bannerman speak.

"He could have killed us all yesterday."

"But he didn't." Cipher's gravelly voice reached Tristan as he walked down the hallway. "That room was shredded, yet we don't have so much as a scratch among us."

There was the telltale sign of a chair scraping against the hardwood floor, then footsteps exiting the dining room. Cipher must have had enough as well.

77

Tristan found Caleb outside in his tree by the lake. The sun was already shining down over the water, giving it a glow that would give a cinematographer chills. The entire property was truly a beautiful place, with its preserved antebellum beauty still present on the grounds and throughout the mansion.

Caleb and his relatives took care of the property with loving respect and it showed in great detail, from the manicured lawn and trees around the property to the choice of modern yet old style appliances and furniture that filled each room.

Taking a moment to enjoy his surroundings, Tristan didn't speak right away. He just stared out over the lazy water not really knowing what it was he actually wanted to say. There were so many emotions swirling around inside him. There were so many things he wanted to say.

He was angry with himself. He felt frustrated that seeing he was alive didn't make Cianne as breathless as it made him when he laid eyes on her.

Why didn't she run to me?

Why didn't she wrap her arms around him and bury her face in his neck?

Tristan was anxious to do something, anything to make things right. But what he felt underneath everything was slowly eating away at his resolve, his focus.

What if she is done with me?

His fear was like that. It lay in the background, hidden until something triggered it to rise to the forefront. Tristan would like to say that he was completely fearless, but the truth was, he just lived his life by accepting the things he couldn't change and working hard to change the things he could.

When his grandfather passed away, he knew then that death was inevitable and permanent. He just didn't allow it to break him. But since Cianne came into his life, fear was ever present.

The day he saw Bianca standing over her with that gun, his heart stopped. It was as if every fear he ever ignored rained down on him all at once. Losing her…losing his children was what scared him more than anything in this world. It was that fear that made him walk away from them when he saw Cianne commit to mating with Whodai.

He'd done what he thought was right.

"It wasn't," Caleb said. His voice was softer than it ever was. "A man's family is all he has."

"Stay out of my head please," Tristan gritted the order out through clenched teeth.

"Push me out," Caleb challenged.

Tristan wondered if all their interaction would be based on anger, life lessons, and defensive/offensive training. It reminded him of the relationship he had with his own father, but much more physical.

Comparing dangerously volatile Caleb to his business-minded, mostly genteel father, made him laugh.

"Technically Tristan, I am your father," Caleb said, in the most genuine of Darth Vader voices.

One corner of Tristan's lip turned up slightly. "Father-in-law old man," he corrected. "I didn't take you for the Sci-Fi type."

Caleb shrugged, "I've watched a film or two. I prefer historical dramas and comedies but every now and then I find something in a different genre that appeals to me. With Star Wars, I enjoyed the simplicity of the characters and the ease of the storyline."

"Ah," Tristan said, smiling now, "It spoke to you."

Caleb laughed.

In their current situation, there was really no reason to laugh, but Tristan found himself joining in. After their laughter died away, Tristan sighed. It almost felt as if they were just two regular men sitting under the sky discussing something as simple as a movie; not a Coesen Protector shooting the shit with the mortal enemy of the Coesen people.

"Weirder shit has happened," Caleb offered his opinion on Tristan's thoughts.

Looking up, Tristan sighed loudly. "Okay, how do I keep you out of my head?"

"It's simple really. Think of a vault."

Frowning, Tristan questioned, "A vault? It's that easy?"

"No. We were talking movies and that's what they usually say," Caleb said dryly. "I will stay out for now." Something resembling regret passed over Caleb's face momentarily before he straightened his back and returned to his usual stoic demeanor. Breezy conversation on a mild morning was probably not a common thing for him.

Be more normal around Caleb. Tristan logged the information.

"You have to be able to sense when someone is prying in your head. Some are untrained so the intrusion is sloppy and rough. It feels like you've been punched in the head by a cast iron pan. If the person has some skill, the invasion feels like a slight tickle in the back of your neck. If they are an expert at retrieving and combing through thoughts, you won't feel a thing. But you, you are the Protector of the most powerful female on this planet. You may not have her abilities, but I sense that she has endowed you with the means to protect yourself, and by doing so you will be able to protect her. The stronger the Coesen, the stronger the Protector, which means you are the strongest."

That sounded good on paper but…

"So more of you beating me down to build me back up," Tristan groaned.

"You need to be able to hold off a mental attack long enough to strike. The defense is basically the same for a mental attack and mind reading."

It might help when he confronts Cianne again. "Let's get started." Tristan was eager to see her again. On their next meeting, he'll block her mental ability and speak his piece.

"There's no real defense against her when she's like *that*, aside from me." Caleb pinched the bridge of his nose. "The abilities she inherited from me should be growing stronger yet

I barely sensed them. Her Coesen abilities should also be unbinding, granted slowly, but even those were muted greatly. I fear she is holding them in, binding them herself. At some point, they will erupt, and when they do it may not be good for those around her."

Squatting, Tristan lifted a piece of flat tree bark and slowly peeled pieces off and dropped them to the sand. "You'll save her and us," he said with conviction.

"I may not be around to help."

Tristan looked up at Caleb. He smiled. "Right," he said, shaking his head before returning his gaze to the lake. It was a good thing Tristan wasn't the jumpy type because when he glanced up, Caleb was standing beside him. As usual, the man emitted no sound to indicate he moved at all.

"Pythos has awakened," Caleb transferred.

Tristan frowned, thinking of what happened yesterday. "You were losing control," he mumbled. "But you reined it in and made sure no one was hurt."

"Yeah," Caleb said sarcastically as he raised a brow, "their safety was my main concern."

Regardless of Caleb's sarcasm, Tristan knew he didn't take pleasure in killing people even though sometimes it seemed he did. "You can keep him from gaining control, right?"

"Pythos is awake but weak," Caleb said with a shrug.

"But is he going to stay weak?" Tristan knew from reading the Annals that the Coesen acquired their abilities from the essence of the Ilterian race. Caleb's long-life span, preternatural strength, and his unmatched abilities were a direct result of Pythos, who seemed to be anti-Coesen.

Caleb bent down and picked up a small shiny rock beside his foot. He tossed it up in the air then caught it a couple of times before turning his gaze back to Tristan. "I've got it under control," Caleb assured him.

The word of Caleb Scott would normally be enough. As far as Tristan knew, the man never told a lie to him or anyone else. Caleb did, however, take his sweet time supplying important information until he saw fit to share. But he never lied.

That was until now. There was something Tristan never saw before in those familiar eyes. It only lasted a split second and it was a look he'd seen before, but never on Caleb. It was a look Tristan knew well because he saw it often in Cianne's beautiful eyes.

It was uncertainty.

"You need to worry about how you're going to convince Cianne that you left her and the children only to keep them safe. Considering your last meeting, I'd say your next will be just as difficult." Caleb threw the stone at an angle and it skipped across the water, touching down several times.

Tristan didn't follow its path but he was sure if he crossed the lake he would find the stone on the other side, resting on the shore.

"And we still need to find out who wants you dead."

Tristan shook his head again as if doing so was going to fix the mental shit storm that was building inside it. He pissed Cianne off by just breathing. How in the hell was that possible?

Damn…don't I have enough to deal with?

No doubt whoever wanted his head was going to be a little peeved that he was still alive. And to top off his ever-growing problems, Caleb, the man he wanted to hate but ended up actually caring for, was a walking time bomb. Taking into account what happened the last time that bomb exploded, Tristan was pretty sure losing a hidden village would pale in comparison to the destruction Caleb's parasite would do now.

But everything meant nothing if he didn't get Cianne back.

Does she still love me? Has she really moved on?

"She *is* engaged," Caleb shrugged, throwing another stone across the lake.

Tristan narrowed his eyes. The need to put Caleb on his ass was overpowering. "Stay. The. Hell. Out. Of. My. Head."

"Again," Caleb said then sighed, "keep me out."

Tristan rubbed both hands over his head before locking his fingers behind the back of his neck. God, his life was so frustrating. He tilted his head back and roared. It sounded more animalistic than human as it shattered the early morning silence around them.

Caleb rolled his eyes. "Sound the all clear, please. I really don't want to hurt your friends."

Tristan looked over to the grand deck stairs then to the back patio. Cipher was sitting on the railing with a book in hand but his head was raised and he seemed to be peering his shaded eyes at Tristan and Caleb. Zeta was leaning out of the French doors, looking their way.

He knew they were on edge. Shamed, Tristan waved.

"White Lion, huh?" Caleb grinned. "Look, I doubt she's fallen for the taller, darker, and more handsome guy. But I bet he's head over heels for her."

Tristan pinned Caleb with an angry glare.

"What?" Caleb glared back. "Look, I've never seen a woman love a man the way she loves you. This coming marriage is nothing but a Coesen union based on tradition. I haven't been able to watch her like I want now that I'm enemy number one again, but I know she has been doing nothing but existing since you've been gone. What she did when you went to her was unexpected but she has a reason. More than one. If you can get her to just listen to you, I'm sure she will understand."

A hollow empty laugh was all Tristan could muster. "Yeah, if..." He picked up a stone and hurled it sideways into the lake. "I guess I should practice skipping stones too."

"Maybe, but since we have little time to spare, I suggest we get to business." Caleb hurled another stone into the lake. "I won't delve too deep into your mind. It isn't something I like doing which means I almost never do it. Even though it's an advantage in some instances, I find that people rarely do what they're thinking. I've learned the hard way that thought and intent are very different. When you read minds, you have no way of knowing which is which. And honestly, I couldn't give a rat's ass about what a person wants for lunch or who their neighbor is sleeping with. So," Caleb turned to face him, "let's keep it clean. Block me out of your mind."

Tristan fisted his hands and foolishly tried to prepare himself for the pain that was coming. His lips curved upwards. There was a part of him that took pleasure from his physical pain. It was the man inside him who would never forgive the boy who willingly walked away from his family. He would gladly suffer the fires of Hell to win them back.

...and when he did win Cianne and his children back, he was never letting them go or allowing anyone to hurt them. If that meant enduring unimaginable pain to be the best, then so be it. Nothing was ever coming between him and what was his again.

Caleb raised a brow, "The best? You would be more like third at best."

"Whatever old man," Tristan grinned wickedly, "Don't hold back. I have a family reunion to plan."

Chapter Six
May 13ᵗʰ

Zeta examined the large foyer at Ark Manor. Everything looked the same, but the mode of operation was different. When she last visited Cianne, it was as if her prior status and respect as a Royal Protector to Sovereign Harper were of no consequence. Security was heavy and visitors were almost always turned away.

Even her.

Today, she was scanned at the gate and allowed entry without an escort. It reminded her of the way things once were.

Zeta inhaled. The scent of Sovereign Harper still lingered inside the walls of the mansion. It was lavender with the subtle scent of what Zeta referred to as "Born Rich". It was a scent that she was familiar with. After she Transitioned at age twelve, she moved in with her ward, Felipe, who came from a very wealthy family. With her being an orphan, her living with him made it easier for them both.

When Zeta saw a woman wearing all black with soft soled shoes pass in front her, she held up her hand. "Excuse me," she called out.

The woman stopped and offered Zeta a wide smile. "Yes, Miss Zeta?"

Zeta frowned. "I'm sorry," Zeta said, moving forward, "have we met?"

"Not formally, Miss." The woman bowed her head. "I am Glenda. I oversee the domestic operations here at Ark Manor now. Mrs. Higgins and her husband decided to retire, after… Yes well, I had the good fortune of securing a position by her referral." Glenda waved her hand, silently telling Zeta to lead the way. "I was informed, as was all of the staff, that you were here through these nifty ear communicators." She tapped her left ear.

That explained why there was no one to greet and follow her around like she was a threat. Apparently, the new Captain did things differently.

"Did you not get the new introduction packet that was sent out last month? All of the Royal Guards should have received one."

Zeta winced. "I haven't exactly been home in the last few months."

They arrived at one side of the large staircase. "Well then, that explains it," Glenda said, with a smile. "I will inform Captain Rey that you will require a packet. Soahn Cianne is currently in the playroom. Enjoy your visit."

"Thank you," Zeta said before turning toward the stairs.

Zeta heard the children as she approached the playroom. The doors opened as she reached for the knob. Before she knew what was happening, Cianne was there launching herself into her arms. Zeta was taken off guard, considering their last visit didn't go over so well. The hug was tight and long. It was something Zeta needed.

"How have you been?" Cianne asked, holding her out at arm's length.

"I've been good. How are you?"

"The children keep me busy." Cianne smiled.

Speaking of the children, Nadia was making her way over to them. "She's walking!" Zeta leaned over and lifted Nadia up in her arms. "You're walking princess. Look at you."

"I walk," Nadia said. She threw her hands in the air, and her beautiful green eyes sparkled.

"And talk," Zeta said as she lifted Nadia and spun her around in a circle. "Where's my big man?" Zeta looked around the room for Aidan. He was standing near the link block table watching her.

His adorable face always seemed eclipsed by his soulful eyes.

"Hi," Aidan said with a wave.

"Hey, big man." Zeta made her way over to him. She eased Nadia to the floor and extended her hand to Aidan. He placed his tiny hand on hers and she gave it a little shake. "What are you building?"

"We," Cianne said, joining them at the table, "are building a zoo." She lifted some little gray blocks and attached them to a structure that resembled a small house. "I am in charge of the gift shop. Nadia is in charge of the penguin habitat and Aidan is partial to the lions so he is making their habitat." Cianne placed another gray block on the structure. "Would you like to help?"

"Sure would." Zeta got down on her knees. "I can totally build the reptile house."

As they built, Zeta noticed an object peeking out of Aidan's shirt pocket. It was a miniature white lion with a golden crown upon its head. Zeta looked over at Cianne, who was watching her. Cianne gave Zeta a weak smile then began talking and praising the children for their creations.

"Our zoo rocks," Zeta said an hour later. She peered down at the table, admiring their hard work. "I totally rocked this play date. I could give up my day job and work in a daycare."

Cianne raised her brows, "Says the woman who fought with a one-year old for the last brown building block." She picked up two large colorful floor pillows and moved them against the wall next to two other pillows.

Zeta placed several books on the bookshelf that covered an entire wall. She picked the last book up off the floor. It was thick, just like the others she placed on the shelf. Curious, she turned the book over to view the title. Her brows rose and she smiled.

"You're reading this to the kids?"

Cianne looked over her shoulder as she placed several pieces of doll furniture inside a huge doll house. "Ah," she said focusing on the book Zeta held up. Cianne looked away, her expression guarded. Then she straightened and shrugged with a look of resignation. "No, Aidan reads them to himself."

"He reads this?" Zeta asked skeptically.

Cianne nodded. She looked nervous as she swept her hair back from her face but the thick mane of dark brown hair fell back in place and settled, cupping her jaw on both sides.

"And he understands it?" Zeta flipped through the pages.

"We discuss them in detail after he's done," Cianne shrugged. "Aidan speaks differently when we communicate telepathically. If he's vocal, his words are broken and pieced like a child his age. Telepathically, he sounds like a young boy with an extensive vocabulary. He doesn't like the restraint of speaking." She smiled tightly, "Want to go for a walk? The children are scheduled to eat dinner with their grandparents and will be occupied for a while after."

Zeta placed the book on the shelf and crossed the room. She followed Cianne down the hall and steps. They avoided the common areas to get outside and took the servants hall to get to a back door. Neither spoke, which gave Zeta a moment to digest that the Bertrams were at Ark Manor. She knew that they visited with the children often but she assumed Cianne would want to visit with them as well.

It was probably best that Cianne didn't visit with them. Her avoiding the Bertrams most likely made it easier for them. Tristan advised his parents that in order to keep them, the children, and Cianne safe, they would need to keep his return a secret until he took care of the threat. They agreed, but Zeta knew it was a struggle for them as well.

After they were away from the main house and into the cool night's air, Zeta spoke. "You should talk to Dr. Bannerman. He may know a specialist who you can speak with, someone who can gauge how advanced Aidan is and can challenge him."

Cianne chuckled but there was no humor laced within. "Aidan reads books that some twelve-year-old kids can't read but he is a toddler through and through. Though, he may understand more than he lets on." She shrugged then said, "I didn't even know he could read or even speak telepathically until I caught him reading a princess book to Nadia. You should have seen them nestled together on her bed, him turning the pages and her following along."

They followed the path of the paved walkway. Zeta exchanged a bow of courtesy to two passing guards on patrol then glanced over at Cianne.

"Aidan is smart," Cianne continued when they were alone, "really smart, but he is still a toddler who loves playing with blocks, tummy tickles when he allows, and bubbles. His brain is advanced but his body and desires are that of a one-and-a-half-year-old. And he is so self-conscious about being different that he hides within himself."

Wow. Zeta thought of how confusing this all was for the children and Cianne. "I guess I wasn't really thinking about his feelings. It's kinda hard being a mom, huh? Having to be responsible for someone else, making decisions for them."

"Even harder when you have to make all the decisions alone." Cianne led them along the familiar route. It was the same path Sovereign Harper used to walk.

"I imagine so," Zeta said. Parenting issues weren't the perfect segue to Tristan but it would have to do. "You know," Zeta took a deep breath and looked at Cianne, "I'm sorry about not believing you when you said that Tristan was alive. If you say he's alive then—"

Cianne stopped and turned to face Zeta. "Don't," she whispered. "Please don't do this. This is a good day. I spent most of it awake, with my children, and with you, my dear friend. I haven't fallen asleep, had a day or nightmare, and I haven't seen any apparitions of my...him." Cianne lowered her head.

Zeta heard Cianne's pulse pick up and her breathing deepen. It seemed that Cianne was trying to calm herself. It was an awful thing to do but Zeta needed to know. They all needed to know. "You've seen Tristan," she asked, "recently?"

Cianne took another deep breath, this one slow going in and even slower coming out. "When I'm awake, I see Tristan everywhere. Standing, sitting, smiling at me. I see him whenever I sleep, but in my dreams, he is usually trying to kill me. In my dreams," she whispered, "he always turns into Caleb before he deals the death blow. But a few days ago, my nightmare was different. Instead of him trying to kill me," she trailed off, "I tried to kill him."

"Oh God, Cianne," Zeta grabbed her hands. "How do you know that you were dreaming? What if—"

"Don't!" Cianne yelled. A rumble or a shifting sound came seconds before the ground beneath them started to vibrate. "Tristan is gone. It was a nightmare." The ground vibrated again, this time stronger. "It felt different." She all but whispered as she shook her head. "His eyes were the same as I remember...but he smelled odd and his aura was like...it was like Caleb's." Cianne's eyes narrowed but after a few breaths, she frowned then looked in the distance as if she was working something out. The ground shook for a few seconds. "He had a smell. Nightmares don't have smells. Do they?" She raised her hand to her head. "No...no...no, the wall was fine. No blood was on the hallway floor. A dream, it was just a dream."

The ground beneath Zeta's feet settled. Zeta watched in silence as Cianne sank to the cool cement, rocking back and forth, holding her herself tight. Bending down, Zeta helped

Cianne to her feet. She wrapped her arms around her friend and held her close as they slowly strolled back to the house using the same door they exited from earlier.

Zeta used her enhanced hearing to avoid running into any of the house staff, guards, or the Bertrams while she escorted Cianne to her bedroom.

She sat in the sitting area of Cianne's bedroom after putting Cianne to bed. Zeta wanted to get back to the others to report her strange findings but she needed to make sure Cianne was alright before she left. She was just rising to her feet to check on Cianne when Cianne shot up and swung her feet off her bed and stood.

Taken by surprise at how fast Cianne moved, Zeta froze. She watched as Cianne moved to the vanity and began brushing her hair without even acknowledging that she was in the room.

"Cianne?" Zeta slowly walked over and stood beside her friend. "Cianne, are you alright?"

Cianne suddenly stilled. Her raised hand hovered with the brush halfway down the length of her hair. Cianne tilted her head to the side and pinned Zeta with a cunning gaze and a knowing smile that set off every self-perseveration alarm Zeta had, then Cianne faced the mirror and continued to brush her hair out.

An icy chill ran down Zeta's spine.

"What...The...Hell?" Zeta backed out of the room with her eyes fixed on Cianne. It wasn't until her back hit the wall in the hallway did she realize that the bedroom door had somehow opened.

The sound of Cianne's bedroom door slamming shut caused Zeta, an experienced Coesen, to jump with fright. She sucked in a gulp of fear-laced air as she descended the stairs in a rush. Gail or Gwen called out to her as she ran out of the front door but Zeta ignored the woman. Her pulse was still racing when she jumped in the rental car and tapped the stored number on her cell.

"Hello," Langley answered. Him answering on the first ring and his anxious tone said that he was very interested in her visit with Cianne.

Zeta took some deep breaths but she was unable to speak, and she had no idea what she was going to say. She really didn't know what just happened or why she was so unnerved, and even a good two miles away from the Manor she still was.

Why was she running?

"Zeta, what's wrong? What happened?" Langley's concern broke through to her.

"Umm," she began. The low sound of rustling fabric beside her caught Zeta's attention. When she glanced over to her right, she screamed or thought she did. She wasn't sure if she screamed or cursed because her brain literally shut down in that moment, and the left turn she was in the process of making was going horribly wrong.

As she tightened her grip on the steering wheel of the rental car with her left hand, she dropped her cell phone and reached for her firearm with her right.

A steady hand took hold of her wrist, effectively restraining her ability to pull the trigger. "Get control of the vehicle." Caleb's matter-of-fact tone both gave her a sense of relief and tipped her mounting anxiety over the edge.

When he released her wrist, she grabbed the steering wheel and steadied the car. Somehow, she managed to avoid the oncoming cars and swerve back into the lane she needed to be in. The string of curses that spilled from her mouth as she banged the steering wheel was a shock to her own ears but it was all she could do to express her frustration with everything.

It took Zeta a few minutes to calm and Caleb allowed her the time without saying a word even though his jaw was tight and his eyes betrayed his forced appearance of serenity. It took a while but she was noticing those subtle nuances of his, more and more. He was irritated, but still, he gave her time.

"You don't think she's in immediate danger," Caleb stated.

Just when she was thinking of him as being human… Zeta didn't like him reaching inside her head even though he claimed he never reached further than what was on the surface.

Sighing, Caleb said, "Fine, then drive to where you rented the car and tell me what has you so uneasy."

Chapter Seven

Whodai held his cellphone to his ear. He listened intently but thought that Cianne sounded distant, lonely. That shouldn't be the case because she was surrounded by staff and she had her children. Not to mention that the Bertrams were at the Manor and he was told that Zeta just visited the day before.

It confused him that she seemed so alone, though he would prefer that she received no visitors at all. When he was acting Commander of the Guard, he went through many steps to isolate Cianne from those who could put chinks in his plans. But Jamiah was in charge now and he did away with almost all of the protocols Whodai put in place.

When I am King…

Whodai focused on Cianne's voice as she reviewed her day without him. It was his daily ritual to check in on his intended while he was away but she called him tonight. A pleasant surprise, but the loneliness in her sweet voice actually pained him.

"Any more nightmares or blackouts?" Whodai asked when she paused.

Cianne sighed, then softly said, "I was thinking of doing something special for Aidan and Nadia."

Whodai didn't like that she changed the subject. He longed to be the male she trusted with her problems, her secrets, her heart. He wanted that now. Yet, he was willing to wait. He was willing to wait for her.

Smoothly and gently, he responded without indicating how frustrated he was with the progress of their relationship. "I have something perfect in mind. I was planning to discuss it with you when I returned."

"Really?" Cianne's voice lifted as if she was smiling.

Whodai closed his eyes for a second to imagine Cianne lying on her bed, covered in a soft satin silk nightgown as she spoke to him. He saw her beautiful smile stretching those succulent lips of hers.

"Really," he said, smiling too. "Now I have to go but I'll be home Sunday. We'll discuss it then. I will set everything up."

"I thought you were coming back sooner? It's Tuesday."

He loved that she was counting the days until his return. Whodai knew it would take time for her to see him the way he saw her. It would have happened sooner if she wasn't so haunted by the memory of her dead mate. The worst thing for him to face was that she might have gotten over Tristan's death sooner had he not intervened. Now, there were times that Cianne's link to Tristan seemed even stronger.

"An important matter that I have to handle myself has come up. I'll be *home* soon. Now try to get some rest and I'll call you tomorrow afternoon."

"Alright," she said. The smile in her voice faded.

When Whodai heard the disconnect sound, he pressed his palms to his forehead, sliding his hands outward until he reached his temples. *Give her time.* He sighed. *You'll have all of her soon enough.*

He dropped his hands to the steering wheel and sighed again. How had things gotten so complicated? All he needed to remember was that Cianne was his.

She has always been mine. That fact was evident, but at what cost?

It truly didn't matter the cost. He'd pay any price.

Toggling his gear shift to make sure it was in neutral before turning the key in the car's ignition, Whodai put the car in gear, managed the pressure on the clutch and gas, then steered the car back onto the road.

Those damn nightmares were going to ruin her.

Twisting Tristan into a nightmare seemed like a good idea. Whodai thought it was a way to snuff out the connection between Cianne and her dead mate so that he could easily gain her trust then her love. Invading and molding her dreams to his benefit seemed to be the only way a Coesen's ability worked on her back then. Her mind and defenses were at rest when she was asleep, only he didn't factor that Cianne's subconscious mind would take those initial artificial nightmares that were fed to her and mold them into something much darker.

Felix, a Royal Guard and one of his trusted men, paid for their tampering with his life, and now those once suggestive dreams were an entity of their own. Even more troubling, when in the sleep daze of one of her nightmares Cianne was someone wholly different and extremely dangerous.

Hindsight was 20/20. He should have never listened to his partner and had Felix mess with her dreams.

The ringing of his cell phone drew Whodai's attention. There was no need to pull over to take the call. He only gave Cianne his full undivided attention. Plus, he was running late and he wasn't in the mood to talk, but he did glance at the number.

I thought up the devil, he told himself. His partner in this little coup was checking on his progress. Whodai allowed the cell to ring again before answering.

"Is it done?"

That husky voice always made his skin crawl. Whodai straightened in his seat. "I was delayed but I'm on my way," he responded. In his tone, there was none of the soft gentleness that he reserved for Cianne. He said nothing, nor did his caller, for several beats. "Is there something else you need?" he finally asked.

"Your progress with the girl, or lack thereof, concerns me. The children still live. That's not what we originally discussed. Secure their deaths so we can move forward."

"I know what needs to be done." Whodai glanced up at the street sign he was passing. He made a slow right turn, paying attention to the addresses as he drove. The houses were spaced out the more he drove. That was good. "Are there any more *concerns* you would like to voice? I have business to take care of."

"Failure is not an option I'm comfortable with," the caller said.

"Yeah, I'll make note of that." Whodai rolled his eyes.

The laugh on the other end of the call was not comforting but Whodai shrugged it off. He had everything under control. Things were more or less moving along as they should. Cianne will be his mate in a little over a month. After the nuptials…after Cianne gives him all of herself, he planned to take everything she holds dear from her.

Whodai planned to take her children from her first then her throne. If things went as planned, he should already have her heart by then. If not, he'd have it soon enough, because he planned to be the one holding her tight through those trying times.

"Business I'm sure you will enjoy more than I would," the voice held no disdain or disgust. As always, his collaborator didn't judge the manner in which he handled things. The concern, apparently, was with the timeframe in which he handled them. "I'll leave you to it."

There were no goodbyes or promises to speak later. Each of them knew that the other was vital to their operation to gain control of the Coesen nation. They both understood that Whodai was not to just be a figurehead but the sole leader in the end. His collaborator was happy to remain in the shadows, satisfied with what bringing him to power would do for them.

There were some Coesen who romanticized the old ways, some who thought the old ways were to be honored. They didn't agree with mixing business, family, or recreation with Middlings unless absolutely necessary. They believed in archaic laws and punishment. In their eyes, Whodai won the Tandot and he was the rightful mate of the Sovereign. To them, he was the perfect male specimen and the perfect instrument for the rebirth of the Coesen, a rebirth to bring back the ways of old.

Whodai chuckled as he continued driving down the street lined with craftsman-style homes. He didn't care about politics or the ways of old. His parents were raised in the old ways and even though they raised him and his sister the same, they encouraged them to have knowledge of the world and the Middlings who governed it. Whodai had no preference for either way of life. In all honesty, he couldn't care less. His own interests were his only concerns.

Lampposts lit up the numbers on the mailboxes for him to read in the darkness. Whodai passed his destination and drove to the end of the street then made a turn at the corner. He rode several more blocks before parking alongside a cluster of cars near a house that was in full swing of a party that didn't seem to be slowing regardless of the late hour.

It didn't take long for him to walk back to the house he sought. From the outside, the interior seemed quiet and dark, with a low glow from a television downstairs. Whodai heard voices but couldn't determine if they were coming from a television on the ground floor or upstairs.

He moved around to the rear of the house, avoiding a wide variety of children's toys. After checking for an alarm and finding none, he pushed the rear door open, dislodging both the top and bottom locks to get inside.

Whodai saw no reason to rush through this so he opened the refrigerator, pulled out a beer, and had a seat at the kitchen table.

George Kent blew out a long pent up sigh. "Go to the bathroom, Myra," he ordered. "I'll pause the movie."

"Fine, I'll be right back," she said as she struggled to her feet.

He would have helped her get up but she hated when he tried. As if he could coddle Myra Kent. She was and would forever be independent. That was the very thing that caught his interest when he met her at Gering, the Coesen U.S. campus located in Texas.

George pushed himself up from his laid-back position on the sofa and glanced at the TV. The movie they were watching wasn't bad but it wasn't good either. He had trouble staying interested in the comedic antics of a new father trying to hold on to his old life while being pushed into a new one that involved diapers, a family van, and maintaining a relationship with his childless friends.

The truth was, the movie hit too close to home for him to enjoy. The main character was going to find his happy medium by the end of the film, while George continued to struggle with those problems and a few more.

Unlike the star of the film, money was a very real problem for George and his family. Since the birth of Fran and Jake, their four and six-year-olds, money was tight. Even with him making good money at CoTech as a biochemist, he had to dabble in things he shouldn't just to make ends meet.

George stared at the frozen image on his television. How easy life would be if he was born with a silver spoon in his mouth. He scrubbed a hand over his tired face.

Getting involved with his department head, Professor Zuri seemed like a blessing at the time. After saying yes to the top-secret project Zuri offered him, George was given a promotion almost immediately. He received a significant bump in pay and a new respect at the job just from being linked to the highly-respected Professor.

That respect was long overdue, in his opinion.

What George didn't understand then was that he made a deal with the devil himself. Zuri wasn't the fine upstanding Coesen everyone thought him to be. He had the right lineage, the status of a hard working successful male of worth, and the trust of all the Coesen who counted. But he was evil incarnate, dressed in high-priced suits and wielding a forked tongue.

Zuri dealt with the black arts called Jzerect, a forbidden form of science laced with Coesen abilities that were outlawed. Anyone found using Jzerect was dealt death by the Coesen Guards.

George learned too late that the secret project he and Zuri were working on was a poison he thought was nothing but an urban legend. Not much different from the tales of the Boogeyman used by Middlings to scare their young. By the time he realized what Zuri was up to, it was too late and he was in too deep.

Yawning, George slipped into his slippers and pushed off the sofa. He headed for his remodeled gourmet kitchen. A few cookies for him and some popcorn for Myra might throw them back into movie mode and take his mind off his worries.

Only, the thought of going inside the kitchen triggered mixed emotions. It was the first investment he and Myra made after his promotion. At that time, he was still in the dark about what he was really doing. He was only subjected to partial data and experiments that were eventually completed by Zuri. It wasn't until a few months later that he stumbled onto the real reason for all his hard work. When he approached Zuri and was given an ultimatum—make the money he needed or die— of course, he chose life.

George desperately needed the money being as his family just kept growing. Not to mention how he enjoyed all the new attention from his co-workers. Even Myra was acting differently toward him. She always loved him but for the first time in their marriage, she wasn't the one bringing in the most money.

If he wasn't such a worrier, he might enjoy the benefits of his walk on the dark side more.

George flipped the light switch on the wall then went to the custom-made cabinet where he stored the popcorn. As he removed the wrapping and placed the pack into the microwave, an odd sensation ran through him. George lifted his chest and straightened his back.

He felt like a man. He *was* a man and now he finally felt like one. That was why he needed to continue with the special project.

As George moved toward the cookie jar that sat on their new marble countertop, he thought he saw something. He glanced over in that direction, expecting to see one of the dogs trotting by, but what he saw made him gasp and jump back, almost completely onto the countertop.

The cookie jar shattered as it hit the floor.

Sitting at his table was the first son, Royal Guard, and the Sovereign's intended, Whodai Tam.

"Did I frighten you, George?" Whodai asked.

George didn't hear any mischief or fake comfort in the voice. It was a simple question and though they both knew the answer, it was just a question.

"Yeah, uh yes, Soahn," George stuttered, "you frightened me." He slowly placed his feet back on the floor as he took a quick look at the kitchen entrance for Myra. When he didn't see his wife, he turned his attention back to Whodai.

Did she hear the commotion? Will she be running in at any moment?

Whodai nodded his acknowledgment. There was no smile of accomplishment on Soahn Whodai's face like there would be if it were Zuri or one of his minions sitting at his table.

Complete silence filled the room until George heard water running through the pipes from the upstairs toilet flushing. Myra never much liked the downstairs powder room. Plus, she took any opportunity to check on the children.

"I…did not expect you to come to my home, Soahn. Not in person."

"You contacted me, didn't you?"

George wanted to deny it, but lying to a Guard, and one such as Whodai Tam, was foolish. He didn't know what abilities the Royal wielded. Feeling frayed, George looked down as he fisted his sweaty hands. Instead, he chose to evade the question. "I, I should inform Myra we have a guest."

"Don't move."

George felt as if those mere two words wrapped around him like a noose. They were simple words, yet the sound of the voice that spoke them was equivalent to the most beautiful song he ever heard. He wanted to turn his head, to find the Angel who was sent to him from the heavens, but nothing else mattered to him other than following the voice's instruction.

Yet, in the far reaches of his mind, an itch of a thought kept trying to push forward. There was a feeling that called to his base instinct to protect something or someone, but George couldn't get hold of who or what he should be protecting. The voice was his main concern, his only concern.

Whodai sat with one leg crossed over the other, at the small kitchen table. He sized up George Kent, a brilliant scientist, and family man. He was youngish, maybe in his early thirties. He was handsome enough and had a beautiful wife.

"Look at me, George."

George turned around to face him.

"Now, I want you to respond with short honest answers. Did you contact me?" Whodai loved controlling people with his Wheddler's ability. The high was heady and he got things done much faster than the use of physical force.

"Yes!"

"How did you know I conducted business with Castor Zuri?"

George swayed then said, "I partnered with him on the secret project."

"My Project," Whodai sneered. He tilted his head and took in a calming breath to rein in his anger. Zuri should have known better.

"Yes," George admitted.

"Did Zuri tell you about me?"

Shaking his head frantically, George spoke, "No...no. When Zuri didn't show for our weekly meeting, I suspected he was taken by the Coesen Guard. I went to his office to make sure there was nothing linking me to our work. I discovered a hidden cabinet and found out who the project was for."

"Have you told anyone of my involvement, George?"

"I am the only one who knows."

"Good," Whodai said.

George sighed as if he was pleased that Whodai was pleased. "George, do you have the information that links me to Zuri?"

"Yes."

Whodai sat forward, dropping his foot to the floor. "**Get the evidence**."

George turned to the refrigerator and reached for the cabinets above. He pulled out a locked box then reached inside his t-shirt and pulled off a long chain with a round disc from around his neck. He walked them over and handed them to Whodai.

"I will not be blackmailed by you or anyone else. If you were a smart man, you would have burned that evidence and forgot you ever knew it existed. But instead, you make demands and gained my attention. Do you own a gun, George?" Whodai asked as he stood.

"Yes."

"Good. **I want you to get your gun, then I want you to shoot your wife and children through the heart. After you've made sure that they are dead, I want you to shoot yourself in the head, directly between the eyes.**"

"Yes, between the eyes."

Whodai didn't follow George as the man left the kitchen and climbed the stairs.

◉

George saw his wife as she ushered Jake, their six-year-old, back to bed. He walked forward with his orders replaying in his head.

He needed his gun.

"Jake woke up. I gave him a glass of water and I'm putting him back in bed," Myra said as she passed George.

"Daddy?" Jake's voice sounded drowsy from sleep. "Can I come downstairs too?"

George ignored them as he made his way to his bedroom. None of his fatherly instincts rose as he heard his wife kiss their son then told him to get back in his own bed. He did hear his wife's footfalls as she followed him inside their room. He noted that he wouldn't have to go after her.

"George, is everything?"

He felt his wife's eyes on him as he took down the lock box from a top shelf in the closet. The key was on his nightstand, so George carried the lock box with him as he crossed the room to retrieve it.

"Oh, my God, George, what are you doing?" she asked, her voice sounding high.

George unlocked the box and didn't hesitate as he rose up and aimed at Myra's chest. A scream barely escaped her mouth before the bullet hit her heart, dead center. Myra dropped to the floor like a sack of potatoes.

Inside George's chest, an ache bloomed into an unforgiving pain of red hot flames. Tears streaked down his face as he walked into the hallway, yet he was so determined to follow orders. Even as his heart broke for doing something so vile, so unforgivable.

Whodai sat behind the wheel of his rental car, thinking of Cianne as he took the off-ramp that led him to the hotel where he was staying. He realized now that it was a mistake to mess with someone in such a fragile state the way they did. The damage could be permanent. It certainly was the reason for her sleepwalking episodes.

This latest one, with the kitchen knives, was unexpected. If Kim wasn't doing a walk through since the kids' usual Guard was out of town, it could have been bad. But Kim was there and managed to cover it up before the entire house discovered the blades embedded in the wall across from the children's bedroom the next morning.

Kim, a trusted subordinate, oversaw the repairs with a prepared story about something along the lines of an electrical problem inside the walls. Thankfully, there was no need to explain anything to Cianne. She slept through the entire repair.

Pulling up to the hotel's valet stand, Whodai got out of his rental and handed over the keys. He ignored the practiced smiles and greetings of the hotel staff as he moved through the large grandiose lobby to get to the elevator.

As the elevator rose to the penthouse suite, Whodai wondered what Cianne was doing with those knives. Per Kim, they were clean. Whodai also entertained the thought that he may have caused Cianne irreparable mental damage.

No. He wouldn't entertain such thoughts.

His Queen was perfect. She was more powerful than any Coesen before her. With his love and encouragement, Cianne will pull out of the depression that was plaguing her. He was going to give her the strength to be the leader she was destined to become. Under his tutelage, unbeknownst to his supporters and conspirators, they will rule together.

Whodai had no intentions of ruling the Coesen without his beautiful bride. Unlike his accomplices, he cared nothing about who her father was or the whisperings among his Pure Bloodline supporters about her Breed status. He wanted

Cianne's body and soul. All he needed was to accept her oath and claim her during the mating ceremony. They were to be joined as one, and only then, will he sever her connections to the boy who tried to take what was his by right. Only then, when they were made whole, would he rid himself of her offspring to make way for an heir of his own loins.

"Until then," Whodai said under his breath. He smiled as he walked through the large suite toward the bedroom. He unbuttoned his shirt and hung it over a chair's back in a sitting area of the bedroom. Until he had Cianne, he needed to satisfy his needs with less than adequate look-a-likes.

He quickly showered, dressed, and exited his swank room. It was hunting time.

Chapter Eight
Quende Territory, Brazil

Chandra inwardly sighed but gave her guest her best business smile. "I am a very busy woman Mr. Yarell." She waved over the waiter who stood at the ready a few feet away to refill her cup and serve her guest.

"Soahn Chandra," the male greeted. He took the hand she offered, turned it so the back was facing up, and placed his lips firmly on her skin. "I'm happy that you finally agreed to meet me."

When he loosened his hold, Chandra pulled her hand away. "Making time for everyone who wants an audience is difficult. You have my attention now." She lifted the steaming cup to her lips and took a sip, speaking when the waiter returned to his station. "How may I help you?"

Mr. Yarell smiled as he took a seat across from her. "Of course," he agreed, "but it is I and my associate who can help you. We understand that you have separated from the collective. I…I mean we, the Kytel, have been watching you and we feel that a partnership would benefit all involved."

"And why would you think that, Mr. Yarell?"

"I've read your theory on the Breed. The examples you gave on how they weaken our nation on a molecular and social level are unparalleled." He pushed the tea away and leaned forward. "No one has ever made it so clear," he added.

Chandra took a moment to really look at Mr. Yarell. He was tall, like most Coesen men. He wore an expensive suit and was well groomed. He was possibly around her age, give or take a few years. His smile was genuine but his eyes were calculating.

She didn't like him.

Of course, she knew of Yarell for some years. He and his group, the Kytel, spewed their message to anyone who listened. Talking wasn't against Coesen law but she always suspected the Kytel of more.

"I was nineteen when I wrote that paper. Life was simple then and my views at the time were motivated by a cushy upbringing, a sheltered mind, and the fact that my ego was bigger than the planet." Chandra shook her head as she placed her tea cup on the saucer. "You are mature enough to recognize the ravings of a child." Mr. Yarell began to speak but Chandra cut him off. "I don't want to waste any more of your time, Mr. Yarell. I have separated from the *collective* but not because Sovereign Bertram is a Breed. I've separated myself because she has no loyalty to our people, as a whole. It is no secret I have issues with the diluting of our blood lines. I also have issues with fast food, but I do not seek out Blimpy Burger's employees to terrorize them. Hate is not my goal here." She smiled. "No, I don't think we can help each other at all."

Mr. Yarell sat back stiffly before getting to his feet. He straightened his suit jacket. "With your pool of supporters thinning in light of the media selling the Breed Queen's fairytale wedding, I would encourage you to reconsider. We both could benefit from a union."

"I can see how you might think so." Chandra placed her napkin on the table and waved for the check. "Oh, and Mr. Yarell…although I am separated from the collective, the Coesen in my territory, Breed included, are still under my protection. You have a great day."

Chandra watched him walk away before she made her way to the lobby to get to the elevators. Victor and her other two Guards surrounded her and her assistant, ushering them into the elevator when it arrived. As she stepped inside the lift, she noticed the new fire emblem over the Coesen tribal birthmark on Victor's neck.

Had she gone too far, rebranding her loyal supporters, creating her own clan of Dregans?

No. I only want to protect what the forefathers created.

But, that meant protecting everyone.

It wasn't until Chandra reached her suite did she speak. "I want him watched."

Ark Manor, Canada

Cianne glanced at the alarm clock as she pushed away the damp hair that was plastered to her face. She reached over and switched on her bedside lamp then stared up at the ceiling. Waking up damp was a constant thing but tonight's nightmare was the worst yet. The dreams were so bad lately that she reached out to Whodai a few nights ago for comfort.

He offered what he could.

She sighed as she reached for the bottle of water she always kept on her nightstand. As she drank the water down, her eyes caught a glimpse of something on her bed.

Cianne slowly lowered the bottle as she focused on what lay before her. The blanket covering her was littered with photos. Dozens of images of her with her children, her and Tristan, and her with Tranae and other friends, were splayed out all around her. It took only a glance to know that there was something not right about this or the pictures.

With a feeling of dread spreading through her veins, Cianne lifted one of the pictures. It was of her but it was terribly altered. Her face was scratched away. Confused and a bit scared, she grabbed several photos at a time.

In each picture she held up, her face was scratched out.

There was also something else. *Blood.* Dried blood was smeared on just about every photo. Drops of dried blood also covered her blanket and sheet.

As panic set in, Cianne's mind posed the question of where the blood came from, or more importantly, from whom.

Did I hurt someone? Oh God, did I hurt the children?

Almost instantly her thoughts were calmed in that regard. A part of her linked to the connection she shared with her children. Her fears regarding them fell away from her mind. They were fine and unharmed.

Cianne's worry then shifted to the others in the Manor. Her connection to the staff that resided on the grounds was nonexistent, but somehow with just a thought, she was able to tap into her unused abilities. How she did or how it worked, she didn't know. She didn't care. All that mattered was she knew everyone was safe. Cianne checked three more times that everyone on the premise was unharmed to ease her mind.

The question of the blood was answered when Cianne pushed herself up to get into a better sitting position. The sting from her thighs shot up her pelvis to her stomach, catching her off guard. She stifled a scream as she lifted the sheets. Cuts and dried blood covered her legs.

I did this?

Cianne gently touched the stinging cuts. She glanced over at the destroyed pictures of herself and treasured memories of her with her friends…and with him. Confused and angry, she swung her legs off the bed, stepped into her slippers, and crossed her room to enter her bathroom where the light automatically came on.

Cianne frowned as she wondered if the light was automatic? *No.* That meant it just came on because she wanted it to. Shaking her head, Cianne turned on the shower, removed her gown, and immediately stepped inside. The spray cooled her marred skin. After several minutes of rinsing, Cianne grabbed a towel and patted the cuts dry.

As she did, a cool tingle overtook the stinging sensation she felt. Cianne focused on her injuries so there was no missing it. Her breath hitched and she blinked several times while her skin stretched and mended before her eyes.

It wasn't as if she hadn't healed herself before. After she gave birth to the twins, Caleb helped her to release the power she inherited from him, and she repaired her damaged body with just a thought. She felt the strongest she ever felt that day. Since then she buried the memories of that day, and soon after Vivian's death, she buried her abilities.

Cianne hated what she was capable of and didn't want any part of it. She saw her rejection of those powers as a way to be free of Caleb. But, her cuts were now healed and Cianne realized that her father's power will always be alive and waiting inside her. *The power of a murderer.*

Her breathing picked up but Cianne forced herself to calm as she stared at her reflection in the mirror over the sink. She thought of the pictures that lay on her bed and the damage that was done to them. As much as she tried, she did not remember doing it. Though, from the gashes on her body and the fact that she lost time to blackouts before, Cianne had no doubts that she did it.

But, why did she?

Weakling, a disembodied voice hissed.

Surprised by the voice, Cianne bit her tongue when she jumped, drawing blood. "Shut up, shut up, shut up," she chanted as she gripped the edge of the sink. After a few seconds of silence, she relaxed and focused on her image again. Her eyes were their usual vibrant hue but then the eyes in her reflection flashed red and the corners of her mouth lifted into a wicked smile.

She wasn't looking through a red haze and she didn't move her mouth.

Cianne backed away from the mirror until her back and heels hit the far wall. "Go away," she ordered, staring at the monster of her nightmares. She closed her eyes tight. "Just go away, please."

She hesitated before opening her eyes and exhaled with a sigh of relief when she saw that her image was normal again.

"What is happening to me?" Cianne sobbed.

The cold chill from her exposed thighs touching the marble floor was the only indication that she slid down the wall to the floor. Feeling defeated, Cianne let her head rest on her knees and began to rock back and forth.

Vivian Harper's private study could only be reached through Vivian's bedroom suite so Cianne crossed the length of the opulently furnished bedroom and stepped up to a set of large dark wood double doors. She stopped in front of a shelf that had a single stone sitting on a small display shelf. The stone seemed to glow as she moved closer.

A Rootstone.

Cianne placed her palm over the stone like Cassius told her. After a few seconds, she felt the stone warm then cool. Soon after, the sound of several sliding pins filled the room before the doors opened. The air in the room was a bit stuffy but that made sense being as the room had been closed tight since Vivian's passing.

With a quick look around, Cianne took in the contents of the room. Most of the walls were covered with floor to ceiling dark wood bookcases or shelving. The center wall in front of her was filled with photos on floating shelving. A workstation sat on one side of the large room. A sitting area was in the center and on the other side of the room, in front of one of the bookcases, was a larger than life pedestal display case.

Cianne trailed her fingers over one of the shelves as she made her way into the room. When she heard the doors close and seal behind her, she fought back the wave of fear that crept over her. Being locked in a room sparked her fight or flight instincts, triggering memories of her abduction.

"I'm Cianne. Mother of two and sovereign of a nation," she weakly reminded herself.

She unconsciously raised her chin and straightened her back before moving toward the sitting area. She headed for the two oversized recliners that looked more homely than elegant. Though both were similar, one was more masculine and more weathered than the other. She walked around to the backs of the chairs and noticed the insignias on the headrest. Both had Arkean brands but under each brand was two letters, GH and VH, respectively.

Cianne grazed her fingers over the VH monogram. This was Vivian's chair. It was Vivian's chair in the place where she kept all her beloved treasures and spent most of her time.

Langley told her that Vivian never allowed anyone in this space but him, and he rarely imposed. How the room was now accessible to her and only her, Cianne didn't know, but Langley assured her that the stones knew; plus, Vivian wanted her to have access.

With a sigh, Cianne traced the soft lined fabric of the chair. There were no lingering scents of the woman who'd spent her time here, though her style was evident. From the homely seating to the modestly framed artwork and knick-knacks, there was no doubt that this room held the real woman her grandmother was, and not the composed elegant leader with the severe bun hairstyle.

I miss you…grandmother.

Cianne moved her fingers from Vivian's chair and traced the back of Gaither Harper's chair. It was the most worn of the two, with a faded seat cushion and worn arm rest. She walked around and sat down in the chair of the man she would never know on a personal level. Guilt that she never once thought of her grandfather suddenly filled her.

There was never a thought or care of the man. She asked no questions about who he was or what he meant to her mother or Vivian. It was as if he was nothing but a silent partner in the world of the Coesen. An afterthought.

Cianne relaxed in the comfortable chair and let her eyes close. It was clear that after his death, Vivian made Gaither's chair hers, instead of using her own.

Did Vivian love Gaither?

Cianne realized then that there may be a photo of the man on the wall. Her eyes popped open. Getting to her feet, she rushed to the wall of pictures. Vivian chronicled everything on the wall. There were pictures of her father, Joe, the twins, and even one of Tristan and his three friends who participated in the Maatii together.

Cianne avoided all the photos of her and Tristan together to focus on the others. One photo stood out immediately. She reached for the photo of a small group of teenagers. The way they were dressed told her the picture was old. It didn't take her long to make out who the people in the photo were. She easily found a young Vivian in the center. Her hair was loose, wavy and flowing down around her shoulders. Vivian wore a simple summer dress but she looked as elegant as ever.

Wow.

There was no doubt that the young man who had his arm around Vivian's shoulders, pulling her to his side, was Langley. His blonde hair was practically falling into his eyes. His smile was easy and he looked genuinely happy. Beside him was a woman who had to be Deni. She looked exactly like Brenna, her daughter. She was resting or leaning on Langley and her legs were crossed at her ankles. She also had an enormous smile on her lovely face.

On the other side of Vivian was a young Eldra. Her hair was parted down the middle and braided into two neat sections. She leaned on Vivian in the exact same way Deni was leaning on Langley. Cianne never saw the woman smiling as brightly as she did in the photo.

Kneeling in front of Vivian was Chandra. Her hair was pulled into a loose ponytail and her beautiful face was full of surprise as the camera caught her mouth in the shape of an O. Chandra's surprise may have come from the fact that two guys, one kneeling on either side of her, were kissing her on her cheeks. Both men were extremely handsome.

Cianne didn't recognize the men right away but when she looked closer, she saw that one of the men's eyes resembled Whodai's eyes. She placed the photo back on the shelf then continued to look over more of Vivian's pictures until she came to a shelf with only two photos.

Cianne stepped closer to one of the photos but didn't dare touch it. Touching the beautiful image almost seemed wrong so she left it in place. Vivian and a man, who had to be Gaither Harper, were immortalized in their wedding clothes holding each other as if the photographer caught them during their first dance as man and wife. Both of them had a faraway look on their faces but they didn't seem altogether miserable.

The other guy kissing Chandra's cheek was Gaither.

I wonder if he and Vivian were a couple then?

The other photo of the couple looked completely at odds with the wedding photo. It was of Chandra and Gaither during some kind of party. Cianne assumed they were caught off guard because neither of them was facing the camera. They looked a few years older. Vivian was sitting in a chair, and her hand was in Gaither's as he stood over her, but her attention was on a little girl who stood beside her. It looked as if Vivian was wiping something off the smiling child's face. Gaither was watching them, and all the love he felt for them was clearly expressed in his eyes.

Cianne instantly felt love for the man she never knew. She took a deep breath then turned to view the rest of the room.

There was a small desk and even an old-fashioned typewriter in a far corner, but it was the large glass display case that stood a few feet in front of the two recliners that caught her attention. She walked over and peered inside to see a large beautiful bracket-styled Arkean Royal family tree on a wood plaque that resembled the weathered look of a piece of old parchment paper. The names were scripted in fancy print-signature penmanship. Arkean and Eyet, names she never heard before, were at the very top, in bold type. Their Coesen classification and their dates of birth and death were beneath that.

Cianne skimmed over the names of each Sovereign and their children with great interest, promising herself that she would read each of the Annals on these shelves to get a better grasp on who her ancestors were. A few generations in, a name stood out among the others. It was darker and thicker than the rest.

"Ilias," Cianne said out loud, "the last Coesen King."

She continued to look over the document until she came to where her name was listed. Beside her name was Tristan's name, no date of death was filled in. Cianne ignored the pang of loss that vibrated through her and read the last two names. They were the names of her children.

Several minutes passed as she read some of the names of her ancestors. With a final glance over the names, she turned to the bookshelves that were encased in locked glass doors. The spine of each book had the name of a Sovereign, and the years covered in that Annals, imprinted on it. Some names were repeated only on a few books and others were repeated on more.

Cianne's eyes roamed the shelves looking for Vivian's Annals. Just as she found that section, her thoughts turned to Caleb and how he was perceived by the Coesen. She wondered if he was referenced in these personal journals.

Remembering the time period when Caleb became known to the Coesen, Cianne moved over to the journals that were dated around the 1800's. She touched the glass door, only realizing then that she didn't know how to open it. There were no handles or locks. Just as she pulled her hand back she heard the soft sound of a pressure lock being released. She looked at her fingers.

Am I the key?

Cianne giggled then reached for one of the ancient-looking leather journals when her eyes caught a little metal plate secured on the shelf. She lowered her hand as she read. "Delicate and priceless. Please refer to digital versions unless absolutely necessary. If you must refer to original journals handle with care."

She glanced over her shoulder at the desk and computer. She closed the glass door, satisfied when she heard the lock secure, then went to the desk. The system booted up quickly, revealing a large black circle that was surrounded by a thick outer ring. It was her birthmark. Then a beautiful moving waterfall scene appeared with words that read, 'All my faith lies with you...'

Cianne pressed the enter key then an assortment of random keys but nothing happened. "Maybe it needs a password," she said to herself. "All my faith lies with you...," she repeated.

Vivian didn't seem the religious type but Cianne typed the word 'God' anyway. The screen faded then reappeared. "Not God."

She shrugged. Then, it came to her. She wasn't God but the Coesen felt that she was the savior so she quickly typed in the word "Halo". Again, the screen dimmed then reappeared, unchanged. She typed the name "Zaria" because it was once her name but that did nothing as well. Maybe she was being arrogant. Maybe she hadn't earned Vivian's faith.

She typed several names, including Gaither's and her mother's before pushing the rolling chair away from the desk in frustration. Cianne glanced around the room as if looking for something that would give her the password. Her eyes fell on all the pictures of her as she grew up. Cianne didn't feel the smile that stretched her lips as she noted the milestones of her life. She didn't have a carefree childhood but she felt loved and would not have chosen any other life for herself if given the opportunity.

Then it became clear. She was always going to be exactly who she was and would always do what she felt was right. Vivian knew that. She even said so once. Cianne was always going to be herself even if she took the crown, and Vivian still thought she would succeed. It was the ultimate gift, her grandmother's faith.

Her fingers glided over the keyboard, tapping the letters C.I.A.N.N.E with confidence. As before, the picture of the refreshing waterfall faded before the Coesen Directory popped up.

It was easy to navigate through the directory. Cianne went straight to the day Vivian explained to her who she was. Most of what Vivian wrote about the meeting was sort of clinical but after the informative parts, the journal entry became more personal.

Annals of Vivian Harper
The Year of Cianne's Recovery
May/Entry 001

Tristan Bertram. I sigh with just the mention of his name. The young man is going to be a thorn in my side, this I know. Stubbornness has been ingrained into his DNA, inherited from Patrick Arlington, I am certain. Among the obvious reasons, I must discourage his claim to Zaria. He is arrogant, headstrong, and ambitious. One could argue that these same qualities are mirrored in my dear Whodai and that I encourage them with him. I will admit that may be true but I remind those that Whodai is a Coesen. He was bred to be Zaria's help mate in every way.

I shudder to think how this Tristan will find my granddaughter and ensure that she is unharmed when he cannot understand the full scope of what gifts he's been given. What was Kayla thinking, hiding this boy from me? We could have done something then. As it stands, Oma has informed me that this boy has to bring Zaria home without my interference. Heaven knows that I have never questioned her rarely spoken words before but allowing this boy to hold our future in his hands doesn't sit well with me. I must admit that his devotion to Zaria is admirable and his lack of respect is refreshing.

June/Entry 002

Nothing could have prepared me for the moment I saw the beautiful creature that is my granddaughter up close. Her spirit has been beaten but she bears the strength and the resolve of a warrior. I have no doubt she will prevail. And though her world has been forever changed this day, she is determined to covet who she thinks she is.

It took all I am, to restrain myself and keep my distance and not pull her to me and cuddle her like I once did many years ago. She only sees me as her flesh and blood right now but I hope one day she will cherish me as I do her. I cannot thank the heavens above enough for the man that I once thought incapable of fostering my heir. It would pain me to admit this to anyone other than myself and my most cherished friends, but Joseph Baxter has done well in raising her. My Kayla, for all her secrets and personal agendas, chose well. Oh, and she prefers Cianne vs. her given name.

Cianne went through page after page, skimming over the textbook parts and reading the personal entries. She ignored the burning in her eyes and continued to read through Vivian's thoughts and small events that happened in her life.

July/Entry 020

Tristan Bertram never ceases to amaze me. The Middling convert is hands down one of the best Warriors Cassius has ever trained. These were Cassius' words, not mine, but it is clear when watching the boy train.

He is focused and determined to be invaluable to our people even though my granddaughter wants nothing to do with our politics. Somehow, he has managed to balance our two worlds. He navigated through the Maatii with the skill and intelligence of a Coesen who trained since birth. The boy is a definite enigma and I couldn't be prouder. The source chose well when linking my Zaria/Cianne with this male of worth.

September/Entry 029

Today, Cianne and Tristan shared their afternoon with me. It was informal, yet my family doesn't quite know how to relax around me. Hopefully, in time they will see me as someone who loves and accepts them as they are.

As I write this, I see the truth in my words. I love both of them for who they are and have no intentions of molding them to what I view as acceptable. I wish this revelation had come to me with my Kayla.

Gods, I've made so many mistakes in my life, so many regrets haunt me. But I will endeavor to not waste another moment on the past unless it is to reflect on the few times I saw the love Kayla and Gaither had for me reflected in their smiles, though those times grew few as the years passed.

As I watch them, Tristan and Cianne, while they sit on the terrace, I can't help but embrace the future with hope. The love I see between them is so physically powerful that I want to reach out and grab hold of it. The way she looks at him. It's as if nothing and no one else matters to her but his happiness. I believe that is the case.

What astonishes me the most is how he cherishes her. Cianne is the Halo, the soon to be leader and wielder of an unrivaled power the world has ever known, but he treats her as if she is the most delicate, the most precious being in this entire world. I have never seen such devoted, uninhibited, soul encompassing love in my life and will venture to say that no one ever will again.

Their love for one another and their unborn daughter is indeed a gift from above and I am forever grateful because they *will* need it to govern our people. Cianne has expressed that she wants no parts of my world but I know it is her, *their* destiny. One cannot run from their destiny no matter how fast they are. I pray that she will accept her role before she is thrown into it like so many before her. All I can do is be here when she needs me.

Chapter Nine

Cianne didn't know that her eyes welled up with tears until they began to fall down her cheeks. The pain that she tried so desperately to bury was now clawing its way to the surface once again. It was a fierce pain so severe that she temporarily lost the ability to breathe. The stinging burn in her throat as she gasped for air was second to the ache in her chest as her heart threatened to stop beating.

The memory of that day, the one Vivian logged in her Annals, crashed into her so hard, Cianne found herself yanked from Vivian's private library to that day, which seemed a lifetime ago. The smells and sounds of that day drifted all around her as her consciousness seemed to hover in the bright daylight. Cianne tried to focus on the insects in the distance, the smell of a nearby garden, anything to ground her spiritual essence because she was afloat.

She was not familiar with her abilities and didn't really know what to do but she was certain this was a Coesen ability. She learned to manage some of them without really trying while others didn't answer to her commands but rather were triggered by emotions or another ability. Whodai attributed the lack of control to her refusing to accept her father's abilities.

"Stop that," a familiar yet foreign voice called out.

But it was the thick sultry laughter that centered Cianne's drifting soul and made her focus. That uninhibited laughter,

Tristan's laughter, was what she needed to zone in on. She saw her physical self but just as she did, she felt a magnetic like force pulling her. Before Cianne knew what was happening, her physical form and her spectral form merged.

The combining of her present consciousness and her body of the past felt like she was being pricked by tiny needles. Just like it felt when her hand or foot fell asleep. What was even odder, her body didn't rebel. It embraced her Specter as if it was a part of it.

Well, she was.

Can I effect this time? Change it?

As soon as the thought manifested, a jolt of pain shot through her. Cianne imagined that her specter form bent in pain but her physical form didn't seem affected at all. She shuddered inwardly as her specter silently vowed to only watch this weave of time play out. Besides, she knew the dangers. Changing the slightest thing in time could start a ripple that could unmake events and lives, or even destroy the planet.

Her mother, Kayla, may have changed the direction of the future and ultimately paid for it with her life. Who knew what kind of life they could have had if her mother lived? Cianne was sure she would have eventually met Tristan but would they have fallen in love? Would he have seen her in the same light?

Cianne was certain her physical form in this time wasn't aware of her specter form. All hell would have broken loose if it did. But the two were merged in a way where her Specter was capable of experiencing all five senses but only as a silent partner. The air was scented with flowers. The fork in her hand felt solid. Her vision was clearer than ever. And her hearing...

She gripped the fork in her hand as she turned her head to the man whose laughter could pull her from hell. It was a dizzying experience, seeing the real him. In that moment, Cianne knew then that she would willingly lay waste to the world to have him back. She knew that the inexperience with her abilities was the only thing stopping her from having him.

I will learn, the Specter of her consciousness thought. But for now, she planned to watch and listen to this moment. To appreciate the mundane.

September, over a year ago

"She can see us,"** Cianne warned. She saw Vivian on the balcony, looking over the expanse of the property. It was only a matter of time before her grandmother's gaze swept over the terrace where she and Tristan sat, enjoying breakfast.

Cianne looked to Tristan. Face to face, her hand rested on his tight chest as he leaned in with the intention of kissing her. She gave him a slight shove but he didn't budge. Instead, the next thing she knew she was cradled in his lap.

"I am sure our Sovereign Queen is not the least bit concerned about what we're doing. And even if she is watching, I'm certain she is all smiles."

Cianne closed her eyes. She didn't want to see the grimace on her grandmother's regal face. Tristan knew better than to behave in such a…a "normal" manner in front of Vivian. Vivian was accustomed to grace and etiquette, not the behavior of average teenagers. Tristan, of all people, should know this. He trained, studied, and saturated himself in the Coesen way of life.

When she felt Tristan's warm lips on hers, Cianne squeezed her closed her eyes tighter as the taste of him clouded her anxiety. He held her very essence in the palms of his hands and she was inexplicably at ease with that. When Cianne opened her eyes to peer up at him, she blinked several times. Just looking at him was overwhelming at times. The man was truly beautiful.

"You are not acting like a soldier, or whatever it is you are," she finally said, glancing at the Maatii brand that was tattooed on his arm. "Don't you need to be bowing to me or something?" she asked as she stared into his crystal blue eyes.

"Or something," he said. He leaned forward to kiss her lips again.

This kiss was longer and deeper than the one before so she couldn't help the needy moan that escaped her swollen lips.

"How're my girls?" he asked when he pulled back.

Cianne whimpered as she tried to get her head together after such a scorching kiss. Tristan graced her with an arrogant, knowing grin.

She felt the baby move under her skin, seeming to follow Tristan's movements as his hand gently rubbed her extended belly. "Hmm, she likes that," Cianne said with a sigh.

Tristan leaned over her belly and said a string of foreign words to their unborn daughter. He spoke in the native Coesen language. "Daddy loves you very much. I can't wait to hold you in my arms, little one," he translated as he pinned his gaze on her.

That he chose to translate was charming. Cianne knew that Tristan knew she understood the language.

"I want you to know that I will always love you. I will always be yours, Cianne."

Both her corporeal and spiritual awareness shivered in the wake of his vow, the intensity in his eyes, and the sincerity in his voice.

"Promise me that you will always be mine," he said. "Promise me that no man will ever have your heart, your body, your soul. Just me."

There was no thought about how she would respond. Immediately, Cianne began to nod as she gazed into his eyes and said, "I promise that no man will have my heart nor will I ever give another my body. You are my soul, Tristan." She tried desperately to express this verbally and physically like he did but she knew she would fall short. Tristan was the passionate one and no one ever questioned the emotions he so easily conveyed.

He smiled and Cianne felt as if her heart would stop. It wasn't that he rarely smiled. It was that his smile was so beautiful, so radiant, it made her weak.

Tristan sighed. "Good," he whispered as if relieved. "Good, because no other woman will ever have my heart." He placed his forehead on hers as his thumb rubbed her shoulder where he held her to him. His eyes were closed and he didn't speak until his breathing was even which was odd because she watched him train and fight. Never did he seem short of breath.

Cianne placed her hand on his cheek, wondering what happened just now. They had a lovely lunch with her grandmother and Langley. The conversation was light except for a brief mention about the ongoing investigation into the murders of her kidnappers, Nick and JC. When Langley noticed her discomfort, he changed the subject after confirming that Tristan was still a person of interest for the local police department, but nothing more.

Tristan seemed to have no interest in discussing her attackers or the ongoing investigation of their deaths, so Cianne was sure it wasn't what had him so wound up.

"What's wrong?" She used her hand to hold his face still as she rubbed her nose against his.

Tristan took a deep breath before he answered. "I never want to lose you. There are times that I am so damn happy… I just…" He shook his head as if clearing it. "It's just that I can't help wondering when it will all fall apart, Cianne. I've never been a pessimist, but I've never had something so precious to me before now." He lightly kissed her nose then placed his forehead back on hers. "You and this kid," he said, putting a bit of pressure on her belly, "are my life and I worry that one day you will wake up and realize that you don't want this, me. Or worse, that something will harm you both. I have to be the best, train the hardest, know the ends and outs of this world of yours to keep you both safe. But I'm so damn scared that I will not be enough or that I will fail you."

Cianne was panting now, her breathing matched the rapid beating of her heart. As far as she knew, Tristan feared nothing. He was a force of nature, always in control, always the epitome of intelligence, strength, fearlessness, and poise. She only saw fear in his eyes once and that was the day after she gave herself to him when he thought he'd hurt her.

Yet, this was different, more intense. She could hear it in his tortured tone, she felt his tightly coiled body as it shivered around her, she saw the difference in his glossy eyes.

"I will always want you, Tristan. Every day since the first day of high school, I carried on because I wanted, needed to see your face. You are the beginning and end for me. But you must know that you can't do this to yourself. You cannot drive yourself into the ground, to be this super soldier just because you fear what may or may not happen to me. No matter how much you want to, there will be a day when you won't be able to save me. Life is unpredictable Tristan, but my love for you, my devotion to our life together, is indestructible."

Tristan exhaled then a slow grin spread across his face. The tension in his body eased and he loosened the protective grip he had on her. That was good because he wasn't hurting her, but her muscles were beginning to cramp in the cradled position she was in. The change in him was fast and so polar opposite from several seconds ago, that she wondered if it had happened at all.

"I like that," he said. Lifting his head, he peered into her eyes.

It was as if he could see all her thoughts, her fears, and her soul in that moment. He smiled her smile.

"Indestructible," Tristan said it as if was a declaration, a vow. Then he righted her so that she was sitting upright on his lap, making sure to move slower. He wrapped one arm around her and used his free hand to lift one of her favorite little petite cakes Vivian specially ordered for her when she visited. He placed it to her lips. "I will always save you, my queen."

Cianne leaned back into Tristan's chest and turned her head to kiss his cheek. *Who is going to save you?* she thought but dared not ask. He shook off whatever he was feeling seconds ago, and was again the confident man she fell in love with.

Tristan popped a few of the cakes in his mouth before reaching for his glass.

The Present

Cianne's Specter jolted then was yanked from the scene without warning. The unmistakable scents of Vivian's private library filled her nostrils. She dropped her forehead on the desk as she tried to calm herself.

All the emotions she felt that day, a little over a year and a half ago, ran through her full force now. Those emotions were coupled with the knowledge of what happened next in their tragic love story.

Would he understand the decisions she had to make? That she was finding it hard to keep sane without Whodai's support.

"Why did you abandon me?"

Cianne touched her fingertips to her temples to quell the ache mounting in her head. Her chest rose and fell in tune with her frantic heartbeat. She was vaguely aware that she was approaching dangerous territory but she was beyond helping herself at this point. With her forehead still resting on the edge of the desk, she looked at the white carpet through red tinted eyes. Two words ricocheted through her mind because she was unable to speak them.

"Help me."

Caleb was asleep when he felt Cianne's distress punch into him. It jerked him to an upright position as he mentally reached out to her, but she was closed off to him. Even in a moment of need, she managed to keep him at bay.

She was losing herself.

"Aidan," Caleb transferred to his grandson. He needed a link. *"Your mom is hurting and the only way for me to help her is for me to make her sleep. I don't want you to be afraid because though your mother's conscious mind has retreated, her instincts will always be to protect you and Nadia. I would come but my presence will only make things worse in her current condition."*

"I'm not afraid," Aidan transferred back.

A light chuckle came from Caleb. *"No, you wouldn't be. Let's help your mom. I'll need your help to get to her, just relax and try not to fight me."*

Caleb felt Aidan tense as static charged the air around his small body. Power like his would make anyone nervous, let alone a small child. To ease his grandson, he talked. *"I'm going to take control, seeing and acting from inside you but you have to let me in. I'll have to force you into spectral form. You'll feel a light tickle beneath your skin."*

Before Aidan could question him, Caleb merged his mind with Aidan's and forced the change. Aidan shivered as his body faded. *"Take us to her, son."*

Aidan's spectral form appeared in a barely-lit room. Cianne was seated on the edge of an office chair with her head resting on the desk a few feet away. She was struggling for breath.

"Her basic instincts are going to take control any minute now, so she'll be in battle mode, but you have nothing to worry about. Her sense of smell will be heightened so if we can't help her in time you will still be fine."

"What do I do?" Aidan asked.

"You're going to be a conduit so all you need to do is touch her head and I'll do rest. Do it now!" Caleb told him.

Aidan moved forward to place his hand on his mother's head just as she lifted up to peer at him. The eyes that focused on him were blood red.

"They're unfamiliar, but still your mom."

Cianne sniffed the air as she tilted her head to regard Aidan.

Caleb felt Aidan's fear but knew it wasn't for himself. Aidan was scared for his mother, and he was wondering if the state she was in might be better than the way she lived day to day. Unfeeling, no memory of her pain.

She can be free.

"Listen to me, Aidan. Pain is what lets us know we're alive. Loss makes us appreciate what we hold close to our hearts. Without loss, we cannot be who we are and who we will become. I know it is hard to watch your mother suffer day to day." Caleb sighed then transferred, *"It hurts me to see her grieve but I had to learn to accept that this is life and that it can't be lived to the fullest if we, who have the ability to intercede, don't allow the ones we care for to just live. Your mother loves to say 'just because you can, doesn't mean you should'. Now touch her head before she senses me with you."*

A single tear trailed down Aidan's cheek. Caleb knew he was upset with himself. Ashamed that he thought his mother would be better off in this state.

Aidan shook his head to clear it then raised his hand slowly. Caleb felt Cianne's soft as silk hair through his grandson's touch. He took a second or two to really enjoy it and realized that Aidan was enjoying the feel of her just as much as he was.

Apparently, his grandson wasn't fond of touching or being touched. Nadia was the only person Aidan didn't mind being close to for long periods of time. It seemed he allowed his mother to touch him often enough, but not as much as she would like it seemed. Aidan seemed to think that he was the man of the house and men were strong and capable, not soft and cuddly.

"Even I enjoyed my mother's touch, Aidan. It's alright."

Aidan sighed as he moved his small hand over the crown of his mother's head then came to rest on her forehead. Her unblinking eyes just stared into his as if searching for something.

That was when Caleb acted. He entered her mind and called to her.

As if she'd been shocked by lightning, her eyes widened and an ear-splitting scream came out of her mouth. Her reaction was so sudden, so random, that Aidan jumped but managed to maintain contact.

The crescendo of her wail only lasted for a moment before her eyes returned to their normal radiant greenish blue. Her lids slowly closed then opened before slowly closing again as if she was fighting sleep. Then just like that, she slumped forward.

Aidan easily pushed her back in the chair so she wouldn't fall forward, without Caleb's help. "*Is she going to be alright, now?*" He brushed her damp hair from her brows and looked at her.

"*Use your own body, your heartbeat, brain activity, organ function, as a baseline then scan hers to compare,*" Caleb told him.

With awe, Aidan did what he said and Caleb was able to read her vitals with his grandson. She was fine.

"*You are capable of so many wonders, Aidan. But you will find that some of our abilities take much more effort. Just remember that it is our responsibility to police ourselves and make responsible decisions.*"

Caleb stayed connected to Aidan but reached out to Cianne's unconscious form and transported her body to her bedroom. Aidan shivered again as Caleb faded his form then returned him back to his own room and his own bed.

"*How…*"

"*I am the patriarch of a power that connects the four of us. That means that I am able to connect to you three and manipulate that power.*"

"*Can I, one day?*"

"*Manipulate our abilities, no,*" Caleb said, then he chuckled as he separated from Aidan. He allowed his grandson to see his spectral form. "*You showed compassion and strength that some men do not have. What we did has drained you. Sleep now, and no more worries tonight.*"

"I wish I was as powerful as you and as strong as daddy," Aidan whispered. He sat sluggishly on his bed. Caleb saw a rare smile on his grandson's face as he slumped onto his pillow and closed his eyes.

"*You will be, little one. You will be…greater than the both of us.*"

Chapter Ten

Bannerman drove through the last security checkpoint before pulling up to the main house. Ark mansion was always imposing, but now it was somewhat scary. The few times he visited in the past, he felt welcome. Today, he just felt the need to retreat.

He glanced over to the passenger seat where Langley sat, looking straight ahead. Though Langley didn't seem troubled, Bannerman knew that being here affected him deeply. Langley was not only Sovereign Harper's lawyer but it was widely known that he was also her closest friend and confidant. Some say they were related by blood. Needless to say, the man was quiet and stiff as they drove around the circular driveway and exited the car.

After Zeta's call Saturday evening, Caleb felt that she should bypass the long flight home. He did that teleportation thing, popping out of Maiden Hall and back mere minutes later with Zeta in tow. Uneased by the report from Zeta, coupled with Caleb's insistence due to some situation last night, Bannerman and his cohorts agreed that Cianne must be examined as soon as possible.

The big questions were, would they be allowed to see her and would she allow him to examine her? The answer to the first question was now in play.

Bannerman and Langley walked toward the main door but both stopped at the base of the stairway when the doors opened. Jamiah Rey looked down at them.

Caleb briefed them on Jamiah but seeing the young impressive male made the situation more real as he stepped down the grand main stairs then strolled toward them.

"Good morning, Dr. Bannerman. I'm Jamiah Rey, Captain of the Royal Guard," Jamiah extended his hand. Bannerman shook it. "We processed your request just minutes ago. I apologize for the new security procedures but it's necessary." Jamiah released his hand and looked at Langley. "Good morning, Counselor Langley. It's good to have you home." Jamiah held his hand out to Langley. "Will you be staying for a while?"

Langley's eyes widened for a moment before he looked at Jamiah and took his hand. "I wasn't sure I would still be welcome at Ark Manor."

It was Jamiah now who seemed taken aback. With a confused expression, the young Captain said, "This is your home, isn't it?"

Langley nodded but seemed a bit flustered.

They all moved forward and up the steps as one. "I won't be staying long. I have to fly out tonight but wanted to check on Cianne," Langley said.

"I see." Jamiah nodded as they reached the large double doors that were pulled open for them. "I informed Soahn Cianne as soon as we received your request, Dr. Bannerman, to see the children." He focused on Bannerman. "I have to say she is a little worried because their scheduled check up isn't for another two months."

"I'll do my best to calm her worries," Bannerman said, following Jamiah's and Langley's lead as they entered the mansion. Each visit felt like a first when it came to the floor plan. He paused to glare up at the large crystal chandelier in awe, again.

"Well," Jamiah said as he looked at Bannerman, "I have some business to attend to. I trust you remember the way to the medical wing, but I ask that you allow Dennis to escort you." Jamiah turned his attention to Langley. "Counselor, I'd like to speak with you before you leave."

Langley nodded. Jamiah bowed, then took his leave.

As if on cue, Dennis walked up. He looked like he was in his mid-twenties. He had a hard look to him and was built for physical combat. "I'll follow up the rear, sirs," the Guard said, sounding formal.

"Is Soahn Cianne with the children?" Langley asked.

Dennis nodded, "Yes."

Bannerman shot Langley a questioning look but Langley only shrugged. For the past six months, only a select few were granted access to Cianne and the children. Now, it seemed they would be able to see her.

"Sirs," a woman dressed in all white nodded as she passed.

Bannerman noted that she flashed Langley a welcoming smile before moving on to her destination. As they passed a few more house staffers along the way, each gave them both welcoming smiles.

According to Langley's report of his last attempted homecoming to Ark Manor, this experience differed vastly. It seemed they were going to be given access to the Sovereign, and Langley was openly being welcomed with sincere smiles and greetings.

As they made their way through the common area toward the back of the mansion where the elevators to the medical bay and lower floors were located, Bannerman cleared his throat. He glanced over his shoulder at Dennis. "Things seemed to have changed around here since my last visit."

"Yes sir," Dennis answered but said no more.

Fine, I'll just ask. "Why?"

Dennis didn't answer right away. He was most likely thinking of what he should and shouldn't reveal. He swallowed, then said, "Captain Jamiah was not pleased with the old-new rules, so he did away with them and enacted some new-new rules. The new way will still keep our Sovereign safe but also involved," he finally said. "Like Sovereign Harper was," he added quietly.

The young Guard seemed to still be feeling the loss of losing Sovereign Harper, like so many others. Already, Bannerman liked this kid Dennis.

Before her death, Sovereign Harper decreed that Bannerman was to be the Arkean Royal physician, which meant he would treat the royal family and all the Royal Guards employed by them. That meant that he might come to know Dennis better.

All three men entered the elevator and were silent as it descended. No one said a word as they stepped off the elevator and navigated the tunnels until they came to the medical wing. A newly installed large glass sliding doors blocked what looked like a newly remodeled facility.

Wow!

Dennis advised, "Just step up. If one of us isn't welcome, it won't open."

Bannerman stood in front of the door. A small image of him, Dennis, and Langley appeared on the door, along with the word "Accepted" displayed in green above the door.

"Nice," Langley said.

"Yes," Dennis agreed. "They found a way to link facial recognition to the Rootstone

The glass doors separated. Bannerman and Langley stepped inside but Dennis didn't cross the threshold. When Bannerman looked back the Guard didn't move, so he and Langley moved forward without him.

Behind a long desk that resembled a nurse's station, a pleasant looking woman sat.

"Hello, Dr. Bannerman, Counselor Langley."

Both Bannerman and Langley offered a greeting.

Bannerman noted that she wore light gray scrubs. He watched her swivel around in her chair and place a folder in one of several large file cabinets behind her. She lifted a key that was attached to a long chain around her neck, stood, then placed it in the keyhole of one of three cabinets and sorted through some folders.

"Aidan and Nadia are waiting in the sitting area. Room three is prepared," she said, spinning around and handing him two file folders.

Bannerman took the files handed to him. "Thank you, Nurse..." He looked at her questioningly.

"Dodson," she offered as she felt around the desk then produced a name tag.

"Nurse Dodson." Bannerman smiled. He gave the remodeled area a once over, wondering where room three was located because he was pretty sure that where he was now standing used to be the only room.

"Right." Nurse Dodson giggled. "You don't know where room three is. Forgive me, Doctor." She stepped from behind the desk and pointed down a hallway to their right. "That hall is where your office and all exam rooms are. There are ten rooms in total." She then pointed in the opposite direction. "Down this hallway are the operating and recovery rooms. And there, down this section, are the extended stay rooms. Behind me is the break room which has a full kitchen, our supply rooms, and overnight rooms for staff." She smiled then continued. "We plan to be fully operational in the next few weeks. Of course, you must hand-pick the rest of the staff." She shrugged. "We have our own private entrance separate from the mansion and no one can access the upper floors except for you and a few other VIP's."

"Impressive." Bannerman nodded as he took the folders.

"Yes." Nurse Dodson smiled. Her focus wasn't on him when she spoke. But rather, she was looking at Langley. Her eyes brightened with admiration and something Bannerman couldn't place.

Langley must have noticed. He cleared his throat as he took hold of Bannerman's arm and led him down the hallway where room three was located. He seemed flustered.

"Your idea?" Bannerman waved his hand that held the folders out in an attempt to reference the entire space.

"I proposed a remodel of the mansion and some other properties to Vivian months before her death. I had no idea that someone would implement them," Langley said with a shrug.

Bannerman was sure that Langley felt more than what he was showing. Ark Manor wasn't the only home where Langley laid his hat, but it was his first home after his parents and siblings were murdered. Langley's ancestors and the Sovereign line were closely linked for as long as anyone could remember so it was no surprise when Vivian's parents took him in and raised him as their son.

However, when Sovereign Harper passed away, Langley was virtually dismissed.

Of course, he didn't complain. Bannerman realized after coming to know the man better that doing so wasn't his style. So, like the rest of them in their little group, Langley simply chose to quietly fight the changes. Bannerman suspected that losing his home wasn't what hurt Langley the most, but rather the forced separation from his only link to Sovereign Harper, whom he loved like a sister. His separation from Cianne and the children probably hurt him even more.

They passed four brightly-lit good-sized exam rooms before they came to a small lobby. A dozen chairs with a couple of side tables, a few vending machines, a stocked coffee cart, and a flat screen television filled the space.

Bannerman saw Eleanor, the twins' nanny, first. She sat in one of the chairs, reading to the children who were sitting on the floor facing her. Aidan was peering back over his shoulder at him and Langley. Nadia was still looking at Eleanor, her eyes wide and her hands clutched as if the story was just getting good.

A couple of seats away from the kids and their nanny was Cianne. She sat there stiff, with her eyes forward and focused on the wall. She looked extremely tired, her skin was pale, the whites of her eyes were red, and their once vibrant green-blue hue was dull.

Clearly, she was sleep deprived. Bannerman didn't need to examine her to get to that diagnosis. But he would need to examine and talk to her if he wanted to know why she wasn't sleeping and if there was more going on. She didn't even seem to notice that he and Langley were in the room.

When Cianne didn't move or speak, Eleanor did. "It's nice to see you, Dr. Bannerman," Eleanor folded the thick book closed and stood. She extended her hand and Bannerman shook it. "Sir," Eleanor said then bowed her head to Langley instead of shaking his hand.

It was then that Bannerman realized that everyone who greeted them bowed their heads to Langley. Even Jamiah bowed in respect. Bannerman thought it unusual because a great deal of Coesen felt one of three ways about the Children of Jai.

Some, the Kytel, believed that all Breed should be disposed of. The Purists only recognized pure blood royalty and regarded the lesser blood Coesen as disposables—that included Langley's bloodline. Then there were the Coesen who felt that your character proved your worth.

Because Langley was Vivian's attorney and her closest and dearest friend, he was at least tolerated by many. To Bannerman's knowledge, no one ever gave Langley the respect of a bow. Only Royals were respected in that way and the Captain of the Guard was also, but only by their officers. Though, per the gossip-mongers, Langley's ancestor was legally adopted into the Arkean tribe. That meant that with Tristan missing in action, Langley was technically lord of the manor.

Maybe Langley is finally getting his due, Bannerman thought with a grin.

Bannerman watched Langley lifted an excited Nadia up in his arms. The bowing was a big deal and Bannerman wanted to say something, to ask Langley how long he knew about being the lord of Ark Manor. But Langley seemed oblivious as he smiled at Nadia, who was playing with his tie.

"Dr. Bannerman!" Cianne stood. Recognition, that wasn't there before, flickered into her eyes as a slight smile pulled her lips upwards. "How are you?"

"I can't complain, Soahn Cianne. And yourself?" Bannerman took her hand and used his other to encase it. Her grip was hesitant and her hand felt slightly chilled.

Odd.

"I won't complain," Cianne said. She lowered her gaze for a moment before returning it. She produced another halfhearted smile. It wasn't until she moved her gaze to Langley that her smile was bright and genuine. "Langley." She sighed. Her movements were slow initially as if she was contemplating what she was going to do, either shake his hand or hug him.

Bannerman accepted Langley's hand-off of Nadia right before Cianne went in for the hug. He wasn't sure how many times Langley was hugged in his life, but the man looked uncomfortable. It took a few seconds for the counselor to lift his arms and hug her back. It took several more seconds for Cianne to lift her head off Langley's shoulder and separate from him. The smile on her face held as she continued to look at Langley.

"I was hoping you would come home," she said, beaming. "I've wanted to speak with you. Cassius tells me that you have some of my grandmother's private Annals. I was wondering if you would allow me to read them."

Langley wasted no time in replying. "Those volumes are yours," he said, lowering his head. "I will personally deliver them to you myself."

"Maybe we could have dinner tonight. You could tell me about how she grew up. What she was like," Cianne said shyly.

"I'm sorry," Langley said, looking pained, "I have to fly out before dinner but we can talk a little now, and when I have a few days to myself, I promise we can sit down and I'll tell you everything I know about our Vivian."

Cianne's smile dimmed a little as Langley spoke but lifted again by the time he finished. "I'd like that." Cianne nodded.

"Well then," Bannerman lifted the file in his hand a little, "I will go ahead and examine the children and leave you two to talk."

Cianne turned to look at him then looked around the room, pausing on each person in the room for a second before moving to the next. It was as if she forgot that anyone other than Langley was in the room. In Bannerman's opinion, she recovered quickly and nodded again before taking a seat.

Langley nodded to Bannerman before sitting beside Cianne.

Bannerman heard Langley's voice as he carried Nadia toward exam room three. Eleanor and Aidan followed.

Examining the twins for any reason was a treat. There was no one on record who compared to them. They weren't developing at all like average children, Coesen, or Middling. As the offspring of two anomalies, they were stronger, smarter, and some of their abilities—such as healing, were already present. They were perfection in Bannerman's eyes.

From a medical standpoint, to watch and log their development was the most exciting thing Bannerman was ever a part of, aside from doing the same for their father. Being involved on a personal level was a mind-blowing experience.

Because Bannerman held Nadia in his arms, he placed her on the scale/weight table first. He ran through the basics first, always opting to take his patients' temperatures, weight, and height himself. After placing Nadia on the exam bed, he began the physical exam starting with her head. As he made his way down her tiny form he briefly looked behind her left ear.

Even now, he was stunned that Nadia and her brother's skin didn't bear the one telling sign of a Coesen. No birthmark was present on the skin behind her left ear. Shrugging, he quickly looked the rest of her over before handing Nadia to Eleanor then helping Aidan up on the standing scale with the height measuring device.

He examined Aidan.

"We are just finishing up," Bannerman said to Cianne as she entered the room. "Eleanor, can you take the children out to the waiting room so I can speak with, Soahn Cianne?"

He didn't watch as Eleanor carried Nadia and took Aidan's hand to exit the room. He kept his eyes on Cianne. He spoke when the door closed. "Have you noticed anything unusual about the twins? Or anything you'd like to talk about?"

"Unusual?" Cianne raised her brow. "You *are* kidding right."

Bannerman chuckled. "Right, have either of the children shown any supernatural abilities?"

"Nothing that I've noticed," Cianne answered with a shrug then looked away.

He didn't believe her. Bannerman would swear to the Source that he witnessed a silent conversation between the children on one occasion. Aidan was beyond his years physically and in intelligence, and though he tried to hide that fact, it was obvious. Nadia was a little more advanced than a child her age physically but she too was very intelligent. If Cianne wanted to keep that private, he wouldn't push…today.

Besides, he wasn't here to learn about the twins and their abilities or lack thereof. He was here to see how he could help Cianne, even if she didn't want it.

"Fine. How are you?" Bannerman stepped forward and took her wrist in his hand and felt for her pulse.

Cianne jerked her hand back before he could finish the count. "I'm fine," Cianne spat out. Her eyes, focused and determined, were on him. "…and I don't need a checkup. I never ever get sick." She made sure to enunciate the words "never" and "ever".

He understood her just fine but what she wanted didn't matter. She was here. He was here, and they were doing this, now.

"Look, Soahn," Bannerman began, "you look tired. You're thinner, and you seem distracted. You may not get physically ill but you can still be in poor health. Let me look you over, you answer a few questions about your diet and sleep habits and we'll figure out how best to treat you."

"Nothing's wrong with me. I'm just tired and nothing you prescribe can help that." Cianne turned to leave. Her hand was on the door when…

"Just sit down," Bannerman ordered.

Cianne stopped. The door she was pulling open sat halfway ajar. Her hand dropped, she turned her entire body around, then walked to one of the chairs against the far wall where the computer station was, and sat down. She said nothing, just stared straight ahead.

It took Bannerman a few seconds to realize what he did. In his frustration, he gave Cianne a Wheedled command. What tipped him off kilter was the fact that she actually followed it. In the past, he may have given her a command or two, just to see if it would work. To his utter shock, they never did, and his Wheddle charted as one of the highest since the Original Four.

There was only one other person who was immune to his ability. Bannerman didn't take offense that Caleb was immune. Hell, the man flicked away most attacks like a mild annoyance and it seemed Cianne was similarly capable, until now.

What's changed, he thought as he closed the door? That thought was quickly followed by the answer.

"Sit still and be quiet until I say, all done," Bannerman wheedled. He walked across the room and began to gently probe Cianne's head. She didn't move while he moved his hands over her head and through her hair. It was much shorter than it was when he first met her so he had no trouble getting to her scalp. He moved his hands behind her ears and then to the back of her neck.

Bingo.

It was small, but there was no question what it was that sat on her spine just below her hairline.

"**All done**," Bannerman offered as he sat down at the small desk. Just as he began typing his notes, the door to the room swung open. Bannerman looked over his shoulder.

"What's going on here?" Whodai demanded as he entered the room. He moved toward Cianne but kept his eyes on Bannerman.

"Sorry we took so long," Eleanor sounded winded as she rushed into the room with Nadia still in her arms and Aidan trailing behind. She handed Nadia to Cianne who held out her arms and took her daughter. "We couldn't find Aidan's book." As if on cue, Aidan lifted the book up. "He's ready to show it to you now." Her eyes were wide and focused on Bannerman.

Cianne smiled, "Are you going to read your book to Dr. Bannerman?" She stood, balancing Nadia on her hip while helping Aidan, who was already trying to climb up on the exam table.

Bannerman got up and walked over to the exam table beside Aidan but spoke to Cianne. "I'll need to take some blood samples next time." Cianne nodded. Bannerman glanced over at Whodai who looked both confused and irritated. "Alright little guy, what have you got there?" he asked Aidan.

"Cianne," Whodai said, "can I speak with you in the hall?"

Bannerman gave all his attention to Aidan and didn't look up.

He wasn't sure if Whodai was behind the inhibitor chip attached to Cianne's spine or not, but he was the obvious suspect. He surmised that it was a powerful piece of tech too, one that Whodai would have no issues commissioning. But to accuse a Royal of such an offense was punishable by death if it couldn't be proven. Removing it would be a mistake. So, for now, he would share what he learned with the others.

◉

Cianne allowed Whodai to hold her hand as they left the exam room and moved into the hallway. She tried not to pull away from him due to his hand resting on the small of her back but it took a lot of effort. It wasn't as if his touch made her skin crawl.

Whodai was all man, handsome, confident, and protective. Any woman would love his attention, but she craved only one man's touch. No other would ever compare and after reliving that moment with Tristan a few days ago, Whodai's touch felt wrong.

Cianne felt wretched. For whatever reason, Tristan was never coming back to her. Why did she hold on to hope when she should be embracing the man in front of her?

Turning to face her, Whodai placed his palm on her cheek. "Are you alright?"

He looked at her with such concern that Cianne suddenly felt the urge to step back. She mentally kicked herself for not being able to give Whodai what he wanted. Did it matter that she warned him that she was broken? Did her honesty absolve her of the pain she will undoubtedly cause him?

No. Cianne sighed.

"I'm just tired," she answered honestly. Yes, it was her go-to answer but it was also true. "I thought you wouldn't be back until tomorrow. Tomorrow is Thursday, right?" Keeping days straight was a challenge.

Understanding reflected in his chocolate eyes. Whodai knew of her nightmares and seemed so desperate to help her, but as much as he tried, he wasn't able to run them away like Tristan had. Cianne knew this pained him.

Whodai glanced at his watch. "Yes, I'm a day early. Have you had your energy drink today?" Cianne shook her head no. "Have you eaten?"

She looked around him, then down at her feet, then at her hands. She looked anywhere other than at the disappointed look on Whodai's face.

Sighing, his hands moved through her hair to palm the back of her neck. He spoke low. "I know you get sidetracked with taking care of the kids and with your job," Whodai moved closer, "but you must take care of yourself first. Those nutrition drinks are sometimes all you have the entire day. You have to promise me you'll take better care of yourself."

With her neck held firmly in his grasp, there was nowhere else to look but into Whodai's eyes. It took all she had not to squirm under his intense gaze or to move away entirely. "I'll try," Cianne whispered. Her heart raced as she saw something flicker in his gaze.

Is he going to kiss me?

Whodai moved slow as he leaned into Cianne. Her palms itched as the need to push him away became almost overpowering. Her breaths came out short and quick. Cianne's chest visibly rose and fell as he came closer. His lips were mere inches from hers when he stopped and tilted his head forward to meet hers. Their foreheads touched.

"Try harder," Whodai said. His words were spoken so softly she barely heard him.

It was then that Cianne realized that his chest was rising and falling just as fast as hers. His hold on her neck was tighter than it was seconds before, and his body seemed strained and coiled. He was holding back and it was evident that it took some effort to do so.

She relaxed a bit but it didn't escape her that Whodai wanted more, yet he took nothing.

"I don't deserve you, Whodai. You deserve someone who will—"

"*Shhh*," Whodai moved back but didn't let go of her neck, "I want you and *you* are more than I deserve." His grip tightened before he released his hold from around her neck. "Are you going to let Dr. Bannerman look you over?"

Cianne tensed again.

Whodai held his palms up. "I'm not saying that you have to. I'm just concerned; I'm not going to make you do something you're not comfortable with." He looked over her shoulder at the exam room door for a few seconds before focusing back on her. "I'm going to go up and make one of those shakes you like so much, and some lunch for you and the children. When the doctor is done, you guys come eat with me."

Cianne nodded.

Whodai opened his mouth as if he wanted to say more then closed it. He looked worried but he didn't say anything more. He just smiled then turned and left her standing there.

If he had concerns about how she felt about him, he should. She was never going to love him. If he worried about her health, he should. She was cracking, and sooner or later she would shatter. What he didn't have to worry about was their mating ceremony. She was going to show up and when she said "yes" she was going to work real hard to be the wife he deserved.

Cianne gently rubbed the back of her neck where Whodai's hand was. She closed her eyes and tried to prepare for a headache that was already mounting.

Chapter Eleven

Cassius glared at the charred contents spread out over the motel desk. They were taken from the home of Evelyn Bogdon several months ago. None of it yielded any solid evidence then and still wasn't now.

He let his head fall back and peered at the dust-covered popcorn ceiling. He wasn't getting anywhere. He was no closer to Caleb, of whose involvement in Sovereign Vivian Harper's death was now uncertain. He was no closer to figuring out why Bernard Givens was found in Evelyn's burned down home. And, he was no closer to finding the reasons for all the mayhem that plagued his people lately.

Cassius focused again on what he knew about Givens. The man's body was burned to a crisp, the obvious target of the fire no doubt. Evelyn was always good at commanding her fire ability. He just wished she hadn't died by the likes of Givens. She was labeled as a Dregan for her political beliefs but she was nothing like her murderer.

Givens was a Sodreg, the worst kind of Dregan. They cared nothing for human or Coesen law. He was a murderer, a thief, and an all-around piece of shit. Evelyn Bogdon would never associate with someone like Givens. His kind of tactics and practices were beneath her.

So why was Givens there?

Cassius looked at the surveillance disk that sat on the desk. It featured Perkins dropping Evelyn's lifeless body off at a Coesen medical facility, already thoroughly cleaned and prepared for Fasen. Then Perkins disappeared.

Apparently, Perkins found out something. *But what*? And, was what Perkins found out related to Vivian? The investigation of his Sovereign's murder was still open, and though his Protector abilities had mostly faded with Vivian's death, it was still his job to solve the crime and bring her murderer to justice.

Following his initial instincts that Caleb was the killer, Cassius attempted to hunt his bane down. His search led him nowhere. But that wasn't a surprise. Caleb was good at hiding. He successfully hid for decades from the Coesen.

Cassius was stubborn, but he could admit now that there were some issues with his original theory. Perkins may have been right. Why would Caleb kill her, and so sloppily when he was the master of stealth?

Cassius' investigation did give him a bit of insight. Caleb had plenty of opportunities to kill them all. Evidence showed that though they didn't know where *he* was through all the passing years, Caleb knew exactly where *they* were.

And Perkins…

The fool was going to get himself killed. Cassius hadn't heard or seen the man in almost a year since Perkins gave him the slip in New Orleans. That was the night Evelyn died. He should have at least listened to his old Guard. Then maybe he wouldn't be staring at the last written thoughts of Evelyn Bogdon, looking for something, anything.

Cassius lifted two of the few scorched papers of Evelyn's day planner he placed in clear protective skins. Again, he tried to piece together what was written on it. There were fragmented words with missing letters that he could make no sense of. He placed the charred pieces of the planner down and lifted the only piece that was clear. He read the name over and over in his head.

"Zuri," the name was hissed in a whisper.

It took only a second for Cassius to realize he was the one who whispered the Coesen's name so low that the average man could not hear it. Though his abilities had almost completely faded, he still retained some quickness and better than average hearing.

It was a step above a middling's speed and sight, and it wouldn't last too much longer but he hoped to solve his Queen's murder before he was completely useless. It seemed his uselessness was mounting sooner than he hoped. The fact that he still had some of his Protector abilities several months after his ward's death was unheard of but she had been one of the strongest Coesen and they were linked for a long time.

Cassius stared at the name on the paper again. Castor Zuri was a prominent Coesen of worth. He was a scientist of some sort at CoTech, located in Texas, and a good one according to his co-workers. Cassius met the man only a handful of times but he was sure they never spoke to one another being as Zuri, who was from an old family and a Royal, would have had to engage him in conversation first.

The Coesen, like most of society, had a class system in place. The Royals were the uppermost echelon of their race known as Royals or Soahn. Only three living generations of the family line and their offspring were acknowledged as such, leaving the unfortunate fourth and subsequent generations as average citizens.

The ringing of his cell phone pulled Cassius from his thoughts. Cassius placed the scrap of paper back on the table, then crossed the room and lifted his phone, checking the number. The phone was fairly new, only a few months old. He purchased it in an attempt to leave his old world behind in order to focus on what he needed to do. If he was needed, really needed, he was sure he would be tracked down.

The number on his view screen was one of the few he programmed in the phone and the call was one he was expecting but not so soon. The noise of a busy office in full swing could be heard through the line.

"Hello, Jamiah," Cassius said, sitting on the edge of the most uncomfortable bed he ever slept on.

"Sir," Jamiah said.

Cassius liked the confidence he heard in the voice of the young man he chose as the new head of the Royal Guard. "We spoke a few days ago. Is there a problem?"

"Honestly, I'm not sure and I require your counsel in an attempt to decide. A Coesen by the name of George Kent was found two nights ago in his home. Apparently, he killed his family then turned the gun on himself."

Cassius assumed that his choice for the head of the Royal Guard would step into his role seamlessly. Jamiah stood out among the candidates, and aside from Whodai, who was unable to take the head of the Royal Guard position due to his recent engagement to the new Sovereign, Jamiah was the best choice. Now, Cassius wondered if he made the right choice.

"Jamiah, though it is rare for a Coesen to do something so heinous, it happens." Cassius frowned. "You haven't the ability to predict or always prevent a crime. You must accept the losses. Some will affect you more than others but you can do this. You are the male for this job, Jamiah. Now, you are head of the Royal Guard which means that these unfortunate events must be reported to you but cases such as this can and should be handled by the local sentries unless it involves one of the royal families."

"I understand completely, Sir, but this case...I thought might interest you," Jamiah said, his tone even.

The sounds that were in the background when Cassius answered the call had all but faded into silence. "Alright," Cassius prompted.

"George Kent worked at CoTech. He worked there for seven years in the development department but was pulled from his normal duties to work on a special, yet secret project.

The man who recruited Kent was none other than Castor Zuri, your missing scientist."

Cassius felt his heartbeat increase but his mouth was suddenly dry, making it all but impossible to respond.

"Sir, I just assumed you would want this information," Jamiah said after a few seconds of silence. "If I was wrong…"

Cassius swallowed the lump in his throat. "No, no," he said. He knew he sounded overly excited but in truth, he was. "This…information does interest me." The sound of Jamiah quickly tapping computer keys filled the silence.

"I thought it would, Sir."

It didn't take long for Jamiah to fill him in on the details of the gruesome Kent murder-suicide. By all accounts, the case was exactly what it seemed. George Kent murdered his family then himself. Normally no one would have looked into the tragedy any further, but Jamiah did. When he was informed of the Kent tragedy he flew to the home in Louisiana and took a walk-through. Maybe it was curiosity or it was just Jamiah wanting to touch every case…literally. Whatever it was driving the young man; Cassius was extremely happy with his choice.

"What information didn't make it into the public file?" Cassius asked.

It was common for Coesen to keep certain aspects of their crimes from Middlings and Coesen citizens alike. It was obvious why the Guard kept certain details from Middlings. The Coesen citizens were left out of the loop about most crimes due to ongoing investigations.

"There's no doubt that Kent did what the evidence suggests but…" Jamiah let the word linger then went quiet.

Cassius was aware of Jamiah's reluctance to mention any information he derived from the use of his ability. Per his words, Jamiah thought it was useless in the grand scale of abilities other Coesen possessed. If he wasn't chosen by the Source as a Protector for his ward and gained the additional gifts of strength and speed, Cassius wondered if Jamiah would have gone down a different path versus one of justice.

"This issue you have concerning your ability needs to be addressed. It's your issue, not everyone else's."

Jamiah was silent for a few more seconds before he spoke. "From the gun...I know that Kent's heart was in turmoil. The man wasn't angry or hurting from some kind of betrayal. I felt only love and devotion for his family that he took from the world. I sensed confusion and helplessness but no splinters in his mind."

"Then why would he kill his family?" Only a few seconds passed before Cassius gasped with awareness.

Jamiah grunted his agreement as if he was reading Cassius' mind.

"A powerful Wheddler is responsible. Maybe even the same one we've been hunting for over a year," Cassius mumbled.

"Sir?" Jamiah questioned.

Though Jamiah was a Royal Guard at the time, he wasn't privy to all of the attempts on Sovereign Vivian Harper's life. He was thoroughly briefed on all the cases but some details may have been kept secret.

"There was an attempt on Sovereign Harper's life a few months before her murder. The Coesen was under a Wheddler's orders. We had to put the puppet down." Cassius fisted his hand as he pushed off the bed. "They're all connected. The last attempts on Vivian's life, her murder, Castor Zuri's disappearance, and the murder of an entire family." He just needed the person behind it all.

"Seems so, sir."

"What else?"

"One room in the house didn't feel like the others. I sensed deep-seeded chaos, turmoil, and anger. I think the one pulling the strings, the person we're are looking for, was there in the house. In the kitchen. The chair he sat in..." Jamiah paused for a shallow breath. "I only grazed it but I sensed intense, horrible things. Sir, I also saw things."

Cassius recalled Jamiah's Coesen Abilities Registration Department file or CARD registration. CARD was similar to the middlings Social Security Agency. A Coesen's birth, lineage, and abilities after manifestation were logged. This information was kept private, for only the eyes of the Royal Guard, but key Coesens could gain access by submitting a formal request if a crime was committed, for safety and medical emergencies, or special employment circumstances.

According to the CARD, Jamiah's ability was similar to that of an empath, sensing the emotions of others from objects they came in contact with. What Jamiah was telling him now, was that he saw images related to this person.

"Have you seen things before when using your ability?" Cassius asked as he walked over to the chair and sat at the desk.

"Only recently," Jamiah responded, his tone soft and low. "When I spoke with Sovereign Bertram, I took her hand and I…I felt a great loss. It felt like a dull knife cutting into the most sensitive parts of me. Her loss haunts her to such a degree that I fear…" Jamiah's words broke off and he cleared his throat. "I've gone off topic, I apologize Sir. When I touched Sovereign Bertram, I saw Soahn Tristan Bertram. It was brief, just a flash in my mind but it was him."

Cassius said nothing for a while but took a few quiet breaths. "Are you sure it was Tristan you saw?"

"I was a part of the security detail at their mating ceremony. I'm certain it was him," Jamiah said with conviction.

Neither spoke for a moment, both taking in the information.

"Do you know what seeing him means?" Cassius asked. Cianne always felt that Tristan was still alive. *Could he be*?

Sighing, Jamiah said, "I don't know. It's never happened to me before. It could just be a reflection of her desires." He cleared his throat. "About this Wheddler," Jamiah began again, "he has a great amount of depravity. Never have I seen such vivid images. Women, Sir…he has a taste for their pain. I sensed that he finds some sort of comfort in what he does. As if he needs to do these horrible things."

"Have you combed through the missing women reports?" Cassius asked. His mind was racing.

It couldn't be *him*… Akil?

Cassius was certain the nightmare who stalked the women of the Arkean Royal bloodline was no more. He saw to his end himself, just days before Sovereign Vivian went to the Baxter home to finally see her granddaughter for the first time since Cianne's childhood. Cassius still felt the loss of the good men who died that day while trying to take down that bastard, Akil.

Cassius allowed doubt to creep into his already weary mind. Did Akil die that day or had he screwed up?

"I have," Jamiah said. He spoke with confidence again. "There was an influx of missing Coesen women about two years ago but the report is coded confidential and I do not have access to them yet. The number of missing women decreased not long after, but I'm sure you're aware of this because you handled that investigation yourself."

Then it's not Akil.

Jamiah went silent and Cassius knew why. Jamiah wanted to know the details of that investigation. Cassius squeezed the bridge of his nose. Akil was indeed dead. The relief he felt was overwhelming. It meant they had at least sixteen more years to prepare. After he brought Vivian's murderer to justice and Jamiah's probationary period as Head of the Guard was fulfilled, Cassius planned to hand over all of those confidential codes.

"Since then," Jamiah went on, obviously sensing he wasn't getting more information, "Nothing unusual, but I have a feeling I wasn't looking in the right place. I've got a man searching state and federal databases for missing Middling women."

There was no need to tell Jamiah to keep what he found to the select team of men. Each Captain was told to select an inner circle of three to five people they trusted with their life. Cassius had only two men he trusted until Tristan Bertram came barging into their lives. Then there were three, Whodai, Langley, and Tristan.

"Keep me updated," Cassius ordered. He would be kept in the know until Jamiah's probationary period of a year was over. After that, Cassius would be a regular citizen again.

"There's something else. The images I saw, the women, they all have specific characteristics. Each of them, though they pale in comparison, resembles our current Sovereign."

It just keeps getting better, Cassius thought as he rubbed a hand over his face. "This guy is top priority as of now. We need to put him down and we need to do it fast. Have you located Perkins yet?"

"No. He's completely off grid—"

"Just inform the Royal and Sentry Guards to keep a look out," Cassius quickly cut him off. "If Perkins sticks out his head, I want to know. And Jamiah," Cassius said.

"Sir," Jamiah responded.

"I want you to speak with Dr. Bannerman. Inform him of what you saw in detail when you touched Cianne. Her safety, health, and general happiness are our priority and though her heart has been broken, I hope with all I am that Whodai will be able to give her some part of what she lost when Tristan died. Until she allows him that, it is up to us, her people, to care for her when she or her mate can't."

"I understand, Sir."

"Good. I'll expect information about our mystery Wheddler as soon as you get it. I'll talk to you next Thursday," Cassius told him.

"Next week then, Sir," Jamiah said before Cassius disconnected the call.

Cassius rubbed his head as he tried to piece together all the new information. The man he was after was linked to Zuri, linked to this George Kent, and linked to Evelyn and Perkins. He just needed to find the missing links to bring it all together. He needed to know what Perkins knew and he needed to know it now.

It was time for answers.

A Week Later

Caleb smiled. It was something he didn't do often and it was only reserved for those he cared deeply for. He sat on a branch of his favorite tree, his hands wrapped around the precious little girl who held tightly to his neck.

"Are you ready to let go, sweetie?" Caleb asked Nadia.

"Uh un," she said, shaking her head rapidly in the crook of his neck.

Laughing was also foreign to him but damn if he wasn't laughing now. He kissed Nadia on her forehead.

Caleb looked up to see Aidan sitting on the branch above them, further out with his feet swinging back and forth. Aidan seemed content with just sitting there. He didn't say much since they mentally linked up and entered the projected dream-like landscape that was an exact replica of Maiden Hall. Aidan didn't really talk much when they had their secret visits.

"Would you like to go for a swim, Aidan? The water's real enough." Caleb watched Aidan's brows draw together with confusion. "This place is as real as we make it, Aidan. You can smell the grass…" He peered down at the ground below. "…and feel the sun on your skin," Caleb said as he looked up at Aidan, who inhaled then glanced at his tiny arm.

Sometimes Caleb saw some of his Samuel in Aidan, but the two were different enough that he could never confuse two of them.

"Your capabilities are limitless here because this place is the creation of our minds. You can do whatever you dream, be whatever you want."

As soon as the words left Caleb's lips, Aidan transformed himself. Not into a superhero or some exotic animal like most kids dreamed up. No. Sitting on the branch above him and Nadia was the likeness of Tristan, and from what Caleb could tell it was a near perfect copy.

Nadia lifted her head from Caleb's neck and looked up as if she sensed a change around them. When she saw Aidan in Tristan's form, she smiled then giggled. Caleb found himself laughing once again.

They met on this plane of existence for months now. Caleb adopted the idea from the Coesen Veris, the meeting place of The Four. It was after Caleb took Tristan, after the attempted shooting and poisoning, that he decided to pull his grandchildren into this place, "their place". The act was more for him than them, he soon realized. He was sure they would have gotten along without him but he knew now that he could have never gotten along without them.

When Caleb first began these meetings, Aidan was apprehensive. He was cautious and seemed to think everything over before acting. It was a trait many adults never master, yet his grandson easily did. Nadia, on the other hand, embraced him from the start. She was sweet, innocent, and loving.

Aidan—Tristan got to his feet, balancing on the branch as if he was in his own skin. It seemed he was going to swim after all.

Just as Caleb was going to ask if he'd ever gone swimming, Aidan stilled.

The bright sunny sky of their made-up world darkened.

Caleb wasn't responsible for the change in the atmosphere. "What's wrong?" he asked.

Aidan's anxiety was as potent as his own. Neither child had time to answer before a vision took Caleb's attention.

He wasn't in their virtual world any longer. Caleb wasn't even himself. His body was lean, feminine, yet familiar. He was Cianne, or he was seeing the world through her red-tinted eyes as she moved through a deserted cemetery. It was freezing out, gray and cold enough for him to feel the blistering chill in his, her bones. The trees were barren and brittle; frost and residual snow covered the hard-dried grass that snagged at the long black gown that she wore. Her frozen wrinkled hands and fingers clutched the worn fabric, probably an unconscious reaction so she didn't trip over her dress. The emotions he felt coming from Cianne were nothing but despair, misery, and loneliness.

Caleb instantly knew this was being projected from Cianne directly. He also knew that she was doing it unconsciously. She was most likely dreaming.

In her dream that she inadvertently pulled him into, Cianne continued to move through the barren cemetery, passing headstones that were covered with overgrown grass, roots, and debris. She stopped when she came to three pristine gravestones. The center marker was taller but the two that sat on either side of it seem like they were hovering in the air. She moved around those large black stones until she was facing them and could read the names.

Caleb heard Nadia inhale.

"She can read her name, but that's all so far. Ms. Eleanor and I are working with her. Nadia does understand death, though," Aidan informed Caleb mentally.

Of course, she could read her name.

What worried Caleb more was that Aidan showed no emotion at what he was seeing. He understood death too. Aidan already witnessed things far beyond the boyish, sheltered life of most babes his age. That saddened Caleb, but Aidan's reserved demeanor gave him a sense of pride.

"I'm sorry," Caleb transferred. He thought of closing his mind off so Aidan wouldn't be able to read his thoughts, but decided not to. What was happening, what they were seeing, he had to discuss with them.

"We are used to the nightmares," Aidan sent back. *"She has them often enough. We don't need to discuss it."*

"Alright, but if—"

"I won't, and I'll help my sister. I'm the man until dad returns. He said so…"

Caleb closed his thoughts off from Aidan and Nadia. He would discuss the matter with Tristan later.

Focusing on the nightmare as it continued, Caleb watched as Cianne fell to her knees and sobbed in front of the three headstones that memorialized Tristan, Aidan, and Nadia. In their virtual realm, Caleb rubbed Nadia's back gently as she silently cried.

"Has your mother always projected these nightmares to you and Nadia?"

"No. We started seeing them a little while after our birthday. Until then, I think she had enough control to keep them to herself."

Caleb felt the connection to Cianne's dream sever for them all. Aidan looked down and met Caleb's concerned gaze.

"Mamma wake up?" Nadia moaned. Looking up she unlocked her hands from around Caleb's neck to reach for her brother's hand.

"We have to go," Aidan said as he appeared beside Caleb and Nadia, reaching for his sister's hand.

He was himself again, small. No matter his maturity, he was still only just a babe.

Caleb looked at his grandchildren, standing hand and hand. He failed to save Samuel, Marda, and Kayla, but he wouldn't fail them. He wouldn't fail Tristan. Though Cianne thought him the enemy, he would not fail her.

"Your father and I are going to fix this. We're going to make things right for you again," Caleb promised.

Aidan tilted his head to the side and looked at Caleb as if he were studying him. Then he held his head up straight and said, "I know, Pop-pop."

Caleb blinked, and when he opened his eyes the twins were gone and he was in his room, lying on his bed, looking up at the ceiling. He then sat up and swung his legs off the bed then looked at his door. The door to his small one room cottage swung open.

"I saw it as well," Caleb said.

◉

Tristan found it difficult to hide his joy. Aside from the dark content of the shared dream, the implications were big. The connection between them was severed to save his life. The thought of that day still pained him. He could have lost the woman he loved and his children that day, all because he didn't understand how desires and mental illness could push people to do the unthinkable.

He only had to think of Aidan and Nadia when he felt the weight of that day, and his joy would come rushing forward. He was filled with that same joy now as he stepped into the small cottage without invitation and closed the door.

The light switched on as he walked over to the small kitchenette set and pulled out a chair.

"I saw it as well," Caleb said again. "Except, I'm not sure we saw the same thing because what I saw didn't stimulate my happy reflexes."

Tristan scooted the chair closer to the bed. "Because you're not seeing the big picture. Our link, it's back. Well, not *back* exactly," Tristan waved his hand dismissively, "but it's a start. Right?"

Caleb looked around him to peer at the wall. Tristan glanced over his shoulder to see a round clock on the plain wall. It resembled the ones he used to see in schools, round and big with black trim and black numbers on a white surface. Tristan took a moment to look around the cottage. The small space was updated—clean but plain—yet it held none of the opulent beauty of the main house. Yet, it was where Caleb preferred to spend his time. And it had indoor plumbing, which was a plus.

"It *is* a start," Caleb said, pushing to his feet. He walked over to a beautifully restored wardrobe and began moving things around. "We're not sleeping tonight so we might as well train. You need to be at your best when the two of you meet again."

Tristan shook his head. "Did you not hear me? Our connection is re-established. Not like it *was*," he mumbled the last word, "but that's because of the distance between us. Once we are together in the same room, Cianne will feel me." He pounded softly on his legs to give emphasis to his words. "She'll feel what we had, what we were, and what we will be again. I just need to be close to her."

"I don't think it's that simple, Tristan." Caleb pulled out a short sleeve shirt and pulled it over his head. "I don't want you going to her. Let's talk with Tranae first. Bannerman thinks he can make the chip inoperable without setting her off or alerting whoever placed it in her."

Tristan shook his head as he got to his feet. "What are you saying? It's been a week since Bannerman discovered she had an inhibitor chip embedded under her skin. We all know who put it there." To Tristan, all roads led to Whodai. "Cianne needs me now. You said so yourself. I need to go to her."

The air in the room seemed to thicken. A low hum surrounded them. Curious, Tristan glanced around the room. When he turned back to Caleb, Tristan realized the change in the room and the low humming sounds were coming from Caleb.

"When she kills you, and she *will* kill you, it will haunt her for the rest of her life." Caleb's head hung and his fists were clenched at his sides. He made no moves to attack, though he looked like he wanted to. "You saw her nightmare, but you are so high from the possibility of a renewed connection that you didn't really see." Caleb looked up and stared at Tristan. "Let me refresh your memory. She was alone, wrinkled, and aged. Those gravestones had you and your children's names on them. Her sadness was palpable but did you notice the things you didn't see? Like the fact that there were no other sounds around her. No birds, no traffic in the background, no signs of life near her or in the distance. Alone. She was completely alone and aware enough to know it."

"It was a goddamn nightmare, Caleb. Just a nightmare." Tristan sighed. "She had them all the time and will continue to have them unless I go to her."

Tristan watched Caleb close his eyes and take several deep breaths. When he opened his eyes, Tristan saw so much pain in them he almost moved forward to offer assistance. The only thing that stopped him was the sound of Caleb's voice.

"You know of the time I tried to end it all," Caleb began, "…after I killed everyone in the Coesen village all those years ago and I jumped from that cliff."

Tristan nodded.

"Well, that wasn't the only time I tried to end it. After losing Kayla and not being able to find her, I tried to end it a few times. Learned some things about myself. Like that little teleportation trick, you hate. I discovered it when I tried tossing myself into an active volcano."

Appalled, Tristan glared at Caleb.

"Don't give me that look. Fire and lava that hot would destroy anything…and a bullet to head and heart didn't get the job done so…" Caleb sighed. "Anyway, it didn't work. Pythos was dormant but apparently, its self-preservation function knew when to kick in, because one moment I'm falling into a scorching red inferno, and the next I'm a continent away, lying on the floor of one of my properties." Caleb paused, looking ashamed. "If things don't go as planned, I will be here when all that surrounds me is gone."

Frowning, Tristan opened his mouth to ask, *What the hell do you mean? What plan?*

But Caleb lifted his hand. "I suspect that what we saw tonight wasn't just a nightmare. I believe it was a vision of the future I thought I prevented when I brought you back to life after your ex-girlfriend shot you. What we just saw was what her mother feared. We avoided a Cianne-atomic-bomb when you went MIA from her life because she believed you were still alive. Now, it seems she's losing faith that you are, but she has the kids. They are keeping her going, barely.

"If you go to her and she succeeds in killing you, then she comes to her senses afterward, Cianne will never forgive herself. I can't allow her to live with your death on her hands. So, until we fix what's wrong with her, you do not go to her." Caleb brows tilted downward. "I'll kill you myself before I allow her to suffer through that and see her nightmare become reality."

"And you can live with that, killing me?" Tristan sneered.

Caleb looked him square in the eyes as he arched a brow. "With ease, if it meant saving my daughter," Caleb answered without blinking.

◉

"If you think you can keep me tethered here, you've got another thing coming. I'm not the boy you once knew." Tristan rolled his shoulders back as he glared at Caleb.

He wasn't as fast as the man standing in front of him, and the fact that Caleb could literally put him down with a thought meant nothing. Being without Cianne was killing him and she wasn't faring well without him either. His own stupidity kept them apart all this time but he wasn't going to let anyone or anything keep him from her now.

Before Tristan knew what happened, he was on the hard floor gasping for air. The scent of wood polish was damn near overwhelming from the position he was in. On his back with his head hanging to the side, Tristan worked to focus on what the hell just happened. His ears were ringing and his head drummed a beat he came to know intimately over the months he spent with Caleb.

This time, the SOB moved so fast that Tristan didn't see a thing. The only reason he knew Caleb moved was because he actually felt the man's hands on him before losing his footing. Even with him trying to rewind and slow the movements in his head, he still couldn't resolve when or how Caleb came at him.

From the pulses of pain on his body, Tristan could ascertain exactly where he was hit. He felt the pain from the severe blow to each ear, to disorientate him. A swift skull crunching punch to the left temple and a fist to the chest (almost simultaneously of course) challenged his balance. And a wicked chop to the neck damaged his windpipe. The exact order of the actions that resulted in his ass being handed to him, Tristan didn't know, but the aftershocks of getting handed said ass was still in full effect.

Tristan rolled over to his side and moaned. He actually moaned.

God, Caleb has a way of making himself clear.

"Even in my youth, I hated repeating myself. As a person, you're likable. But that means nothing to someone like me. You get in my way, you die. Now, my daughter and grandchildren love you and I will admit they need you, so that gives your life value. That means you live and all those who mean you harm, die. But don't for one-minute assume you are the one making the decisions here, Tristan." Caleb looked away. "I don't like this chip thing any more than you do."

Tristan tried to speak but coughed instead. "Then do something," he hoarsely demanded, eventually.

"Don't you think I want to lay waste to all who oppose me and take my family from all of this?" Caleb spat, "the treachery, the politics..." Caleb walked over to the bed and sat down. He shook his head then scrubbed a hand down his face and sighed.

Tristan clumsily got to his feet and fell into a nearby chair.

"As much as I want to..." Caleb shook his head again. Then he suddenly straightened. His mind seemed to be made up. "I can't. For one, she would not allow it, and a confrontation between us would be disastrous, especially with Pythos nipping at my heels. Then, there is the matter that she is a Coesen. As much as I hate it, she has taken on the role of Sovereign. It is her right and her life is her own to live. I keep reminding myself of that. All I can do is help out where I can.

She is stronger than you both think. My unbidden and public assistance would only bode ill for you both when this is all over. In the precarious state, I'm in right now, all I can do is walk in the background and be there when I'm needed."

Tristan sighed. It seemed that their hands were tied, for now.

Chapter Twelve

Cianne rubbed her temple. He wouldn't leave her alone. Two and a half weeks passed since that horrible, all too real nightmare, and his presence in her mind was chasing away every bit of her sanity. It seemed that there was nothing, not a single thing, she could do about it.

Tristan haunted only her dreams at first, but now he was constantly on her mind. His voice saying her name, his fresh masculine scent, she could almost feel his touch. Just the thought caused her to involuntarily shiver.

Cianne forced Tristan from her mind and tried to focus on the reality she lived in. So, she looked to the only beings who anchored her—her children. They sat nestled in-between her and Whodai, both of their expressions forever opposite—Nadia's with a smile and laughter that was just beneath the surface and on the verge of spilling out; Aidan's was curious but restrained.

Cianne glanced over at Whodai, who either just turned to look at her or already was watching her. His deep brown eyes always spoke to her, saying the words he abstained from saying out loud but she somehow heard them anyway. She wasn't ready to acknowledge those things yet, and she may never be.

She forced a smile then stifled a sigh as she looked over her shoulder. Jacobi frowned when their eyes met. He moved forward, toward her, but Cianne shook her head. They didn't have time to reconnect since his return yesterday from an assignment that took him away for three months.

When she saw him walking down the hallway toward the children's room earlier, she forgot how a Sovereign was supposed to act and jumped into Jacobi's arms. She sensed he didn't know how to respond, but after a few seconds of hesitation, he returned her tight embrace. It was nice having Jacobi back as the twins' personal guard. He was now more family than friend.

Tristan's Maatii brother forever.

It was also nice to see Zeta last week. She called twice since her visit and even though their conversations were short and full of Zeta's concern for her health, it was nice.

Cianne realized that she was wrong that she pushed her friends away in the first place. None of them seemed to hate her for it and they seem willing to pick back up where they left off, with no reservations.

Though, it still bothered her that neither Zeta nor Jacobi requested to stay on with her. Even after she had Whodai offer them both permanent positions with her and the children, Whodai reported back that they both graciously declined.

Cianne felt the sting of their rejection then but now she was just happy to have Jacobi back, and Zeta visiting again.

Maybe they realized how grief struck she was...*is*. She lost so much...her father and her grandmother whom she just found. She was reluctant to admit it for months, but she also lost her life. Tristan was her life.

Cianne felt a calming warmth settle over a section of her hand. She looked down to see Aidan's small hand over hers. She looked up to see Nadia watching her too, her daughter's small eyes searching, her smile gone. It was amazing how in-tune her children were to her, and no matter how she tried to remember this, she often failed to keep her emotions locked away.

She forced a smile as she closed off the connection with her children. Cianne also locked away her thoughts of loss and decided to give her attention to the show. Whodai must have pulled a lot of strings to arrange a private showing for the children. It was her idea to include the staff and their families in the fun. Their numbers were small but that meant that everyone had great seats. The least she could do was enjoy it with them.

Holding onto the joy she felt when seeing her kids happy, Cianne rubbed Aidan's hand and pointed to the center ring. A man with a painted face and dressed in a white suit and a top hat balanced on high stilts as he announced that the world-renowned Utopia Circus was overjoyed to be welcomed at Ark Manor to perform for them.

Cianne's heart warmed as children's laughter filled her ears. Even the twins seemed to have forgotten the sadness she felt minutes ago, their eyes were glued on the performers. Extravagantly dressed men, women, and animals filed out from behind a pair of large curtains to fill all three rings.

The Utopia Circus was one of the best and renowned in the world and she always wanted to see a show but never went to one.

Not with my random visions back then.

During a quick introduction of the main acts, Cianne noticed that each group lowered their heads when she looked their way. Apparently, back in the 18th century, a story was told to the Middling world to explain the wealth, security, and sovereignty of the Arkean family. Today, it was well known that she was royalty to that nation, so the bowing was expected and she didn't mind it so much now. She returned the bows with a nod of her head in acknowledgment.

Once the introductions were over the ring emptied, leaving the Ring Master in the center. A harmonious sound filled the extra-large tent and the show began.

Cianne let out a deep breath. She was going to enjoy this. She had to, for her children's sake.

The day was turning out to be surprisingly nice. The circus was a hit with both of her children, though Aidan was harder to read because he usually gave no physical response other than his concentrated attention and a slight smile.

By the way, Nadia's face lit up, especially when she saw the acrobats and dancers dressed in their beautiful costumes, purchases of tutus and plush animal were definitely in Cianne's future.

They all clapped when the music signaled that the show was over. It was indeed magnificent and Cianne was pleased she finally got to see it.

She got to her feet and held her arms out for Nadia, who readily reached for her. Aidan slid from his chair and moved down the aisle with Whodai following behind him. They moved toward the end of the row where Jacobi waited. They could turn one way to leave the huge tent or the other way which would lead them to the center ring.

It was weird, but Cianne didn't want the day to end. The circus took her and the children to another world, where sadness, loss, and pain weren't welcome. Once they left this tent and stepped one foot toward the Manor, her life and all its problems would crash back into her. Under this tent, it was as if she was normal, with two normal children and her normal fiancé.

"Is something wrong?" Jacobi asked when she didn't move forward.

At the same time, Whodai touched her arm, "Cianne?"

Confused about what she wanted to do, Cianne looked up to see the Ring Master approaching. The Ring Master stopped his forward stride when Jacobi held up his hand.

"Excuse me, Soahn," The Ring Master said, "would the children like to see some of the animals up close?"

Cianne noticed that he didn't look offended or confused that Jacobi, who looked like a high school girl's crush, gave him the subtle order to stop.

Jacobi waited for her to respond but stepped between her family and the Ring Master.

"Want to see the animals?" Cianne looked to the children. Both nodded.

"That would be wonderful. Thank you," Cianne smiled. She moved Nadia over to her other hip and took Aidan by the hand. They followed the Ring Master, who was still rather tall without the stilts, down the bleachers, and through the rings to the rear of the tent.

Going through an opening in the tent, Cianne thought that the magical atmosphere which enraptured her was lost when the show was over, but that wasn't the case. The spell of the circus was still in the air as they followed the Ring Master to where a handful of smaller tents and trailers were set up.

Performers moved about, doing their designated chores, stopping to bow whenever they happened to look up to see their group. She noticed that some of the performers had the Coesen mark.

"Are they all Coesen?" Cianne looked to Whodai, then gazed up at the Ring Master who walked in front of them. She couldn't see if he bore the birth mark.

"He's a descendant of Jai," Whodai offered as an explanation. "And yes, they are all Coesen."

They are all Coesen, she thought with awe.

The information shocked her. Why, she didn't know. Did she expect every Coesen to be Royals, Guards, or lawyers? She knew there had to be others, with normal jobs and lives. She knew some. The cooks, domestic workers, and the children's nanny were all Coesen. Yet, she still was slow to see them as people with regular lives.

They are just people.

It was ridiculous, but her new-found awareness eased her mind in a way.

Whodai touched her shoulder. "I'll be right back."

Cianne gave Whodai a small smile before he walked in another direction.

Her, the children, and Jacobi reached a hay enclosure where elephants were being tended. Nadia wriggled in her arms to be free, so Cianne lowered her daughter to the grass and watched her look at her brother, who managed to climb up on one of the hay stacks.

The Ring Master leaned over them. "Which one first?"

Nadia pointed to the elephants with barely-contained excitement as she bounced up and down.

The Ring Master laughed as he stepped up on the hay enclosure. "Well then, let's get a closer look."

Nadia attempted to pull herself up over the hay but Jacobi was there to lift her in his arms. "I'll take them," he said, reaching for Aidan's hand after stepping up over the haystacks. When Aidan didn't take his hand, Jacobi paused. "You don't want to go?" Jacobi asked, looking down.

Cianne watched as Aidan looked up at Jacobi and shook his head once then turned and focused on Whodai as he approached.

"She'll be safe with me," Jacobi said as he looked to Cianne.

When she gave him a nod, he walked Nadia to the elephants.

"You having a good time?" Whodai asked as he walked up holding a couple of hot dogs and a small container of fries. He handed Cianne the hot dog and bent to give Aidan the fries.

Aidan looked at her, only taking the food after she gave him a nod. When Whodai straightened beside her again, she smiled. "I'm having a wonderful time. Thank you for…" she said, as she looked around, "all of this. It was so thoughtful of you."

Whodai handed her a few napkins. "It is my pleasure to please you and the children."

Cianne lifted her hot dog to her mouth. It smelled amazing so she took a small bite. The weird thing was, everything smelled amazing yet they were near the animals. She hadn't been around large animals in a long time but she remembered the smell.

Shrugging, she chewed her food. The hearty appetite she once had was still absent but she chewed the small bite, trying to savor the flavor, hoping to jumpstart her interest in food. It was really good so she took another bite, this one bigger.

They didn't speak as they ate. Cianne watched Jacobi and Nadia as they rode on one of the elephants. Another kid who looked about six years old rode another elephant beside them. Other children waited in line for a ride.

Cianne took the silence as a moment to look around. People waited in line for cotton candy, while others ran by with balloons. A jovial clown blew bubbles for no one in particular, but a few people stopped to pop them. A few games were set up and people tried to win prizes.

This day made her life almost seemed normal.

Cianne's gaze fell on Jamiah. He was speaking with a woman she met earlier. She was the business manager for the circus but Cianne failed to recall her name.

Jamiah tilted his head when their eyes met, and Cianne smiled in response. He wasn't happy with her decision to extend an invitation to the staff and their families but she felt it would be a waste for the circus to only perform for just her and the children.

Her decision made the Royal Guard's jobs harder, but when she saw the smiles on everyone's faces she felt it was worth it. Jamiah felt the same, she could tell. Or maybe he was just happy that he was able to talk her out of inviting the entire county or town.

I wonder what Canadians called their towns.

Cianne's gaze landed back on Whodai. He was offering Aidan a cup of what looked like orange flavored slush. Again, Aidan looked to her for approval. She gave him another nod so he placed his fry container on the hay he was sitting on and accepted the drink.

Whodai chuckled then joined her a few feet away. "Do you think he will ever accept me?"

Cianne mentally winced, expecting the discomforting feeling she always got when someone asked a question about or mentioned her upcoming nuptial. Surprisingly, this time there were no feelings of dread threatening to send her into a panic. She didn't experience warm happy fuzzy feelings either, but this was a start.

A start to accepting what must be done to ensure my children's safety.

"He can't read you," Cianne said as she wiped the corner of her mouth.

Whodai stared at her. He gave the impression that he was studying her then he raised a brow. "You're serious, aren't you?"

Cianne twisted her mouth and shrugged.

"Read me how? Aidan is just a baby."

"I don't know how to explain it." Cianne looked away, focusing on Nadia laughing and pointing at a kid on the elephant as she waited in line for another turn. Cianne swept a few strands of her loose hair away from her face with the back of her hand, then looked back at Whodai. "It's almost like an aura or rather a sense, a feeling. You're open but at the same time closed off. Aidan senses that."

"Is that what you're sensing from me too?"

"Yes," she admitted, "but I can also sense that you are determined to see us succeed, as a couple and as leaders."

Whodai's tone was lower, thicker. "Is that all you sense from me?"

Cianne didn't want to answer his question. Of course, she sensed more. She couldn't step in the same room with him and not feel his desire. If she was honest with herself, it was always there, lying in wait just under the surface of their friendship. Maybe she was oblivious then. Now, his want was like ropes that were slowly tightening around her neck, wrists, and ankles as each day passed. With the end of each day, those bonds tugged and tightened as their mating ceremony drew closer.

"Yes," she forced out. Lying never came easy for Cianne but to admit she knew how he felt might encourage him to seek more from her sooner rather than later. They will be mated soon and she will promise to be his wholeheartedly, but for now, she was still Cianne Bertram.

"Have you tried to look deeper? I mean, no one really knows all you'll be capable of as the Halo, but it's assumed you will have use of every known Coesen ability, along with whatever powers your father wields. So, it stands to reason that you can or will have a number of mental abilities at your disposal." Whodai stared into her eyes as if looking for a telltale sign to see if she may or may not be forthcoming with her answer. "Have you ever looked deeper than what lies under the surface?"

The fact that he repeated the question and the way he emphasized it made Cianne wonder what she would see if she chose to delve into Whodai's head. What would she find there? The thought sent a chill up her spine.

Cianne never invaded his privacy or anyone else's, but now...

She grabbed on to the power she often ignored in an attempt to get into Whodai's head.

"Ah," Whodai said then grinned.

It was a welcoming smile even though he clearly knew what she was doing.

"I've worked you up," he said. "Your fear of what I may be hiding has you ripping into my head instead of gently nudging your way in to get what you want. We can work on this but for now..."

Whodai opened up to Cianne, but she realized not completely. His feelings toward her children were...curiosity and uncertainty. She felt no danger to her, only approval, respect, and a passion for her that bordered on the extreme.

Cianne released the connection and fought the impulse to run from Whodai. She could no longer pretend that this was a political mating for him. Not now, knowing what he wanted of her.

"I...," Cianne began but paused, "I don't..." She lowered her gaze. What could she say?

Whodai lifted her chin with his finger. "Don't overthink what you sensed. Remember that I knew of you long before we met. The way I feel," he said as he shrugged, "is how I feel. It has nothing to do with how you feel. You agreed to this mating for your own reasons. I have my reasons. I only want what you are willing to offer, nothing more."

The gentle way he touched her and the tone in which he spoke calmed Cianne's racing mind. If there was one thing she knew, it was that Whodai never treated her like an outsider. From their first meeting, he seemed kind and understanding.

Why couldn't she try to give him a chance to win what little of her heart she had left? It wasn't as if he was unattractive. Whodai was the embodiment of tall, dark, and gorgeous. In another life, another time, he would have her interest. But as it were, she felt no pull, no quickening.

Cianne sucked in a breath when Whodai leaned forward. Only a few inches separated their mouths. She lifted her hand and wrapped her fingers around his wrist, the one with his finger under her chin, as a warning.

"I can't apologize for the way I feel, Cianne. I won't." Whodai slowly closed the minute space between them, turning at the last moment to place a chaste kiss on her cheek.

Cianne allowed her eyes to close in relief as her chest slowly deflated with the air she held in. Was she shaking? Her nerves were shot.

"*You're about to marry him but you can hardly stand his touch,*" a little voice in her head taunted. "*You're weak. Not fit to be a leader, their mother, or Tristan's wife.*"

Startled by the fact that her self-loathing suddenly had a voice, Cianne gasped. She tightened her hold on Whodai's wrist; her manicured short nails dug into his skin.

"Call me Gemini. Self-loathing is your bag, not mine."

"I've overstepped," Whodai said. He lowered his finger but covered her hand in his.

Maybe it was because Whodai sounded so wounded, or maybe it was a way to assert herself against her inner voice, but Cianne reached up and pulled him close and buried her face in his neck.

Whodai sighed as he drew her closer and buried his face in her hair.

Cianne felt his chest move when he inhaled her scent. She still didn't swoon but she felt a sense of acceptance she hadn't felt in a long time. For the first time in over a year, she was ready to believe in someone again.

"Really now?" the inner voice teased, "as *opposed to believing in yourself?"*

Cianne couldn't help the grievous moan that escaped her. She was bat shit crazy and who knew how long she could hold on to the speck of sanity she still had?

Whodai pulled back, holding her at arm's length. "Are you all right?" His concern reflected on his handsome face.

She wasn't, but she couldn't admit that. "Yes," Cianne answered. She forced a smile.

A light tap on Cianne's leg drew her attention to Aidan, who was looking up at her. He also looked concerned, for her. Cianne stepped away from Whodai and lifted her son up in her arms.

He didn't protest.

"I'm fine, AJ," Cianne told her son, as she stared into his soulful blue-green eyes. He stared at her for so long that she was about to ask him what he saw but she wasn't sure she really wanted to know.

Aidan wrapped his arms around her neck and held her tight. He was strong. That was good because he will grow into an even stronger man, mentally and physically, who will watch over his sister. That was comforting because it was time to begin planning for the worst.

The children's care needed to be settled before her complete descent into madness, along with the reigns of the Coesen Empire. But there were other matters she needed to tend to first so she made a mental checklist:

1. Eliminate Caleb.

2. Fix the mess with Chandra

3. Choose and brief the person who will be her children's guardian.

Planting a smile on her face, Cianne pushed what she needed to do out of her head and again decided to try and enjoy herself.

Chapter Thirteen

May 27th

Tristan glanced down at his cell phone and noted the time. He covered his head with a worn baseball cap, placed a pair of dark sunglasses over his eyes, then opened the driver's door and stepped out of the car Langley loaned him.

He moved through the crowded sidewalk with little effort as he made his way to the drug store. Opening the door, he held it for a woman and her small son before entering himself. Tristan lowered his head as he strolled down the cosmetic aisle of Hammond's Drug store. The aisle gave him the perfect view of the pharmacy counter that was bustling with the Monday rush. He didn't see who he was looking for but he knew she was here.

He saw her when she walked in almost eight hours ago.

Tristan wished there was another way to do this. The way that he planned to do it plagued him the entire time he waited in the parking lot. He didn't want to drag someone else, someone he cared for, someone so vulnerable, into his mess but she was all he had. Since Zeta, Langley, and Bannerman's visit to Ark Manor, they noticed a pattern.

Zeta returned home, back to France. Her ward, Pierre was involved in some kind of attack. He wasn't badly hurt but she had a need to get to him as soon as possible. Caleb stepped up and teleported her home. She reluctantly allowed him.

Both Bannerman and Langley were suddenly pulled away as well. Bannerman was called away on a medical emergency and Langley was called away to handle a legal matter that his law firm somehow couldn't solve without him.

To Tristan, it was apparent that someone was intentionally keeping them away from Cianne. He had his suspicions of who, though his cohorts felt differently. It was unheard of for a Royal heir to do what Tristan was accusing. But the way he saw it, Whodai was the only one with something to gain from Cianne's controlled acquiescence.

According to Bannerman, the chip embedded in the nape of her neck was not one that could be easily found. Most inhibitor chips were placed and attached on the outside of the body. This one was embedded under her skin with no tell-tale surgical scar. That was new and innovative. Bannerman was anxious to get his hand on the tech.

To Tristan, the sophistication of the tech spelled money, time, and influence. All of which Whodai had in spades.

Tristan heard the familiar voice of his friend telling her co-workers that she was leaving for the day. He moved to another aisle after he heard the gears of the ancient time clock punch her time card, knowing she would use the cosmetic aisle to leave. He tuned his hearing to her heartbeat, breathing, and footfalls to separate her from the people around them, to make it easier for him to follow her without her noticing him.

Tristan's first side view of Tranae sent him spiraling into the memories he held close to his heart. His first day at West Hills High, the second time he saw Cianne, she and Tranae were talking as they moved down the main entrance hall. When his and Cianne's eyes met for the first time, his heart seemed to stop, and he felt as though it didn't start again until she gave him a subtle smile before shyly turning away.

Even back then, Tristan knew she didn't give just anyone her smiles.

Following Tranae now, Tristan eased the memories of his past aside so he could focus on his future. To get to that future, he needed to get this over with.

Tranae's phone rang as she walked toward her vehicle. She answered the cell phone as she juggled her purse and clicked the button to open her car door.

Tristan hid behind a tree as Tranae sat down in the driver's seat and started her car while speaking to the male caller.

Tristan took that moment to study Tranae. She was always beautiful, and he admired her zest for life and fun, but he could see a change in her. The spark that was uniquely Tranae, dimmed a bit. Her tone was polite as she spoke, but her usual vigor was nonexistent. The conversation was mostly one-sided and ended after only a few minutes.

He watched as Tranae backed her car out of the parking space then pulled into traffic. He could approach her now but he suddenly feared her reaction in such a public place. Tristan wished he planned this better but there was no time. No, it was better for him to follow her home.

Making his way to the car he drove, Tristan got behind the wheel and took off after Tranae.

Tranae sighed. She glanced at her favorite photo then threw her purse and keys on the end table as she kicked her apartment door shut with the back of her foot. Her apartment was small so it only took a few strides to get from the front door to the cozy kitchen. Once inside, Tranae grabbed her favorite mug and placed it under the spout of the one cup coffee maker her mom bought her as a housewarming gift. She inserted the single serve container then pushed the brew button before heading for her bedroom located just down a short hallway.

Feeling infinitely better now that she replaced her work clothes with yoga pants and a long sleeve gray shirt, she made her way back to the kitchen. Tranae doctored her coffee to her liking, snatched up a donut snack pack, and headed back to her living room.

The space was compact but it was useful, and it was hers. Her red sofa and loveseat nearly touched as they sat side by side in an L-shaped pattern. Her television, another housewarming gift from her parents, sat directly in front of the sofa and was possibly her favorite item in the entire world. Pictures, decorative baubles, and whatever else caught her eye, filled her space, giving the apartment a lived-in look.

Moving her routine along, Tranae pointed her remote at the television, and seconds later sounds began to steal her away—away from her loneliness. Movies and reading propelled her into worlds where she could experience life through the lens of someone else.

When she was in high school, reading and television were the furthest things from her mind. Hell, sitting for just a few minutes felt like punishment back then. Her cell phone was the only technology that held Tranae's attention at the time. Now she loathed the small electronic device.

The fact that it was ringing now really irritated her.

At the same time, there was a knock at her door. Standing, Tranae reached for her cell as she made her way to the door. She sighed when she saw the bold large letters that spelled out 'Jessie' on the screen of her cell as she opened the front door.

"Hello," she said as lifted her head, coming face to chest with the person standing in her doorway. A well-sculpted chest.

"Nae, you have to talk to Vanessa. She won't listen to reason."

Jessie continued to talk but Tranae didn't hear him. She felt dizzy as she stared into a pair of familiar crystal blue eyes.

"Oh. My. God." she gasped, repeating it several times as she dropped her phone while backing away from the open door. A shriek bubbled up and burst out of her mouth as her butt hit her side table before she stumbled back over the arm of her sofa. She would have landed awkwardly if it wasn't for a pair of strong hands grabbing hold of her arms and hoisting her up on her feet. She was placed on the sofa in the same spot where she sat before she heard the door.

"Calm down Tranae, or you're going to pass out."

Tristan?

He placed her coffee in her hands, hands he had to hold up.

"Drink," he ordered.

Confused and still chanting her disbelief, Tranae shook her head until he took hold of her face between his hands and spoke slowly.

"I need you conscious."

"Oh-kay..."

With a nod, Tristan released his hold. After over a dozen deep breaths and excessive blinking, Tranae adjusted herself on her sofa. "Ok," she watched as he moved away and sat beside her. "You're not dead. She *said* you weren't dead. Why aren't you dead?" Her mind raced with questions and comments but she couldn't focus, she could only ramble. "Not that I want you dead, but Cianne..."

Tranae gasped, covered her mouth then jumped forward suddenly, spilling coffee on the floor and table. She placed the dripping mug on the table as she tossed magazines and random items aside.

"Where's my phone?" she called out.

Cianne needs to know. Does she already know? She couldn't know and not call me.

Tranae froze. *Cianne might already know.* They weren't close anymore. Cianne all but shut her out. *She would have called to tell me Tristan is alive, right?*

It didn't matter. Either way, Tranae was going to call her best friend. She searched the room with her eyes before seeing the cell by the door where she dropped it. She turned her back to the door so she could face Tristan, hoping he didn't disappear but he wasn't by the sofa.

"Please Tranae," Tristan said.

"Where'd you…?" she asked. She turned back. "How'd you…" He was right in front of her. How did he move so fast?

He took hold of her hands. "I need your help. Cianne needs your help."

Tranae watched Tristan closely as he tilted his head toward her, then he…

He was now standing in her hallway. Tranae covered the gasp that threatened to come out of her mouth as she pointed at him.

"Your brother is coming."

"You're like Cianne. Well, not like her, but like her," she squealed. Tranae's heart was in an excited frenzy. She was about to ask him how did he move so fast but he held up his hand.

"Get rid of Jessie."

"First, are you here? Am I crazy?"

"You're not crazy, but you must get rid of Jessie."

"Ok…not crazy," Tranae whispered as she slowly walked toward her door…the door that sounded like it was being beaten down.

"Get rid of him, as fast as you can."

Tristan's voice was coming from someplace in her apartment, but from where she didn't know. What she was going to say to get rid of Jessie after she opened the door, she had no clue, but she pulled it open anyway. Before she could even speak, Jessie took hold of her and pulled her into a hug then pushed her back. His wide eyes raked over her.

"You're alright," Jess breathed as he pulled her into another hug. This one was bone crushing. "Damn it Nae, do you know how many laws I just broke to get here?"

Pushing, or at least attempting to push him away, Tranae mumbled, "I can't breathe."

"Shit," Jessie released her and gave her another quick look over. "Sorry," he grinned, then his expression turned serious. He pushed her aside and stalked into her apartment as if he was on a mission. "What happened earlier? Why did you scream? Is someone here?"

"What?" Tranae glared at him. It took a moment for her to get her mind right. She did scream, then she dropped her phone. "Oh, nothing's wrong," she said as she bent to pick up her phone. She watched as Jessie looked around her living room. "I saw a spider," she offered as an excuse.

"A spider?" Jessie turned and pinned her in place with his disbelieving stare. "You scream like a Freddie Krueger victim and you tell me it was because of a spider?"

Tranae nodded sheepishly, hating the reference to her only lingering childhood fear. It wasn't Michael Myers, Jason Voorhees, or killer clowns who had her hiding in her parents' bed under impenetrable (because everyone knew that their parents' bed sheets were made of bad guy repellant) linen sheets that covered her small shaking body.

It was Freddy Krueger who earned the title of scariest bad guy of all. Until this day, she believed that he was the most realistic bad guy because dying in your sleep seemed more realistic than a corpse that couldn't be killed.

Jessie twisted his lips and narrowed his eyes, then turned toward her bedroom. Calling over his shoulder he said, "I should probably find and kill that spider then."

Tranae reached out to her brother but...she dropped her hand. Maybe if he found Tristan hiding in her room she could believe he was actually here, alive. She followed Jessie and watched from her bedroom door he searched her room, in her closet, and behind her long ceiling-to-floor curtains. Tranae sucked in a breath when he pushed open her ensuite bathroom door and stepped inside.

She couldn't see her brother from this angle but she didn't move. Tranae just stood in the doorway of her room staring at her purple and gray patterned bedspread. Questions, lots of questions filtered through her confused mind but one thing stood out like a beacon.

"Cianne needs your help," Tristan told her.

Concern for her best, yet estranged, friend made her call out. "Jess!" She moved as quickly as possible without running. Jessie had a hand on the opaque shower door. It was pulled back enough for her to see some of the dark blue wall tiles but nothing else.

"Jess, get out of my bathroom. My whole purpose of moving out on my own was privacy." She tried to sound as irritated as possible while placing her hand on his shoulder and pushing him out of the bathroom. She sounded like the old Tranae, and Jessie must have thought so too because the slight lift at the corner of his mouth didn't escape her notice. "No one's here but me so you can stop searching my tiny apartment. As if there was a place to hide," she added under her breath.

She managed to get him to the front door without him saying a single word. Jessie just turned and stared at her. He didn't stare long but it was long enough to make her wonder what he was thinking.

"What?" she demanded, placing her hands on her hips.

He gave her a full-on smile this time. Jessie had always been handsome but his immaturity and desire to make her life as his little sister hell diminished his good looks in her eyes. But women noticed what she didn't, especially her friend Vanessa.

"It's just that you seem different," he told her. "Better," he quickly added when she frowned. Jessie took her in his arms and spoke. "Since that dick Brian left, you haven't been the same. Then Mr. J was killed and Cianne had the twins. Now she's off playing princess of Zamunda or some remote place I've never heard of, leaving you here. You haven't been the same, is all. Till now." He held her at arm's length.

It was true. She wasn't the same. After Brian went away to college, she panicked and ended things between them. Then Cianne's father died. That affected her deeply. Joseph Baxter was another father to her. Bianca's actions that day not only took away someone she loved, she injured and almost claimed the lives of her two closest friends and her godchildren and set in motion what her life soon became.

In a word, her life was lonely without her friends. She hadn't seen or spoken to Cianne or her godchildren for some time.

Jessie squeezed her hands, pulling Tranae out of her head. His eyes bore into her, reflecting sorrow, and maybe shame. "I'm sorry, Nae. I shouldn't have mentioned any of that stuff up." He reached up and brushed away a tear she didn't realize was sliding down her cheek.

"It's alright Jess." Tranae placed her hand on his cheek then let it fall to his chest, and smoothed out the silk tie she bought him when he began working for the financial agency in historic West Hills, a few blocks away. "I *am* better." She smiled, realizing she didn't have to fake it. Tristan showing up was a game changer, or at least she hoped it was. "I'm sorry I scared you so badly that you left work for nothing."

Jessie glanced down at his watch. "I still have a few minutes before my break is over. Besides, you are my little sister and you come before any and everything." He kissed her on the forehead then turned to open the door and stepped outside.

She watched him descend the stairs, and the thought of how to make him happier came to her. "I did talk to Vanessa," she called out, "she called me yesterday."

Jessie spun around on the step that was one above the bottom. "What did she say?" he asked, sounding nervous and excited at the same time.

"She wants to move in with you but she's scared you might change your mind about her living there when the newness of your relationship wears away."

He moved up a step and braced himself on the rail. He looked hurt. "She…she thinks I would put her out?"

"Don't be like that," Tranae said, moving outside to lean on the rail that prevented her from falling over onto her neighbor's patio. "Vanessa has been infatuated with you for years and you did nothing but ignore her. She'd come over the house just to get a glimpse of you, but she had to endure listening to your romantic phone calls and sometimes even seeing your temps."

He frowned up at her.

She continued. "Your temps Jess, you know, the chicks who filled the position as your girl for a limited time before you let them go. God Jess," she shook her head, "I swear it takes you inhumanly long to get the simplest slang."

Jessie raised his brow, giving her another partial smile. Then his expression got serious. "She was just a kid then, Nae. It wouldn't have been right if I encouraged her, no matter how bad I felt exposing her to those *temps.*"

"Oh my God, you liked her this whole time, haven't you?" It all made sense now. Tranae thought back to how Jess would bother her only when her friends were around. No, it was only when Vanessa was around. He would show up at her school dances and sports games, but she thought he just liked being the big fish in a small pond.

Now that she was thinking about it, Jessie was popular no matter where he was. Some people had that certain something. People like Jessie and Tristan had the world flocking to them no matter where they were.

Jessie stared at her for a moment, saying nothing, then he sighed. "I couldn't, wouldn't do anything about it until she became an adult no matter how I felt. It was better to not encourage her," he said again as if trying to convince himself. "But it seems my tactics in trying to not encourage her ruined whatever we could have now."

"Tell her," Tranae urged. "Tell her that you've been into her all this time. Tell her the truth, Jess."

"She'll think I'm some kind of creep," he huffed.

"No," Tranae smiled, "she won't. Vanessa is a romantic, Jess. You must have figured that out in the last four months. And she loves you."

"She's…huh? Vanessa has never said that."

"Have you told her that you love her?" He shook his head. "Then you're both fools. Life is too short to play games, Jess. Now," she waved him off, "I have to see a man about a horse. Talk to Vanessa and be honest with her."

Tranae just stared at Tristan. He sat on her sofa, where she found him after coming back inside her apartment. What he told her was unbelievable yet she knew every word was the truth. Cianne's long lost father intervened during the attack on Tristan's life but kept him hidden, away from Cianne and the twins. His reasons, Tristan explained, was to train Tristan to defend himself and his family, and to discover who was behind the attack.

Why Cianne's father kept Tristan against his will and allowed Cianne to believe he was dead was beyond Tranae. But it pissed her off.

"She's suffering without you," Tranae said once Tristan finished his explanation. "She still believes you are alive." Tristan didn't respond but Tranae saw in his eyes that he suffered too.

Good, she thought as she sighed. Apparently, it was Tristan and not Cianne's father who delayed their reunion six months ago, so she laid fault on him as well. "What can I do?" she sighed.

According to Tristan, there was a mystery person who wanted him dead; there was some kind of civil war going on among Cianne's people; and apparently, someone was influencing Cianne's decisions. No one knew if all these situations were connected or if they were just having a shit storm of unrelated problems.

Tristan scooted to the edge of the sofa and leaned forward. "What I've told you so far has been my and Cianne's personal business and limited information regarding her father. I will need to tell you more sensitive information that concerns Cianne's people. Discussing them with outsiders is against their laws."

Tranae grimaced but nodded.

"I know what I am about to ask is unfair to you but I must have your word and you need to agree to be all in before I reveal more."

Cianne told her when she was reunited with her grandmother that she was unable to be as forthcoming as she used to be about her abilities. The secrecy that surrounded these people concerned Tranae, but nothing, not even a few secrets, could sever the bond between true friends. If Tranae was being honest, she did miss knowing what was going on in every aspect of her best friend's life, but to maintain some semblance of a relationship with Cianne, she accepted her terms.

She was done standing on the sidelines though.

"When it comes to Cianne or you," Tranae leaned forward and touched his hand, "I'm always in. So how do we do this?" She stood. "Do I sign some kind of gag order? Let's get the paperwork out of the way so I can get your wife and my bestie back."

Chuckling, Tristan pushed off the sofa. He regarded her with a slight smile but it wasn't forced and it mesmerized. "Feet first, huh?" Tristan smirked. Tranae gave him her signature eye roll. "I have to warn you," he said pulling out his cell phone, "you may see and experience things that can't really be explained."

"My best friend gets premonitions. I think I'm a little familiar with the unexplained."

Tristan shrugged but didn't reply. He spoke into his cell phone instead. "Tranae is onboard." He listened then said, "No, I don't want to freak her out so soon after my resurrection. We'll fly to Memphis to link up with Langley since he is on official business there and can't come to us."

Tranae wanted to ask who it was he was speaking with but she didn't, deciding instead to go to her room and pack a bag. She quickly called her job and told them she had an emergency and needed the rest of the week off. Then she called her mother and explained that she was going to visit Cianne. She figured that she should stick to the truth as much as possible. When she finished placing her toiletries in her bag she returned to the living room.

Tristan wasn't alone.

Tranae stared with wide spellbound eyes at the guy standing next to Tristan. It wasn't as if she wasn't used to seeing someone so thoroughly handsome—she spent years watching Tristan and Brian around school before becoming close friends with them. It was just…this guy with his blonde hair, strong chiseled jaw, and perfect lips had a certain energy about him that intrigued her but at the same time set her internal alarms on alert.

…and he looked familiar.

She let her eyes take in his whole form. He was dressed in a pair of dark jeans and a long thermal gray shirt that hugged every toned inch of his upper body.

Tranae heard herself sigh in appreciation but didn't know if it was a mental sigh because lord knows, she would never embarrass herself and openly let him know that she thought he was scorching hot. But then, she *was* gawking at a complete stranger, with the most amazing familiar green-blue eyes.

A corner of the stranger's lip curved up and a hushed chuckle came from Tristan who stood beside him.

God, did she sigh out loud? Tranae closed her eyes, berating herself for acting like a school girl with a crush.

When she opened her eyes seconds later, deciding to face her embarrassment head on, her focus fell on the long chain around his neck that held a gray ring with a blue line around it. Her feet moved forward and she reached for the familiar ring. Only, she didn't get hold of the ring because the guy grabbed her wrist in a death lock before she could touch it.

Tristan wedged himself in between her and the stranger, his back to her.

"Caleb," Tristan's tone was cautious.

That was odd because for as long as she'd known Tristan, he was rarely cautious. He was usually confident and approached everything with determination and strength, with no visible fear when he moved head-on into any situation. If he thought about his actions ever, it was with a quickness she wished she could because his response was always immediate. That was why he was great at football, academics, and just about everything else.

So why is he cautious with this guy?

"That's Cianne's ring. Why is it around your neck?" Tranae looked around Tristan to peer at the stranger.

The stranger's brows furrowed but he didn't let her wrist go as he stared back at her.

"Caleb," Tristan said again. This time his tone was one of warning.

Tristan was so close to Tranae that she felt the tension coiling through his body. If she felt it, she knew this guy, Caleb, did too, but he didn't seem to care. He did let go of her wrist and stepped back.

Caleb lifted his hand and Tranae watched his fingers gently brushed over the ring.

"It isn't Cianne's ring. It was her mother's, and for now, it's mine." He turned and moved toward the door. "If we must travel in a way to appease the *girl*, I suggest we get going." He left through the front door, leaving it ajar.

"Who is the girl?" Tranae frowned and placed her hands on her hip. "Was he talking about me? The girl has a name," she called out in the direction Caleb headed, hoping he heard her. When she turned to face Tristan, he looked almost ashen. "Who the *hell* is that and what the *hell* is his problem?" she demanded.

Tristan wiped his face with his hand and sighed. Tranae had a feeling that the answer was one of the many secrets kept from her. The ones she was soon to be told because her assistance was needed. *Good*, because she wanted to know about Cianne and she also wanted to know about the hot prick she was going to be traveling with.

"There are some things we need to discuss but we can do it on the flight. Are you packed and ready?"

"As I'll ever be." She rolled her eyes then lifted her keys and purse from the table before glancing at her favorite photo. She chanted, "This is about Cianne," over and over to herself as she got into the backseat of the car they were driving in.

Tristan took the front seat, and the guy, Caleb, drove.

Caleb, was he...

No. He couldn't be. She relaxed and let the passing scenery lull her.

They were treated to a light meal on the private jet. At least that was what the stewardess called it. The seasoned beef medallions and roasted potatoes with mixed veggies were, in a word, succulent. The peach sorbet was to die for.

It's treatment like this that has a large percentage of the world wanting the millionaire lifestyle, Tranae thought as she took another sip of her wine.

Her eyes fell on Caleb, who was seated near the front of the plane. His seat was reclined and his eyes were closed. He was asleep, which meant it was the perfect time for some answers.

"Soooo...Caleb?" She glared at Tristan expectantly.

As he looked away from the window he was staring out of and glanced over at Caleb, he seemed troubled, as if he were having an internal debate. Then he turned his gaze on her. It appeared that he had come to some decision.

"We told everyone that Caleb is Cianne's brother but he's not. He's her father. He's over a hundred years old, human but he is also something else, something...supernatural. Caleb is very powerful and has little to no patience when it comes to anyone other than Cianne, the children, and me—from time to time, as far as I can tell. So please, please try not to piss him off," Tristan warned.

Tranae tried to swallow but the sudden dryness of her throat made it impossible. The fact that she was able to close her gaping mouth was an accomplishment in itself. The way Tristan looked as he stared back at her, defeated and sincere, she knew again that he was telling her the truth.

She pried her eyes from Tristan to look at Caleb, who still slept.

"And he isn't sleeping. He hears and sees just about everything," Tristan informed her.

"Supernatural, like seeing visions and moving like light, supernatural?" she whispered even though Tristan told her Caleb heard everything.

"No, Tranae." Tristan scrubbed his hand over his face and said, "Much, much more."

Tranae wasn't sure if it was the warning about Caleb's temper or the knowledge that this twenty-something-looking gorgeous guy's super powers rivaled Cianne's, but she was a little freaked.

She swallowed again, needing something to drink. Her eyes moved frantically around the cabin for water, only to hear a light tapping on the glass she held.

Tristan poured her a drink.

"Thanks," she said to Tristan. Tranae lifted the half-filled glass and gulped the contents down. She placed her glass on the fold-out table and lifted Tristan's full glass to her lips and gulped that down too.

"You need to try and relax. Your heart is working double time and I need you to soak up what I'm telling you, because…" He glanced at his cell phone. "In about an hour, your world is going to get a lot more complicated. I'm sorry," Tristan said as he looked over at her.

She didn't notice before but he looked tired and his eyes didn't hold the vibrant life that normally gave his breathtaking beauty an unneeded but appreciated boost. It was then that she took a deep breath, placed his glass down, and lifted her chin. Tristan was worried because whatever was going on with

Cianne was dangerous, but Tranae wanted to do what she could to help.

Though, she thought as she made an attempt to slow her breathing, now realizing she was panting, Tristan had the decency to appear genuinely sorry.

"I'm a ball of steel," her words dripped with sarcasm. "Wait," her eyes widened, "you can hear my heart beat?"

For the rest of the flight, Tristan refused to answer how he could hear her heart beat or anything she asked about him or Cianne. He did, however, answer all questions she asked that were related to Caleb.

Apparently, Captain Caveman's abilities were ok to discuss because he was considered "independent". Independent to what, exactly, she had no idea and no one seemed inclined to clue her in right now.

The plane landed at a private terminal all too soon. She only asked a handful of questions about Caleb and had many more, but Tristan shut down when the plane began its descent. Now she was being ushered off the jet to a small office inside an airport hangar on the side of the runway.

When she stepped into the office behind Caleb, her attention was instantly pulled to a very handsome blonde gentleman clad in a black designer suit, a man she was also sure she saw before. He stood beside a conference table with several office chairs that took up most of the space in the room. The stranger regarded Caleb with a slight smile but didn't shake his hand. He nodded but bypassed her to shake Tristan's hand, holding onto it longer than she felt necessary.

The man then focused on her. "Hello Tranae," he took her hand and kissed it, "I am Langley, Cianne's family lawyer, but foremost I think of myself as a member of her family. I appreciate your willingness to offer your assistance with little to no explanation."

"Whatever I can do to help," she told him. Tranae looked over her shoulder at Tristan, who positioned himself by the only exit. He gave her a small smile and nodded toward Langley.

"Why are we even here? I checked this girl myself. She is devoted to my daughter. She's known about the visions and could easily have told someone but she didn't." Caleb's eyes were focused on Langley then moved back to Tristan. "She can be trusted to keep your little secrets."

"Protocol," Tristan offered.

Langley nodded.

"Right." Caleb's tone dripped with sarcasm.

"Oh-kay," Tranae dragged the word out, "can one of you GQ cuties fill me in on what's happening right now, because I'm lost. And my name is Tranae, not *the girl*." She pinned Caleb with a glare only to be shocked by the twinkle of amusement in his eyes.

Great, she rolled her eyes. *He's even hotter when he isn't brooding.*

Langley sat down on the edge of the table in front of her. "Tranae, I am going to give you information that middlings— normal humans—aren't privy to and then ask you a few questions. Would you please have a seat?"

Did he say, normal humans, she asked herself? Tranae pulled out the chair in front of her, which was beside Langley, and sat down.

"Cianne's mother was what we call a Coesen. As am I and all the people that Cianne now governs. Most of us are capable of doing supernatural things due to our DNA mixture with…something else. To save time and any questions you may have…" Langley motioned for Tranae to look at Tristan.

She looked over her shoulder to Tristan who was standing by the door. He gave her a wink, waved and then was gone. Tranae gasped as she blinked several times. She spun around in the office chair in almost a complete circle before seeing Tristan standing next to Caleb.

"A small show of your strength please, Tristan," Langley requested.

Tristan seemed to look around the room for something before his eyes landed on Caleb. Tranae watched some kind of silent communication cross between the two of them, then Tristan moved, fast. Lifting Caleb with one hand, Tristan threw him over her head and into the far wall. Only, Caleb didn't hit the wall. He disappeared completely.

"How?" She jumped to her feet, knocking over the chair. "...how did you, he...do that?" She pointed to where Caleb was before he disappeared. "He just vanished into thin air." Tranae stood against the wall Caleb should have hit. She gripped the hem of her shirt, twisting it in her hands.

A second later, Caleb appeared in front of her with something in his hand that he extended to her. *"I won't harm you."*

Is he in my head?

The whisper of a promise, telling her that she would not be harmed, overrode the drumming of Tranae's beating heart. She glanced over at Tristan then back to Caleb, as she stopped twisting her shirt in knots to extend her shaky hand out to take what was being handed to her. She stared into Caleb's green-blue eyes as she took the item. At once, she recognized the weight and design.

Tranae looked down at the picture frame, a treasured gift given to her by Brian on their first Christmas together. She would know it anywhere. She always looked at the silver framed photo before leaving or returning to her apartment. She saw it when she left earlier today.

Her gaze lovingly caressed the image that Jessie took of her, Cianne, Tristan, and Brian. It was a time when life was still innocent, and promises and love were forever. It was before Nicholas and his obsessive greed, before Bianca snapped, and before everyone left her behind.

Tranae's eyelids fluttered as strong arms encompassed her.

"Awesome," Tristan said.

His voice sounded a thousand miles away.

"She's blacking out because you had to go all Night Crawler on her," Tristan growled. "Did you not hear me when I said that I wanted to ease her into this slowly?"

She barely saw the faded image of Caleb moving toward her.

"Night Crawler, Captain Cave Man," Caleb said as he shooed Tristan out of his way.

A warm hand touched Tranae's temple, then a jolt sparked something inside of her. She jumped to attention, feeling renewed.

"Know that I resent being compared to your fictional characters. You need to stop placating the girl or we are going to be here all night. Now back away so she can sign the privacy clause or whatever it is you need to get us on our way," he ordered.

Tranae blinked twice as she stared at Caleb. Included with that amazing feeling running through her, her resolve was renewed. She was going to help her friend, her amazing, selfless, beautiful friend.

"Where do I sign?" she asked, looking at each of them. "Because you can trust that I will never share your secrets with anyone. Captain Caveman is right; we need to get this moving."

Langley touched what looked like some kind of Bluetooth device that was lodged inside his ear. "I sense no deception in her words," he told someone.

Chapter Fourteen

Tranae peered around the lab they were in. Caleb was not only capable of teleporting himself, he could carry passengers. He took them from the airport and popped them here about twenty minutes ago. It took her most of that time to stop vomiting. A few saltines and a ginger ale later, she still felt ill.

She sat on a stool that was pulled from under a large lab table, twisting the saltines pack in her hand. She had no idea where she was or even what time zone she was in. All Tranae knew was, at some point, she stepped into the Twilight Zone.

Tranae shook her head to dismiss her thoughts of fantasy and fiction in an attempt to stay in the here and now. She focused on the conversation at hand, even though she had no clue what the discussion between a man who she thought was a doctor, and a woman who she thought was a scientist, was about.

"The device that is attached to Cianne is made to inhibit her abilities. It is unlike any we've seen before. We know nothing of its effects on her. An experiment was performed using Caleb and an enhanced version of an inhibitor that was confiscated by one of our Sentry Guards," the man named Bannerman said. "I feel that the results aren't typical."

"The device could hardly contain…" The scientist, a middle-aged woman, nervously looked over at Caleb then to

Bannerman. She cleared her throat then seemed to realize she stopped talking. "The device could inhibit Caleb's abilities for half an hour before I had to replace it. We have to take into account that he is mentally and physically healthy. According to reports, our Sovereign is experiencing sleep deprivation and severe depression."

Tranae frowned as she gave the female scientist her full attention. The woman had perfect mocha-toned skin, beautiful hair and... *Oh heck, she's just perfect.* Like Tranae, the woman was either scared of Caleb or totally entranced by his hotness. Either way, Tranae could tell it took the woman some effort to stop staring at him.

"If she is being influenced by any other factors, those along with the advanced tech of the inhibitor may extend the effects on her. What I am sure of, by studying Caleb..." she paused, "is that her body will ultimately attack and destroy any foreign invaders, even in her weakened and distracted state. Someone has to be replacing the inhibitor regularly to maintain her weakened state. We can counter that by introducing these."

Tranae focused on the glass vial that looked like fine granules of sugar. *What are they going to do with sugar?*

Bannerman reached for the vial and held it in the air. He looked at the contents closely then offered the container back to the woman, but Caleb reached for it before the woman could. The woman quickly pulled her hand back before Caleb could touch her, letting him grab the vial.

Tranae didn't see Caleb, who was beside her, move; she doubted anyone else did either because the tension in the room definitely raised a notch. Now she knew the woman wasn't impressed by Caleb's looks. She was terrified of him.

"Are those what I think they are, Anoda?" Bannerman asked, watching Caleb inspect the vial.

Tranae noted how Anoda dragged her attention away from Caleb before she looked at Bannerman.

Anoda nodded, "Yes, we have made great strides since the last time you visited our home lab." She seemed to realize something then. Anoda's eyes widened as she turned her attention back to Caleb.

Caleb placed the vial in Tristan's hand then turned to Anoda. "There's no need to worry. I have no desire to step foot on the continent of Africa or anywhere near your research facilities. Nor will I use what I've heard and seen against you or your people in the future. I have family that are part Coesen and that means I will not harm anyone unless they are a threat to what I hold dear. So, try to relax and tell us what we need to know."

Anoda stared at him for a moment then frowned.

Caleb continued, "It's not too hard to pull information from someone's head, especially when they so vividly project the secrets they want to keep. As I have already stated, you have nothing to fear from me."

With wary eyes, Anoda nodded. She cleared her throat then noticeably tried to relax. It was obvious that she was still scared of Caleb but Tranae commended her attempt to push that fear aside to continue. Yet, aside from sensing that Caleb could lay waste to all of them, Tranae couldn't help wondering why everyone feared him.

"We've designed these little guys to mimic our immune systems." Anode reached out her hand and Tristan placed the vial in it. She gave Tristan a respectful nod.

Everyone they ran into bowed to him. That was cool.

"I won't bore you all with scientific terms. Basically, when they enter the bloodstream, they find whatever is wrong and aid your body in healing or in expelling the problem causing the patient's illness."

"Cianne has a unique immune system," Tristan said, shaking his head. "Her body, just like Caleb's, will fight *any* foreign invader. You said that the inhibitor had to be reintroduced into her system every few days. We don't have that kind of access to her to keep immunizing her with those." He pointed to the vial.

Bannerman spoke up. "That is why they were imprinted with her DNA. Hopefully," he shrugged, "the micro-orgs should go unnoticed by her body's natural defenses. They will aid her body in expelling the inhibitor. They are micro computers so they will adapt and expel any inhibitors that are subsequently reintroduced as well."

"And you want *me* to give them to her?" Tranae asked, looking at Tristan. Once again, she noticed that everyone in the room tensed. Well, everyone except for Caleb. It seemed that it may take a lot to get him visibly pissed.

#UnwantedGoals

"I do," Tristan told her, "but not without you knowing what you may encounter." He sighed before turning from her and looking at Caleb. "Show her."

Before Tranae could object to his touch, Caleb grabbed hold of her shoulder. His other hand was around Tristan's wrist. Everything went black then Tranae saw Caleb and Tristan talking before Tristan attacked him. It wasn't really a fight. Caleb grabbed Tristan by the neck but then Tristan's face twisted in pain and he was yanked through the air by something unseen. Miraculously, he landed on his feet and began moving. That's when Tranae saw Cianne standing in a doorway of her bedroom in the house Tristan built for them.

Tranae looked at Cianne. She really looked at her and what she saw in her best friend's glowing red eyes and face was pure, unadulterated hate.

Cianne raised her hand toward Caleb as Tristan moved toward her, speaking softly. Instead of attacking Cianne before she attacked him, Caleb raised his hand toward Tristan, somehow pushing him out of the way in time but leaving himself open to Cianne's invisible attack.

How do I know that Caleb was trying to protect Tristan?

Tranae saw it reflected in Caleb's eyes and in his expression of determination.

Tranae saw Caleb's body fly through the window at the same time Tristan's body flew out of the room and over the stair banister. Tranae heard her own distant voice calling from...*downstair*s.

"Oh God, I remember this." She remembered seeing Tristan dangling from the second-floor stair rail that night.

As suddenly as the scene began, it switched. Tranae was watching Tristan, who was pinned to a wall. *Cianne?* Cianne was his attacker, but it wasn't the Cianne she knew. It was the same Cianne from the previous scene. Again, her eyes were blood red.

Tranae watched in horror as sharp utensils were hurled into Tristan's body. All through the ordeal, Tristan watched Cianne with love in his eyes, even though he was clearly in severe pain.

How? How did he hide the pain?

"She wasn't herself," Tristan explained, "If I had died, I wanted her to remember how much I loved her."

The scene dissolved and Tranae felt Caleb's hand move from her shoulder. "Soooo," she dragged out the word, "you both are on her shit list and if you go near her, she attacks. You think she won't get all "Witchy" with me trying to trick her."

No one said anything. They all just watched her warily, waiting for her to say something. Tranae took a deep breath, her shoulders moving up and down dramatically.

"Alright," she said with a raised brow, "what do I need to do?"

Cassius moved slowly along St. Peter Street toward Congo square. It was mid-day but the streets weren't too busy. He'd been in the French Quarter for more than a week now, making his presence known.

He tried to find Perkins through official Coesen channels but failed. Now he was just hoping to get noticed and that his arrival in New Orleans will spread enough for Perkins to come to him.

Cassius crossed N. Rampart and found a bench under a large tree to sit. Someone was following him and he had an idea who it was.

Finally, Cassius inwardly sighed as Perkins crossed in front of him.

"I hear you've been looking for me." Perkins sat next to Cassius on the bench. He handed Cassius a small bag then opened the one he kept that looked the same. He pulled out a sugary beignet. "Bet you haven't relaxed enough to enjoy your stay in this lovely city," Perkins said as he popped the treat into his mouth.

Cassius looked at him for a few seconds then to the bag Perkins handed him. He brought his eyes back up to look at Perkins who was now handing him a cup of steaming coffee, by the smell of it.

"Breakfast," Perkins motioned to the bag and coffee with his own coffee in hand.

Cassius frowned but nodded his thanks.

Perkins sipped his coffee then popped another beignet in his mouth. "I know you are a get-down-to-business, no-nonsense kind of guy, so I'll try to limit the small talk. Caleb didn't kill Sovereign Harper."

"You say his name as if you are well-acquainted," Cassius accused.

Perkins lowered his head, seeming to consider Cassius' comment. "No-nonsense," he said, then shrugged as if convincing himself of something. "We share a common goal, Caleb and I."

"A common goal," Cassius raised his tone, "with a murderer."

"I don't need to be reminded of Caleb's crimes." Perkins popped his last beignet in his mouth. "Right now, there are more pressing matters that need my attention, and so far, Caleb has done nothing but protect the Sovereign and her consort."

Cassius' brows furrowed as he stared at Perkins, his face reflecting a hint of surprise. *Why did he say the 'Sovereign and her consort'?*

He absently took a drink of the coffee in his hand. "What protection did he offer Tristan?" Cassius spat out in disgust.

The death of the young man he once labeled an "over-eager middling", was still a sore subject. And the fact that he was no closer to knowing who killed Tristan or Sovereign Harper was a stain on Cassius' stellar career as a Royal Guard. Apparently, clearing that stain and his hatred had him pointing a finger and pursuing the wrong man. The evidence he once ignored pointed in a different direction.

But, Caleb was in no way a victim.

Cassius realized then that Perkins never responded to his question. "What is this common goal you two share?"

"First things first," Perkins said as he balled up the empty bag and tossed it over his shoulder into the garbage can. "You were looking for me for a reason and I need something from you. Under the circumstances, allies we once trusted are now suspects." Perkins shrugged. "So, I will offer the first signs of trust. What can I do for you, Captain?"

Looking around suspiciously, Cassius wondered if he just walked into an ambush. The thought was fleeting because, in all honesty, he was no longer the Guard he once was. If Perkins and his *allies* wanted him dead, it wouldn't take much to make it happen.

"Givens...who was he to Evelyn Bogdon?"

Perkins visibly stiffened.

There once was a close connection between the Bogdon girls and Perkins but Cassius didn't pry then. Now, things were different. Cassius needed to know everything, even the things that seemed insignificant.

"He was nothing to Evelyn," Perkins growled. "Givens was a hired enforcer who was sent to stop us from snooping around. I'd like to tell you that we were getting closer to finding out who was connected to Sovereign Harper's murder but we weren't. The person behind it is very smart, seems to be well connected, and reacts quickly to quash leaks. We still don't know who's behind it but whoever it is, knows about our investigation. Givens was sent after us but he underestimated Evie." Perkins turned his head and looked at the tops of the trees, then took a deep breath.

"I was careless after Evie..." Perkins focused on his coffee cup, rubbing the cool-touch cozy with his thumb. "I got myself captured by Castor Zuri, who Evie linked to the poison 'Death's Door'. Zuri would have killed me but Caleb was on the trail of a special bullet. That bullet led him to a warehouse where I was bound and beaten. He saved me."

Despite what he already knew, and this new information from Perkins, Cassius was stunned.

The connection was Zuri...

But with Zuri being from a family of worth... Someone of his status associating with Dregans was just unheard of unless their job called for it.

"Those are strong accusations you make about a worthy male, Perkins. Do you have proof?"

Perkins' dry laugh was humorless. "I am still a Guard, though not active. My word is testimony enough. I saw Zuri with my own eyes. He participated in my torture and he spoke freely. He intended to kill me so he saw no reason to be secretive. The only thing he didn't discuss was who he was working with or for. It was clear there is someone else pulling the strings but Zuri was the only one privy to who that is. His men thought he was the head but I heard him on the phone when it was just him and me in the warehouse."

Cassius nodded, not knowing what to ask first. After a short mental overview, he asked, "And Zuri, where is he?"

Perkins chuckled again. This time it was full of reflective satisfaction. "Well, I did say Caleb saved me. Zuri didn't survive the encounter."

"Is that why he has your loyalty?" Cassius asked as he prepared to study Perkins' reaction.

They looked each other directly in the eyes, each looking for the other's tell, but they were both Guards and were well trained. Neither would give away anything unless they wanted to. Cassius reeled in his disgust and judgment; he was certain whatever trust issues and personal feelings Perkins had for him would not be shown plainly on the man's face.

"No," Perkins said as they continued to stare at each other. "My loyalties are forever and always with my Sovereign." After a slight pause, Perkins said, "It is hard for you to understand why Caleb is pertinent to our success in keeping Sovereign Bertram safe. I understand. I do, but you must set aside your anger if we are going to succeed. The only way to do that is to work together." Cassius said nothing so Perkins continued. "You must see to believe. I had to as well. Give me a few days, I will show you proof."

This time Cassius laughed as he said, "That Caleb is on our side?"

Perkins stood. He took one last drink of his coffee and tossed the container in the garbage.

Cassius smirked at Perkins' arrogance. To turn his back on him was either stupid or a show of trust. But Perkins was safe with him, even if Cassius thought the man was too damn easy to manipulate.

Looking over his shoulder, Perkins raised his brow. "God no, Captain," he said then frowned. "Caleb isn't on our side. The only side he favors and will die for, is his daughter's, her true mate's, and the twins'. We are just lucky enough to be their subjects; and as long as we have their best interests at heart, we get to live." With that revelation, Perkins walked off.

Cassius didn't follow.

He sat there on the park bench for hours, lost in his thoughts. *Caleb tracked a bullet to Zuri.* Cassius wondered what were the circumstances in which Caleb got a bullet and traced that bullet back to Zuri. *Was Zuri after Caleb, and if so, why?*

If someone was after Cianne, they will need to take out her protection first. Were Zuri and his backer the ones who killed Tristan?

Then they went after Caleb because apparently, everyone besides me knew that Caleb wasn't a threat to Cianne.

But how did Zuri and his men pin Caleb down? Or did Caleb know of the threat and go after them? And who was Zuri working with or for?

The questions kept coming but it seemed he would have no answers until he and Perkins met again.

Am I to sit here for a few days?

Cassius wasn't given any details on where and when to expect Perkins again. With his mind racing, but knowing he would get either some answers or death in a few days, Cassius got to his feet.

Surprisingly he had a taste for some authentic Creole cooking. His appetite wasn't the same since he lost Vivian, but today...today he could eat.

Koves Glenn, California USA

Tristan looked out of the window of the four-bedroom house at some kids playing basketball in the cul-de-sac. "Tell me again why we're staying the night here."

After entering the tranquil gated community named Koves Glenn with no questions asked other than a request for their ID's, they rode down several streets until they came to the home where they were now holed up. It was a furnished house with all the desirable amenities.

Tristan moved his finger from the blind he held up then looked over his shoulder at Caleb. The sound of chimes, a cell phone ring, caused Tristan to raise his brow. "I thought you didn't care for our 'tech'," he said.

Caleb sighed but pulled the small cell phone from his jean pocket. "I don't, but no one wants me in their heads. Though they can't keep me out if I really want in, I respect their need for privacy until I sense they're a threat. So, it's the cell phone or…telegrams." Caleb answered the phone as he walked down the hall where the room he chose was located.

"I'm going to make a food run. What do you have a taste for?" Cipher asked as he came down the stairs. He headed for the door.

"We are here because the girl needs some rest before she goes to Ark Manor. Langley and I have our reasons for choosing this place," Caleb said as he reentered the living room. "Bannerman is going to stay with the girl. We're taking a walk." He glanced at Cipher then to Tristan. "You can eat while we're out."

Both Tristan and Cipher looked at each other. Cipher looked as confused as Tristan felt. It was obvious that neither of them had a clue to what Caleb or Langley planned. If Caleb was involved, Tristan surmised that whatever it was, it related to Cianne. So, he followed Caleb outside.

As he moved over the threshold, just as he did when they drove through the front gate, Caleb changed his appearance so that his skin was a smooth caramel tone, his hair was short and curly, and his eyes were brown. He looked the way Cianne would if she was a boy. This time, Tristan noticed the Coesen birthmark that appeared behind Caleb's left ear.

Stopping on the sidewalk in front of the house, Tristan took a moment to watch the children play. His mind must have been somewhere else because he didn't notice before that more than half the children, who were of various skin tones, had Coesen birthmarks as well.

"Have you never been to The Glenn?" Cipher asked as he patted Tristan on the shoulder.

"No, I'm pretty sure I've never even heard of it." Tristan searched his memory for any mention of Koves Glenn but recalled nothing.

He and Cipher moved forward, bypassing the car they arrived in to catch up with Caleb.

"Koves Glenn is a community Sovereign Harper founded. The majority of the residents are made up of Coesen and

Middling pairings and their children." Cipher bent to pick up the basketball that rolled up beside his foot. He tossed the ball over to the waiting children.

"Thanks, mister," a small boy said. He smiled as he caught the ball that was almost too big for him.

Tristan looked at the boy who was no more than five years old, as he ran over to several children who ranged in age. "How?" Tristan focused on the little boy's birthmark, "I mean...how?"

Cipher waved at the rest of the children then he and Tristan continued to follow Caleb. "Well you know that the mating between Coesen and Middlings is forbidden, but when Sovereign Harper learned of her grandchild's existence, changing those laws got her undivided attention. Apparently, my father was already working on arguments for abolishing the law but he was met with resistance. It's rare for the Sovereign to override the Council but my father said she eventually did, to protect Breed. Soon after, she welcomed her own Breed, her grandchild. The Glenn's existence is still largely a secret though."

"I didn't ask before, but you and some of them have the birthmark."

Cipher nodded. "Some do."

Cipher said no more so Tristan let the inquiry go. "Is this where you grew up?" Tristan asked. They passed a couple walking by who nodded their greetings. Tristan nodded but turned his attention back to Cipher, who seemed to have mentally drifted off. "You don't have to answer that."

"No, it's cool. I grew up with my maternal grandmother. I always knew who my father was but he didn't know about me until I was seven, when my grandmother's search for him came to an end." Cipher adjusted the dark glasses over his eyes. "I could have come here to live or moved with my father but..." Cipher shrugged then added, "But with my father being a Child of Jai, everyone thought that I would be safer if I remained with my grandmother."

"You were kept a secret?" Tristan asked, then he laughed and said, "Vivian was good at hiding people."

Cipher chuckled as he playfully elbowed Tristan in the arm. "Yeah, our family is…different, to say the least. Aunt Vivian was awesome though a bit wound tight. She also talked about Cianne a lot."

Our family. Tristan found himself smiling at how Cipher so easily regarded him as family.

As he walked along, Tristan gauged how far Caleb walked ahead of them. He was about a few feet away. He wondered what Caleb and Langley were working on, and why they didn't include him and Cipher in the plan.

"I will tell you later. You both can get something to eat," Caleb transferred.

Cipher tapped his shoulder. "This way to the grub. The Glenn has its own little shopping district on Shoppers Row."

Tristan watched Caleb continue the way he was going while he and Cipher turned right, toward the shopping center.

Later then.

He and Cipher continued past a large park that was full of people having what seemed to be a good time. None of the children with the birthmark seemed introverted or shy as they played with the children who didn't have one. He couldn't help but think that Cianne would have had a better life if she grew up here in this accepting and beautiful place, where her abilities wouldn't have made her feel like a freak.

Glancing over at Cipher as they walked, Tristan wondered about his upbringing. "Was it hard, you know…with the eyes?" Tristan asked.

Cipher's head bobbed from one side to the other as he shrugged. "It caused some issues with some of the elders, but it wasn't negative. When I was younger, I didn't hide my *abilities* well. So, I caught the attention of some who thought I could be of use. There were a few children and parents who thought I was evil incarnate, especially because my Grands didn't offer up who my father was, and because my mother was a drug addict." Cipher looked at Tristan. "My mother's people are very superstitious. I suppose living here could have been 'different' but I loved the time I had with my Grands."

Tristan was sure Cianne would probably say the same thing about her time with her adoptive father, Joseph. Plus, he may have never met her if she lived here at the Glenn.

They stopped at a street corner and waited to cross. Across the street, Tristan saw over a dozen commercial establishments offering a wide selection of services and foods.

"You don't look like a usual Child of Jai," Tristan said. He stepped off the curve.

"Strong genes I guess." Cipher rubbed his chin arrogantly. "I feel like tacos," he announced. "What are you craving?"

"Actually, tacos sound good," Tristan said as they moved toward the Taco Stop.

Once inside, he looked over the menu then gave the cashier his order. Cipher added his order and beat Tristan in handing over the money to the cashier. When the order was filled, Tristan carried the tray to a small table near the windows that offered a view of the street.

The food smells amazing, Tristan thought as he unwrapped a crunchy taco. He lifted one of the bottles of hot sauce on the table and shook a good helping of it over his taco.

"Thanks," he said before taking a bite.

"No problem." Cipher said. Then he shoved almost an entire taco in his mouth.

Tristan thought he was a fast eater but he couldn't help watching Cipher inhale his food. Nothing, not even a piece of shredded cheese, hit the table. Watching the guy scarf down food was oddly entertaining.

"Sorry," Cipher mumbled then covered his full mouth. He swallowed the mouthful then said, "Used to eating fast. When enlisted, you never know when all hell is going to break—" Cipher froze and cocked his head to the side. He gave Tristan a questioning glance then stood.

"I hear it too," Tristan said, pushing away from the table.

Caleb walked across the crowded parking lot with his new cell phone pressed to his ear. "Did your informant tell you where exactly the bomb will be?"

Just as Langley informed him, Harper Elementary was bustling with students, parents, and faculty. Caleb trailed a group of people as they made their way to the entrance. He looked up at a rather large flag pole where the United States flag, and what he assumed was the Coesen flag—based on the design of Cianne's birthmark—flew in unison.

"No…if I had to guess I would check the basement."

Langley's voice came through the new more modern cell phone as clear as if they were standing side by side. He could admit that this model was better than his basic flip version. Modern wonders never ceased to amaze Caleb.

As Caleb approached the building he noted the banner above the main doors that read Welcome to Harper Elementary showing of "The Wizard of Oz". He chuckled because he once used the moniker "Oz" when he helped out one of Langley's kin. It crossed his mind to check in on Jason and Evelyn Jones.

"Because anywhere other than a school would be too original," Caleb said to Langley, then sighed as he followed the group up the main steps. He looked to his right and frowned. "Did anyone else get this tip?" he asked as he climbed.

"Can't be sure," Langley answered. "I don't even know if it is valid. You three being there is just a precaution. I would have alerted the Guard but I just got the details minutes ago and the informant, an avid liar, is a go-between. If it turns out to be a hoax…"

"Your credibility, which is already fragile because of who you are, will be shot to shit. I get it, but what I don't get is why the acting Captain of the Guard is here." Caleb and Jamiah made eye contact briefly before they both turned away. "From the way the Captain is watching the crowd, he seems to be waiting for something or someone."

"Jamiah's brother is mated to a Middling and they have a daughter who attends the elementary school. Jamiah rarely misses an opportunity to see his niece when she has a game or a performance. I suspected he would be there with his personal Guards."

"Good to know." Caleb entered the school.

"Are Tristan and Cipher in place?"

Caleb smiled at a woman at a desk when she handed him a program. "They're in the center of town, eating I presume. I've kept them in the dark like you wanted. Remind me again, why?"

"There's no need to unnerve those two unless it's necessary. Unlike you, they are both driven by emotions. I know they're capable but if it does turn out to be an assault on Koves Glenn, I'm sure they will do whatever it takes to keep the community safe."

Caleb would bet his life on that.

He stopped before entering the auditorium and looked down a hall to his left, then another to his right. "I'll keep you posted."

Langley didn't respond.

Caleb sensed the man's anxiety even though they were thousands of miles away. Comforting someone wasn't one of Caleb's strong suits but he hadn't completely lost his humanity. "Getting me involved couldn't have been an easy decision for you, but it was the right one. It means a lot that you would trust me with your people."

"I've never had a reason not to trust you." Langley sighed.

"Good," Caleb said before disconnecting the call. "Excuse me, miss," he said to the woman standing just inside the auditorium doors. "Would you mind pointing me in the direction of the men's room?"

"Of course." She smiled. Her eyes brightened when she turned away from the people she was directing to face Caleb.

Her smile faltered a bit then shined even brighter. She sauntered over to him, slipped her hand under his elbow, and led him half way down a hall. "The men's room is around that corner." She pointed the way.

"Thank you," Caleb told her.

Caleb gave her a smile before walking away. He glanced over his shoulder at her before pushing the bathroom door open and taking a step inside. His guide was again engaged in conversation and was walking back the way they'd come with a couple who seemed to be lost.

He was certain she would have waited for him. She wore her availability on her sleeve.

Thankful that some strangers unknowingly came to his rescue, Caleb exited the bathroom. He moved down the hall and away from the auditorium until he came to a wall plaque that mapped the school. Memorizing it, Caleb took off toward one of the doors leading to the lower level.

It didn't take long to find what he was looking for after walking through a maze of halls, doors, and pipes. The bomb sat on the floor with nothing around it. It was quite large as bombs go, but that wasn't the only thing out of place here. Caleb heard a heartbeat that was coming from behind a large boiler that practically took up most of the room.

…and there was a body in the corner.

"I expected a little more than just a boy," the heartbeat said as he stepped out of the shadows and glared at Caleb. The man shook his head. "Langley is a fool," he said more to himself. "It doesn't matter." He moved closer. "I gave him fair warning to save his people. What he does with it is his business."

"Don't either of you move," Jamiah ordered, with his gun trained on the man.

Caleb didn't have to turn around. He knew the acting Captain was following him since he entered the building.

"Turn around. Slowly," Jamiah ordered. When he stepped into the room beside Caleb, he spied the bomb immediately.

"It's not set to go off until twenty minutes into the show," the man offered. "Stefan figured me out... Knew that I wasn't on board."

He pointed to a body in the corner, the one Caleb saw earlier.

"The Boss has his own remote detonator. Whatever backup you have you best get them prepared."

Jamiah lowered his gun an inch. He looked to the bomb then he raised his weapon and pointed it directly at the man. "You bought that, here?" he asked in disgust. "My niece and fifty other kids and their families are right above us."

Caleb moved toward the bomb. He heard when Jamiah pulled another weapon and trained it on him but he didn't pause.

"I said don't move," Jamiah gritted out.

Jamiah tapped his earpiece with the butt of one of his weapons and was about to speak when Caleb turned and raised his hands. Both guns shot from Jamiah's hands and landed in Caleb's. He hated the process of convincing someone he was there to help and he was certain it would take eons to convince the young Captain, who was staring at him with shock and anger.

"You alert your men, you alert this guy's buddies, and I won't be able to get rid of this." Caleb pointed to the bomb with the guns he held in his hands. "You," he said as he looked to the man, "what's the range of the remote detonator?"

"About five miles. He'll stay close so he can watch the mayhem."

Caleb tossed the guns back at Jamiah. The Captain's eyes widened when his weapons burrowed into their holsters. Caleb was sure Jamiah would have gasped if he didn't already take away his ability to speak.

Only a few steps away, Caleb closed the distance to the bomb. He paused before placing his hands on it. He wasn't afraid of explosions—he'd been in a few; the last was during World War II. The pain was severe, and the healing he endured in a cave so no one would come across a mangled but living man, was even worse. He paused because bombs were so damn complex these days.

Wasting no more time, Caleb called upon the ancient power that fueled his body. He transported himself and the bomb to an abandoned warehouse he owned in New Mexico that was located more than twenty miles from a human population. In the blink of an eye, he was back at the school, standing in front of an open-mouthed man, whose name he chose not to pluck from his head, and a stunned Jamiah, whose eyes gave him away. With a flick of his hand, Caleb released the Captain, giving him full control over his body and voice again.

"Who are you?" Jamiah asked.

"Right now, I'm a concerned citizen whose daughter happens to be Breed." Caleb saw more questions forming in Jamiah's head, but to his surprise, the young Captain held them in.

Caleb knew from picking Langley's brain that Jamiah could touch objects and get information about the person who last touched it so he made sure to leave no trace of himself on those guns, one of which Jamiah was now brushing his fingers over the handle. Satisfied the Captain would sense nothing, Caleb turned to the man who still seemed shocked over what Caleb did with the bomb. "How will I know your friends?"

The man shook off his stupor then focused on the spot where the bomb previously sat. "Uh," he finally answered, "you won't. They've blended in with the residents. After the bomb was supposed to go off, they are to begin their assault on unsuspecting locals."

"I need to call this in," Jamiah announced.

Jamiah began to touch his earpiece again but Caleb held up his hand, freezing and silencing the Captain again. This guy and his dependence on his damn backup was beginning to annoy Caleb. Caleb continued to stare at the man, not sparing Jamiah a glance. "How are you communicating?"

The man pulled off an ear communicator similar to the one Jamiah and the rest of the Coesen Guard wore. *Maybe I can do something with this.* "May I?" Caleb held out his hand.

Without hesitation, the man placed the communicator in Caleb's hand.

"What is the agreement my associate made with you for your…tip?"

The man shrugged.

For the first time, Caleb noticed the tired resolve in the middle-aged man's eyes.

"I made no deals. I've always felt the Breed were evil abominations, but what we set out to do here, to kill children…Breed or not, killing children doesn't sit well with me." He shrugged again then said, "I don't deserve any pity and—"

Caleb struck, and his aim was precise. The man's words were cut short by a sharp intake of breath. It took only one carefully positioned blow to the heart and the man dropped to the floor. His dead eyes stared out, seeing nothing.

Caleb released Jamiah.

"You killed him," Jamiah accused, "without allowing me to interrogate him or a trial."

Caleb moved past Jamiah, toward the stairs. "He was guilty. He was punished." Although he shattered some of the man's ribs, Caleb knew his death was instant and virtually painless. "Worrying about the dead won't save the living, including your niece."

Jamiah had to jog to catch up to Caleb.

The anger radiating from him was palpable. Of course, the young Captain was all about the rules. Cassius would have made sure his successor was a straight arrow, and a straight arrow wouldn't like the way Caleb handled things. *Too bad.* Caleb was too damn old to care and never liked dancing to the common beat of others.

"You may want to alert your backup now," Caleb said as he lifted the ear communicator to his mouth then whistled.

Anyone close enough to hear the whistle would think it sounded a little high pitched but basically normal. To the people with the buds in their ears and on that particular frequency, the whistle was excruciatingly loud, enough to cause damage to their ears.

As he and Jamiah came to the auditorium where people were still being seated, Caleb noticed two men stumbling as they pushed people out of their way. One was covering a bleeding ear and the other was frantically trying to get the small communicator out of his own ear.

Before Jamiah could raise his gun, Caleb raised his hand, sending the two men flying out of the auditorium and out of the open main doors. Both Jamiah and Caleb quickly followed the pair as they tumbled down the stone stairs.

"Everyone get inside and lock all the doors!" Jamiah yelled to several adults who were ushering their children into the building. He tapped his ear-comm as the rest of the parents and children disappeared inside the school. "I need everyone on guard. Hostiles in the Glenn. They're armed and dangerous. The residents are their targets. Look for anyone with bleeding ears."

Two of Jamiah's Guards were coming around the corner when one of the assailants Caleb had thrown out of the school drunkenly raised his gun at them. Before the man could fire, Caleb summoned the weapon from the man's hand.

The gun flew into Caleb's waiting hand and he didn't hesitate to shoot both men dead.

"Don't move," a female Guard yelled as she pointed her gun at Caleb.

She stood about ten feet away and didn't seem to notice Jamiah yet. Her partner, a male, had his gun drawn as well but he didn't appear as nervous as the female.

Caleb ignored her as he walked over to the dead men. The female Guard's heart was racing and Caleb could smell her perspiration, so it wasn't a shock when she pulled the trigger as he bent down to get the other dead man's weapon.

Caleb shifted his upper body slightly to the left but raised his hand and caught the bullet. He relieved the dead man of his weapon as he turned his head to pin the female Guard who shot at him with an annoyed look. Caleb opened his hand and let the bullet drop to the ground before standing to face her.

He made certain to leave no trace of himself on the bullet or anything else he came in contact with.

"Stand down, Deanne," Jamiah said. He descended the stairs and pushed her weapon down when he reached her. "I need you and Howard to protect the people in the school."

Caleb eyed the female who was still watching him with a confused expression instead of listening to orders from her superior.

Coesen are so annoying.

Jamiah snapped his fingers in front of the woman's face. That seemed to pull her out of it. Jamiah repeated his orders and both Guards took up defensive positions in the front of the school. He also ordered an arriving pair of Guards to cover the back of the building.

Jamiah faced Caleb when they were alone. There were several beats of silence as Jamiah and Caleb stood facing each other. Caleb knew that questions and indecision were swirling in the young Captain's head. It was clear that he had no idea what to do with Caleb, but the sound of shooting about a block away made the decision for him.

They ran toward the gunfire together.

Chapter Fifteen

Tristan glanced at Cipher, who was ushering patrons to the back of the restaurant, as he dove for a woman who was eating near them when the windows of the Taco Stop shattered inward. He ignored the glass cutting into the front of his body as he slid toward the screaming woman. There was no time to placate her so he lifted her in his arms and ran for the rear of the store.

Tristan pushed the woman inside the storage room where Cipher was calming down a small girl. "See if anyone was left behind."

Cipher agreed with a nod of his head then ran toward the front of the store.

Tristan glanced at the dozen or so people huddled together. "Stay hidden," he said as he turned to leave.

"Wait." A young man, no more than twenty-one, grabbed Tristan's arm. He and a boy who appeared to be about fourteen stepped forward together. "We can help," the young man said.

Tristan sized them up. Visually, they didn't look to have much fight in them. The boys looked related, brothers maybe, but they bore no Coesen birthmark.

"No Adam." An older woman pushed through the group. She grabbed the young man. "You mustn't do this."

According to the Coesen, the gift almost never survived in Breed due to their diluted bloodlines. Tristan only knew of one Breed who had abilities. Cipher seemed to have superhuman reflexes and eyesight but that was all. As for Cianne and the children...Tristan wouldn't necessarily classify them as Breed though most did. To him, they were extra, due to the impact of Caleb's blood.

As he watched the exchange between the boys and their grandmother, he suspected the Coesen were wrong to discount the Breed.

The younger boy pointed to Tristan, "It's alright, Grandma. He and his friend are Breed like us. They can do things too."

"We need to help, Grandma," Adam told her. "This is our home. These are our friends," he said, looking over the huddled people.

"I can't stop you from going out there but know that this isn't some video game," Tristan interrupted. Both boys nodded. He looked at the older woman, who now seemed to look much older than she did when he first stepped inside the Taco Stop. She gave him a reluctant nod then stepped back.

Tristan carefully but quickly made his way to the front of the store. Stepping outside he and the boys walked into total chaos. He saw at least four men shooting at people who were trying to take cover, and another three who were using knives or their hands to harm the townspeople.

Tristan started to walk, then full out ran to the closest gunman. Using speed that was rivaled only by Caleb's, Tristan surprised the man. Face to face, he took a gun that was secured in one of the man's chest holsters and shot him with it. Turning, Tristan aimed at another gunman who was shooting at a group of people who hid behind a small sedan a few feet away. The bullet entered the man's head dead center. Before the man fell lifeless to the ground, Tristan moved to another.

In less than a minute, Tristan took out three of the enemy. Then it dawned on him that he didn't ask the boys about their abilities. He turned around to look for them but saw Cipher first. Cipher was in hand to hand combat with a very large man.

Tristan noticed two things immediately. The large man was a Coesen, and by the way, he moved, he was a Protector. Cipher was strong but he was in no way as strong as the guy he was up against. The giant of a man connected a blow to Cipher's chest, knocking him on his back a few feet away.

The large man stood over Cipher, raising his foot to stomp him, but Tristan noted that Cipher's reflexes were extraordinary; he rolled out of the man's reach, then jumped to his feet and went on the attack again. Both men were just about evenly matched when it came to speed but it was Cipher who seemed to be better trained because just as Tristan was about to assist, the giant dropped to his knees. A large dagger protruded from his massive chest.

"I see you brought back-up." Cipher motioned to the boys with his head.

Tristan didn't notice that the boys immediately stepped into the fray. The younger one's hands were raised while the older one, Adam, had his hand on a light post. Tristan actually saw the electricity enter Adam's body then shoot out of his other hand toward his younger brother who stood a few feet away. The electric spear made contact with an invisible barrier the younger brother seemed to command. Sparks flew but the electric spear deflected, shooting into a gunman positioned on the roof of a nearby building.

A sniper on another roof noticed the two boys took out one of his associates and aimed at the younger brother.

Tristan knew he couldn't make it to the sniper in time so he frantically searched for something to throw, to maybe change the trajectory of the oncoming bullet but there was nothing. So, he called out to the boys to take cover as he made his way to the building where the gunman was posted.

That asshole is dead, Tristan promised himself as he heard the shot ring out. He didn't stop scaling the building but did look over his shoulder to trace the bullet. He saw the bullet hit some invisible barrier the younger brother used to shield himself.

The boy grinned at Tristan as the bullet fell to the ground. A crooked electric spear flashed toward the boy from his older brother. The kid used his shield to deflect the spear, taking out the sniper.

"Snipers zero…Wonder twins, two," Tristan said as he propelled himself off the windowsill to the sidewalk three stories down. He landed like a feline then made his way over to the brothers.

"Take cover," Cipher ordered a few people hiding in the doorway of a storefront.

Tristan continued toward the brothers as he looked over at the people Cipher was yelling at. It was a bunch of six, four women and two men.

Without warning, Cipher tossed one of his knives into the group of people he ordered to seek shelter. The man who was hit with Cipher's knife dropped to the ground. A woman screamed as she stumbled over his body.

Tristan furrowed his brows. He didn't notice any weapons on the man, and the man looked as if he was no threat. In fact, the man was moving along with the crowd as if he wanted out of the chaos.

Cipher met Tristan's confused gaze then tapped his right ear.

It took only seconds for Tristan to make the connection. He smelled blood on the assailants he took down before he even touched them. Of course, Cipher smelled it too. Tristan focused on the man's ear and noticed the blood. The guy was trying to blend in with the locals but he was bleeding from his ear. Tristan used his keen sight to look from one downed shooter to the next. All of them were bleeding from one of their ears.

It was a dead giveaway.

Just as Tristan and his allies came together under a light post in front of a movie theatre, the earth started to shake beneath them. In the distance, a ball of flames lit the sky. The boys glanced at each other. Concern and a touch of excitement were what Tristan saw in their eyes. They both seemed eager as they peered at him. They were waiting for his command.

Tristan also noticed that their group was growing. A few of the residents picked up some of the guns the assailants brought. *I like this town*, he thought as he said, "Kill any verified outsider threat. No one walks away."

"No one," a woman nodded as she grumbled the declaration.

A man who carried one of the assailant's guns and looked like he knew how to use it, came forward. He was older but looked battle-born. "We'll protect the people here."

Caleb and Jamiah ran the short distance to the center of town. It was also the location of the small explosion they heard. He noted that the buildings—a post office, a library, a small security station, a few more service buildings and a supermarket, sat unmarred.

Littered on the street and sidewalk were over a dozen people lying unconscious or dead. Some were shot but Caleb detected that something or someone else killed the assailants and injured the Guards.

One of Jamiah's Guards, a female, groaned.

Caleb stayed where he was while Jamiah ran the few feet to get to her. The charred buildings, vehicles, and dented asphalt told him that the spot he was standing in was near the center of the localized blast.

Caleb looked at one of the smoldering vehicles closest to him. The fire was already dying out so he walked a few feet to two bodies that lay in the street. He kicked one, the corpse of an assailant, away from the body of a small boy who lay in the center of a scorched hole. Caleb squatted beside the boy and checked his vitals without touching him. The boy was alive but his heart was racing and his body was emitting enough energy to power a city.

"What happened?"

Caleb heard Jamiah ask the female as he glanced their way. She was sitting up on her own but rubbing her head.

"The kid," she moaned, looking at the boy.

"Explain," Caleb called.

The Guard sat up straighter, seeming to realize who was assisting her. When she spoke again, her voice was clear. "Bach and I were engaged in battle when the kid came out of nowhere. All he did was touch three of them and they dropped, just like that. I don't know how he did it but I was grateful. He saved a lot of lives," she said. "But he's just a kid and we needed him safe, out of the way, so I ran over here to tell him to take cover." She shook her head. "He was just touching another Asshat when I came upon him. The look in his eyes was so intense. He was in pain but I don't think he wanted me touching him. Because when I tried, everything went black."

Caleb looked down into the boy's face. His European and African mixed heritage was apparent immediately. Like most ethnically diverse children, he had the perfect skin color that a lot of people envied. His hair was short but long enough to bend, hinting at dark silky curls. His eyes were shut, so the color was a mystery, but his lashes were dark. The boy was just that, a boy of no more than thirteen years old, but in Caleb's younger days the boy would have been considered a young man.

A young man brave enough to fight back.

Caleb liked the boy. His Samuel may have been as gallant if he lived.

"Is he alive?" a concerned voice asked.

Caleb heard the Coesen approaching but he didn't turn to face the man. "He lives," Caleb answered. The man kneeled on the other side of the kid. He reached out but Caleb grabbed his wrist before he could touch the boy. "Don't," he warned, "unless you want to end up like him." Caleb tilted his head to the crispy assailant he kicked earlier.

With his hand around the Coesen's wrist, Caleb read him easily. This was Bach, the one the female Guard spoke of. Unlike the female, Bach was not a Protector. He was a Coesen with an odd ability. Once Bach got hold of someone; he could inflict enough pain or pleasure with just a touch that could kill if he chose. Though, it seemed Bach often chose not to kill unless it was totally necessary; and when that was the case, Bach often chose to kill the cruelest among his adversaries with pleasure instead of pain. Apparently, he felt it was the worst way to go.

The guy brought a whole new meaning to the phrase "Killing with Kindness".

Caleb released the Coesen's wrist without alerting him that his mind was breached. If he allowed himself, he was sure that he could actually like some of these Coesen. He barely tolerated Bannerman; the man was a know it all, and even worse he fancied his Kayla once. The reverence in his voice when the doctor spoke of her was laced with unfulfilled desire. It was only because Kayla respected and trusted the man that he still lived.

Langley was…well, if Caleb really thought about the past, which he didn't like to, the lawyer was family. He was a descendant of Jai and Jai was family. He could never discount her worth and that meant he could never discount her bloodline. His ties to the Coesen were limited but he was aware of Langley and most of his ancestors.

Hell, he watched some of the Children of Jai and positively intervened in their lives when he felt the need, but mostly it was unbeknownst to them. Though, he had no prior knowledge of Cipher. Now Langley and his son were added to Caleb's umbrella of protection. If he kept meeting Coesen like the boy at his feet and the worthy male in front of him, the mental armor he erected a lifetime ago, the one that kept him indifferent and distant to mankind, was in danger of cracking.

Gah…when the hell did I start giving a shit? And more importantly, *why do I now give a shit?*

As he reflected, Caleb used half his consciousness to fade to where Tristan's aura was the strongest. He noted that Tristan and Cipher were a few blocks away, not on Shop Street anymore, but still engaged in combat with a small group of assailants. He sighed with relief that his son was unharmed. Though, if Tristan was harmed, he would have felt it.

My son?

Yeah, he taunted the boy with the word "son" but that was because it upset Tristan and fueled his hate and determination. If anything, he should blame Tristan for all these new, unwanted connections. Spending time with the hybrid awakened something Caleb thought long dead. Even returning to Maiden Hall didn't upset him like he thought it would. The bad memories were still there but there was always a longing to reconnect with his past and the family he once knew.

There was no anger, just…

Caleb placed his hand over his heart.

"Hey guy," Bach said, "you alright?"

Damn it.

Caleb felt an ache in his chest that he once only allowed himself to feel for Kayla and his unborn child after he lost Marda and Samuel. He once explained to Kayla that love was not a worthy word. Love was mysterious and difficult to understand. It was gentle, strong, and impossible to control. Love was all-encompassing and it was definitely a gift and a curse. And though he still felt the word "love" was unworthy for what he felt, the word was exactly what he had for his daughter, her mate, and their offspring. It was the easiest word, to sum up the wide plethora of emotions one felt.

"Captain," Bach called out as Caleb swatted the man's hand away.

Caleb, so wrapped up in his emotional moment, looked up to see Jamiah and the female named Feria, standing over him.

The looks on their faces and the concern in Bach's voice actually annoyed Caleb. He steadied himself as he stood.

"I'm fine," Caleb said. He took a deep breath then cleared his thoughts and trapped any and all emotions he just discovered in the back of his mind. If he learned anything in life, it was that emotions got people killed.

With his focus back on his senses, Caleb tilted his head in the direction of the new energy he was receiving. He looked at Jamiah, "If anyone touches that boy, they will die." He looked off in the direction of the energy, where the park was located.

The park was near the house where Tranae and Bannerman were holed up. "Something is happening at the park," he announced.

"Bach," Jamiah said, moving around the boy, giving him a wide berth, "you stay with the boy. Feria, you secure the area and eliminate any threats. I'll go with..." He looked at Caleb.

"Guy," Caleb answered then stepped in front of Jamiah. "We can't get there on foot. There's no time." Confused, Jamiah moved back but Caleb was fast. He felt Jamiah's alarm but he placed his hand on Jamiah's shoulder anyway and said, "Try to relax."

"Relax?" Jamiah questioned, "wait...no."

Before Jamiah could finish, Caleb faded them into the park to find the source of power before he teleported them there. He sensed the power was there but still had no idea who was the source of it or their exact location. He just knew that it was very strong and foreign to him. At no time in his long life did he feel this particular energy from a Coesen.

Unique...

Caleb took in his surroundings, ignoring the nausea that followed teleporting. Jamiah apparently didn't take his advice about relaxing. The Captain was on his knees retching up what was in his stomach. He hoped the man recovered fast.

Ignoring the sickening sounds of the Captain spilling his guts, Caleb reacted to the scene he stepped into. With one hand, he sent a wave of energy in the direction of two gunmen. With the other hand, he moved a family van through the air to cover a group of children running from spraying gun fire.

Jamiah was up and sprinting with Coesen speed toward the gunmen Caleb just knocked back. With those two taken care of, Caleb spun around to the face what brought him to this park.

Across the grass near a baseball field, a large group of people was huddled together under a set of bleachers. Just a few feet in front of them was a young girl who wore a sports uniform of some sort. Her arms were raised in front of her with her fingers spread outwards.

She is the source.

Caleb followed the direction of her intense stare. Twenty feet in front of her was an armed woman who was fighting for her life. But she wasn't defending herself from someone who was beating the hell out of her. No, this female assailant was fighting animals—birds, rats, squirrels, deer, a few foxes, and coyotes, among other wildlife. They were all attacking the screaming woman. And more animals were coming out of the forest to get to the woman.

Are those mountain lions?

The scene itself was grisly, and the assassin was giving them a good fight but she was no match for the onslaught.

Caleb walked toward the girl as he mentally touched her mind. He sensed her confusion and pain, smelled her fear. He also smelled blood. Her blood, he assumed. He visually scanned her for injuries as he approached. There was a large stain of blood spreading through her shirt near her shoulder.

"Cassie sweetheart," Caleb spoke as softly as he could. "Can you control them?" He kept his eyes on the girl while keeping his senses open, listening to the assault behind him. Caleb knew exactly when the female assassin fell.

He wasn't sure what the girl did to get those animals to help, but by her trembling and with the thoughts running through her head, he was sure she didn't know how to rein in the ability.

She shook her head as she began to openly sob. She thought of how much trouble she was going to be in with her parents. She thought about how no Breed was supposed to be able to do these kinds of things. But she and some of her friends were just like the Specials. Specials was the name they gave the Coesen with powers. They were Specials too, but they had to keep it secret from everyone. It was their club rules, after all.

"Do you prefer I call you, Cass?" Caleb took a few steps toward her, not wanting to spook her more than she already was.

Cassie nodded.

"It's alright, Cass, I can help."

"H-how do you know my name?" Cassie asked. Her arms wobbled like they were getting heavy.

"I'm sort of like you…and your friends. I'm Special too." Caleb noticed that Jamiah eliminated the human threat and was now moving the people out of the park to safety from the new threat.

Cassie's tears continued to fall as her sobs got louder. "I can't hold them. It only works for a little while then they pull away." She kept her eyes on the animals.

Some already began to bore of their kill.

"When they do, they're always…they will be angry with me. They will hurt me…after."

Caleb continued to move toward Cassie. Her gaze was pinned on the gruesome sight in front of her. Without turning around, Caleb could tell that some of the animals were now focused on her. He stepped in front of the young frightened girl and pulled her to him. He could tell she was exhausted but she attempted to fight him anyway.

"I can't lose focus!" she cried, "They'll attack us."

Caleb rubbed Cassie's back as he cradled her in his arms. "*Shh*, you are safe with me, Cass. I promise." Her struggling stopped as she turned her head to look at the animals again. She tensed when she faced the narrowed eyes of her former rescuers.

The animals' ire was definitely spiked and their undivided attention was centered on Cassie.

The mountain lions separated from the other animals first. They stalked forward, heads low, eyes on Cassie. Caleb placed his hand on the side of her head and gently pushed, laying it on his shoulder. "Relax," he told her. She again tensed when he began to walk them toward the parking lot. They had to walk by the animals and their discarded chew toy to do so.

Caleb would spare her the discomfort of teleporting her. She didn't need nausea on top of fear and blood loss. Plus, there were the animals he had to see to.

He didn't see it but he felt the shift in the air as one of the mountain lions leaped. Cassie wrapped her arms around his neck and squeezed her eyes shut as if that was her only defense. The large cat never reached them, falling in mid leap to the grass. The other mountain lions attacked, only to fall as well.

As Caleb strolled toward the parking lot, more animals attacked. Birds flew at them, deer charged, rats and other small animals scurried in their direction, but each one fell.

By the time he reached Jamiah, Cassie was moaning. It was due to the pain in her arm. After handing the girl over to Jamiah, Caleb ripped open her sleeve to expose the bullet wound. Usually, he would keep his abilities hidden from the Coesen, but things had changed.

He changed.

So, Caleb raised his hand over the wound and caught the bullet that burst out.

"My arm burns," Cassie said drowsily, peering up at him. Her eyes blinked several times.

"Only for a little while, Cass." Caleb looked down at her wound. He watched Cassie's skin knit back together, knowing that whatever damage inside was healed too.

It was tricky healing someone. Doing so always came with discomfort for him and the person he was able to heal. Most of the time it didn't work; humans were usually too fragile and died anyway. He couldn't heal Coesen. He tried. But Tristan and Breed were, well it seemed that they were different. Maybe the combination of human and Coesen DNA was the deciding factor for them. In Tristan's case, his DNA had restructured itself during his transformation into Cianne's Protector which probably allowed Caleb to resurrect him.

"Lots of tricks up your sleeves, eh?" Jamiah said.

Ignoring Jamiah, Caleb pocketed the bullet then brushed his hand over Cassie's brows. She was going to be out for a few hours. "All intruders have been dealt with. Headquarters, Captain?"

Frowning, Jamiah gave Caleb a questioning look. It seemed the Captain was full of questions but he rarely voiced them. Caleb liked that about the man. Plus Jamiah, like most, was easy to read. Without breaching his mind, Caleb knew that Jamiah wanted to know how he knew about their hidden headquarters in The Glenn.

"There isn't much I don't know," Caleb offered before transporting Jamiah and Cassie to headquarters.

Chapter Sixteen

Tristan backed against the wall, trying to make himself as small as possible as three hospital workers hurried by with a man on a gurney. After they passed, he peeled himself away from the wall and continued down the long hallway where he stepped into an elevator.

Beneath the Glenn's town square was a medical facility, sophisticated and efficiently staffed to handle the mayhem that interrupted the tranquility that once was. The staff seemed to work like a well-oiled machine as they assisted the injured who were brought in.

The medical ward was located on Level B2, so Tristan hit the button for B1. The elevator traveled up one floor and opened. A Guard, a female, was waiting for him.

"I'm to take you to the Captain and your friends," she said before motioning for him to follow her.

He followed.

They passed a manned guard station with over a dozen security monitors that displayed points of interest in the hospital, along with images of the front and rear views of the street above. The Guard led him down a few hallways to a closed door that she opened for him.

Inside the room was a long conference table and chairs. In the corner was a small work station and a file cabinet. Caleb leaned against the edge of the workstation table. Strategically the spot placed the door, and everyone in the room in Caleb's view.

Cipher sat in front of Caleb, at the conference table. He looked like he was about to stand to bow but caught himself. Instead, he kicked his feet out and acted as if he was getting more comfortable.

Across from Cipher, two males Tristan didn't know were seated beside each other. Both men were dressed in dark gray but he noticed that one of them wore the same necklace the female who escorted him wore, a thin silver link choker with a small stone.

The female Guard who escorted Tristan crossed the room and stood next to the two unknown Guards, who got to their feet when she entered the room.

Tristan closed the door then chose the seat next to Cipher. Everyone sat down. The room was oddly split in a "them versus us" way with Jamiah standing in front of a large observation mirror.

Without moving a muscle, Caleb transferred, *"The Captain and these three others are devoted to Cianne, the idea of The Glenn; and at one time they were ready to embrace you as their Sovereign's Potentate. We have to be cautious but they could be useful. Though there were some unforeseen obstacles, our goal remains the same, to get you back where you belong."*

"Ok," Tristan transferred back.

"With your disguise, they won't know you but Tristan...don't let Jamiah touch you or anything you're touching at the same time."

Tristan mentally nodded, then tuned into the conversation Jamiah was having with his Guards. The Captain took a few steps toward the door then turned and closed the short distance to the conference table as he spoke. He stood still for a few seconds then repeated his pacing.

"Fourteen residents are dead, thirty-six injured," the female Guard reported. "Dr. Bannerman is overseeing things at the hospital."

Jamiah nodded, took two steps toward the table as if he was going to sit then turned and looked up. He glanced at Tristan and frowned then spoke again. "And the kids?" he asked.

The man with the silver choker spoke. "Luckily Dr. Bannerman is in town. He didn't need to patch up Cassandra Vaughn. Thanks to our mysterious friend here." The man nodded to Caleb, "Ethan Emery I'm told will make a full recovery. Adam and his brother Luke Webb weren't injured but are staying for observation."

"Have their families been notified?" Jamiah asked. He glanced at Tristan again then returned his attention to his Guards.

The other man, who had very light brown eyes, spoke up. "I took care of that myself, Captain. The children's families are with them now."

Jamiah touched the bridge of his nose and sighed. "The media?"

"Nothing has been leaked so far. We were able to block all incoming and outgoing communication five minutes into the attack." The female added, "We are monitoring all Coesen media outlets."

"What are you going to do about the kids?" the man with light eyes asked.

Sighing, Jamiah sat down in a chair at the head of the table but was far enough away that he hadn't touched it. He lowered his head a little. "What is required," he answered.

"But…" the light eyed man began but stopped.

Jamiah lifted his head. He looked at the man and waited. When the man didn't speak, Jamiah said, "You can speak freely, Anton."

Instead of finishing his comment or question, Anton turned his attention on "them". "Are you certain I can speak freely? These three don't check out. No hits on the ID's they supplied. There's no record of them living here, or ever being here before today."

"Dr. Bannerman has spoken for them," the female said.

"I agree with Feria," the man with the matching choker spoke up. "Plus, they kicked ass," he added with a grin that hinted to a playful side.

Jamiah stared at Tristan for several seconds. It was clear that the man was looking for something or seeing something.

The disguise Tristan wore only consisted of contacts that made his blue eyes brown; his hair had grown down past his ears and had a wave to it now but he wore a wool hat. His face was covered in a few day's growth. Tristan had Caleb do his mojo on his Maatii tattoo so even that was mystically covered. Although he resembled his old self, there was no way Jamiah could ignore the lack of those key components that made Tristan into the White Lion and the Sovereign's missing, and presumed dead, Potentate.

"Thank you, Bach and Feria for your seal of approval," Jamiah said mockingly. "Anton, I'm aware of the lack of information on our new friends. These men weren't required to help us tonight but they did with no care for their own safety. So, for now, they are on the in..." he looked over at Caleb, "regarding the Glenn, anyway."

"Since we are on the 'in'," Cipher said, "I'd like to say that reporting those kids to the Council would be a mistake."

Jamiah focused all his attention on Cipher for the first time since Tristan walked in the room. His gaze took in Cipher with a scrutiny that people with authority liked to use. Jamiah's authority came off him in waves.

Jamiah scooted his chair forward and reached for the table, but just before Jamiah's hands touched the table, Caleb moved from leaning on the desk and laid his hands on it. Remembering that Caleb said to avoid Jamiah's touch, Tristan guessed that the Captain had some kind of psychometric ability and he wanted to read Cipher.

It didn't take long for Jamiah to figure out that Caleb was blocking his attempt to read Cipher or any of them for that matter. The Captain turned his gaze to Caleb and the two men stared at each other for several heartbeats. The three guards noticed, and though they gave each other questioning looks, no one said anything.

The removal of Jamiah's hands and him relaxing back in his chair signaled the end of the standoff, but Caleb didn't move his hands. Instead of returning to leaning on the desk, he sat down in a chair, leaving one hand on the table.

Jamiah didn't seem at all worried about the exchange, which led Tristan to believe that something similar had already transpired between the two men.

"The Glenn was set up so Coesen and their Middling mates could live safely together as one. This is only possible if the Coesen agree to the Council's terms. One of those terms is that each Coesen must have his or her abilities bound if they are to reside here."

Cipher smiled. An almost silent intake of breath from Feria momentarily caught Cipher's attention but no one seemed to notice the exchange except for Tristan.

"Then none of those terms have been broken. Those kids are Breed, and according to current law..." Cipher shrugged. "...they are not considered, Coesen. That means you do not have to turn them in."

"At least not right now," Feria added. She immediately dropped her eyes and blushed when Cipher gave her a thank you nod and smile.

Rolling his eyes, Bach said, "Romeo has a point, Captain. Those kids helped to protect their home. We were unprepared for this attack. If we hadn't had those kids and these guys," he said, flicking his thumb at Tristan and his friends, "there would have been many more casualties."

Jamiah didn't respond right away. He just focused his attention on the table. Tristan suspected he was fighting a silent battle in his head over what he wanted to do and what he needed to do about the children.

Duty was important to Tristan as well and had been, since the moment he found out who and what Cianne was. He accepted her and her role immediately, then modeled himself to be a man she could be proud of. He embraced the Coesen ways because he admired their loyalty, sense of duty, and their honor. He believed in their way of life so much that he convinced himself that his family would be safer if he was out of their lives.

Doubts of his worthiness was the issue of late. He now understood Vivian's campaign to convince Cianne that he was not the right choice in the beginning. Tristan knew Cianne feared her power and that, among other reasons, why she chose not to acknowledge her role; but he couldn't help thinking that a part of her didn't think he could be the husband a Sovereign deserved. That he wouldn't be able to be what she needed him to be.

"You people, your beliefs, and your misplaced loyalties," Caleb said. He sighed.

Tristan looked over at Caleb, who was looking at him.

"When faced with a hard choice, you do what you feel is right. If what you've decided ends up being the wrong move, stand by it but do what you can to fix it." Caleb shook his head then said, "Keep life simple. Be devoted to doing what's right. Honor the people you can't live without. Your only duty in this world is to them. Life isn't that complicated unless you make it so."

Tristan stood. Without a word, Caleb and Cipher got to their feet as well. "These people here are guilty of no crime, but they are kept here and their abilities are bound because they want the right to choose who they love and who they spend their lives with. A person has the right to defend themselves and that right should never be taken away."

"I feel like I know you from somewhere," Jamiah stood. His brows furrowed as if he was thinking deeply.

"We're leaving," Tristan announced. He moved to the door.

Jamiah blocked Tristan's and his group's only physical exit. "Have we met before?"

Tristan stopped in his tracks, fully aware that the Guards were on their feet as well. His mind processed several possible outcomes if Caleb felt that his safety was threatened. Tristan had no doubt that these people's lives would mean nothing to Caleb if they moved to harm him in any way.

"You're beginning to understand how I think." Caleb's words brushed Tristan's mind. *"Cianne, the children, you…that's what I honor. That's what I fight to protect."*

Tristan turned his head and met Caleb's stare. In that moment, he *knew*. He knew that Caleb had and would forever have his respect, loyalty, and affection. Tristan lowered his head in respect but said nothing, not sure if he wanted Caleb to know what he was feeling because their relationship may flow better with the distracting undercurrent.

Looking back at Jamiah, the desire to reveal himself was overwhelming but he knew that the place and time weren't right. "We have," Tristan answered honestly.

Lies tasted like acid to Tristan. They always did, so he never took up the practice of lying.

Jamiah reached for him and though he could have, Tristan didn't move away. He wanted his identity known more than he would admit. If anything, he was sure once the Captain knew who he was, an order to keep quiet about the children and their abilities would be followed.

"Why can't I read you?" Jamiah asked, his hand resting on Tristan's shoulder. "Why can't I read any of you?"

"Because I don't want you to," Caleb answered.

It was then that Tristan realized Caleb moved past Cipher and was touching his back.

"What are you?" Jamiah asked, dropping his hand.

"Someone who doesn't see you as an enemy," Caleb told Jamiah.

Jamiah gave a slight nod.

Tristan thought the nod may have been done without Jamiah really thinking about it.

"I won't report the children," Jamiah said; his gaze moved to everyone in the room.

Each of his Guards seemed relieved by his words.

Jamiah looked back at Tristan. "For now, anyway. But I think you know I will have to eventually. I'm not getting what I want from you three but I can sense that you all are Breed of worth. I will accept that for now." Jamiah took six steps back, clearing the way for them to leave.

Anton, one of Jamiah's handpicked Guards, was charged with taking them to the house they were staying in. The community was a bit calmer since the battle but things weren't yet settled. It may take a while for that to happen.

Tristan realized that he wasn't yet settled either, as he sat in the rear of the car watching the people of the community clean up. This incident was his first real engagement with an enemy to the death and his first time protecting someone other than Cianne. It was also the first time he witnessed the deaths of people he wanted to save, yet couldn't.

It felt like hell.

"You can't save everyone," Cipher said from beside him.

Tristan turned from looking out of the car window to Cipher. He knew Cipher was a soldier in some secret special-forces team for the U.S. military but he didn't know the details. All he knew was the man who headed the unit was somehow related to Caleb and that Cipher purposefully set himself apart from the other soldiers to gain the man's interest and entry to the secret team in an attempt to locate Caleb.

"Believe me, I've tried." Cipher looked haunted for a moment. He fisted his hand then stretched out his fingers. "It's not easy, but if you can accept that, you hang on to your sanity."

Turning back to the window, Tristan didn't focus on what was going on outside. He looked beyond what was happening, giving nothing his full attention. When they arrived at the house, he noticed that Anton didn't stick around. Jamiah was keeping an eye on them, but not a close eye.

Inside, Tranae sat up on the sofa. She rubbed the drowsiness from her eyes as she looked to each of them. "We heard gunshots. Dr. Bannerman had me hide upstairs while he stood guard then someone came for him," she said. "Is everything alright?"

"For now," Cipher said as he moved around Tristan. He headed for the kitchen.

Tristan took a seat beside Tranae who continued to rub her eyes. He glanced at Caleb who started climbing the stairs as he spoke. "This is a place where people like Cianne and normal people can make a life together. Some think that mixing both races is cause for war. Tonight, some of those people attacked."

"Glad you guys were here to stop them," Tranae said. The drowsy look in her eyes was gone, replaced with anger. The fact that she wasn't asking if they protected the community but assumed they did, made Tristan feel like he was the hero Tranae thought he was.

"We stopped them but people got hurt and some even lost their lives," Cipher said.

Tristan and Tranae both looked up as Cipher walked into the living room. In his hands were a cup of tea and some miniature chocolate glazed donuts. He handed the tea and donuts to Tranae then sat in the chair across from them.

"Thank you." She smiled. She took a bite of one of the treats then frowned. "Cianne can stop this kind of thing. She's queen or something now, right?"

Tristan had faith that Cianne would do her best to protect her people if she was in her right state of mind. He also wanted to believe that she would need him by her side to do just that, but he knew better.

Tristan nodded. "When she's able to focus and see the forest instead of just the trees, I'm sure she will make a lot of changes."

Tranae sipped her tea and finished her treats in silence.

Tristan noticed that Cipher's head had fallen back on the chair's headrest. He liked that the soldier felt comfortable and trusted him and Caleb enough to close his eyes. But he suspected that Cipher would be up and ready in no time if he sensed a threat.

After Tranae finished her tea, she retired to her room, leaving just Tristan awake.

Eventually, Tristan stretched out on the sofa, and for the first time in a long time, he was able to close his eyes with a pinprick sense of calm. He knew that there would be an end to this. What that end would turn out to be was not written, and each of the players had a part.

His part was big but he needed to rely on his friends to help him. He was confident they were going to succeed. But his goal was more complicated. Yes, he wanted Cianne to reign with her sanity, confidence, and compassion. To be at her side while she did was what he wanted most. To raise his children with his wife as a couple was what he needed. Today wasn't one of his best, but the day was fast approaching where he would hold Cianne again.

Tristan drifted to sleep, with his hopes high and for the first time in a long time, completely trusted Caleb to watch over them.

"And I will."

Chapter Seventeen

Cianne wondered if Tristan's spirit didn't just latch onto hers. Theirs was a love so deep-seated that she thought it possible.

As she drifted down the hallway on auto pilot, saying good morning to the staff, Cianne couldn't mask the pain she felt today. Even being around her children, her sole reason for trying, she couldn't fake it.

"Morning, Soahn Bertram," Tally Newsome said with a bright smile.

Inwardly, Cianne groaned her displeasure. The happy-go-lucky event coordinator was hands-down the bubbliest person she ever met. Cianne's mood was, at best, low tolerance for bubbly.

A look of mild interest was all Cianne could muster when she returned the greeting. "Good morning, Mrs. Newsome."

"Soahn," Mrs. Newsome bowed, "you must call me Tally."

Mrs. Newsome's smile was so bright, Cianne found herself squinting. Or she was squinting from the pounding headache that just reached atomic level?

"Do you have a moment to look over some of my plans for the Ceremony?" Tally pulled her shoulder bag around to rest on her hip and took out her tablet. She used a stylus to tap the screen over a dozen times in quick session then said without looking up, "I've left you several messages to get your approval on a few major things."

"I gave you total autonomy with the ceremony." Cianne stepped around the cheerful decorative diva and continued on her way. "I'll show up dressed in whatever you've chosen."

The Meriotia ceremony, a three-day event, was similar to a wedding with a rehearsal dinner, but along with the wedding party, VIP's were also in attendance. Tally did give Cianne a write-up of what will be expected of her. The first day was basically a celebration of the mating couple. The second day was the Mating (marriage) and Blooding ritual. The next day the couple is separated, and later that evening is brought together for the Showering, where the mated pair will be presented with gifts.

The Blood Ritual or Sharing was expected of the Coesen mating pair. Cianne wasn't particularly on board with that but everyone who had an opinion told her that she was expected to comply with tradition. All the Sovereigns before her performed the Blood Ritual.

The thought of giving her blood to someone other than Tristan made Cianne sick to her stomach.

Tristan never pushed her to marry the Meriotia way, knowing that she wanted nothing to do with Coesen traditions at the time. Now, she wished she had because Whodai was to have her blood. And she, his.

Cianne held in a sigh when she realized that Tally caught up with her.

"Yes…" Tally said as she looked up from the tablet, "your attire has been chosen. I would love your approval though." She held up the tablet.

Cianne's eyes swept over the image without really seeing it. She nodded.

"What I would like to speak to you about now is the Shower and your choice for a stand in."

"I haven't decided who will be giving me away." Cianne sighed.

Tally winced, shrugging her shoulders. "We like to call it 'offering'."

The woman actually did the air quotes. "Of course," Cianne said. She rubbed her temple. "I haven't decided who will be 'offering' me."

They rounded the corner at the end of the hallway, Tally keeping pace with her while consumed with tapping away on her tablet. "May I suggest Jamiah, Soahn? It will show unity at the very least."

The door to Vivian's personal library came into view. When it was clear where Cianne was headed, Tally stopped. There were wards in place that kept everyone except for Cianne out. If by chance someone happened to gain entry, they wouldn't make it out alive.

"I'll think on it, Mrs. Newsome," Cianne said, moving closer to her destination. The library was a great wealth of information but it was also Cianne's sanctuary of sorts.

"Please, call me Tally."

Cianne said nothing as she disappeared into the library. Inside, she lifted the book she placed on the side table the night before and took a seat in Vivian's chair. She settled comfortably in the chair, opened the book, then started where she left off. She skimmed most of the entries in silence until one piqued her excitement.

Annals entry of Vivian Keen
Twentieth Year/book 3 entry 45

I know that my time of being carefree is coming to an end. No one has said as much, but I can feel the inevitable crush of expectations weighing down on me.

To make things worse, Taio keeps disappearing. I don't want to be one of those girls. The ones who accuse and yell but I am worried that he has fallen for another. Someone who can give him the things a man desires.

Annal entry of Vivian Keen
Twentieth Year/book 3 entry 47

Today, my faith in love prevailing above all things was validated. Deni confided in me last year that she was interested in a boy named Devin, the son of one of the professors at Gering, who showed romantic interest in her. I know they never broke the rule of fraternization but I've noticed the way they look at one another when they think no one is watching.

Devin showed up at mid-day break today. His face was battered, beaten, and he had a bad limp but he won the Tandot for Deni's hand and she accepted him. I am so happy for them both. But I silently prayed to the Source that the man I wanted above all others can win my hand like he won my heart.

Annal entry of Vivian Keen
Twentieth Year/book 3 entry 48

Taio has broken me. He came to me with anger and hurt in his eyes. When I asked him to confide in me, his response... He lost. He lost the Tandot for my hand that I never even knew was underway. He could barely look at me. If he had only accepted all of me when I offered.

He failed me, us.

Annal entry of Vivian Keen
Twentieth Year/book 3 entry 59

Today, at my parents' end of the year gala, I found out that Gaither Harper is my intended mate. Though we've been friends for years, I feel nothing akin to romance for the male. Our friends seem to think we are well matched but it will be a union of duty. Nothing more.

Taio requested reassignment. I won't fight it but my heart will go with him.

Cianne traced her fingers over Taio's name, then raised her head and peered over at Gaither's worn chair. Based on the chair's appearance, among other things, it seemed Vivian eventually opened her heart to her mate.

Whether Gaither knew it or not, was the question.

Cianne returned her attention back to the book. The last entries barely filled the page and there was nothing else written. She turned the page, then the next, finding them blank. In fact, the rest of the book was filled with blank pages.

Why?

Cianne closed the book and placed it on the side table and picked up the next one. She lifted the hard cover then flipped to the first entry.

Annal entry of Vivian Harper
First Year of Union/book 1 entry 01

I am mated. The ceremony was grand, just what my mother wanted. Everyone who is anyone attended. Yet, Gaither and I seemed to be absent. I think he had someone too, someone he loved.

Annal entry of Vivian Harper
First Year of Union/book 1 entry 03

Last night, I gave all of myself to my mate, as per the law of Coesen dictates. Gaither did what was required of him. We started off a bit clumsily, not really knowing how to touch the other, but it seemed our bodies knew what to do. I'd be lying if I said that it was unpleasant.

I think that being sexually compatible, from my perspective, makes it all the more awkward. Though we've been good friends practically our entire lives, I find it hard to communicate like we used to. I'm told the awkwardness of our situation will wear off in time. I don't know if I want it to. I want to blame him for winning the Tandot. But like Gaither, I didn't stand up to my parents or tradition either.

At least we don't have to see one another until the Showering this evening.

Annal entry of Vivian Harper
First Year of Union/book 1 entry 45
Mated Four Months

For his part, Gaither has been everything a mate should be. He was always a male of worth but seeing him in the role of Potentate, the way he handles everything with ease, I am impressed. My parents are as well.

As a mate, he listens, he's caring, he's tempting. But I believe it is an act that he has been perfecting from an early age. Just as I have. I've made my terms clear. That, he will have my friendship but my heart will never be his. Also, that once we have an heir, I will no longer welcome his touch. Every time the man touches me, I feel as if I am betraying Taio. That I now crave Gaither's gentle, yet demanding touch makes this situation worse.

Gaither agreed with a smile. That worries me. What is he up to?

Cianne grinned as she thought of how stubborn Vivian was. She turned the last page then closed it. Absently caressing the spine of the volume, Cianne shifted in Vivian's chair as she thought of what she read.

The Vivian Harper she knew was all rules and regulations. Yet, Vivian Keen seemed to be a normal young adult reluctantly accepting her duty. The difference in the two personalities was intriguing.

Cianne pushed to her feet. She collected the Annals she already read and carried them to their new home in Vivian's section of the protected bookshelf labeled Personal. Personal Annals weren't required to be included in the historical library of Sovereigns by law. They were usually given to the closest living relative. When she asked Langley if she could read Vivian's, Cianne never imagined he'd gift them to her.

She was eternally grateful to be given such a precious gift. Knowing Vivian went through what she was going through now, and that her grandmother seemed to have handled the situation with grace, as far as she read, was inspiring.

Cianne lifted the glass door and placed the volumes neatly on the shelf, then reached for the next in the series. As she wrapped her hand around the spine, the crackle of the intercom disrupted her calm. She pulled her hand back and sighed as she rolled her eyes to the sky.

"Didn't even know this room had an intercom," she whispered to herself.

Cianne didn't recognize the voice, but that meant nothing. In the past few months, more and more strangers were included in her circle, something she would not have thought possible a couple of years ago.

With Caleb and a good portion of Coesen against her, Whodai recruited security and those he trusted to help keep her safe. Though she often had to remind herself that she was grateful, she truly was.

"Soahn Bertram, I know that we are not to bother you and I apologize for the interruption but you have a guest."

Cianne didn't focus on the last piece of information because the first bit had her curious. Frowning, she asked, "Who said that I shouldn't be bothered?"

"Royal Tam, Soahn," the Coesen said over the intercom. "He insisted that any and all issues, including state business, should be directed to him. That you should be allowed to focus on your upcoming—"

"The ceremony," Cianne interrupted as she bit down on a sigh.

"Yes," the voice simply stated.

"I'll be right down." Cianne lowered the glass door to the case that held Vivian's personal Annals then exited the study. Once the door sealed behind her, she nodded to the Guard waiting outside the room, allowing her to lead the way.

She didn't like being shadowed but her personal set of revolving Guards were professional enough, discreet, and for the most part, they stayed hidden, so having them around wasn't too bad.

"*None of them are Tristan, are they?*" the disembodied voice taunted.

Though Cianne was prepared with an instant response to her inner demon, she refused to engage Gemini right now.

"Soahn Bertram, I'm glad I've run into you again." Tally sang from below.

Cianne looked over the railing as she descended the stairs. Tally stood at the bottom of the staircase. The woman expertly managed to hold onto a large binder as she pulled out her tablet and began poking the screen.

Kim, her Guard, glanced over her shoulder, catching Cianne's eye roll. Kim gave her an "I'm sorry that I can't defend you from this" shrug then a grin.

Cianne offered her an 'it's alright' nod before the Guard faced forward.

As soon as Cianne reached the bottom of the stairs, Tally was shoving the electronic device at her. A beautiful off-white strapless dress with a pale green and peach sash was featured on the screen. If it was presented to her for some other affair, Cianne would have absolutely loved the dress, but knowing it was for her upcoming nuptials had her clutching her neck, virtually loosening the noose around it.

"It's lovely Tally, but—"

Tally cut her off with, "Before you say no, know that I think that these colors are perfect for your complexion. Your friend totally thinks so too."

"Yeah, but I don't really have time to try..." Cianne frowned.

What friend thought so?

Cianne pushed the tablet away as she looked up. "Tranae?"

◉

Tranae held in her breath of surprise, swallowed, then almost choked on it. Cianne looked tired but was still beautiful.

...and she cut her hair. How could she cut her hair without telling...?

Tranae remembered they weren't the close unit they used to be. Hell, she didn't even know if Cianne was going to order her to leave.

The look on Cianne's face, an irritated and confused look, had Tranae nervously looking over her shoulder, in the direction of the front door.

"Tranae?"

Hearing her name, spoken so shakily and unsure, slowly Tranae turned back around to see a blur of movement. Next thing she knew, she was fighting for her next breath.

"Cianne," Tranae grunted, "I can't breathe."

"Oh," Cianne said, releasing Tranae. Her face was lit up, diminishing her worn-out appearance for a moment. "I'm so sorry. What are you doing here? How did you get here?" Cianne rubbed her hand down Tranae's arm, down to her hand, then linked their fingers.

Tranae took in a deep breath. She couldn't keep the grin from spreading across her face. Letting out a relieved chuckle, Tranae gripped Cianne's hand. She was prepared for a whole other kind of welcome, but this one was much better and a lot less scary.

"I flew in last night," Tranae said as she raised her shoulders and scrunched her nose, "and was hoping that you'd let me visit with the twins."

"Of course, you can. Come on." Cianne turned but kept her hold on Tranae's hand. "They will be so happy to see you."

Tranae let Cianne lead her past a woman dressed like security and the bubbly wedding planner, who seemed to be waiting for a response. With a tug of her hand, Tranae got Cianne's attention. She motioned to Tally with her head.

Cianne looked back at Tranae, then to the wedding planner. "Oh, yeah. I absolutely love the dress, Tally. It's perfect!" She then turned her attention to the security woman. "Personal space," she said.

The woman gave her a nod.

Then they were on the move again, jogging up the stairs and down a hallway, then another hallway. The house— mansion—was huge, so much bigger than the estate in Arizona, but Tranae wasn't able to appreciate the details of the place due to their hurrying.

"Details of the mansion's layout and décor is of no consequence. Study it later. You have a job to do."

Tranae stopped short. The momentum jerked Cianne back, but she managed to stay on her feet.

"Tranae?"

"Get it together, bestie. I'm just keeping an ear on you to make certain things don't get hairy," Caleb transferred.

Tranae glanced over at the huge vase that sat in the corner. She pointed to it. "That is so pretty. Where's it from?"

*"I'm on a mission of my own but I'll be monitoring your vital signs and emotions. If you need me, I will know and I **will** be there so, relax,"* Caleb told her.

"Yeah? You better be, Mr. Hotness," Tranae sent back.

Frowning, Cianne's gaze followed in the direction Tranae pointed. "Um, I actually don't know."

Shrugging, Tranae smile. "Nice though."

"Yeah," Cianne said, offering a twisted lip smile, "Come on, I'm sure they are waiting for us."

Waiting for us?

"Oh-kay," Tranae said as she raised her brows.

Chapter Eighteen

Caleb kept his link with Tranae in Canada partially open as he focused his attention on Tristan, who was staring at him with expectation. In fact, everyone in the room was waiting for him to speak.

"She's fine," he said then stepped forward. "Everyone ready?" Caleb looked at each of them, one at a time.

Tristan nodded.

Caleb partially faded to where they were going, to check the surroundings. Once he was certain things were optimal, he reappeared in the library at Maiden Hall. He grabbed Tristan's left shoulder, gripping it tight.

"I'm ready," Perkins said. He squeezed the strap of his shoulder bag that was across his chest.

Langley sighed. "As I'll ever be," he said, "but do we have a contingency plan if things go left?"

"I'll kill him." With that said, Caleb placed his hand on Perkins' shoulder and waited for Langley to grip his forearm. Without a word of warning, Caleb teleported them from Maiden Hall to a small alleyway in the District of Columbia.

Langley stepped forward then bent over as if he was going to be sick. Tristan, who teleported a few times already, seemed somewhat agitated but didn't move. Perkins wobbled, and swallowed a few times but didn't get sick.

"He's in the Chili Bowl, buying a Hot Smoked," Caleb said.

Perkins frowned at Caleb.

Caleb continued, "I'll give you thirty minutes to get him to the hotel."

Perkins bent and pulled the strap of his bag over his head and passed it to Caleb. He then nodded before walking toward the end of the alley that opened to a busy street. Caleb waited until Perkins turned the corner before teleporting the rest of them to the room he procured at a hotel a few miles away from where he dropped Perkins off.

Langley hurried inside the small bathroom and slammed the door.

Tristan leaned against the wall beside the door. He crossed his arms over his chest, glaring at Caleb who turned around and peered out of the window.

"What?" Caleb asked after fifteen minutes. He turned around as he hung the messenger bag strap over his shoulder. He looked to the bathroom.

May have to leave him here, he thought to himself.

"How did you know Cassius would be here?"

"Your 'general' in arms is a creature of habit and is predictable." Caleb moved to the bathroom door and tapped it twice. "Join us downstairs when you can."

Langley groaned a few unintelligible words.

Caleb crossed the room and was opening the door when Tristan pushed off the wall. Caleb held the door open, allowing Tristan to pass through first. He waited for the next question but it didn't come until they were in the elevator.

"Predictable, how?"

Caleb pushed the lobby button on the elevator, taking note of the security cameras, then said, "Obviously, I didn't have to hide to survive…"

"Obviously," Tristan said. The one word dripped with sarcasm.

Caleb raised his brow and chuckled. He knew Tristan loved the Coesen, so defending their honor was paramount, even if they both knew that he could wipe them from the face of the planet. "Cassius' survival meant that he and I couldn't cross paths. To do that, I needed to know where he and Vivian were, mostly. Cassius was in love once."

Seeing the look of surprise on Tristan's face was worth the tale, so Caleb continued. "She worked as an intern for a state senator and lived here in DC. They used to frequent that food spot. Dorothy loved those Hot Smokes. Whenever Cassius is in the area, he drops by there."

When the elevator doors opened, Caleb led the way to the bar and grill located in the building. He noted all the security cameras as they passed through the lobby. Caleb glanced at Tristan, who walked beside him with his head hanging, his brows creased.

"Dorothy died fifteen years ago. Now, smile for the cameras," Caleb said as he nodded at one of the security cameras.

Tristan removed the baseball cap he wore, rubbed his head, then glared at the camera long enough for any facial recognition software to have a clear image to work with.

Caleb stopped in the entryway of the bar and grill and scanned the area for threats. He logged the details of their surroundings to memory. It took a ton of concentration to keep alert and teleport him and the others while keeping an ear on Tranae from over three hundred miles away, but he was confident in the power he wielded.

The amount of energy he was using was great but he was sure it didn't scratch the surface of his limits. *My limits*. Caleb didn't fully know his limits. He grew tired of testing himself decades ago. Though, he worried that the more power he used, the sooner he would have to deal with Pythos.

Caleb spotted Perkins and Cassius at a large table in the corner.

Tristan noticed them as well. "Don't kill him."

Caleb felt his patience wane, that he needed to lay out the rules again.

Instead of causing a scene by breaking all of Tristan's ribs, he weaved through the tables at a normal pace. He ignored the anxiety seeping from Tristan as he sat beside Perkins in the booth, across from Cassius.

Cassius did a double take, but to his credit, he didn't jump up or attack. He looked to Perkins and said, "What is this, Perkins? A setup?"

"If I wanted you dead, kid, I've had plenty of opportunities." As proof, because he was sick of these "people", and their shit, Caleb mentally reached out to Cassius.

Tristan arrived at the table just when Cassius grabbed at his chest and moaned in agony.

"Stop," Tristan demanded as he stared at Caleb.

"What are you doing? You haven't even given him a chance." Perkins grabbed Caleb's arm.

Caleb broke eye contact with Cassius to glance down at Perkins' hand that gripped his arm. Perkins pulled his hand away.

"Please," Tristan pleaded.

Caleb met Tristan's unflinching gaze. When Tristan lowered his head, Caleb narrowed his eyes, but he let go his hold on Cassius' heart.

Cassius coughed as he lifted the glass of water Perkins pushed across the table. When he looked at Tristan beside him, he coughed more.

"Is…is he alright?" A concerned waitress stood over them.

Cassius glared at the waitress but it was Tristan who answered first.

"He's fine, just swallowed his drink wrong." Tristan rubbed Cassius' back.

"Alright." The waitress smiled. She twisted the cloth in her hand as she stared into Tristan's eyes. "Alright," she said again, shifting from one foot to the other. "If you need something, just wave me over."

Caleb watched her walk away then focused again on Cassius who stared back at him. The man sipped the water, maintaining eye contact with Caleb.

"How are you alive?" Cassius managed to sputter the question but he didn't move his gaze away from Caleb's.

Tristan pointed at Caleb and said, "The old man saw the threat before I did. He saved me the day of the crash, killed the bad guys, then kept me hidden to find the ones behind the attack."

Cassius coughed a few more times before quietening. "Prove to me it's you and not some trick of his."

"After training, you…" Tristan said, then whispered the rest in Cassius' ear.

Caleb didn't listen. He waited. He held no favor in Cassius' eyes and he didn't care. What irked him though, was even when the truth was staring some people in the eyes, most will still refuse to believe it.

If he doesn't believe, death is still on the table.

Cassius turned his head, taking his eyes off Caleb to look at Tristan. He inspected Tristan's face for a few minutes before turning his attention to Perkins. "What do you want from me?"

Cassius placed his open hand over the folder Perkins slid across the table to him. It took a great deal of effort to keep his attention on Perkins' words and not on Caleb. He surmised that Caleb wasn't responsible for Vivian's death some time ago. That didn't mean he was ok with them breaking bread together.

He raised his eyes from the closed folder, thinking of the last few words of Perkins' as they replayed in his head. "You say a bullet and poison were linked Zuri?"

"Yes," Perkins said. "He was behind Tristan's attack and Evie's death." He lowered his eyes for a moment before looking up again.

Cassius knew how Perkins felt about the Bogdon sisters. He knew how the man felt about Evelyn, even if Perkins didn't want to admit it. Her opposition for The Four was a nuisance but her death was a great loss.

"I'm sorry for your loss," Cassius told Perkins.

Perkins shook his head. "It can't be in vain. We need to bring down whoever is running this shit show."

Sighing, Cassius turned his gaze on Caleb. "Let's say that I believe *he* didn't kill Vivian, that I was wrong," he sneered, "why would I ally myself with this murderer?"

"If it soothes your Coesen ego, we can pretend that you are the leader." Caleb offered a plastic smile.

"Hasa, please," Tristan said dismissively as he patted the air.

Hasa?

"Look, Cassius," Tristan started, "Caleb has Cianne's best interest at heart. I know for a fact that he doesn't want to hurt anyone who isn't a threat to his family. He isn't proud of the things in his past, but I fear that the Coesen will have no future if he doesn't help."

"...and *he's* gonna help. In fact, *he's* already helped by killing the woman who killed Vivian," Caleb chimed in.

Cassius looked over at Tristan. He heard Tristan's words. He even heard Caleb's arrogant response. But he was still reeling over the title Tristan didn't seem to realize he gave Caleb. From the fleeting flicker of confusion on Caleb's face, Cassius knew the murderer heard and understood the term. *Hasa* was a Coesen title of respect, used for someone who is a paternal protector, or progenitor.

"What do you have on Zuri Castor?" Perkins asked.

When Cassius just stared at him, Perkins sighed.

"We're not asking you to do something you're not comfortable with. As of today, Tristan is no longer in hiding.

He just wants to talk to the Sovereign before going completely public." Perkins tapped the table. "It will take us longer to connect the dots, to know who wants him dead, but we will connect them."

"Then you don't need me." Cassius shifted to move.

"Just look at what we have." Perkins tapped the top of the folder that still sat in front of Cassius, unopened.

Scrubbing a hand over his face, Cassius closed his eyes. When he opened his eyes, the scene was the same. "Fine," he grunted out. He opened the folder. The first thing he saw was a plastic bag with an oddly shaped bullet. He held it up.

This was used on Tristan?

Cassius placed the plastic bag down, knowing he wouldn't be allowed to take it with him to give it to Jamiah for analyses.

"Take it," Caleb said, "I know all I need to know about it."

Cassius frowned, but clenched the protected bullet in his hand then slid it into his breast pocket. He looked at a drawing that was placed in the folder.

"Alicia Reynolds was an amateur artist, though her work was impressive. I retrieved these from a waitress she befriended at the diner beneath her apartment."

Cassius flipped through the images of scenery, nature, and people. None held any significance, as far as he could tell. He needed to decide if he was going to break Coesen law and share what he knew.

Cassius heard Caleb sigh. His impatience was almost tangible.

"Tristan is still your Sovereign's mate," Caleb reminded him. "By Coesen law, that makes him your ruling Potentate."

Cassius and Caleb stared at each other. Each second that passed was one of indecision for Cassius. He wanted to solve this, to protect Vivian's heir, Tristan, the twins. But as a Quende, how could he justify working with "The Boogie Man"?

"*I don't think we need you but they want you as an ally. To be honest, I can just pluck the information from your tiny little brain but I'm trying to be respectful...for Cianne and Tristan.*"

Cassius frowned, hearing the voice inside his head.

"*Know, I want what you want,*" Caleb transferred. "*nothing more.*"

Cassius sat up straight. "Stay the hell out of my head," he warned as he tried to shake the feeling of being disjointed. After a few seconds, Cassius looked over at Tristan and bowed his head. "Jamiah discovered that Zuri employed a scientist, George Kent, to possibly make Death's Door. The Kent's and their two small children were found in their home after his mother asked for a welfare check. It was made to look like a murder-suicide but there was a strong trace of a Wheddler inside their home."

"The same Wheddler who sent Alicia Reynolds, I bet." Perkins reached across the table and tapped one of the drawings.

"There is also..." Cassius let his words die away. He didn't think the murders of the women resembling Cianne were related to this Zuri, but if they weren't then that meant the Evil One was back. They would need...

"*The Evil One?*" Caleb raised a brow.

Dismissing Caleb, Cassius said, "Middling women who resemble the Sovereign are popping up dead. Never the same city or state so the Middling authorities haven't connected them yet but we believe the killings are being carried out by a Coesen. Jamiah made the connection and is investigating."

Tristan tensed beside him but didn't speak.

"Could be some sick admirer," Perkins announced. "She's bound to have a few."

Cassius turned another page in the folder. He was about to turn the page again when he looked at the image. "Yeah," Cassius agreed as everything around him faded away. He gawked at the lines, shades, and shapes on the white paper. It was a drawing of a skyline view from a rooftop, window, or balcony, that looked familiar. Yet, he couldn't place it.

"You know this place?" Tristan moved closer then peered down at the drawing.

"I... I don't know." Cassius furrowed his brows as he picked at his exceptional memory. He looked up after a few seconds of fruitless pursuit. "So, what's next? The union between the Sovereign and Whodai Tam must not proceed."

"*He* *doesn't need to know the details or the plan concerning Cianne just yet,*" Caleb transferred to Tristan and Perkins only.

Tristan tried to relax and not let on how hearing Whodai's name irritated him. He tapped the tabletop a few times. "I'm going to her." Tristan dug the burner cell out of his pocket. He waved his hand to indicate all of them. "We stay connected. We share information. We work as a team to weed out the Dregs." Tristan slid out of the booth and stood.

Cassius took one last look at the sketch then eased out of the booth. He performed a subtle head bow then extended his arm and said, "It's nice to know you are still with us."

Tristan extended his arm, gripping the inside of Cassius' upper arm, and leaned forward and touched foreheads. The embrace was as intimate as a hug. "Thank you, Cassius."

Cassius backed away from Tristan, pivoted to get the burner cell, then regarded Perkins and Caleb. He nodded to Perkins. When he looked at Caleb, he felt he needed to...he wasn't certain. They weren't friends, but the man saved Tristan's life, killed Vivian's attacker, and was helping to secure Cianne's rule. It seemed they were in a truce.

Caleb quirked a brow.

"Take it," Perkins said as he tore the sketch out of the book.

Cassius bowed his head but kept his eyes on Caleb's. He hurried out of the bar with one thing on his mind. The damn sketch he held in his hand.

Caleb leaned against the table in the hotel room, glaring out of the large picture window. He melted into the background and inside his thoughts while Tristan, Perkins, and a worse-for-wear Langley discussed the meeting with Cassius. The plan, the possible outcomes, and how to adjust if things went south, were on his mind.

"So, what do you think?" Perkins asked from a few feet away, where he, Langley, and Tristan sat.

"The more players on our side, the better," Langley said.

Caleb felt a wave of vibrations in the room. He looked to Perkins, who was shifting in his seat.

"Sides," Perkins said, "are we choosing sides?"

"If the visit with Cianne doesn't go well, we will be basically storming the castle." Langley shrugged, then added, "With her being controlled, even slightly, she is our greatest threat right now. One we need to handle delicately. We don't need added opposition."

Tick tock, tick tock, tick... The voice in Caleb's head sang out.

That Pythos was aware infuriated Caleb. "*Leave me be.*"

I've learned so much, sitting here in the darkness of your mind, Caleb. I know what you know, feel what you feel. I've enjoyed...what is the term...sex. It is something I've never experienced before. I should thank you. You should be thanking me as well.

"*Thank you for what? Taking over my body to kill innocent people, children? Oh, for giving the Coesen reason to hunt me, which only gained death for those who were brave enough.*"

Laughter sounded in Caleb's head.

Don't forget, Caleb. You volunteered, for your precious revenge. You welcomed me. You were and always will be a natural born killer, embrace it. How do you think I was able to merge with you? You had the Right Stuff. Now, do us both a favor and fade into the background so that I can finish what I started. I promise, when I'm done, I'll give you the death you've wanted all those years ago.

"Never," Caleb hissed with disgust.

"Caleb?"

A rush of sounds, vibrations, and colors hit Caleb all at once. All the stimulation he worked so hard over his long life to effortlessly mute, overpowered him.

Caleb managed to keep his surprise silent but he closed his eyes. He was aware of the unfamiliar coil of his body, the strain of his muscles. He took a labored breath. With a slight shake of his head, he gained control of himself and the abilities he wielded.

Easing his muscles into his usual relaxed state and erasing the scowl he knew was on his face might have seemed instant to an observer, but it took an instant too long for Caleb. When he opened his eyes, he sought out Tristan, who sat beside Perkins on the sofa a few feet away.

"We need to go," Caleb announced as he pried his hands from the damaged table beneath them.

"Now?" The color drained from Langley's face. He pursed his lips to say something else when the sound of a ringing phone distracted him. Langley looked to his breast pocket then reached inside and pulled out his cell.

Caleb blocked out everything in the room, feeling as if his abilities were new and untried. He focused on Tristan, reading his lips.

Tristan stood. "Is something wrong?"

Caleb watched as Tristan's eyes fell on the damaged table then moved to his face. He also knew from the subtle shift in Tristan's posture that he knew something was wrong.

"*There's a red ring around your eyes*," Tristan transferred. "*Can you mask it*?"

Caleb focused on the strength that carried him through his long life, then pushed at it. The effect was a burst of heat that radiated from him in a wave much like heat rising from concrete on a blistering hot day. He couldn't ease the anger inside him, which he suspected was how Pythos was able to gain the minuscule amount of control that resulted in the overload. What he could do was pinpoint the ability that allowed him to mimic appearances, and use it to hide the red rings around his irises.

Tristan nodded as he moved forward.

Caleb opened his senses, effectively blocking what he didn't want filtering through. He felt warmth on his shoulder from Tristan's hand. He bit down on a flittering sense of anxiety when Perkins placed a hand on his other shoulder.

Hearing only what he chose, Caleb pinned Langley with a questioning stare.

A shade redder, Langley held his phone away from his ear and pressed the mute button. "I uh, it seems I have a sudden unavoidable appointment." He moved to hit the button to unmute the cell when he added, "I think I will fly back."

Hell, Caleb hated teleporting too. If there was a faster way to traverse the globe in the current situation, he would. As it stood, teleporting was the fastest way to travel. Caleb nodded his understanding then teleported with his passengers.

Chapter Nineteen

Maiden Hall
June 6ᵗʰ

Tristan stood in front of the bathroom mirror, staring at his reflection. His back was straight, his hands were loose at his sides, and his face was unchanged. He glared into the reflection of his blue eyes, attempting to look beneath the surface.

"I am the same man who worshipped her from the first moment I saw her. The man who was desperate to kiss her on our first date. I am the man who did and will die to protect her."

I am that man.

Now all he needed to do was prove it to Cianne.

Sighing, Tristan closed his eyes then ran his hand from the back of his head to the front. He repeated the movement, remembering how his wife loved to touch his hair. He scrubbed his hand over his face then opened his eyes.

Tonight, was the night.

After their return to Maiden Hall two days ago, Caleb retired to the cabin. He stayed there, isolated from everyone until he teleported to get Tranae from Ark Manor.

According to Tranae, the plan went swimmingly. She was able to slip Bannerman's concoction into Cianne's water. It took a while, but she watched Cianne finish the bottle. She reported the only snag was when, for a moment she had a sudden feeling of disconnect like she was all alone. Tranae said the sensation passed just as quickly as it began and though her time with Cianne wasn't like old times, it was pleasant.

Tristan believed that the disconnect Tranae felt was connected to what happened to Caleb in D.C., but Caleb refused to talk about it. After returning Tranae to her apartment, Caleb locked himself in the cottage.

I'm up at bat.

Tristan let out a humorless chuckle.

I haven't thought of sports in so long. I haven't thought of my life before Cianne, since...Cianne. Because Cianne is my life.

Tristan gave his reflection a nod then unzipped the small case he placed beside the basin. As he lifted the syringe he heard a knock on the bathroom door. Tristan opened his senses, only noting an abnormally slow heartbeat and nothing more. That was enough to ID the person on the other side of the door.

He set the syringe on top of the remaining secured injections then walked over to the bathroom door. What stood in front of him wasn't the man he knew. Instead of a stoic warrior who dealt death, Caleb's brows were pinched, his posture limp, and one hand was in his jeans pocket and the other was running through his blonde hair.

Caleb lifted his eyes that were focused on the doorknob to look at Tristan. He slowly stood up straight, pulling his other hand free of his pocket. He was certain that he looked disheveled. Hell, he felt like shit.

He felt.

His attention fell to the leather case and the syringe that sat on the countertop behind Tristan. It was the reason he ventured out of his cave tonight. It seemed his timing was perfect.

"I know why Cianne is attacking you. Or at least, I have a theory," Caleb said. He turned away from Tristan and walked over to the other side of the large room, putting space between them. Just in case things got physical.

"Why?" Tristan asked as he followed Caleb into the bedroom.

Caleb faced Tristan. Staring into hopeful eyes never bothered him before, yet...

Hasa.

That was the word Tristan used to defend him to Cassius. The thing was, Caleb didn't think Tristan even knew he said it. It meant something.

"To save your life, Bannerman needed more than what the Coesen had available to them. He made a suggestion, and though you may want to take my head off, it's a decision I don't regret making." Caleb looked at his feet, then rolled his neck as he stood straight.

He didn't plan to retaliate. There would be no great and powerful Oz tonight. In fact, he decided that he wasn't going tap into his power until needed, in the hope that the less he used the slower Pythos would emerge.

...and Pythos *was* emerging.

...and Caleb knew there was nothing he could do to stop it.

Tristan's demeanor appeared calm as he waited. For some, that would seem less threatening but Caleb knew the boy.

"In a nut shell, those injections you take," Caleb said as he watched Tristan's body visibly deflate, "are a cocktail of Coesen science and my DNA."

Tristan just stared at him for several heartbeats then he turned around and strolled back to the bathroom without speaking a word.

"Cianne senses me when she sees you and that's why she attacks," Caleb added as he followed.

He watched as Tristan pumped his left fist then slid the tip of the needle into one of his raised veins and injected himself. With both his brows raised, Caleb just stood there in the doorway between the bedroom and the bathroom.

"Look," Tristan said as he placed the syringe back inside the bag and secured it. "I didn't want to make this awkward for you but the look on your face tells me that you might need awkward right now." Tristan looked in the mirror as he rolled his sleeve down. "I figured that little tidbit of information out at the cabin. After I fled the cabin and broke into Bannerman's lab, I confirmed it. You are the only known organism to defeat death. It was logical to use you.

"I have to say that I didn't put two and two together when it came to Ci." Tristan looked up then said, "But being as you're definitely on her shit list…yeah, that makes sense." He turned to Caleb. "Now for the awkward…and remember, you sort of pushed me to this." Tristan moved to stand in front of him. "I know how hard it must have been for you to offer your enemy any piece of yourself." Tristan placed his hand on Caleb's shoulder.

Caleb turned his head and peered at the hand on his shoulder. He felt the urge to paste a threatening look on his face in response to Tristan invading his bubble uninvited but couldn't muster it. Technically, he supposed he did ask for this.

"That you did it, Hasa, to allow me to live….to allow me more time to love your daughter and our children, that means more to me than you will ever know. I can only offer you my respect, and a promise that I will do my best to honor your gift to me."

Tristan moved in but Caleb raised his hand between them before he could get any closer to hug him. He gave Tristan a gentle push then took two steps back to put some space between them.

"Nice talk," Caleb coughed.

Tristan's light-hearted laughter filled the room. "You really need to embrace your sensitive side a bit more. Nadia is a hugger, she's going to want to hug her Pop-Pop."

"So," Caleb said as he crossed the room, "how will you approach her, knowing what you know?"

Tristan bit back more laughter as he looked at Caleb from across the room. The man really did need to lighten up. "I convince her it's me. Those nanites are working on the inhibitor and I'll have to work on her mind." Tristan shrugged. "Should be interesting."

"Interesting?" Caleb raised a brow. He shook his head then said, "I'll keep a read on you, like before. If things go—"

"I'll wait for you to swoop in and save the day. You ready?"

Caleb closed the distance between them.

"You sure I can touch you now?" Tristan grinned. "Doing so may bring out your inner kitten." He spread his fingers like claws and said, "*Purr.*"

Caleb narrowed his eyes but allowed Tristan to place his hand back on his shoulder.

Langley ambled into the lobby of his East Coast law office, located in D.C. He focused on his footfalls. It was absurd that he felt he needed to look at his feet to feel stable, days after Caleb's teleportation trick. Yet, here he was, watching his feet again.

"Good evening, Mr. Langley," the Coesen said as he nodded.

Lifting his head, Langley spread his lips and nodded at the security guard posted in the lobby. When he stepped up to the elevator, he groaned before he pushed the up button. As he waited, he slid his eyes over the directory.

The building had twelve floors and almost all the businesses were Coesen-owned, though some did employ both Middlings and Coesen. Langley's office was on the ninth floor.

Nine floors, on the elevator.

Remembering there was a staircase, Langley turned away from the elevator, moved to the door marked stairs, and opened the door. Elevators shouldn't be an issue, *but just in case.*

He looked at his feet again before climbing the stairs. He absently touched the little patch behind his ear. Bannerman gave it to him for motion sickness, something he never suffered from before.

Langley reached the ninth floor with no physical discomfort. He pulled the stairway door open and stepped into the outside lobby of his law firm. He crossed the lobby, unlocked the main door, then stepped inside before locking it back.

He walked around the receptionist's desk and had a seat so that he could see through the smoked glass wall and door. Langley glanced at his watch. It was three minutes till eight p.m. The caller, one whose voice he didn't recognize, said they would arrive at eight.

"Mr. Langley."

Langley looked up and to his right when he heard the shaky voice. Raya Tam stood in the small seating area, inside the locked door of the firm. She wore a long shawl with a hood that seemed capable of covering her face completely, but the hood was far enough back for him to identify her.

He didn't show his surprise or confusion as he got to his feet and walked over to greet her.

"Ms. Tam," he said as he extended his hand. "I have to say, I wasn't expecting you."

She shook his hand. Her movements were brisk, hurried. "No," she said as she looked around him and dropped his hand.

"I'm alone," he told her. "But I think you may be more comfortable in my office. It's located at the very end of the hall." He presented the way with his extended hand as he stepped aside.

Raya raised her hand and adjusted her hood to cover her face then led the way, past the glass wall and down a long hallway to the very last door. Unlike the other offices with see-thru smoked glass walls, Langley's office was designed with a frost that gave his clients privacy.

Langley moved around Raya and wrapped his hand around the handle. He felt the knob heat up, then the lock mechanism released and he pushed the handle down. Langley opened the door for Raya and motioned for her to sit. He then closed the door.

"Can I get you something to drink or something to snack on?"

"No, thank you." Raya sat down in a chair facing his desk.

Langley noticed that she didn't relax back in the seat or even pull her hood off. Instead of sitting behind his desk, he chose to sit in the chair beside her. "What can I do for you, Raya?"

Raya looked down at her hands, causing him to glance at them too. He leaned forward and grabbed her hands in his.

"I'm looking for someone. I...," she stopped, "whatever I say here cannot be shared with anyone, right?"

"Raya, you may speak openly. What you tell me will never be used against your interest. Your frankness will help me provide you with accurate, reasonable advice."

"She's dear to me." Raya stared into his eyes, then looked down at their hands. "She's more than a friend." Pulling away, she relaxed back in the chair and pushed back her hood. "Look, I think something's happened to her. I was the one to break all contact but she... She's never dropped off my radar before."

Langley sat back. He schooled his expression. Hearing shocking things through the years meant he needed to be and look impartial. He heard just about everything under the sun but this was a shocker. Raya Tam, the heir to the Bode Tribe, was in love with a woman.

Her sexual orientation didn't matter to Langley but he was aware of the challenges she would face if it were known to others.

"Can I assume you've broken it off before?"

Raya looked at him. "You know that my situation is delicate."

Langley knew the hierarchy of the Coesen better than most. "Have you considered that she just doesn't want to be found this time?"

"I have." Raya slipped her hand under her shawl and pulled out an envelope. "That's why I am here. I've heard my mother talk of how determined, how relentless you are when you work a case. That you will never give it up until you and your clients are satisfied with the results."

Another shocker. Eldra Tam never used his legal services nor would he call her a friend.

"Will you help me?"

Langley wanted to help her. He was a sucker for love, and Raya clearly felt strongly for this woman, but was finding her friend the right thing to do? "I'm passionate about my work because I care about the clients I accept and the reasons they come to me. There is always a personal attachment. Say I do find her," Langley said, "then what? You play this up and down game with her until you take your place on the Council. You break it off again, leaving this woman in more ruin than I may find her in now."

"No," Raya said as she looked him directly in the eyes. "I'm ready to tell our world that I'm in love with her."

Langley's ability, the Sooth or Truth Seer, meant that he heard the ring of truth or the hiss of a lie when people spoke. The problem was, if the person truly believed what they said, he would hear the ring. He had to rely on his gut. That was why he was so passionate about what he did. Even with his ability, he invested in his clients, trusting that they followed through in the end.

He chose wrong before.

"I'll think it over." He stood.

Sighing, Raya stood. "Here is her information, if you decide to help me." Raya held out the envelope and Langley took it. "...and don't be too cross with your security guard. After I convinced him to let me inside, I erased his memory."

Langley raised a brow. The abilities of an intended Four are usually a well-kept secret. Either Raya trusted him explicitly or she planned to erase his memory at some point as well.

"How about you use my alternate entrance the next time." He led Raya to the large bookcase behind his desk. He placed his hand on top of a faux book. A second later, a section of the bookcase moved back then slid behind another one, exposing an elevator door. Langley bit back his newly acquired discomfort for moving things and escorted her inside, then placed his palm on the panel where buttons were normally displayed. The bookcase door slid back in place and the elevator started moving.

"Is this going sideways?"

"Yes," Langley stated as he placed his hands behind his back, using both of them to hold the envelope.

The elevator ride was smooth and the transition of moving from sideways to vertical was seamless. When they stopped, Langley placed his hand on the panel again. The elevator door opened in a small room with a closed door with no knob.

"Beyond that door," he told her, pointing to a door a few steps ahead, "is a twenty-four-hour garage I own." He reached into his breast pocket and pulled out a business card and a key chain with a single key.

Raya took the key and card. She looked at the white card, flipping it over to view the back. Only a number was displayed on both sides. No name no address.

"Use the car to take you back to your car or anywhere else you choose to go. Just leave the key inside, I'll retrieve it from wherever you leave it." He used his hand to hold the elevator door open. "In the future, when you make an appointment and want discretion, you can park here, dial the number on the card and I'll grant you access. There are no surveillance cameras here or surrounding the garage."

"Thank you, Langley."

"I'll be in touch, one way or another." Langley smiled when Raya nodded at him.

He watched her click the button on the key to unlock the sedan's door. The flashing lights on the vehicle alerted her where it was parked. She gave him a last look as she opened the door and climbed inside.

Langley waited until she pulled out of the space and the car was out of sight before he allowed the elevator door to close. As he rode the elevator back to his office, he unsealed the envelope she gave him and pulled out the contents. He moved the paper aside to look at the image.

"Damn," he whispered. Langley pulled out his cell phone. The line rang twice before the voicemail answered. He hung up and dialed another number. "Are you at Maiden Hall?"

"I am," Perkins answered.

"Tristan isn't answering. We have a problem. Or a break…depending on perspective."

"He and Caleb may have already left for Canada. Lay it on me," Perkins said.

Ark Manor

Tristan felt Cianne's presence as soon as Caleb teleported him inside her ensuite. He knew she was on the other side of the door.

"If she senses me—"

"I understand," Tristan cut Caleb off as he squeezed his shoulder.

"I won't listen in but I will need you to let me know if she attacks before she attacks."

Tristan nodded.

"If this doesn't work, I'll have to subdue her then take her and the children to the cabin before the wedding."

Tristan nodded again. He didn't want that but they had few choices. Caleb gave him one last look then teleported out of the bathroom.

Steeling himself, Tristan gripped the doorknob then turned it and opened the door. His eyes locked onto Cianne immediately. She was in front of the window with her back to him, wearing a floor length lace nightgown that displayed her body in such a tantalizing way. Her profile showed off the cut of her hair, high in the back but angled and growing longer as it flowed to a point in the front.

Tristan stepped inside the room. He knew Cianne heard when he opened the bathroom door. If not, he made certain she heard him close it. But she didn't react.

He noted that she was even more beautiful today than she was when he first saw her. But she looked different; she wasn't the innocent angel he once knew.

Or is she?

As if she heard his thoughts, Cianne tilted her head down then looked at him in such a darkly seductive way that Tristan shivered. Her lips spread but Cianne turned her head and attention back to the window. She lifted her bare arms, gripped the edges of the curtains and pulled them together.

No, his innocent angel is gone.

Right now, Tristan saw a seductive femme fatale who looked as if she knew exactly what effects she had on a man. The need to fist her sleek new hairdo and kiss her hard, harder than he ever did, made his fingers twitch.

"Is hard…" Cianne slowly spun around, "the way you like it, Tristan?"

What?

Tristan frowned but lost all reservations when she sauntered over to him. His eyes locked on to her bare feet as she moved toward him, up to the sway of her ample hips, then to the way the gown dipped in a V over her chest. He couldn't help focusing on the way the lace hugged her perfect breasts.

Cianne placed her hand on his shoulder, dragging her manicured nails down his chest then up. Tristan shivered as her hand moved up his neck to scrape over his hair just above his ear.

"You like them…" she said as she leaned in closer, "my nails? I did them just for you."

Tristan could hardly remember the color of the polish. All he could think of was her sweet breath brushing over his lips. She was so close. He missed those lips.

She was so close, all he needed to do was…

But no.

"Where is my wife?" Tristan asked as he grabbed her wrist.

Sly laughter wrapped around him like a warm blanket.

"Silly, I am your wife." Cianne turned from him and walked over to the bed. She sat and crossed her legs, exposing more smooth skin, then patted the space beside her. "Come, sit with me."

"Where is Whodai?" Tristan asked.

"He's away, cloaking himself as usual. He thinks we can't track him, see what he is up to if we wanted to." She rolled her eyes then said, "As if we cared."

Tristan stared at her for a few seconds before he walked over to her. He squatted in front of her, resting his elbows on his knees and clasping his hands together in an effort to keep them to himself. He peered into her eyes, noting that the thin red ring around the iris wasn't growing. It seemed stable.

"Are you Pythos?"

She smirked. "Oh, come on, handsome. Do I strike you as a murderous parasite? I am the product of Pythos and Caleb, but I am not my fathers." She leaned forward, grazed her lips over his, and leaned back.

Flames of desire shot through Tristan, hardening every inch of him. He fought every natural instinct to push her down on the bed and thrust inside her, rough and hard, exactly the way they both wanted it.

"Don't you want to sit?" she asked.

He just looked at her. "I'm sure you've noticed I haven't been around, so what I really want is to know more about you, Cianne."

Uncrossing her legs, she smiled. "Alright, but first off, I prefer Gemini. At least until my other half has accepted me and my needs."

"Your other half being...Cianne."

She scrunched her nose in a playful way. "She's so uptight."

"So, you're a different personality."

Sighing, she placed her hand on his shoulder. "If you want information from me, you are going to have to pay for it." She touched her finger to her lips.

Tristan narrowed his eyes but moved to his knees and leaned forward. The kiss was quick and chaste. Then he glowered at her...waiting.

"Fine. No, I am her. We are one. The Four suppressed us, bound me. What resulted is the demure frightened princess you came to know and love. But, one could argue that you fell in love the moment you saw the united us at the zoo, before the binding." She held her nails up and inspected them. "I am her abilities, her true power. The power she's fought to dim. I've been fighting for years to break free but all she does is try to hide me away.

"Caleb freed her...you...Cianne's power, the day our babies were born."

"He freed us but she keeps me locked away. She's afraid to embrace me, to accept herself for what she was meant to be.

She'd better decide soon, or Pythos will decide for her. No one wants that," she said in a matter-of-fact way.

Tristan grabbed her wrist. "What does that mean?"

Gemini grinned. Then she tapped her lips with the finger of her free hand.

Tristan leaned in for another quick kiss, but this time Gemini grabbed the back of his head with her free hand. She mashed her lips to his with surprising strength.

Fighting her hold and his own desires was a losing battle, and when she pried open his mouth with her tongue, he lost.

He let go of her wrist and slid both his hands through her hair. His kiss was infused with what felt like a lifetime of pent-up need, anger, and love.

She eased her hold when he took over.

Tasting her was all he dreamed it would be and he wanted her with every beat of his heart.

But…

Tristan fisted her hair to the point of causing her pain, held her head in place, and broke their connection. Breathing hard, he asked, "What do you mean?"

He affected her the same way she affected him. Even more so. Her breathing was labored and her breasts rose and fell as if she'd run a marathon. She offered little resistance. When she bit her lip, Tristan realized she liked him handling her. He kind of liked it too.

I need information, not sex, he told himself.

"It wants to inhabit us. It knows we are the strongest being on this planet and it wants us. It will take us if she doesn't accept me. It will take us and kill every Coesen who lives, including the children."

Tristan's anger rose and his grip tightened. He also noticed that she hissed the last part, the threat to his children. Was it because she wanted their death or to protect them?

"They are mine too," she hissed. "They are a part of me. Cianne and I are one and we love you and our kids the same. It's just…" she paused.

She took hold of Tristan's arm and applied enough pain and pressure to make him let go of her hair. She held his arm in her grasp, raising him to his feet as she rose. Tristan narrowed his eyes but didn't cry out in pain.

"When she fights me, we are weaker. We have to be one." She let go of Tristan's arm. "We are weak divided, unbeatable when synced. Understand?" she asked.

Tristan fought the urge to rub the spot where she held his arm. He nodded. "How do we do that?"

"She must accept her power, me, on her own."

"Can Caleb—"

"She will kill him. The only reason he isn't dead now— that you aren't dead because you smell just like him—is because there is something newly introduced inside of us; it is draining her. Her will is strong though, strong enough to keep me chained, mostly. But she will be herself soon. She's pushing at the boundaries of the dream-sleep I have her in now."

Tristan walked over to where Gemini stood. Facing her, he lifted his arm then gripped the back of her neck. He pressed the spot, feeling the inhibitor chip. "There is an inhibitor chip, here. We gave you something to combat it."

Tristan felt the sting before he realized she smacked his arm as she moved past him. "She doesn't, but don't you think I would know about that trinket? She ignores her full power," Gemini said pouted with a shrugged, "so she should have no power."

"You leave her vulnerable," he said through gnashed teeth as he grabbed her arm and spun her around.

"You think we are vulnerable? How cute." She snatched her arm away.

Tristan felt the atmosphere in the room change. The air felt heavy, too thick to breathe. His heart rate rose as panic set in. He couldn't move or talk.

"Even with that toy," she hissed, "we are more powerful than their juvenile plots to control us. Once she sees that she needs me, all her worries and fears will melt away and we will have everything we ever wanted."

Do I call for Caleb?

"Caleb has been trying to teleport here for the past two minutes. I won't let him in, and I am preventing Aidan from helping as well. Kids," she said wistfully. "Aren't you tired of needing them to bail you out?" She walked up to him and placed her finger on his lips, tracing them as she tilted her head. "So beautiful."

"And what do you desire?"

She rose up on her toes and kissed him on the lips. "You, silly." She backed away. "And for us to raise our children together and live happily ever after." She watched him as if waiting for something.

Let me speak, he told her.

With a raise of her brow, he was able to move his mouth.

"You can have that. Just remove the chip, leave Whodai, come with me."

"No. She needs to accept me. Until then, I am safer here. Pythos is growing stronger. I sense it. I'm not strong enough now to resist him if he breaks free of father's will. Father is weakening by the day. He won't last much longer." She sighed. "Don't you see, Pythos hates them but he fears them too. He doesn't know what reined in his terror and locked him inside Caleb after he killed so many. He fears the Coesen, unsure if it will happen again. He won't act unless he has a stronger host. That host is us. Separate me from his only fear, and it will be your demise and mine."

"Then force her to accept you. Let me try," Tristan ordered.

"You will die." She frowned. "But, you're already dying, aren't you?"

She moved so fast, Tristan didn't have time to move. She placed both her hands on either side of his head. The pressure. The pain... She was killing him.

Tristan shut his eyes as he fought back but the pain only increased. It felt as if someone was pouring hot lava over his entire body. He couldn't maintain his silence. The sane part of him hid in the back of his mind, reasoning that no one could remain silent through the attack.

He cried out until his vocal cords felt as if they were burned away.

In the darkness, he heard voices.

"Tristan, how…?"

Is that Caleb? I need to warn him.

"No, Caleb, leave me. She will kill you."

Maiden Hall

Caleb picked up the antique vase his mother bought in 1812 and threw it across the room. The shattering of it did nothing to calm him.

Somehow, Cianne managed to prevent him from entering the mansion or even transferring to Tristan. She even managed to block him from contacting Aidan.

"Fuck!" he yelled as he slammed his fist into the wall.

"What happened?" Bannerman asked.

Caleb shot him a heated look that made the doctor shrink back a few steps. Cipher chose to be silent.

"Cianne broke my connection to Tristan and blocked me from entering the Manor. He's on his own and there isn't a damn thing I can do."

Caleb tried to teleport into Ark Manor again but nothing happened. He was about to try again when he sensed a ripple in his surroundings. He sensed Tristan nearby. A loud gut-wrenching cry followed. Caleb teleported upstairs to Tristan's room. There he found Tristan on his bed, convulsing and jerking, as if in unimaginable pain.

"What the hell happened to him?" Cipher asked. He stood in the doorway.

Caleb placed his hand on Tristan's chest to keep him from falling off the bed. He needed to do something, but using his powers meant he could be opening the door wider for Pythos to escape.

"He's going to hurt himself," Bannerman said as he tried to catch his breath. He must have also run up the stairs.

Caleb sighed, then he used a small fraction of power to knock Tristan out.

Tick Tock.

Chapter Twenty

Cassius avoided the elevator and climbed the stairs with purpose, but he didn't rush up them. His memory was shot to hell but little pieces of it were filtering in. Like, he remembered a vineyard nearby but now it was replaced with shops. The area had gone through a great deal of growth since he was here last but it was the same.

He watched the place for days, waiting for someone to return for him to question, but nothing happened. He questioned a few locals and shop owners and no one seemed to know who lived in the fourth-floor flat. All anyone could agree on was that someone did, in fact, reside there.

He had his suspicions, but still, he needed to prove it to himself.

At the door, Cassius checked for any visible security. There were no visible wiring or cameras. His Protector's senses were just about gone but he strained to hear if there was anyone inside. He heard nothing but the click of the refrigerator running.

Just in case, he knocked.

Nothing.

Cassius pulled out his old-school lock-picking set and went to work on the lock. It took longer than he thought—his skills were as rusty as the guardrail on the stairs—but he eventually got the door open.

He pushed the door until the knob hit the wall with a low thud. The inside of the flat was in stark contrast to the building. Instead of old world quaint, he was faced with sparkling modernity.

Cassius stepped inside, closing the door behind him. He didn't search the place. The first thing he did was pull the sketch from his back pocket as he moved to the patio doors. He pulled back the curtain, exposing the skyline. He held up the image as he peered at the horizon.

A perfect match.

He spun around to inspect the place but noticed the wall of framed images immediately. All of them were of Cianne at various ages.

His stomach knotted as he crumpled the picture in his fist. "Whodai, you stupid son of a bitch. What have you done?"

Ark Manor
Weekly Security Briefing 6/10

Cianne used her middle finger to push the stylus away from her. She let it roll a couple times before she used her finger to roll it back toward her. She did this several more times before she looked up from her seat at the head of the table.

It felt wrong, sitting here in Vivian's seat, in Vivian's home.

Tristan built you a home. You abandoned it, Princess.

Sighing, she ignored the voice and turned her attention to Jacobi.

He came to us, you know. I think he likes me better. I don't try to kill him when I see him.

Cianne adjusted herself in the chair.

Ignore me, it doesn't matter. Doesn't change the fact that he lives. The disembodied voice laughed.

Lies, Cianne said to herself.

"We've beefed up the Glenn's security. As I mentioned when I briefed you the day after the attack, we're no closer to finding out who ordered it." Jamiah told her.

Embrace me, make us strong. We can discover the treacherous Dregans and make them suffer.

No!

"Have you discovered the identities of the men who assisted you yet?" Cianne asked.

"No, Soahn." Jamiah tapped his screen. "The home they were staying in belonged to a Cipher Shawn but we have little to no information on him, other than he is a valid resident who doesn't come home much."

The image of a man appeared on her tablet. All she could tell was he had black hair, a strong jaw, and sunglasses. Another image flashed on her screen. It was of two men.

One resembled her…

The other…

Laughter filled her head. *You know who they are.*

"Royal Chandra has reached out to give her sympathies. She's requested a meeting."

"Um, that's uh, fine, I will meet with her Tuesday of next week," Cianne said as she forced herself to look at him. "Offer the Glenn every accommodation. I'd like to visit. Maybe Friday, if you can see to the details and security."

Jamiah opened his mouth to speak but closed it. He bunched his brows together then said, "You're flying out Monday for your mating ceremony that begins that Friday, Sovereign."

Cianne lowered her head and closed her eyes. When she looked back up, she nodded. "Right. Yes, I will have to wait until after, then."

"Things will run more smoothly once everything settles," Jamiah offered.

"I think so too."

Jamiah used his stylus to tap on his tablet. "We have the matter of your personal security detail assignments. Royal

Whodai took it upon himself to choose and approve your and the children's team. I'd like to replace them. I want you to know that I am considering Oloyede and Shane. Both have requested appointment as your personal Guards."

Tristan's brothers. Jacobi, Tristan's other Maatii brother, was Royal Guard to the children.

"Oloyede's little girl, she's about the same age as Aidan and Nadia."

"I believe so, Sovereign."

The thought of one of Tristan's Maatii brothers dying while protecting her was too much. It was bad enough that Jacobi slipped in, somehow. "I will have to think it over, Jamiah. If there isn't anything else," she said, "I have somewhere to be."

Jamiah rose then lowered his head. "Of course," he said, "I just need you to give me your final approval for the Meriotia Ceremony."

Cianne stood. "I'll look it over tonight and send you my notes, Jamiah."

"Yes, Sovereign."

"Thank you," Cianne said to Jamiah as he held the door open for her.

As Cianne moved along the hallway, she moved on autopilot. The big day was fast approaching. That she kept forgetting was inexcusable.

If you want to check out again, let me take over for a few days instead of a few hours. All you have to do is fade into the background, Gemini chimed in.

Cianne ignored the voice in her head as she continued down the hallway. She still wasn't sure what happened a few days ago, when she felt so tired that she lost time. What she did know was that even though she wasn't conscious for an entire day, her doppelganger performed in her place.

No one even noticed—that was upsetting. Except for the children. Aidan was the one to tell her not to worry, that the doppelganger was as much his mom as she was. What that meant, Cianne didn't know but it was something she wasn't prepared to hear.

Nadia seemed somewhat disappointed that the double was gone. Apparently, she was fun. *Fun*? That mattered to a toddler, being fun.

Cianne touched her fingers to her temple and rubbed the spot. She really needed to talk to someone about this...alternate personality.

See, that's the thing princess, I'm here to stay. As soon as you accept that, we can be happier than we've ever been.

And what if someone makes us unhappy? We kill them?

Dead, the doppelganger scoffed. *Like that idiot who wanted to mess with our dreams. He won't be doing that again.*

What? *What idiot?*

Ask your intended, he was there. I wanted to kill him too but Aidan stopped me. He seems to think Whodai has a purpose, one we shouldn't interfere with.

Cianne suddenly stopped. Her guard gave her a questioning look but she didn't offer an explanation as she changed direction. The final fitting could wait. She needed answers.

I don't think you're ready for them, Princess. I'm tired of holding your delicate hand, but everyone else fears that too much too soon will send you over the edge where you're precariously dangling. You know, nuclear.

Hearing the sound of her double mimicking an explosion shook Cianne.

"Would you like me to adjust the temperature, Sovereign?"

Cianne stared at her Guard. The man, one she wasn't too familiar with, seemed nice. That he was the eighth one assigned to her by Whodai in the last six months was a bit annoying. As soon as she was used to one, they were reassigned. Whodai told her that it was due to him trying to find the right fit but Cianne wondered if there wasn't more to it. Maybe none of them liked her and Whodai was trying to save her feelings.

"No," Cianne said, "but I won't be needing you for the rest of the night." She left him standing in the hallway.

Her children were in their room, seeming to prefer their privacy more and more lately. Cianne turned down the hall where her and the children's bedrooms were located, noticing Jacobi wasn't outside their bedroom door. She quirked her lips as she got closer to the bedroom door.

Inside, Aidan was lying on the floor looking down at a book he seemed to be reading. As she walked into the room, he looked up at her. Then he lifted the book so she could see the title. Cianne never read the series but she was happy he found something he liked. That he was on book four, meant he liked it.

On the other side of the playroom, in the dress-up area, Nadia looked adorable wearing a flowing princess dress. She stood in front of Jacobi, who was on his knees dressed like a horse. She was feeding him an apple.

When Jacobi's eyes fell on Cianne, he jumped to his feet then bowed his head. "I thought you were Ms. Eleanor, Sovereign. She had an errand so I took over, just for a few," Jacobi explained.

"Momma!" Nadia spun around and ran for Cianne.

Cianne held in her laughter as best she could as she stared at Jacobi in full costume. "No worries," she said as she snickered. Cianne cleared her throat as she held out her arms and bent down, waiting for Nadia to reach her, but kept her smiling eyes on Jacobi.

Jacobi looked down at the full-size costume he barely fit, then looked back up at Cianne. "I'll be in the hallway if I'm needed." He rushed out of the room using his Protector speed, then closed the door.

Nadia prefers to play with Jacobi instead of Ms. Eleanor," Aidan transferred.

Cianne glanced over her shoulder to see that Aidan was sitting up and facing her. His book wasn't in his hands or near him. She turned back to Nadia, hugging her little girl to her when she jumped into her arms, then lowered herself to the floor. She placed Nadia on her lap.

Nadia raised the apple to Cianne's lips. "Eat," she ordered.

The demand was so cute, Cianne bit into the apple. "Thank you, princess. What are you playing this morning?"

"Princess pony rescue!" Nadia smiled. "Wanna play too?"

Cianne shook her head. "I'm sorry princess, but mommy has to be a real queen for a few more hours before I can play."

Nadia's face lit up with a bright smile. "Imma be queen."

Cianne tapped Nadia on the nose. "One day, yes."

Just as Cianne lowered her hand, she felt a ripple of power. It was subtle and would have gone unnoticed if she wasn't as tuned to her children as she was. She watched as Nadia turned her head to look at Aidan.

Something passed between the two, then Nadia kissed Cianne on the cheek.

"I'm hungry," Nadia announced. She climbed off Cianne then walked toward the playroom door.

Cianne watched as the door opened on its own, then closed. She wasn't certain which of the children opened the door.

Nadia did, Aidan answered.

"You know, I've never been fond of Transferring. Someone talking in my head…" she looked at him. "…always seemed a bit invasive."

I know.

Cianne smiled at Aidan. She wanted to crawl over to him and pull him into her arms but Cianne sensed he wouldn't welcome it.

I wouldn't stop you.

Cianne frowned. *But it would make you uncomfortable, Aidan.*

Aidan tilted his head. *Isn't that what love is? Dealing with the uncomfortable to make the ones you care for, happy.*

She smiled again. *How did you get so bright?*

Genetics, Aidan simply transferred.

"Well, yes, there's that," Cianne said as she giggled. When she finished laughing, she stared at Aidan for a few moments. He was so handsome, just like his father. He was a bit darker than his father as if he was of Mediterranean descent and loved the sun. His dark hair was still curly but he liked it short. His eyes…well, she wasn't certain of the real color. She suspected they changed with his mood. He was always stoic on the outside but inside…

Maybe. Nadia hasn't mentioned it and I haven't noticed. He looked pensive then transferred, *the color is like his, but…I prefer to keep them like yours, for now.*

"Oh." Cianne nodded.

I can't tell you what you want to know.

"Why not?" Cianne asked.

Aidan said nothing For a few passing moments, Cianne thought he wouldn't respond. She was about to ask him again when he spoke.

Do you love me and Nadia?

"Of course, I do, Aidan. I know things have been a bit hectic lately but I promise that everything will level out and we will have more time together."

Aidan shook his head. *Do you think we are evil, dangerous?*

Cianne frowned. No one could think them evil or dangerous. Nadia was sweet, gentle, and friendly. Aidan was a bit quiet, but he was fair, loyal, and selfless.

Some fear our power, just like you fear yours. They think we should be destroyed.

"That's never going to happen," Cianne said. "I won't allow it."

How, when you won't trust your own abilities to protect yourself? Gemini sang inside her head.

Aidan lowered his gaze. Cianne followed his line of sight to her hands that were fisted tightly. She sighed then relaxed her hands.

"You and your sister are perfect, Aidan. Just the way you are," Cianne told him. She saw Aidan shift. A half second later he was standing in front of her, leaning in, and wrapping his arms around her neck. Cianne gasped. She slowly wrapped her arms around his small body, squeezing him enough to enjoy the feel of her baby.

"Can't you see that you are perfect too, mom?" Aidan whispered in her ear.

Cianne blinked several times.

Two days later

Whodai climbed out of the car. He listened to the world around him as he adjusted his suit jacket. He walked up the stone path and through the large archway, gazing around the still landscape before moving in the direction of the single heartbeat he heard.

"Cassius? This is a bit off the beaten path, isn't it?" Whodai said as he looked up into the night sky through the open ceiling. He lowered his gaze and swept it over all the greenery. The Solarium Garden was a place he and Vivian used to enjoy together. She loved her gardens.

Cassius stepped from behind a large tree.

"Have you been to the main house, seen Cianne?" Whodai noticed that Cassius didn't move. His mentor also looked tense, like he did when he was confronting a target.

"I haven't. I wanted to speak with you first before I go to her," Cassius said.

Whodai stopped his progression, standing a couple of feet from Cassius. Sighing, he slipped his hands into his pants pockets. "Even when you're painstakingly careful; when you handle most of your plans yourself and tie up all loose ends;

there is always someone who threatens the process." He groaned again. "Call it curiosity, but what do you know?"

Cassius held out his hand.

Whodai looked at the folded paper for several seconds before he moved forward and took it out of Cassius' grasp. Unfolding the paper, Whodai took a look at it. His lips spread into a thin line.

"Tell me that I'm wrong. Tell me that you had nothing to do with Vivian's death. Tell me you knowing this woman is coincidental."

Whodai shrugged. "I don't suppose I can convince you to come over to the dark side?"

"How could you, Whodai?" Cassius demanded. "She loved you like a son and you betrayed her."

"Guess not," Whodai said as he crumbled the drawing in his hand.

It was Whodai who struck first. He backhanded his mentor then grabbed him by the neck.

Cassius grabbed Whodai's wrist and ducked under his arm, then punched his student. The uppercut was swift and solid.

...and stung like a son of a bitch, Whodai thought as he stumbled a few steps back.

"Ah," Whodai said, chuckling as he rubbed his chin, "seems you have a little juice left. It's to be expected, considering how powerful Vivian was."

"I swear you'll get a fair hearing," Cassius said.

"Well, that's considerate of you but I'll have to decline." Whodai moved forward. "I will tell you that I won't enjoy killing you. I appreciated our friendship."

Whodai smirked as Cassius stood his ground. That the old-timer faced him without fear was worthy. So, he didn't drag things out like he would if he was facing someone he didn't care for.

After a series of punishing punches that Cassius couldn't defend himself against, Whodai stood over the barely conscious man. Whodai used his speed and brute strength to overpower his opponent.

"I regret how your life will come to an end, my friend," Whodai said as he walked over to the discarded crumbled up drawing. "But, before you die, I will give you something you've been searching for." He bent and picked up the paper then returned to Cassius' side.

Squatting beside Cassius, Whodai stuffed the drawing into his mentor's mouth. **"Chew this, then swallow it."**

Whodai smiled as understanding lit in Cassius' wide eyes.

Maiden Hall

Tristan stared out over the landscape but found it difficult to focus on anything in particular. He woke with the sun and came outside with the thought that the fresh early morning air might offer calm to help him focus. He wanted the quiet; he wanted to breathe.

It didn't take him long to realize that it was pointless, yet he sat in quiet contemplation. He'd been so sure of himself, of everything. The impact of things being more complicated than he knew was damn near debilitating. He was lost.

He was so lost, he didn't acknowledge his friends when they joined him on the patio, or the curious look each of them gave him as they arrived one by one and found a seat. Tristan chose to tune out, though he heard the conversation around him.

"So, what you're saying is he's cured?" Perkins asked.

"It would seem so," Bannerman said.

Tristan felt a couple of pats on his leg. He looked at the spot on his leg then turned his head to peer at Zeta. She sat beside him, staring at Bannerman with such a hopeful look on her innocent face that he frowned. Tristan returned his gaze to the big oak and the lake.

"How?" Zeta asked Bannerman.

Tristan knew how. It was Cianne or a part of who Cianne could be if she accepted who she was. Whatever she did to him was one of the most painful experiences of his life, for about five minutes. Then Caleb came through for him again, by taking his mind to some alternate plane of existence. Some place where there was no pain. Some place that looked just like the landscape he stared out over now, but it was different. It was a dreamlike world of beauty, peace, and no pain.

No pain.

"We don't exactly know how. All we know is that she did." Bannerman took a sip of his drink.

Tristan felt another pat on his leg. This time when he looked over, Zeta was watching him. She stared into his eyes.

"You alright?" Zeta finally asked.

Tristan didn't respond at first then he said, "I'm fine, apparently."

Zeta brushed her fingers over his jaw. "You're growing it out again?"

The light touch to his overgrowth tickled so Tristan moved his head back, out of Zeta's reach. He turned his head back to the lake, but not before glancing at Caleb's bungalow that sat off in the distance.

"She knows you're alive, why did you come back? Why aren't we there? What's the plan now?" Perkins asked Tristan.

Tristan slowly turned his gaze on Perkins who was propped against the railing in front of the patio sitting area. He looked into Perkin's expectant gaze for a few seconds before turning his attention back to the lake.

"Good, you're all together," Langley said as he walked out on the deck. "We have a problem. Where's Caleb?"

"He's been hiding in his hole," Zeta offered.

"For more than a day," Cipher added. He sat in one of the many seats available. One of his legs was bent, supporting his leaning frame, while the other extended out across the stair.

"Caleb," Langley said with little inflection in his tone.

Tristan didn't react when Caleb appeared on one of the unoccupied chairs on the other side of him, but he noticed how Langley recoiled. Tristan also noticed that someone was inside the house. Zeta and Cipher seemed to notice as well.

"I have someone here who I think we need to listen to," Langley announced. When no one opposed, Langley turned to the patio doors. "Raya," he said, "will you join us please?"

Tristan frowned when he saw Raya Tam step out onto the patio deck. She appeared nothing akin to the woman he saw over a year ago. Her eyes were red and her hair was loosely plaited and hung over her shoulder.

She also didn't look anyone in the eyes. Until she noticed him. Her eyes grew wide for several seconds before she sucked in a breath then lowered her head into a bow. "Potentate, you live?"

Tristan jumped to his feet and lifted Raya into an upright stand by placing his hand on her elbow. "No need for formalities or titles here, Raya. Please…" Tristan motioned to an empty seat beside Zeta. "Sit. Would you like something to drink?"

It was Perkins who got up and went inside, presumably to get Raya a drink.

Raya stared at Tristan for several more seconds before nodding as she took a seat. "God, Whodai, does he know? Does Cianne know?"

"It's complicated," Tristan said as he sat back down.

"Yeah," Raya said. Her eyes watered over and she had to pinch her tears away.

Raya looked up to accept the water Perkins handed her; she thanked him then spared everyone a glance.

When her gaze fell on Caleb, she didn't respond the way Tristan thought she would. She displayed no fear or revulsion. Whatever feelings she held about him, she seemed too upset to care.

Langley sat beside Raya. He placed a hand on her shoulder. "Raya," he calmly said, "As I've previously stated, we've been investigating a series of events, and your situation is connected. I can't divulge some of what I've discovered due to our agreement. So, if you please…"

"I don't know where to start." Raya swallowed. "I met Lexa or Alicia Reynolds when I went to an art convention in New York. Her paintings were beautiful, and when I saw her… I was instantly drawn in." She looked down at her hands as she fidgeted with her fingers. "Our attraction to each other was intense, and a relationship soon followed." Raya looked up.

Tristan met her gaze head on, offering her a slight nod. He understood the significance of what she was sharing and wanted her to know that he held none of the prejudices the elders may, but what she had to say was more important than his assurances.

"Over the years, I've been conflicted over our relationship. I've broken it off several times. This last time was over a year ago. Since then, I've tried to locate Lexa with no success. Langley…" She looked over at Langley then over at Caleb. "…shared with me her fate. I know you did what you had to do."

Caleb nodded.

"Why would she go after Vivian? Did you ever discuss what you are, or the Coesen world with Alicia?" Bannerman asked.

Raya focused on Bannerman, shaking her head. "Never. For obvious reasons, I kept her well hidden from our world."

"Except," Langley prompted.

Raya sighed. "Except for Whodai. He knew of our relationship. But he seemed ok with it. Even helped me hide it from our mother and the rest of the Coesen world."

I knew it. Tristan balled up his fist. "He's behind it all," he hissed.

Raya's bottom lip quivered as she blinked back tears. "I can't believe he would harm her. He loved her more than anyone. More than our own mother. I came here only because

I promised Langley I would listen to what you have to say before I go to him. I know my brother would never—"

"Raya," Langley interrupted, "At any time in your life was there a moment that you felt as if you've lost minutes, maybe even hours?"

Tristan was curious about where Langley was going with the direction of his questions. Raya seemed curious as well, then Tristan noticed a sudden change in her posture and a look of awareness from her.

"I've done a bit of digging," Langley continued, "there are reports of instances when, after doing business with Whodai, people reported being disoriented and dizzy, and feel as if they've lost time. In each instance, the people I spoke with expressed to someone close to them that they were going in a different direction or looking for a different outcome before meeting with your brother, then afterward they changed their minds. To this day, these individuals cannot be swayed to change their position or minds on that particular piece of business."

"Like a Wheddler has influenced them," Bannerman said with awe, to no one in particular. "That would make his influence more potent than my own."

Raya shook her head in denial. "Everyone who manifests is taken to a Reader who has to register their ability."

"Maybe the Reader wasn't as proficient," Cipher said. He looked around the room. "I mean, he was just a kid."

Tristan knew what Cipher was thinking, what everyone was thinking. "Someone was grooming him."

"Not the Reader. He died in an unfortunate accident just hours after he read Whodai. His assistant at the time, Sofia Holloway, Castor Zuri's aunt, completed and filed the affidavit with the Coesen Ability Registration Department."

"My mother wouldn't have allowed this," Raya reasoned. "She would have protected him from—"

"Unless she is the one behind it all," Caleb said then disappeared, giving no one a chance to refute his comment.

The ringing of a cell phone drew everyone's attention to Langley. "Excuse me." Langley pulled out his phone and stood. "I have to take this."

Tristan moved his gaze around the room, focusing on each of his friends. Each face reflected an emotion he was feeling. Cipher looked somewhat annoyed. Bannerman seemed deep in thought as if trying to make sense of the information they received. Zeta's eyes were wide as if she was still in shock. Raya…well…she was still staring at the place Caleb was seated.

A short distance away, Langley spoke in a clipped tone with his back to them. When he turned to face the group, he looked confused. "Something is going down," he said as he closed the distance. He stuffed his cell in his trousers. "The ceremony has been moved up. The Sovereign and the children are en route to Homeland."

Chapter Twenty-One
The Next Day

Jamiah stood in the security room viewing the video he watched more than a dozen times as he traveled to DC, where it was recorded. Yes, he knew what he watched was genuine or looked to be, but he had to see the original for himself. He had to make sure it was authentic before presenting it to his Sovereign.

In the video Tristan, along with a man who looked like Caleb Scott, walked through the hotel lobby. Tristan actually looked up and removed his hat, giving the camera a perfect view.

"This here," the security tech said as he motioned to another screen, "is the footage from the bar."

That, Jamiah hadn't seen. He shifted, leaning over the security officer who sat in the chair and focused on one of a dozen screens. "Can you expand the image to all the screens?" Jamiah could see the video just fine with his exceptional sight but he didn't want to miss a thing.

With a few clicks of the keyboard, the security officer had the video playing as one streaming image on all the monitors.

Jamiah saw Tristan and Caleb, or men who were their exact copies, walk through the bar's doorway. When they were out of the camera's sight, the guard pulled up the next camera view. This wasn't as clear but...

"Can you zoom in more?"

301

"The video isn't that great of quality. Sorry." The guard shrugged.

In truth, Jamiah didn't need the zoom but he had to be sure. The grainy video showed two men arriving at one of the booths where two men already sat. The two men who were already seated at the booth were Cassius Ende and Ryan Perkins.

"Interesting." Jamiah straightened as he dug his cell from his pocket. "May I have a copy of this video please?"

"Sure thing," the security tech answered. "My boss says to give you whatever you need."

"Thank you," Jamiah said before stepping away. He stood just inside of the security room, a few feet away from the monitor station. He dialed his office that was located at Ark Manor.

After three rings, Jamiah frowned.

"CPA home-base, Gregory speaking."

"Howard, I'm in DC. I need to know the Sovereign's schedule for the next couple of days."

"Um," Gregory Howard started, "The Sovereign and the Royal Tam have decided to speed up the ceremony. They left for the airport a few hours ago."

"Why wasn't I informed of this?" Jamiah demanded. He noticed the security tech standing with the disk he requested. Jamiah took the offered disk then said, "Thank you" to the tech while he placed his cell receiver to his shoulder

"No problem. I'm not sure why you need to see the booth. The table and the area around it have since been cleaned, but I'll call upstairs to inform the staff you're on your way up."

Jamiah nodded, then placed his phone back to his ear. "Well?"

There was a moment of silence. "I don't know, sir. It seems that Royal Tam—"

"Has no authority until after the ceremony," Jamiah interrupted. He left the security room and headed for the elevator. "I want to know what time their flight is landing and

I want a team on the ground ready and prepared for… Never mind, I'll see to it myself."

Jamiah disconnected the call as he stepped inside the elevator. "That arrogant prick!" he yelled. He slammed his fist on the closed elevator doors. When the elevator moved, Jamiah stumbled forward.

"Dammit." Jamiah relaxed his hands. He raised his head and silently counted as the elevator rose. When the ring announced his floor, he took a breath and exhaled. As things stood, he had to deal with Whodai or resign.

But, there was the matter of Tristan. If the Sovereign's Potentate was alive, his problems with Whodai will be resolved. For a time, anyway.

With a new sense of motivation, Jamiah stepped off the elevator and headed for the bar and grill restaurant that was located in the hotel's lobby. A woman waited at the door, holding it open for him.

"Good morning," the woman greeted him with a raised brow and a side smile.

"Morning. Thank you for accommodating me."

The woman backed away, allowing him inside. She gave him a seductive grin. "No problem. Just let me know if I can help with anything else you may need."

The invitation was clear but unwanted. So Jamiah gave her a nod then went to the booth he'd seen in the video. There was nothing that stood out. No red flags.

Raising his left hand, Jamiah eased off his thin protective glove that resembled a second skin. He wiggled his fingers then placed his hand on the table. Everyone had a unique imprint, a sort of beacon of emotional energy that Jamiah could read. He didn't care for the ability but was encouraged by his parents to learn to use it.

He did.

It took a few moments to filter through the patrons who settled in this spot after his group's meeting but not long. Soon, he was tapping into the energy he was looking for.

Cassius and Perkins' emotional signatures were more familiar so he recognized them immediately, having sensed them often enough.

Caleb Scott's signature was not unfamiliar. Jamiah was brought in a few times, as one of the stronger Feelers in the Coesen, to read an object that Caleb handled in order to gauge his intent. Jamiah always reported that Caleb wanted peace but held an underlying need to destroy all Coesen. That need, a festering wound, pulsed from the table like never before. So much so, that Jamiah suddenly pulled his hand away.

Jamiah flexed his fingers and his ability, effectively rebooting himself. This time, he dismissed all other energies and focused on one. Tristan's.

Again, Jamiah easily pushed aside the random emotions of others and zoned in on Tristan, who he knew little about. Though, Jamiah knew enough to recognize Tristan's unique signature.

The moment he felt it, Jamiah sighed. The video can be questioned but his gift was irrefutable. Tristan Bertram was alive.

Caleb maintained a partially visible form as he appeared on the grounds of Ark Manor beside an abandoned building. No one on the property could sense him in this state unless they happened to be some sort of gifted empath. Jamiah, the one empath who may sense a foreign presence, wasn't on the property.

As Caleb moved through the dirty window of the garden solarium, he maintained his ghostly form. He glanced around, remembering that this was once a lush and vibrant garden. His feet weren't solid so there were no crunching sounds as he went further into the barren and desolate structure.

It seems little attention is spent on keeping the area up since Vivian's death.

Even in his noncorporeal state, Caleb's senses were active, heightened. The scent of death circulated around him, mixed with a familiar scent of a man. A man who would never hunt him again.

He focused, and within the matter of a second, the location of the body was known to him.

Caleb continued forward, summoning his solid form from Maiden Hall and making himself whole. He noticed the disturbed dirt and rotted plants that were strewn all over the marble floor as he zoned in on a shoe.

When Caleb squatted beside the body that was partially hidden under dried foliage, he took out the cell phone he carried regularly now and pressed his finger on the number two and held it down.

"Perkins is saying the tracker hasn't moved. Did you find anything?"

Caleb used his free hand to move some of the debris that was placed over the body. He knew exactly who it was but...

Did it matter if he softened the blow for Tristan or not? Death was death.

"I've found Cassius' body."

He waited for Tristan's response but the line went completely silent. Caleb didn't even hear Tristan breathing.

"Tristan?"

"I'm here," Tristan said. His tone was low and his voice cracked. "Can..." he cleared his throat, "can you bring him here?"

Coesen Territory, Homeland
Continent of Africa

Cianne reached for Aidan's hand and waited for him to grab it as she looked around the grand hall. Nadia, whose hand Cianne already held, hopped up and down with excitement and squealed as she looked around with wide eyes. Smiling at her daughter's excitement, Cianne turned her attention back to Aidan, who still hadn't taken her hand.

"Is there something wrong, Aidan?" Cianne asked.

Aidan regarded her then said, "Somewhere, something is always wrong." He then slipped his hand into hers as he raised his eyes to look into hers.

Cianne held his gaze. *What is going on in his little head,* she wondered.

Aidan raised his brow.

"I wouldn't pry, Aidan," Cianne assured her son.

Sometimes it is necessary, Gemini chimed.

"...sometimes," Aidan added.

Cianne blinked. Aidan heard Gemini? She was about to ask when Nadia tugged on her hand.

"Whodai," Nadia called out.

Cianne looked up. Her eyes fell on Whodai almost immediately. He stood out, even here surrounded by all this immense beauty. The people, men, and women of various shades, were all strikingly beautiful.

This room, one in the palatial complex used by Royals, was one of luxury and wealth. But in this place, Cianne felt more like a stranger than a Sovereign.

Whodai's look of open adoration and his sultry grin as he watched her approach made Cianne's face heat. Each person in the small crowd he was addressing turned their heads toward her and the children. Her nature wasn't to live in the spotlight but here she was, the center of this confusing world.

Curiosity and excitement covered each of the onlookers' faces.

Aww, they want to see the Mad Queen, Gemini taunted. *All those beautiful smiles. Don't you want to know what they really think of you?*

As if it would change anything.

Cianne paused, not wanting to interrupt Whodai, but he waved her to him. Reluctant, she stepped up to him and the small group he addressed.

"Everyone, I'd like you to meet your Sovereign and my mate, Cianne Bertram," Whodai announced as he touched the small of her back. "Cianne, this is Webster and some of his team who will be in charge of security."

Cianne glanced over and gave them a nod but focused her attention back to Whodai. She tried to keep the frown of confusion off her face when she asked, "Can I speak with you for a moment?"

"Sure," Whodai told her. Then he looked to the group. "Excuse me for a moment, please." Whodai swooped down and lifted Nadia in his arms, spun her around, then took Cianne's hand and led them toward the closest set of double doors.

Nadia's laughter eased Cianne's worry a bit but not for long.

Cianne appreciated Whodai's slow pace. It allowed for Aidan to walk on his own.

They entered the room through the door that Whodai held open. He waited for her and Aidan to walk inside the room before he entered and closed the door.

When she turned around to face him, she witnessed another sweet moment between Nadia and Whodai. They were playing blowing their cheeks up, then blowing out the gathered air at one another.

So, cute. Too bad he isn't going to get what he wants. Gemini sneered.

Cianne let out an internal sigh. Ignoring the voice was becoming harder and harder.

If you think Tristan is going to allow us to marry—

"For all that is holy, please shut up!" Cianne yelled as she squeezed her eyes closed. She let go of Aidan's hand and covered her face. *Go away. He's gone. So, please go away.*

Awareness hit her almost immediately. Cianne removed her hands and looked down at Aidan. As usual, he seemed indifferent. She relaxed some...well until she focused on Nadia who looked sad. As Cianne reached for Nadia, she glanced at Whodai. He looked at her with such love that she had to stop herself from running from the room.

Cianne sighed as she looked to Nadia. "It's fine, Nadia. I was just—"

"Trying to stop the words in your head," Nadia cut her off. "It's ok."

"Do you hear words in your head, Nadia?" Cianne tried to sound calm but her tone was high and full of fear.

Nadia didn't answer right away. Instead, she looked down at Aidan. Cianne sensed some unspoken communication from the two, yet waited to see how Nadia would respond.

A slight wiggle from her daughter let Cianne know she wanted down. She lowered Nadia to the floor beside her brother. Nadia smiled but it was Aidan who spoke.

"We only hear the other you sometimes. Nadia wants to look at the flowers," Aidan said then looked over at the flowers that lined the far wall.

Cianne didn't notice them when she entered the room. She nodded then rubbed her temple. The kids' footfalls, amplified in the quiet room, settled the throbbing of her head enough to address Whodai.

"I apologize for the outburst. I…I'm working through something that I don't want to discuss."

"No judgment." Whodai moved closer. "I understand." He took hold of her hand. "But know I am here if you need to talk, **I want you to talk to me**."

Cianne's headache pulsed, but through the pain, she made out Whodai's words. She didn't deserve him, his adoration.

We deserve more, Gemini said. *He's coming back to us.*

Cianne stiffened. She pulled her hand out of Whodai's grasp and took a step back. "I think I need to…" She looked over at the children. "…rest for a while."

"I thought you wanted to discuss something?" Whodai took a step toward her.

Cianne took another step back. "I did, but I can't right now." She turned to Aidan who was approaching. "Aidan," she pleaded with shame in her voice.

When Aidan motioned for her hand, Cianne shamefully took his. In the blink of an eye, she, Aidan, and Nadia were in her suite.

"Thank you," she said to Aidan, who was already transporting him and Nadia to their shared suite beside hers.

Cianne flipped off her shoes then flopped on the bed. Forgotten were her worries of having another security detail, more people she didn't know and didn't have time to build trust in. She worried about her upcoming Gathering, the first day of the Meriotia ceremony, and her splitting headache.

Cianne felt like she was losing her mind.

Accept me and be whole.

"Go away," Cianne whispered as she fell into darkness.

Whodai eased the door open and looked in on Cianne. She was laid across the bed, still dressed in her day clothing. He'd given her the entire day to rest, due to her earlier headache, handling most of the preparations for the next day himself.

"She seems exhausted."

Whodai went rigid. He closed Cianne's bedroom door then turned around. "She is strong. I have no doubt she'll recover before the Gathering." He offered his mother a practiced smile.

"Walk with me," Eldra insisted, by the tone of her voice. She started off down the hallway.

Whodai quickly caught up with his mother's pace but walked a step behind her.

"Why is it that you have brought in your own security instead of the CPA?"

Whodai bit his lip before responding. "The Coesen Protection Agency is under Captain Jamiah's command. He was not at Ark Manor and we left in a hurry, so I was unable to contact him to make the proper arrangements, Soahn."

"Am I to understand that you've moved up the Meriotia as well?"

"I…I've—," Whodai began.

"Don't stutter," Eldra clipped.

"Yes, I've decided to move up the ceremony. Tomorrow will be the Gathering."

Eldra stopped then pivoted, looking back to see him. Whodai stood erect, presenting the Royal and Soldier she raised him to be.

"With such a sudden change in the schedule, there will be some who won't be able to attend as planned. Make certain you send them our deepest sympathies."

Whodai nodded. Eldra lifted the corner of her lip in a semi grin, spun, and walked off.

He let his chest deflate of pent up air as he watched his mother walk away. Yes, he had deep sympathies to convey, at the tip of his men's blades. His mating with Cianne was going to birth a new Regime. Some of their people were going to resist, and that meant they would die.

Convert or Die, Whodai thought as he balled his hands into fists at his sides. He grinned as he walked to his suite. He smiled because Jamiah and the rest of the CPA, Royals, and common Coesen alike were going to fall in two days' time.

The Gathering

Tristan stood off to the side, away from the friends who were about to risk their lives for him. He glanced over at them: Zeta, Cipher, Langley, and Bannerman. Each of them was dressed for battle in fitted dark clothing. Langley carried guns, Cipher did too but it seemed he preferred his knives. Tristan suspected Zeta would rely on hand-to-hand combat like most Protectors. Bannerman didn't seem like a fighter but looks were deceiving, and he had a powerful ability at his disposal.

They were as ready as they were ever going to be. No one wanted to storm the castle but they had no more time and no more choices.

"Is he alright?"

Tristan heard the question even with his rock music blasting on high volume through his earbuds. He pushed one of the buds further into his ear as he glanced at Cipher and Zeta.

Zeta met his eyes for a moment then looked at Cipher. "He's fine," she answered as she bent into a stretch.

Tristan sank further against the wall. The room they were in was some kind of storage room. The only item here was a small shard that remained of the original Veilex stone. Apparently, anyone inside the room was undetectable to anyone outside of it, and it was the only place they could hide in Homeland until they were ready.

"*Guilt has no place on the battlefield,*" Caleb transferred.

Tristan looked down at his hands. They washed and wrapped Cassius' body in the tradition of the Coesen but Tristan wanted to wait to burn him, in case Cianne…

"*Cianne will want to attend his Fasen,*" Caleb assured him.

"*She might not want to. What if she knows he's dead, ordered it? What if she is right where she wants to be?*" He closed his eyes. "*What if she wants him?*"

"*He wouldn't have drugged her if that was the case.*"

Tristan didn't respond. He couldn't. His words seemed to feed his anxiety. Cianne was more powerful than any drug. Hell, most didn't work on her.

That little inhibitor is child's play. She must…

"Stop," Caleb whispered just as he appeared in front of Tristan. He gripped Tristan's shoulders and said the next words so low no one else heard, "She's lost right now. You have to convince her who she is, who you are, that's all. It's my fault, all of this. I can't fix it and I'm sorry, but you can."

Tristan stared into Caleb's eyes. Some part of him believed his father-in-law's words but another part of him…believed that his and Cianne's time was over.

"You can't be here. What if she senses you?" Zeta said from where she stood.

Caleb looked over his shoulder. "Just giving Tristan something." He looked back at Tristan, cupped Tristan's hand in his, then placed his other hand over Tristan's waiting hand before disappearing.

Chilled metal settled in Tristan's cupped hand. He opened his hand only to see the necklace he gave Cianne for her birthday. Dangling on one side of the key pendant was her promise ring. Her engagement and wedding rings were on the other side of the key.

Tristan watched the jewelry sparkle in his hand for a moment. *"Just be ready to save the kids and as many others as you can if things don't go as planned,"* he transferred.

"You aren't the only ones crashing the party. Jamiah is en route. He is on your side and has a small group of Guards with him. I suggest you wait for the fireworks from his entrance then storm in," Caleb transferred.

By the way everyone looked up, Tristan knew the message had gone out to them all. He nodded, put the necklace on, focused on his music, and waited.

The Meriotia

Cianne sat motionless, uncomfortable and very aware that she was virtually alone in the hall of about seventy VIP guests. She laughed to herself, thinking that only five of the people attending were somewhat important to her.

Beside her, to her right, Whodai sat. He looked stiff and uncomfortable. Maybe their pending nuptials were weighing on him too.

Sitting beside Whodai was his mother, Soahn Eldra Tam. She looked as elegant as ever. To Cianne's left, Brenna sat with her youthful beauty. On the other side of Brenna sat

Soahn Chandra whose classic exquisiteness hid her obvious discontent.

This was a formal affair and everyone was dressed to impress, including Cianne. The gown that was chosen for her was a lace-keyhole tie-back halter dress with a sequin bodice that sparkled under the lights. It was designed to make her feel beautiful and she did. Yet, how she appeared to these people did nothing for her confidence.

"I trust you are feeling well?" Brenna asked.

Cianne felt a hand brush over, then cover her hand. A gentle squeeze followed. Cianne flipped her hand up and closed her fingers over Brenna's. "I'm a bit nervous, I suppose."

"That's understandable. I can only imagine how I will feel when I go through my own Meriotia Ceremony."

"Do you have someone?" Cianne asked.

Brenna shook her head. "There is no one. My mother knew that I wasn't interested in being attached so she stalled the process. After her passing, Vivian, my godmother, never pushed me on the subject."

"Oh." Cianne nodded. She had no idea that Vivian was Brenna's godmother. Cianne let that information sink in, to bring up later. She was about to ask Brenna about her beliefs regarding tradition but a commotion at the hall's doors drew her attention.

One of the men from Whodai's security force rushed inside.

Cianne looked to Whodai who pushed to his feet to meet the man almost in the center of the room, beside the wall. Everyone focused on the two men as they spoke in hushed tones. Cianne frowned with concern when Whodai looked to his mother, then shook his head.

"Well." Eldra stood as she made eye contact with Whodai, "It seems there is a bit of a problem outside. I was hoping this would go much more smoothly, but I suppose that would be asking for too much." She sighed. "I ask you all to return to your quarters through the rear exits and to stay put until we have this matter under control."

Most of the guests stood up and seemed calm as they were led to a back door but Brenna and Chandra stayed at the table.

Cianne stood. She looked to Whodai who was moving through the crowd of people, making his way over to their table. She looked for the man he was speaking with but the man was lost in the crowd.

"Come," Whodai said as he took hold of her elbow, "I must get you and the children somewhere safe."

"*Are you and your sister safe?*" Cianne transferred to Aidan immediately. She sensed they were alright but she refused to rely on her senses alone.

"*Yes, Jacobi is moving us,*" Aidan responded.

"What's happening?" Chandra asked as she pushed away from the table and stood.

"We'd like to help," Brenna said.

"It isn't anything we can't handle," Whodai told them.

By the way he gripped her arm, Cianne found little confidence in his words.

The sound of metal hitting metal and what sounded like yelling reached them from outside the closed doors. With the sounds came a new sense of urgency from everyone.

Whodai led the way, pushing through the gathered guests to the back doors, and she rushed behind him, her arm still in his grasp, when a loud roar of her name stopped her in her tracks.

"Cianne!"

She knew that voice.

"I know that voice," she said as she stopped and whipped her head around to pinpoint the direction from which it came.

The Battle

Tristan saw the doors that separated him from Cianne just feet away. *Doubt has kept me from her long enough*, he told himself as he put another opponent down with a punch to the throat then pushed him out of his way.

Caleb was right. Jamiah and his team arrived in full out battle mode. It took only a word from Caleb, and Tristan and his companions were on the move to join the fight.

How Caleb knew Jamiah was en route and that there would be a fight was a mystery that Tristan would figure out later. What he did know was that the CPA wasn't guarding the festivities. The notorious Kytel were, and though some were dressed for the occasion, most were dressed in their customary blood red and black garb with hoods. That made it easier to determine who was the target.

"Tristan, GO!" Zeta yelled. She spun, kicked one man in the face, then punched another in the chest.

"We got this," Jamiah said as he dodged a knife, caught the arm that wielded it, and broke the woman's wrist.

"Zeta, the kids," Tristan said.

Zeta gave him a nod of assurance then ran off.

Caleb assured Tristan that the twins didn't need protection and that they had Jacobi, but he didn't want his kids dealing death. He trusted Zeta and Jacobi to protect them.

Tristan gave Jamiah a thankful nod then used his speed to breeze past the fray and into the hall. People were moving toward the back doors which had a small crowd around them, making it difficult to find her. But he knew she was here. He felt it.

"Cianne!" Tristan yelled out. His voice carried above the frantic chatter inside the hall and the commotion behind him. He focused on the many faces that turned to look in his direction but didn't see hers. "Cianne!"

Tristan stood unmoving. She was here. She must have heard him call her name.

"He lives," one person said.

Other people spoke the same phrase throughout the crowd. The chatter eventually hushed and the people parted.

Half of them turned to look at him, the other half focused on someone else.

On her.

Their eyes locked. Cianne's eyes grew wide then narrowed with what seemed like confusion.

Tristan stepped forward but leaned to his right when he sensed an attack from behind. The fist aimed at the side of his head missed. Tristan didn't have to attack the assailant because Jamiah ran up from behind the man and body checked him to the floor.

Several more Kytel and Guards spilled into the hall behind him, causing the remaining guests to push their way to the back-exit doors with a new sense of panic. He heard gasps and cries from them but Tristan kept his eyes on Cianne as he took another step forward.

It was Whodai who broke their staring contest. He pulled Cianne behind him. "You live?"

"Cianne," Tristan said again as he held out his hand. He took small measured steps so he wouldn't frighten her away or provoke her rage.

The familiar red haze was absent from Cianne's eyes but she didn't move toward him either. Tristan should feel some relief that he didn't spark her anger yet, but his ego was slowly deflating.

"Those are Kytel soldiers, Yarrel's men," Chandra called out. "Victor."

The summons was barely out of her mouth before Victor burst into the room and was at her side. "Protect the rightful Potentate."

Tristan fought off another attack as he watched Victor look at Whodai, then to him. Then Victor moved, flashing toward him. Tristan didn't want to kill the Protector, but he would if Victor stood in his way.

Tristan tracked Victor's movements easily as he approached. He prepared himself for the attack but it never came. Instead of Victor charging him, the man shifted at the last moment and took down another Kytel.

"Riley," Brenna summoned.

Riley called out with excitement, "Already on it. You get to safety."

Tristan had no clue where Riley or even his team were. All he saw was Cianne. He was also aware of Whodai, who still had hold of her arm yet.

Most of the civilians were already out of the hall so Tristan decided to close the distance between him and her.

Someone had other plans. A gunshot rang out.

Chapter Twenty-Two

Caleb held his breath as he waited for a response. Minutes ago, Aidan sent him a telepathic message that they were under attack and being moved.

I should be there, helping, keeping my family safe, he told himself as he paced the cottage.

You should be, Pythos hissed.

"Aidan," Caleb transferred, *"can you show me what's happening, through your eyes?"*

Aidan didn't answer with words. Instead, Caleb felt the connection between them strengthen. His vision went black, then an image, blurry at first, broke through. Caleb was able to see the scene play out through his grandson's eyes.

Jacobi, the children's guard, was locked in battle with two Kytel soldiers. The Coesen was faster and seemingly more experienced than his Kytel counterparts, using them as cutting boards. Both Kytel fell dead at the Guard's blade.

Caleb watched the kid lift one of the bodies over his shoulder and grab the other by the wrist. He then carried and dragged them out of Aidan's eyesight. He returned a few seconds later.

"Aidan," Jacobi said, "I thought I asked you to close your eyes." He didn't wait for an explanation. He just picked up

Nadia, whose eyes were closed tight. "Can I at least carry you?"

Caleb's line of sight moved, indicating Aidan agreed with a nod.

"Cool," the young Guard smiled. "You guys ever use a secret passage before?"

"Ooh," Nadia said with excitement.

Caleb stayed connected to Aidan as Jacobi sprinted down the hall with the children in his arms until they reached a corner. Before they turned the corner, Jacobi paused, then looked back down the hall they just traversed.

"Keep your eyes closed, Nadia…kay," Jacobi reminded her. "Aidan," he said as he lowered them to the floor, "*Shhh*." He placed his finger to his lips.

Caleb watched through Aidan's eyes as Jacobi stepped away to intercept whoever was following them. A few seconds passed before a figure stepped into view. Caleb relaxed as soon as he sensed who it was.

"Tristan sent me," Zeta said to Jacobi. She looked at Aidan. "Hey there, handsome."

"Tristan?" Jacobi asked, confusion evident on his face.

"I'll explain it all when we get the little people to safety. Uh, Kim…she won't be joining us." Zeta said as she glanced over her shoulder. She shrugged then smiled as she breezed past Jacobi to stand in front of Aidan. "Can I carry you, big guy?"

"You trust her, Aidan?" Jacobi asked as he moved beside them.

Caleb watched as Aidan raised his arms to Zeta.

"Cool," Jacobi said as he lifted Nadia. "Could use the company." He moved to a wall that looked like just a wall. "Open your eyes, Princess. You ready for our adventure?"

Nadia clapped her hands with excitement.

●

Tristan heard the shot before he saw and tracked the bullet with his exceptional sight. The bullet streaked toward its target, but it wasn't headed for Cianne. It was headed in the direction of Chandra and Brenna, who both lacked the speed to dodge it.

Without a thought, Tristan raced to beat the projectile. He reached the two women, launching at them over the banquet table and tackling them to the ground. A gasp came from Chandra, and Brenna grunted.

"Apologies." Tristan got to his feet and did a quick scan of both Council members. They were disheveled but looked unharmed. He looked at the wall and saw the hole the bullet left. It was exactly where Chandra was standing.

When he looked to the Kytel who fired the gun, a woman by body shape, was already cut down by Victor.

"Excuse me. ladies," Tristan said as he focused on Whodai, who stepped in front of Cianne. "Ci," he held out his hand, "we have some things to discuss."

"Who are you?" Cianne asked. Her tone was laced with suspicion.

Tristan glanced at the fighting to his right, then at Eldra—who seemed curious—before returning his gaze to Cianne. He thought of what to say and if it would be the right thing, or if it would be the very thing to set her off.

Coming up with little to nothing, he moved his hands behind his neck and unclasped her necklace with her rings secured to it and held it out to her.

"You said you'd love me forever when I gave you this necklace," Tristan told her as he moved forward. "Do you remember that day, in my bedroom? It was your eighteenth birthday."

Tristan felt a glimmer of hope when he witnessed Cianne's cheeks redden.

"You are a charlatan, a shifter of sorts. Tristan Bertram is dead," Whodai renounced. "**Leave This Place, Tristan.**"

With Whodai's last word, his name was just a whisper but Tristan heard it loud and clear. The order was followed by a rather intense itch inside Tristan's ears. He knew exactly what it was and had to roll his neck just to shake the irritation. Tristan noticed that Cianne must have felt the power of Whodai's words too because she ripped her hand from Whodai's and covered her ears.

Concerned, Tristan moved forward again but Whodai held up his arm in front of Cianne.

Standing mere inches from Whodai and his wife, Tristan chuckled as he thanked Caleb's foresight. "Seems you've been keeping secrets, Whodai. Your Royal Guard registry held no mention of you being a Wheddler. By the way, *my wife* is reacting, you're a powerful one too, but it won't work on me." He leaned to the side and said to Cianne, "Just shake it off, Buttercup."

"I knew something was off about him," Jamiah said in triumph from somewhere in the room.

"I'm a Royal, you commoner. Rules have no hold over me." Whodai laughed.

"Is that what you told Cassius right before you murdered him? That the rules don't apply to you. That killing Vivian was your right?" Tristan heard gasps all around him.

Cianne finally dropped her hands from her head and stared at Whodai's back.

Cianne was trying to wrap her head around the identity of the man in front of her when he spoke the most vicious accusations. Lies...it had to be all lies. But, she *was* affected by something strange seconds ago.

She took a step back when Whodai spun around and reached with both hands to cup her face.

"What is he talking about?" Cianne demanded. She flicked her gaze to the man who looked so much like her Tristan.

...and he called us, Buttercup, Gemini preened.

"Don't let this imposter influence you," Whodai said. "Your husband is dead."

"Another of your failures, Royal Tam," the man said, sounding sarcastic. "My friends stand with me." He glanced over his shoulder, "I doubt they'd align with an imposter."

Cianne took that moment to look around the room. Jamiah, a handful of Guards, and some familiar faces were watching her, the man, and Whodai. It was evident that they won whatever this battle was. Yet each of them was visibly on edge and they clearly waited for the man's direction.

"Come to me, Cianne. He isn't the man you think he is," the man said as he held out his hand again.

Cianne met Whodai's gaze. "Is what he said, true?"

"Cianne," Whodai said, his tone gentle as if he was speaking to a child, "Things aren't as simple as he's telling you." He glanced over his shoulder at the man then back at her. "The Bode clan ruled until Arkean took that right from us. Instead of us taking our rightful place by igniting a bloody civil war, a mating seemed easier. But even with us mated, things need to change. The Council has weakened the Coesen under Arkean rule but I can make us strong again. Bring us out in the world to be feared and respected."

"This was all so that you could rule?" Cianne frowned.

"I love you, Cianne. I've never loved anyone more. You, me, the children, we will rule the Coesen the way it should be. Our son, the one you will carry," his chest rose as he reached for her stomach, "will rule and be respected like no other king before him."

Cianne stepped away before he could touch her. "King? What son?"

Whodai's eager expression melted away. His shoulders fell somewhat as his eyes pleaded. "I know that your bloodline only has one child, a girl, but you had twins. Surely, you must know you are capable of anything. You defy all odds."

"You still haven't answered my question? Is what he said true?"

Whodai closed his eyes and took a deep breath. She was almost his. Just a matter of days and she was his. But now...

It's him...he is the architect of all my problems. He must die.

"This time," Whodai spun around, "You won't survive. I promise you that."

Tristan was secretly hoping Whodai would choose the hard way. Hell, he trained with the Devil for this moment. So, when Whodai stalked toward him, Tristan raised his brow in challenge, then hopped over the banquet table in order to put some distance between them and the others.

As he backed away, he smiled as Whodai changed direction to follow him, throwing tables and chairs out of his way.

Such dramatics.

That was the moment Tristan realized there were no cries of protest. Neither Eldra, Brenna or Chandra protested. But more than that, Cianne didn't cry out for them to stop either.

Tristan kept his eyes on an advancing Whodai as he opened his senses to the room and listened. No one moved. The only indication that they weren't alone was the sound of erratic breathing and pounding heartbeats.

Curious to know what was going on, he looked around Whodai to check on Cianne. What he saw was her writhing on the floor with her mouth opened in a silent cry, seemingly in pain. Concern had Tristan moving toward her.

The distraction was a mistake that cost him a blow to the head and a kick to the chest. Tristan catapulted across the room into a table that shattered under his weight. He got to his feet immediately, looking about the room. Everyone seemed to be in the same state Cianne was in. With narrowed eyes, he approached Whodai.

"What are you doing to her...to them?"

Whodai looked past Tristan, then over his shoulder. "Mother, I'd appreciate it if you don't harm my bride too much. I need her broken, not dead...remember."

Tristan didn't notice it before but Eldra was hidden in the shadows by the exit that most everyone else scattered through.

"You're next," he promised as he pointed to her." Then he stepped up to Whodai, ducked a strike at his face then spun from a few attacks before landing a punch to the side of Whodai's face and side.

Whodai buckled from the blows as he stumbled back.

"Still think I'm out of my element?"

Cianne blinked several times. One minute, her life was imploding right in front of her, the next... Well, she didn't know what was going to happen next. All she knew was that she was no longer in the beautifully decorated hall listening to Tristan, or the man who seemed to be Tristan, accuse Whodai of terrible things.

Now. Now she was...

Cianne looked around, realizing where she was. Fear seeped into her body, penetrating her bones like low temperatures on a freezing day. It was silent, and visibility was hindered by some smoky mist in the air but she knew exactly where she was. Why or rather, how was she in the front lobby of West Hills High, staring at the chain that was wrapped around the doors to prevent an exit, was the question?

Wanting to leave this place, she ran for the doors, hoping the chain wasn't locked. She shook it several times, the jiggle of the lock and chain ringing in her ears. Feeling defeated when she realized the chain was locked, Cianne slowly turned around. Just a few steps away, she focused on the glass trophy case.

She held her breath as she stared at what was to signify excellence and achievement. Her weakness was everything the trophy case signified. She wasn't strong, determined, a leader, or successful. The trophy case was a reminder every time she entered the building that she was a failure, and would never be normal.

Laughter?

The sound of laughter slithered out of the silence. Cianne looked closer at her reflection in the mirrored glass behind the trophies. Gemini, the red-eyed, black-veined evil that lived inside her, was staring back at her.

"Leave me alone," Cianne yelled as she moved toward the case.

Gasps and hushed voices replaced the haunting laughter.

Cianne glanced to her right then to her left. All around her, people outwardly cringed at the sight of her.

Where did they all come from?

Cianne soon realized that she wasn't just seeing Gemini in the reflection of the trophy case mirror...it was her. She covered her face with her hands, wanting to sink into herself, to disappear, but laughter now came from the crowd—it wasn't Gemini this time.

Cianne moved her hands away from her face and searched the surrounding crowd of old classmates to find the source of the chorus of laughter—though she knew before she saw them. It was coming from Brian, Tranae, and Tristan; but it was Tristan who laughed the loudest.

"Did you think that I could ever love a monster like you?" He laughed harder. "You were a notch...a frigid prude every senior wanted to fuck."

"She actually thought we were her friends," Tranae said as she bubbled over with laughter.

Cianne backed away from them. The crowd parted behind her, giving her ample room. But the people in front of her pressed in, following her.

Something flew at her from the crowd and hit her on the arm she held up to block her face. It wasn't hard but she felt it. When she looked down, she realized someone had thrown a balled-up piece of note paper at her.

Cianne continued to back away but her retreat was halted by something solid. She kept her eyes on the crowd, whose fear and revulsion seemed to have transformed into anger and hate, as she felt behind her with her hand.

A wall...she backed herself into a wall.

An object moving above her caught her eye. Cianne moved slightly to the left to avoid another ball of paper. Another ball sailed her way but she wasn't able to move in time. It hit her in the face. She was unable to block the can of cola that hit her in the head next.

The impact of the full can of cola knocked her back into the wall. The pain from it was enough to make her forget where she was. Her vision blurred and her legs wobbled. Cianne touched her head where she was hit by the can, then glared at the blood on the tips of her fingers.

Blood?

Her eyes lifted to Tristan. He looked at her with a hateful grin. She looked at his hands. He held something...a bat.

Cianne sank to the floor and covered her head with her arms.

"*You're just gonna give up, Princess?*" Gemini growled. "*Are you going to let that bitch win? Reduce us to a sniveling weakling?*"

"Go away," Cianne cried. Her tears, warm and salty, leaked into her mouth.

"*She will kill him!*" Gemini yelled. "*He is OURS...and you NEED to fight. Embrace me, EMBRACE YOUR POWER AND FIGHT OR TRISTAN DIES!*"

Cianne screamed as her ears rang from the loud words that vibrated in her head.

"She's so pathetic. Such a loser."

Cianne jerked her head up when she heard the familiar voice. She stared at the ghost from her past. Blood from her head wound burned her eyes as she narrowed them to see Bianca.

Cianne felt anger flood her senses.

Rage.

Hate.

Revenge...

Tristan swung the bat and Cianne screamed. Her voice shook the very foundation of the school. All sound and light disappeared.

Tristan fell to one knee. He gritted his teeth as an immense scalding pressure pushed down on him, but only seconds passed before the pressure was diminished. With relief, he felt the full power of being the Halo's Protector flow through him. Every muscle in his body felt like it was being charged with enough volts to power the world.

"What just happened?" Langley asked.

Tristan looked over to his friends, who still seemed a bit out of it. He wasn't certain if Langley was talking about being under Eldra's influence or if they also felt Cianne accepting her power like he did.

He looked down at Whodai, who lay at his feet, beaten and bloodied, then around the room. Everyone seemed to be coming out of whatever influence Eldra had on them.

He turned to where Cianne was. She was on her feet, staring at Eldra, and she looked, *Ethereal*. Not in the fragile sense, but in the "too perfect for this world" sense. She was actually glowing. *Glowing*, and she looked like an Angel. Her hair rose around her, reminding him of the night they made love and the frame shattered.

"Is she floating?"

Tristan glanced at Chandra, who was rubbing her head as she stared at Cianne and Eldra. He looked back at his wife. She was indeed floating.

◉

Cianne felt her power flowing, moving through her veins; and with it came an immense amount of awareness and knowledge. It was if she was on fire and being frozen at the same time. As if she was connected to every cell in the room, the world.

She felt... *Tristan.*

She took him in. When she met his gaze, her heart drummed with all the love she felt for him. He was here, safe, alive.

"You little bitch."

Cianne slowly turned her attention back to Eldra. Annoyed, she sighed.

"You think you are stronger than me. That you can ruin decades of planning, determination, and sacrifice," Eldra said, visibly incensed. "You're just like her, with that smug look of superiority."

Cianne quirked the side of her lips into a partial grin.

"Vivian thought she was so smart, so perfect!" Eldra yelled, "She stole Gaither from me. She ruined everything. Trapping her in her own mind was too good for her. She needed to pay, and so do you and your abominations for the hoops you've put my son through." Eldra whipped out a blade from her sleeve and leapt at Cianne.

"Stop," Cianne said under her breath.

Eldra froze in place. Her eyes bulged with the effort she used to try to move.

"I don't know what you're talking about, and personally I don't care. You've threatened my children. They are innocent and faultless. You, on the other hand, are a murderess and consumed with hate." Cianne tilted her head as she forced her way into Eldra's mind, breaking her weak barriers. She shivered as she combed through the hateful thoughts and memories. "You feel some small amount of guilt... Because of Raya, who came to you to tell you her most guarded secret, yet you've condemned her to a nightmare like the one you tried to lock us in."

"I will not take your life, Eldra Tam." Cianne straightened her head. "But you must be punished, so you will live in the hellish nightmares you so readily dish out."

Eldra eyes moved past Cianne. "Whodai!" Eldra screeched as her eyes widened. She reached out her hand then dropped to the floor.

Cianne looked over her shoulder. "Tristan, no!" she screamed.

Tristan felt a shift in the air around him just before Whodai jumped to his feet and swung a dagger at him. But for Tristan now, movement seemed equal to thought and just as fast. He moved just enough for the blade to miss his throat by mere milliliters then let instinct guide him.

"Tristan, no!"

Cianne's plea was too late.

Tristan had already grasped Whodai's arm that held the dagger, took control of that dagger with his free hand as he spun Whodai around and in front of him, and then buried the blade in Whodai's heart. Tristan immediately pulled the dagger free then jammed the blade in the side of Whodai's head before the last syllable left her lips.

He looked at Cianne as Whodai's body slid down and slumped to the floor. The pain he saw on her face was hard for him to bear.

...and he knew her heartbreak was for Whodai.

◉

Caleb was seated on the edge of his bed, trying to stay put, when he felt unadulterated power flow reach out to him. It was like a beacon and he knew who it was coming from. He closed his eyes in an effort to stay in control.

There's no use, Flesh-suit. This is what I've been reserving my power for, Pythos chuckled. This is goodbye, Caleb.

Caleb tried to fight Pythos as the entity overtook his mind *and* his body. The entity was much stronger than he thought and it was clear there was nothing he could do to prevent the change.

"Don't you fucking hurt…" Caleb lost consciousness.

◉

Cianne couldn't believe how bad things turned out, as she peered at Whodai's body from several feet away. Her gaze kept flickering from the corpse to Tristan, whose expression was hard and unflinching.

It seemed as if he was silently challenging her.

"Why—," Cianne started, but was interrupted by the onslaught of the aura of a familiar, yet more powerful than she remembered, trespasser.

Disheveled furniture shook as a stifling air of dread filled the room with his…*its* arrival.

When it appeared in the empty space between her and Tristan, Cianne wasn't fooled as to think it was Caleb. She saw the airy figure with its long horn-like appendages resembling those of an antelope, its narrow face with wide eyes, and its long slender body that mystically outlined her father's human form.

"You can save the speech," Cianne said, "I won't let you inside of me."

Brenna, Chandra, and the others were still in the room, which meant they were in grave danger. Cianne didn't offer a warning before she transported them to an offsite location, the same one where her children and their guardians were just arriving.

She kept Tristan with her.

"You misunderstand," Pythos said, using Caleb's voice, "your approval isn't required."

Cianne saw a shift in Tristan's stance, then he moved before she could stop him. She watched as the Entity froze Tristan in his tracks. She couldn't allow It hurt Tristan.

"You distract yourself with him," she said, keeping her eyes on It. Cianne easily removed Tristan from the Entity's mental grasp.

"*Keep out of this*," she transferred to Tristan.

"That's not Caleb," Tristan grunted as he clutched his chest. He sounded hurt but she couldn't let that distract her.

"What happens to Caleb when I destroy you?" Cianne made her way to It.

It laughed. "You are as proud as your father. He thought he could fight me too. Pity." It started toward her. "As a gift, I will tell you that he is holding on by a thread and will die when I take you."

Maybe... Cianne sought out the speck of life she sensed inside the Entity and focused on it. She focused on Caleb's energy, his memories, his heart. She gasped as all of Caleb was finally known to her.

"Caleb...Dad, can you hear me?" Her eyes burned with awareness as she felt the pain and loneliness of his long life. That she added to that pain was almost enough to break her.

"*Kill it, Baby. Don't let it in*," Caleb whispered in her mind.

"I know now," Cianne said as she continued to walk toward Evil. "I know you." It was all she could manage as tears fell from her red eyes. Red eyes from the full power she openly embraced.

"*Don't you dare cry. I have lived long and loved well. It's time for me to rest*," Caleb said, "*Pythos has activated a beacon...you know what you must do.*"

Cianne hiccupped as she wiped her tears with the back of her hand just as she reached out with the other and took Caleb's body by the neck. She easily ignored Pythos' attempts to break into her consciousness.

"Wait...no!" Pythos whined, panic in his/Caleb's voice, "you can't be this strong!"

"Surprise," she sobbed, "I'm the Halo. I am more than you could ever be."

Cianne knew that by choking the life out of Pythos, Caleb would suffer as well, but there was no other way. With the death of its host, the entity's consciousness would die as well, leaving only its power behind. She knew that It had to die slowly so that she could absorb all traces of its power or she would risk some part of It of surviving to find another host.

"No!" Tristan cried out.

Cianne didn't see him move, but somehow, he was there, trying to pry Caleb from her grasp.

"You don't understand. He was trying to help us. Don't do this," Tristan begged. "Don't...don't do this to me."

Cianne closed her eyes as Tristan's strained cries filled the room. But she couldn't let him or her own feelings get to her. She didn't have the time to explain everything to Tristan. If Pythos lived, everything she cared about will die. Caleb fought against that happening, and she refused to dishonor the sacrifices he made.

So, Cianne opened her eyes with a new resolve...and squeezed.

"Don't do this," Tristan begged again.

Cianne ignored his pleas.

"Please," he choked out, once he realized he was unable to match her strength.

Tristan caught Caleb's limp body in his arms when Cianne released him. He used his own body as a shield, covering Caleb's, as he lowered it to the floor. He listened for breath, and when he heard none, he tilted Caleb's head back, pinched his nose, then covered his mouth and pushed his own air inside Caleb's mouth.

"Tristan," Cianne said.

Tristan glanced at her over his shoulder then turned his attention back to the lifeless body of his friend. "He is my friend," he said as he blinked out his streaming tears. He started chest compressions.

"Pythos—" Cianne began.

"You can save him," Tristan cut her off. He looked over his shoulder as he continued to try to start Caleb's heart. "I know you can."

"No," she said.

Her words were said with such a finality that they fueled Tristan's movements. He looked down at his friend's face...his father. "Please Hasa," he encouraged, "you're the strongest man I know."

Tristan was just about to switch back to CPR when Caleb's lips spread into a smile.

"No...you are, son," Caleb breathed before his head fell to the side.

Tristan sat back on his heels, frozen. He sat there like that for what felt like forever before he snapped out of it and started CPR anew.

"He's gone, Tristan."

Tristan felt Cianne's hand on his shoulder. He swung, smacking it away. "Leave us," he demanded. He couldn't look at her. She...she killed him. "You killed him!" he yelled.

He was relieved when Cianne disappeared without saying a word. He might have said something he would regret later.

Empty, he just stared at Caleb's body.

He didn't know what to say... He didn't know what to do.

Caleb had all the answers. Caleb made the plans. Now...now he was on his own and things were never going to be the same.

Tristan sighed as he got to his feet. He turned to face the doorway, wondering what to do next. He stared at the exit for a long time before he realized he had to bury his friend...his father. When he looked back at Caleb's body, it was gone.

Chapter Twenty-Three
A month later

Tristan looked at the wedding band on his finger. He blinked as it reflected the sunlight and sparkled. Fisting his hand, he pushed his car door open, deciding that two hours was long enough to sit in her driveway.

He took his time as he walked to the mansion. There was no need to flash. Actually, there was no need for his Protector abilities at all. When Cianne accepted all of her power, they both got a massive upgrade. Though, if they wanted to fit into both the Coesen and Middling worlds, they both had to greatly mute their abilities.

His new, or rather, old life didn't need him to be a Hybrid Soldier so he tuned his abilities to Middling levels, and lived as one for the past month.

Memories of better days, time spent training with Cassius, his talks with Vivian, and memories of when Cianne loved him, moved through Tristan's mind as he lifted his hand to knock on the door.

Before he connected his fist to the door, it was pulled open.

Tristan took a step back when he saw her.

Cianne. It seemed she was allowing her hair to grow out. The sadness that reflected in her eyes the past few weeks had dimmed some. Her skin glowed with health.

She looked just fine without him.

"I didn't expect you for another hour," Cianne smiled.

If she didn't hear his car pull up, that meant her abilities were tuned way down as well.

"I can come back later," Tristan offered. He started to turn around but she stepped back and held the door open for him to enter.

"No need. It's just that the kids and Jacobi are visiting with grandma-ma Chandra. They aren't due to return for another hour."

Tristan walked inside then turned to face her. "I don't want to be a bother."

She closed the door then leaned into it. "Honestly," Cianne said as she pushed off the door, "it's no bother. I was just going to make a late lunch then take a shower." She walked past him, heading in the direction of the kitchen. "Have you eaten lunch yet?"

Tristan rubbed his hand over his head. This would be his first time alone with her since he encountered her alternate that night at Ark Manor. Bannerman told him that Gemini was long gone since Cianne became whole. They were now one.

Tristan wiped the direction his thoughts were headed from his mind and followed his estranged wife through the first floor. He could eat. Especially being as he didn't eat often enough.

"How's the whole 'back from the dead' thing working out?" Cianne entered the kitchen. She went to the sink and pumped soap into her hands.

Tristan followed her inside the kitchen but didn't take a seat. "Dad has been a great help. I see you're back to running." When she looked over her shoulder at him with furrowed brows, he motioned to her outfit.

Cianne looked down at herself. "Oh," she said as she giggled, "yeah." She shook her head as she tossed the used paper towel in the trash. "I'm using the gym here. I haven't run outside in a long time. I've been trying to get back to the basics, you know."

"You've never been basic, Ci."

He and Cianne locked eyes. They stared at each other for several heartbeats, and all the while, Tristan tried to remind himself not to move. That he can't touch her.

Cianne cleared her throat then turned to the refrigerator and opened it. "Raya is recovering well. She'll be back to herself soon."

"That's great," Tristan smiled. He wasn't quite sure how Raya felt about him since he killed her brother but he was genuinely happy she was recovering well. He put Raya out of his mind and focused on Cianne. The angle at which she stood blocked his view briefly, giving him enough time to think of what to say next. "How are you settling in here?"

Cianne glanced over at him. She got a faraway look in her eyes then turned back to the refrigerator. She rummaged inside then pulled out a few food containers and placed them on the counter. "I used to love visiting Vivian here. Having Cassius make us his famous lasagna..." She looked up at him. "It's not home but Langley said we can stay as long as we like."

Tristan slid his hands into his front pockets and looked down. He focused on his shoes and took a deep breath.

Don't say it. Don't you dare say it...

"You...you can always come home."

Shit, you idiot. You said it.

Silence met his offer.

Now...she's gone silent. Great.

"I mean...I meant..." he stuttered, "if you want." Tristan looked up slowly. "I did build the house for you. I don't *have* to be there, unless..." The last word died out as he stared at his wife.

Cianne was staring at him, her eyes seemed to be...full of hope.

"I mean—"

"I would, if you wanted me to," Cianne cut him off. She placed her hands on the counter and leaned forward. "If you wanted me, again."

"Ci, I've never stopped wanting you. I will always want you."

In the blink of an eye, she was in front of him, inches away.

"You, still want me?"

"Always," he admitted. "The question is, do you want me?"

"Always," Cianne said, staring unblinkingly at him. She lifted her hand up, showing him that her wedding set was once again on her finger.

How did he not notice that?

"Even after I...Whodai?" he stumbled out words that made little sense. In all honesty, he was so nervous he was surprised he was even breathing.

"Tristan," she clasped her hands over his cheeks, "I never loved Whodai, but I don't believe in killing either." She must have noticed the pain he felt, reflected in his eyes.

In answer, Cianne closed her eyes and replayed for him, the events of that horrible day from her point of view. Tristan viewed the scene playing in his head in silence, feeling the same sense of dread and heartache Cianne felt on that day. Except, there was something more. He felt Cianne's pity for Whodai, anger toward Eldra, her respect and admiration for Caleb, and her never-yielding, undying love, for him.

"Always," Cianne whispered.

Tristan blinked a few times then wrapped his arms around his wife. When their lips touched, he...

He pulled away then frowned. "Do you hear that?"

Cianne looked around him and out of the window a few feet away. "There are people outside. A lot of them."

Tristan slowly turned around. He took Cianne's hand and walked to the doors that led to the outside patio. He saw droves and droves of people outside as he opened the doors, some familiar faces and some new. There were even some people he remembered from Koves Glenn.

The vast lawn was covered as far as the eye could see, and in the distance, Tristan heard horns and chaos from traffic. This was an epic gathering on Langley's Arizona estate.

Tristan felt a shift in the air. He looked over to his right in time to witness the twins' arrival, with Jacobi, Chandra, and Vincent in tow.

Vincent looked a bit green. Tristan had to hold in his amusement.

"This isn't everyone," Langley announced. "Just a few who wanted to come."

Cianne looked at the large crowd then up at three circling helicopters in the air. "A few?"

"They're not with us. I suspect they're with the local news." Brenna smiled, then shrugged. She mouthed the word, "*sorry*".

Cianne gave Tristan a questioning look. He held up his hands, "I had nothing to do with this."

"These Coesen and the rest of the Coesen Nation would like to show their respect and acceptance to their Sovereign, Potentate, and the young Royals," Langley announced with his shoulders pushed back and a smile on his face.

What happened next made a sound Tristan would never forget. Even with his "dialed-down-to-middling" hearing, the sound was extraordinary. The ground trembled as every person who attended, everyone...dropped to one knee and lowered their heads in one collective motion.

"Mommy's a Queen," Nadia squealed with awe as she tugged on his hand.

Tristan looked down at his daughter. He lifted her in his arms and kissed her nose. "She sure is Princess. My Queen," he said as he pulled Cianne to him and kissed her.

The Coesen erupted in cheers just as Tristan heard police sirens.

"I'll handle it." Perkins sighed as he stood.

Epilogue

Cianne sat on the lawn located in the backyard of her home; the home her husband built for her. In front of her sat Aidan and Nadia. They were all looking up into the bright moonlit starry sky.

"When, mommy?" Nadia asked with excitement.

"It's not a party, Dia. Stop acting like it is," Aidan scowled.

"Shut up, Aidie." Nadia stuck out her tongue and gave him a nudge with her knee.

Cianne grinned as she held her finger to her lips. "*Shhh*, or you will wake daddy."

"*Too late, Buttercup. Daddy is already awake*," Tristan transferred, from inside the house. "*What are you three up to at two a.m.?*"

"We'll be inside in just a minute, handsome," Cianne said. Their connection was re-established since she accepted her abilities but she still didn't like talking in his or others' heads.

"*Fine,*" Tristan said yawning. "*I'll make us all a snack.*"

"You're not going to tell him?" Nadia frowned. "There should be no secrets between a Queen and her King."

"What is she going to say, Nadia? That six years ago Pythos sent a signal to the mothership of a violent alien race, and that race of aliens are now on the outskirts of our solar system and is ready to attack earth, but we are going to destroy it?"

"You're a turd." Nadia pouted.

"I love you too," Aidan sneered.

"Calm down both of you, and please concentrate." Cianne sighed. "Because I don't know if my reach is long enough without you." She took hold of their hands and waited for them to take each other's. When Nadia wouldn't take Aidan's extended hand, Cianne gave her a hard look.

"Fine," Nadia grunted as she grabbed Aidan's hand.

"Ok, the sooner we're done, the sooner we get to eat our snack," Cianne said.

This is for you, Caleb. I love you, dad.

The End

Look for the Prequel to the Halo Series

Origins

Excerpt Below (Unedited)

Head on over to my website www.SheaSwainWrites.com for

Upcoming Releases,

Character Dream-casting

And sign up for my Newsletter

THANK YOU

Please consider leaving a review!

Origins

Prologue/Unedited

A whisper in the air woke Arkean but the sensation of something touching his arm caused him to move into a crouched position and had him ready to strike. The hairs on his neck stood up and his stomach buzzed with nervous energy but he saw nothing.

As far as he knew, no one was inside the cave but him and his brethren. His brethren were asleep but Arkean clearly heard someone calling out. The words were foreign but he somehow knew that whoever it was, they were calling out for help.

"Wake up," Arkean said shaking each of his companions.

Bode got to his feet, instantly ready for whatever the threat was. Quende and Gedgi were slower to wake but after a few seconds they were up on their feet and looking at Arkean with questioning eyes.

"Do you not hear that? Someone's calling for help," Arkean said.

"Are you crazed, Arkean?" Quende asked, rubbing his eyes.

Bode covered Quende's mouth with his hand, "Shhhhush, listen. I hear it too."

The others strained to hear what Arkean and apparently, Bode clearly heard. After a few quiet minutes, Gedgi jumped back.

"What was that?" Gedgi asked. His eyes were wide as he peered around the dark cave. The moon provided some light but not enough to see in every crevice and corner.

"So, you hear it?" Arkean took a step toward the darkest part of the cave where he found a small opening earlier. It was barely wide enough for him to squeeze through so he didn't think much of it at the time.

Bode used his arm to block Arkean from moving forward. "Wait," Bode whispered, "that isn't any language I know. We do not know what waits beyond that opening."

"Whatever it is, it is in pain," Arkean said, as he gently pushed his cousin's hand away. "It calls us for help. I cannot ignore a call for help from man or animal, Bode."

Heaven on Hell Island

Chapter 1/Unedited
International flight 4816
Dulles Intl. Airport
Swiss Air, Gate 23

Bleu

Bleu lifted her wide lens dark sunglasses above her eyes and glared at the two men who sat in the seats facing hers. One of them had just run off a man who looked to be of Middle Eastern descent and now they were discussing the 'problems' with the United States, rather loudly. Of course, the problem was everything and everyone else.

She didn't spare them much more than a glance and was about to focus on the magazine she just bought from the newsstand when one of them spoke to her.

"What the fuck are you looking at, Dark Meat?" The one who's head was completely shaved except for a long flop of blond hair that covered one of his eyes, asked her.

Bleu smirked as she raised her perfectly arched brow at him. They stared at each other for several seconds before she got bored, lowered her glasses, then stood. She heard Flop-Over say something about hoity-toity dark meat to his friend, a guy who clearly loved tattoos. Their laughter followed her as she found another seat closer to the loading gate. A seat that was out of earshot of Neanderthals.

Chris

"What the fuck are you looking at, Dark Meat?" Thomas asked the black woman sitting across from them.

Chris watched her with curiosity, wondering what her response would be. Why he gave a fuck, he wasn't sure. Yeah, for a darky, the chick was hot. He'd seen a good number of black women he could admit was good looking but he never felt an inkling of interest toward them.

But her... Her skin was smooth and reminded him of warmed walnuts. Her hair was sleek and black, cut short all around but it was long enough in the front that she had to sweep it to the side. Her clothing, a very white shirt and khaki long shorts, looked brand new. He was certain her medium sized stud earrings were real diamonds. Even her sunglasses looked like they cost more than his monthly rent. Her scent–*Gods probably didn't smell half as good*–was heady.

She probably has a 'Sugar Daddy'.

She raised her brow at Thomas, briefly allowing Chris to see her dark seductive eyes, then smirked. Chris couldn't help it, he laughed quietly as Thomas and the chick competed in a stare off for several seconds before she lowered her glasses and stood.

Chris watched her walk...no, stroll away. He *wanted* to watch her.

Some of them darkies pull you in, Chris. It's how they were made. To tempt the better races.

Chris closed his eyes in an attempt to purge his father's words out of his head.

"Hoity dark meat needs to be put in her place," Thomas sneered as *Her* walked away. "Don't know if I want to choke her with my hands or my cock."

"Sara will cut your shit right off," Chris responded. He sounded bored as if he had little interest in *Her*. Thomas laughed and Chris absently joined in but he continued to watch the girl.

Benjamin

Shaking his head, Ben looked back at his cell phone. He'd called Elsie four times throughout the day and her voice mail picked up instead of her.

A few Hours Later
Bleu

The plane shook violently, jostling the passengers from side to side. Several overhead compartments burst open, spilling luggage onto the passengers beneath it. Bleu glared at the Fasten Seatbelts sign that flashed above her head. She leaned out into the aisle and saw two flight attendants who were strapped into their seats. The looked they gave each other before undoing their seat belts and rushing to assist a couple who had been bombarded with the luggage, wasn't comforting.

The sheer panic expressed on their faces shocked Bleu into a silent prayer. She almost felt guilty for not going to church in over five years but that feeling passed with the next series of brutal shaking and shifts of the plane.

When the plane suddenly dipped, Bleu saw one of the attendants grab hold of a passenger. The other attendant flew up, crashed into the roof of the plane, then fell to the floor. Until now, the passengers were trying to stay calm, just as the attendant requested. But now, screams and gasps filled the cabin. No one was buying that this was just turbulence anymore.

"Carla," the attendant's voice bellowed above the screaming.

But Carla, didn't answer. She looked unconscious.

Bleu closed her eyes. Her fingers ached from the death grip she had on the armrest of her seat. Her rigid posture was the only tell that she was scared to death. Her breathing was steady and if she had a mirror she knew her face would reflect a calm expression. She'd been trained her entire life to put her best face forward, to never let anyone know what she felt or thought.

What was she thinking right now?

That she and every passenger on this plane are going to die. It was that simple. Bleu had flown a million time before so she knew that this was different. The other passengers knew it too. Oddly, she had the silliest of thought.

You don't know any of these people you're about to die with.

With her stoic mask on, Bleu couldn't help her perusal of the frightened faces of the passengers. They were all strangers and she knew nothing about them, except that she was definitely going to die among them. Bleu ignored the calls for help and the shouts to God as she looked over her shoulder to her left, at the pair across the aisle and one row behind hers.

Why she looked at the two men, she didn't know. Both had an air of danger about them but with Bleu's sheltered upbringing, the postman could seem a bit nefarious to her. She grasped on to the fact that these men weren't *complete* strangers like the others aboard the flight. Maybe that was why she chose to seek them out.

Bleu recalled the brief, albeit annoying, encounter she had with them right before boarding the airplane.

Now I'm going to die with these Neanderthals, she thought. "*Dying is dying,*" Nana's disembodied voice whispered to her. "*It makes no never mind who you travel to the pearly gates with. Just be happy you made it.*"

Nana, Bleu thought with a sigh as the noise around her increased to deafening levels.

The sound of screams, hushed prayers, and useless instructions filled the cabin of the airplane. The freak storm came about so suddenly, Bleu figured that there was nothing anyone could do. The collective fear on the plane was enough to fuel the jet but sadly it wasn't capable of saving them as lightning struck the back end.

Bleu covered her ears as a loud explosion overshadowed all other sounds around her. She held her scream in but her breathing picked up.

Is my mask still in place? Will I stay alert? Do I want to?

The Island

Bleu

The solid mass of the man didn't register as Bleu swam with him in tow. But his weight mattered now as she dragged him, backward walking through the hot sand that burned her bare feet. She ignored her aches and the burn of each heated step as she struggled to get the man to the tree-lined area just beyond the beach.

Bleu wasn't sure how long it took or how many times she fell on her ass, but she managed to get him close to where she wanted. Exhausted, she took several deep breaths as she looked over the man. Even with his dangerous appearance, he was very attractive. He had short dusty blond hair, long thick eyelashes, a strong jaw, a perfectly straight nose, and generous lips.

What a waste, she thought as she stared down at his chest. His t-shirt was ripped, exposing his body which was a work of art in form and imagery. His entire neck and both arms were covered with tattoos. Just below a design on his neck was a huge winged heart and under that, centered, was the start of a knife handle with a thick long blade that traveled down his stomach. The tip of the knife was hidden under scraps of cloth.

Bleu could appreciate the workmanship of the design, even his beautifully sculpted body was something to admire, but she narrowed her eyes at the two words that stuck out to her above all others.

White Elites.

Sighing, she started CPR. It didn't take long for him to spit out a gush of water after only a few chest compressions.

The guy was a still a bit out of it but he was breathing, so Bleu focused on looking for injuries. The one to his head looked the worst and it still bled. His leg was a bit scraped up and his hands were bloodied but only one of his fingers was twisted, definitely broken.

She ripped a piece of fabric from his torn t-shirt and took off for the beach. Bleu didn't know what the extent of her injuries were so she tried to be conscious of her movement and what hurt, as moved as fast as she could to the water.

She stopped dead in her tracks and shuddered when she noticed a large piece of metal floating in the water, forgetting any aches she felt and her task. Images from inside the crashed plane slithered through her mind. Fear and panic wrapped around her, threatening to pull her into herself.

NO…!

Bleu continued to the waters, drop to her knees at its edge, then vomited all the contents in her stomach. While she battled a bout of dry heaves, several more floating items caught her eye but she kept gaze downward. She refused to look at the plane or what was left of it, as it balanced half on the small island that sat across the water from where she was.

Bleu closed her eyes for several seconds. When she opened them, she cupped her hand, dipped them into the water, then brought it to her lips. She rinsed her mouth. Remembering what she was doing prior to her meltdown, Bleu cleaned the homemade cloth then stood and trekked it back to her patient. His eyes were still closed and considering the kind of person he seemed to be, she figured that was a good thing.

She quickly cleaned his head wound then placed the rag around it. After she was done, Bleu stood and surveyed her surroundings. This place looked like paradise, if it weren't for the whole horrendous accident. The water was clear and beautiful, the beach was covered in light brown sand, a thick lush green forest sat behind her.

Where am I and What do I have to fear here?

Those were her most immediate questions and just as she asked herself, Bleu glanced down at the guy again.

Who, other than him, do I have to fear here?

Chris

Someone was driving a spike into his damn head and that shit had to stop. Chris groaned as he pried his eyes slightly open, squinting because of the bright light. He opened his eyes a little more but a sharp pain made him close them immediately.

He took a deep breath then relaxed enough to try to make sense of the situation. The plane definitely crashed and it seemed he survived. But in what condition? He was about to test his limbs when he felt something wet and cool on his face.

"I hope you don't freak out on me. We may be the only two left." The soft spoken, female tone, said then sighed. "If you can hear me…please don't kill me."

The way she brushed the cloth over his face…it was so gentle. Chris didn't want to open his eyes so he kept them closed.

The woman continued to wipe for what he thought was a couple of minutes or so, then stopped. Chris held back a groan of frustration. He was enjoying what he felt might be his only joy before opening his eyes and seeing his mangled body. So mangled, he felt no real pain because all his pain receptors were burned away.

"I wonder what color your eyes are?"

He didn't want her to stop but when he felt a soft warm hand on his cheek, he couldn't hold in the sigh that escaped.

"Oh, God!"

Dammit, he didn't mean to scare her off. Chris opened his eyes slowly, allowing some light in. For several seconds, he tried to focus but his vision was blurry. After blinking a few times, he was able to make out shapes then objects. He was on his back, looking up at large palm trees and above them, a clear beautiful sky.

Chris tested the range of motion of his neck, moving his head to the side. That's when he saw her. *The girl, dark meat.* The one he tried so hard ignore but failed at every turn. She was a few feet away, sitting on the sand with her hand over her mouth. Fearful wide eyes stared back at him.

He wasn't sure what pissed him off more. The fact that a Lesser had touched him or that he actually liked it and didn't want her to stop. Even knowing the situation, that he just survived a damn plane crash, he didn't want her to stop touching him.

Shaking his head in disgust, Chris spread his fingers out, grounding himself in the feeling of the tiny granules slipping through them. He instantly knew it was sand as he flattened his palms then worked on pushing himself up to a sitting position. His body rebelled with his movements, screaming out that every inch of his body was sore.

"You should take it slow."

Her low, sweet, caring, tone irritated him. "Stop taking to me." His tone held a finality he hoped she heard.

Grunting, he touched his head in the spot he felt the most intense pain. When he pulled his hand away and held it out in front of him, he saw blood on his finger.

Movement to his right got his attention. The girl held out a ripped cloth that looked like… Chris looked down at his shredded t-shirt and bare chest. He narrowed his eyes then snatched the scrap of cloth from her hand. She recoiled but he didn't give a shit. She shouldn't have touched him or his cloths.

"You're welcome."

He noticed her tone was stronger and she sounded offended.

"For what?" he spat back as he looked over at her.

The girl pushed off the sand and stood. Chris gazed at her bare feet, noticing the scrapes and cuts. He then took in her long legs, her disheveled clothing, and the state of her body which also had a few cuts and bruises. Yet, none of that took away from her beauty.

I'm an idiot.

Chris looked away, toward the water and what was left of the plane. Looking at it, at the bodies and debris that floated in the water and the risky state of the crash site, he had to wonder how the hell did anyone survive.

"I don't think anyone else made it. It…it's a graveyard in there," she said, sounding sad.

Why? It didn't seem like she knew them personally. Chris didn't respond to her or say anything that would suggest he heard her.

"You know what...."

Chris turned his head to look at her only to see her stomping away. He rolled over to his knees in an effort to determine his physical condition. Feeling steady, he pushed to his feet.

"Hey. Hey there." A loud masculine voice boomed out.

Chris looked over to his left to see people walking toward him. Well, two people were struggling to carry a third person.

"Oh my god!" The girl rushed past him to get to the trio. "Are you all alright? I thought we were the only ones."

Chris rolled his eyes. He felt no urge to help. Even if they weren't alright, what the hell was he going to for them.

On all fours, Chris watched the girl reached the trio and immediately lift the legs of the man being carried. The four stopped a few feet from him, lowering the man to the shaded sand. Chris didn't recognize the three but he didn't put much effort into committing faces to memory.

He glanced at the girl but quickly focused on the newcomers.

Two men and one woman. The injured male, a mutt of some kind, was unconscious. He looked fairly young, mid to late twenties, he was thickly built, and tall. The other man, looked older, around mid to late forties. He looked white but you can't be sure these days. He wore a torn suit so he was probably some kind of businessman. The woman, who stared at Chris with barely hidden disgust and a shitload of fear, was about the same age as the businessman.

Chris wondered how long the blonde haired blue-eyed beauty would keep her shit together because by the looks of her...the fuse was short...and lit.

"Do you know if anyone else made it?" The man in the suit looked to Chris who just stared at him.

Chris raised his brow then pushed to his feet. Making certain they knew his wasn't no chump, he held in a grunt as he slowly walked toward the water. The girl had said the plane was a graveyard but he needed to see for himself. There was only one person he cared about. He had to look for Thomas. He was sure he'd survived the crash too. If anyone could survive it, Thomas did.

"I only just found him," the girl spoke up after a moment of silence. "…and he was barely…"

Chris heard her telling them she had to help him. It grated his nerves that the black bitch just told them that he needed her. Then he heard the man introducing himself…like he was at a cookout.

"Fuck," he said under his breath.

Don't you ever be indebted to anyone, lest of all those fucking lesser races, his father's angry words echoed in Chris' head.

Chris ignored them and kept walking. He pulled off his torn t-shirt and dropped it to the sand as he eyed the cool water. He heard the Suit call out to him but he dismissed the man. When Chris made it to the shoreline, he undid his boots then waded through the water until he was able to dive in. He had only one thought a he swam.

Thomas. He had to find Thomas. *Fuck them, Thomas was all that mattered.*

The waves picked up the further away from the shore he swam but Chris was a strong swimmer. When he came to the first body floating in the water, he knew instantly that the partially burned body wasn't Thomas. He passed several more bodies as he swam on.

It didn't take long to reach the plane that seemed further away than is actually was. He floated in the water and took a moment to take in the massage wreck. Only part of the plane was visible above the water as it rested precariously on the small piece island.

The craft was split in two but still connected to a large section that was beneath the water but that too was also partially visible. He couldn't see to the bottom of the watery depths because just a few feet down the clear blue water turned completely black so he didn't know how deep the water was or how much of the front of the plane was still intact.

Everyone in that section was probably gone. So, he focused on the part of the plane that rested on the island. Chris didn't know how stable this section was but it didn't really matter. With as much care as he grabbed a section of the plane and tested it by giving it a tug, gently at first then he tested his weight. When it didn't budge, pulled himself out of the water and up into the airplane.

Two things were apparent to him the moment he stepped inside. Thomas was no longer missing. His best and probably only real friend in the world was dead. The second thing that was apparent, was as much as his father had prepared Chris for death, he now realized wasn't prepared at all.

Winter's Icy Heart
A Contemporary Novella

Winter Stratton convinced herself that love was like lightning and it only struck once. She found the love of her life and lost him. Yet, even when she felt nothing romantic for the friend who helped her through hard times, a sense of obligation pressed her to give him a chance. Winter didn't expect her 'friend turned lover' might just be the death of her.

When Cord Kesso decided to step in and rescue Winter and her daughter from what looked like a bad situation during a snow storm, he felt an instant attraction to the pixie of a woman. Offering her a place to wait out the storm through the holidays was the gentlemanly thing to do. If they made a connection, even better. When Cord saw something he wanted, he went all in. Fighting Winter's doubts was one thing. Fighting for their lives…a whole other thing entirely.

Excerpt
December 20

The cab driver swerved to avoid a collision with the sedan that followed. He maneuvered the cab expertly, missed the curb on their left, but spun out in the parking lot of alone convenient store. A scream caught in Winter's throat as the cab skidded sideways across the snow-slicked road then came to a stop inches away from a bright yellow crash post. She clutched her daughter, Andrea, to her chest as she thanked God that they didn't crash.

"Get out of the cab, Winter." His harsh tone was loud and promised pain.

Winter closed her eyes and took several deep breaths. Only, there was no time to get herself together. Her eyes popped just as the passenger door of the cab was pulled open. Cold air and snow overcame the warmth inside the cab almost immediately.

"Leave us alone, Terry," Winter told him.

Terry grabbed Winter by the arm; his fingers dug into her skin as he pulled her across the leather backseat. Winter struggled to keep hold of her daughter as she was yanked out of the cab. Her foot slipped on the snow and she would have gone down but Terry jerked her arm above her head. She had to tighten her free arm around her daughter as she danced on her tiptoes to gain traction.

"Get her fucking bags out of the truck, cabbie," Terry yelled to her driver.

The cab driver looked at Winter with imploring eyes. He stood by the driver's side door with one fisted hand on the hood and the other on the door of his cab. It was clear that he wasn't sure if he should help. This wasn't his fight and Winter had no desire to involve him in her mess. No one else should have to suffer for her choices.

Winter nodded her snow-covered head to convey to the cab driver that it was alright to take her things out of the trunk. Only, the cab driver stayed in place.

"Get. Her. Shit," Terry yelled again.

Winter looked the cab driver over. He was an older gentleman with a studious demeanor about him. There was no way he could win a physical confrontation with Terry, and she hoped he knew that. She was certain he'd get hurt.

"Can you get my things out of the trunk, please?" Winter told the cab driver.

"Are you sure miss?" The man looked torn.

"She's sure," Terry answered for her.

Winter stared into Terry's hard blue eyes for several heartbeats then nodded. The cab driver went to the rear of his cab and took out her two suitcases, then Andrea's little character case and placed them next to Terry's car.

With the luggage out of the cab, Terry relaxed his hold on her. Winter tried to pull her arm free of his grasp but he squeezed tighter then gave her a threatening look before letting her arm go.

Unrestricted, Winter was able to support Andrea's small body better. She used her body to cover her daughter as best she could as she took in her surroundings. They were in front of a 24-hour convenient store that was decked out with red and green Holiday décor. The store and the parking lot were brightly lit but Winter saw no one inside. What she did see was a huge black dog that sat under the awning in front of the store's door. Dogs usually frightened Winter but Terry owned the rights to her fear these days.

"Put the kid in the car, Winter," Terry said from behind her.

Winter turned her attention back to the thorn in her side. He stood there as if he were a King and that all the world should bow to his will as snow fell over him. He picked up one of her suitcases that sat on the ground and held the back door of his car open.

If I put Andrea in that car seat, we will never be free.

The chill she felt was nothing compared to the fear that pulsed through her body. On shaky legs, Winter took a careful step back, then two more. The snow seemed to pick up the moment she made her decision. If that was a good or bad sign, she didn't know, but Winter prayed for the storm to be in her favor. Her name was Winter after all.

"I swear to God, Winter," Terry yelled, "You're pissing me the fuck off."

"Leave the lady alone," the cabbie called out. He sounded scared but he did speak up for her.

That gave Winter a bit of needed strength. She took a few more steps back when Terry whipped his head around to stare at the cabbie.

"Shut the fuck up old man, before I shut you up." Terry turned his angered attention back on her.

Winter backed away from Terry until the heel of one of her feet met the curb's edge. She kept her eyes on Terry and used her foot to feel her way onto the sidewalk that led to the door of the store. If she could just get inside, maybe the clerk had protection hidden in the store?

When she took another step back, something large stepped into her path, and effectively shielded her from Terry.

C

Cord grabbed several fruit and nut chocolate bars off of the shelf then went to the chilled drink case in the rear of the store. If he had to be snowed in for the next few days, he needed to be stocked full of his guilty pleasures.

He picked up a few liter bottles of orange cream soda before he pulled out his earbuds and made his way to the register.

"Are those for you or Onyx?" Remy, the night cashier, glanced down at the items then gave Cord a knowing grin before looking away.

Cord held out his ATM card but Remy occupied with something outside, didn't take it. "What's going on?" he asked. Cord leaned back so he could see around a display case that blocked his view. Outside, a cab and a sedan were parked at odd angles.

Cord also noticed the people whose muffled voices he now heard since he removed his ear buds. He first focused on the man who walked toward the driver's side of a cab, because the person was the one in motion. Next, his attention moved to the other male who stood beside the sedan with the driver's side and passenger door ajar. The third person looked to be a female of small stature, who held a small child. The back of the woman was all Cord could see but he did see the child's face clearly.

The child, a little girl with a round cherub face, had sad, fear filled eyes. Both, her and the woman were covered in snow. They had to be wet and cold. Why in the hell were they out in this damn storm? *Not your party, not your business,* Cord said to himself.

Though, it looked like a bad situation.

"I can't get involved but I've called the police. No telling how long it will take with all the snow," Remy said, shamefaced.

Cord figured he must have looked a little pissed because Remy felt that he had to explain himself. He didn't expect Remy to physically help. The angry looking Asshole outside doing all the yelling, it was clear he'd been in a tussle or two before.

No, Remy already did all he could.

But Cord was a different story. He wasn't on the clock and he was definitely more of a match. He smiled, shaking his head. Well, he was a *closer* match to the guy.

Cord left his stuff on the counter then headed for the door. By the time, he pushed it open he knew that the lady didn't want to go wherever the loud guy wanted her and the kid to go. Cord said nothing to Onyx as he went to stand between the woman, as she slowly retreated, and the man he dubbed the 'Asshole'.

Cord, glanced at the cab as it drove off. *Why can't you mind your own damn business, Cord?* Those harsh words in his mother's angry tone reverberated in his head but Cord ignored them. He planted himself between the woman and the Asshole but stood back enough to see both of them. The woman looked at him with, fear, confusion, then relief. The 'Asshole' grimaced.

"Who the fuck are you?"

Cord focused his intimidating gaze on Asshole but ignored the question and asked his own. "You leaving with him?" Cord questioned the woman.

"No." Her voice was small but surprisingly sweet. Cord frowned because he wanted to look at her face, to see her entirely and not just hear the echo of her enchanting voice, but he had to keep his attention on the threat.

"Then you're leaving him?" He asked, making sure she understood what he wanted from her. She must have understood because she lifted her shoulders and stood taller.

"Yes," she answered with conviction.

That was all Cord needed. He continued to watch the Asshole but said, "Go stand by Onyx. Onyx,"—his dog barked, "protect." Cord pointed at the woman and the child she held. He didn't have to look back to know that his dog got to her feet and now stood in front of the pair, ready to attack friend or foe to follow his orders.

"You should leave," he said to Asshole.

"Fuck you," Asshole sneered, "you leave." The guy looked past Cord and focused his attention on the woman. "You know this piece of shit, Winter? You've been cheating on me...you icy whore?"

Winter? Odd name but he liked it.

Cord glanced over his shoulder and noticed the way she recoiled at the 'icy' remark. Before she could answer, Cord closed the distance between him and the Prick—because yeah, his asshole status has been upgraded. "You should leave now. One: because she's not going with you so you're wasting *my* time. Two: if you make a move to force her, it won't be the last thing you do," he leaned in closer so only the prick could hear him, "but it will be the last pain-free thing you do for the rest of your life."

Prick-the-Asshole stared at Cord for several heartbeats as he flexed his fist and rolled his shoulders. Cord wasn't impressed. Prick-the-Asshole pivoted, kicked one of the suitcases, then gave Cord a scathing look. Cord squared off his shoulders and widened his feet, just in case the prick decided to go against his good advice.

The guy broke eye contact with Cord and pierced the woman with a hard look then slammed the back door of his vehicle shut. He then slowly walked around the front of the sedan, all the while staring her down, and got inside the driver's seat.

Cord grabbed the luggage before the prick could run it over and laughed to himself as the sedan fishtailed as it sped out of the parking lot. He gathered all three pieces of luggage and carried them over to where the woman stood.

When he saw her, really saw her, Cord almost stopped in his tracks. *Winter*, he let her name settle in his head, *is beautiful*. Her coiled curly brown hair with honey blonde tips accentuated her smooth brown complexion. She had an oval face, almond-shaped eyes, her nose was button-cute, and her beautiful kissable lips were shaped like a bow. A beautiful bow on a tiny curvaceous gift who was named Winter.

SHEA SWAIN

About the Author

Shea is a woman in love with the idea of love so it's no wonder she writes Romance Novels. The East Coast native is a romantic to her core and reads and watches anything with a love story. She especially likes binging on the Hallmark Channel around Christmas time.

She enjoys meeting people and chatting, collecting Barbie dolls, toys, and is addicted to The Sims games. Shea also loves music and has mentioned that she writes better when she has movie scores playing as white noise in the background.

This new and exciting author writes Adult Romance in the sub-genres of Contemporary, New Adult, Paranormal, Sci-Fi, and Erotica. Come…Taste A Sample.

Connect with Shea Swain

Website: www.Sheaswainwrites.com
Email: Sheaswainwrites@gmail.com

Coesen Definitions
Words in italics are defined

Coesen: In the *Ilterian* language, the word *Coesen* means the combination of two or more items, particles, or organisms. The Four Originals adopted the term for their classification that defines them as a race of human-hybrids who originated from a single tribe on the continent of Africa. Most are born with birthmarks behind their left ear. Each tribe has a variation of this mark that they are born with. Some *Coesen* are born with an ability. It is present at birth but doesn't manifest until the age of puberty. Most are born with a single ability. A very small percentage are born with two.

Breed: The child of a Coesen and *Middling* coupling. Most of these children do not carry the birthmark of a full blooded Coesen. The law on the books state that Coesen parent and Breed are to be sentenced to death, the human parent's mind is wiped cleaned. 98% of Breed children are born with no abilities but may still carry the birthmark. If they mate a Coesen, their children may or may not have abilities.

Child of Jai or Pet: Jai of the *Arkean* tribe conceived a Breed with a man named Shaw. Even after her descendants couple with only Coesens, each are born with the physical features of a Caucasian.

Middling: Term to define a human with no *Coesen* blood.

Protectors: A Coesen who is chosen by the *Source* and is infused with power during the *transition* stage to keep the Coesen's Ward safe. They sense when their ward is in danger and is able to locate them at all times. These Coesen are stronger and faster than any living entity on earth with exception of one person, *Caleb Scott*. In history only two Middlings have been chosen by the Source. It is believed that Middling aren't capable of surviving the transformation.

Transition: A Coesen abilities become active when they go through puberty. This process is called a Transition.

Transference: When a Coesen is chosen by the Source to be awarded the abilities to become a Protector.

The Halo: A Coesen whose prophecy states will bear a full halo birthmark and have all the abilities known to Coesen.

The Source: What the Coesen refer to the original source of power, *Lette*.

Royals: The bloodlines closely related to the Original Four. Only four generations are referred to as Royals.

Bodai: The Bodai were the original name and leaders of the nation that eventually become known as the Coesen.

Bresi: The Bresi was formed from the original Bodai who decided to opt out of the change when offered power by the *Original Four*. They isolated themselves for a very long time. Eventually they discover *Pythos*. They pray to his cocooned form as a deity.

Four Tribes: *Arkean, Bode, Gedgi, Quende*

CPA: Coesen Protection Agency, the overseeing security and policing branch for Coesen.

Tandot: A competition of strength, intelligence, and endurance, to win the right to mate a Royal. Only those who are considered perfect Coesen specimens are allowed to enter.

Old Age: The time of the gilded age when Coesen were obsessed with wealth, class, and breed. The rich were set apart as elites. Lineage and wealth dictated your place in society. It wasn't until compassion became fashionable that a new way of thinking was adopted and practiced by the Sovereign and most Coesen. Though, with change there is always the few who hold onto the ways of old.

Pula: Curse word, or derogatory name

Maatii: Three round challenge to become a Royal Guard. You cannot die in the dream-like state but you feel all the pain inflicted on you. The challenge is timed.

The Village: The object is to fight your way through a village full of super beings that do not eat, sleep, or feel pain, in order to reach a pearl like sphere that each member needs to touch at the same time.

The Vortex: The object is for each member to cross a wet, slippery metallic pole over a swirling vortex to reach the pearl like sphere that is floating in the center without falling.

The Pride: The object is to get pass the pride of gigantic lions and lioness to reach the pearl-like orb which is guarded by an even bigger, White Lion.

If you should fail these tasks, you must reapply and do trials over…or settle to be a Sentry Guard

Cycling: The process in with a Coesen has been transferred to. These Coesen endures a physical change over a three-day period.

Rotation: Every Protector must enlist in the *Coesen Guard* for a time period of the service. They can choose the branch. The three branches are, the *Royal* (highest), the *Sentry* (detective Branch), or *Guard* (police branch)

Augur: A Coesen who can see the prophecies.

Fasen: Burial ceremony. The body is washed and cleaned by someone close to the deceased. Close family is in attendance when the body is burned. A viewing is held after the body is returned to ashes to show and offer respect to the surviving family.

Soahn: Term for Royal

Potentate: Sovereign's Mate, King.

Rootstone: The power unit of all *Keystones*.

Keystone: An object that denies or allows access to a protected area.

Veilex: A stone that will react to an enemy of the wearer.

Dregan: Coesen who for whatever reason do not agree with Coesen law. Although they consider themselves separate they follow the most important rules which is why they are permitted to live in peace. The name was taken from a Coesen who broke the law a long time ago.

Sodregs: Dregans who care nothing for the laws and break them without care. They are hunted and tried by the *Guard*.

Dardregs: Dregans who practice the *Dark Arts*. They follow no law and most are minions of Dregan, a Coesen Protector from long ago who fell in love with his ward. He eventually killed several Coesen.

Meriotia: Bonding or marriage ceremony that lasts three days.

The first is a celebration or *Gathering*.

The second day is the *Mating and Blooding ritual/wedding*.

The third day is the *Showering* in which gifts and well wishes are given.

Ilterian: The race of *Lette's* people that hail from a planet far from earth.

Ika: A medicine man or woman of the village.

Oracle: The seer or witch that foresees the future.

Jzerect: Black magic, forbidden.

CARD: Stands for Coesen Ability Registration Department, a specialized section of the Royal Guards. Coesen are required to register all abilities to this agency. Information is kept private unless legal, safety, medical, or employment requires to know the information.

Utopian Circus: A circus run by Coesen with Coesen performers.

Inhibitor Chip: A piece of tech that prevents the wearer from using their abilities.

Purist: Coesen who believe the Breed are an abomination.

Kytel: Group who are against Breed and prefer pure bloodlines.

Veris: The only way the Council of Four can meet face to face without fear of being exterminated in one swift move. In a sleep like state, very similar to the Maatii, each of the Four are ushered to a common room in an astral plane by the head of the Four. While in this mental state their physical bodies are vulnerable so they are housed in a secured room watched over by their Protector.

Hasa: A Coesen title of respect, used for someone who is a paternal protector, or progenitor.

Royal Guard: The justice branch concerning royals. They also handle treats, security, and keep the peace. The Sentry

Guards report to them and they report to the Council of Four. They wear a brand, centered on the back of their right hand. A black circle surrounded by the beautifully scripted names of each tribe. A set of knives crossed at their hilts, starting at the wrist, while the blades encircled the script. The tips of the blades ended at the base of their middle finger.

Sentry Guard: The detective and policing branch of the Coesen. They investigate cases for their sector and manage the Coesen Guard. They report to the Royal Guards.

Coesen Guard: Policing branch of the Coesen who handle local cases. They report to the Sentry Guards.

Fading: The stage of becoming invisible before teleporting. The fade can be held as long as the necessary before actually teleporting.

Fader: Someone who can camouflage themselves into the objects around them to become invisible.

The Veris: The act of bringing the Four together on another plane of existence to meet and discuss business.

Monad: A single unit or entity. What the Coesen call the being inside Caleb.

Suma(s): Dry season or summer months.

Rising Sun: 1 day.

Abilities

There are different degrees of these power. The more powerful the Coesen the stronger the effects. Some of the abilities are rare. All abilities are not listed.

Siphon: Can recognize, search, draw the power and ability of another Coesen within range without causing the host harm or alarm. The stronger the Sipher, the longer the distance that they can siphon power. This is a very rare ability.

Empati: A Coesen who can sense power and get readings such as how clean your spirit is.

Engron: A Coesen who can accelerate the growth of living organisms or tissue.

Phantom: A Coesen who can enter your mind and make or produce images that seem real to the dreamer. The recipient will feel the effects as if what presented to them is reality.

Wheddler: A Coesen who can influence another with spoken words.

Time Weaver: A Coesen who can travel through to the past. They can witness events but they cannot interfere mostly because they have no form. People of the past will not be able to see or hear these Coesen. Over time only two Coesen were born with the ability to weave into the future. They both had the ability to be seen and heard, giving them the opportunity to change things.

Fyeah: A Coesen who can wield fire. Two types exist. Some can do it through touch and some can do it through thought.

Seer: A Coesen who can see the future.

Sooth or Truth Seer: A Coesen who can hear the ring of truth from words that are spoken.

Markers: A Coesen who can tattoo skin with only a touch.

Cleoma: A Coesen who can render a Coesen's ability void. This Coesen can make it so you cannot use your ability in their presence.

Toma: A Coesen who can see your inner most secrets, the things you even hide yourself. This is not like reading some one's thoughts, it's reading your desires and fears.

Feeler: A Coesen who senses someone's emotions and sometimes intent through objects they've come in contact with. Some Feelers are strong enough to sense the feeling in a room without touching an object.

Brander: A Coesen who can mark another with tattoo like art by touching a person's skin. The mark is permanent and can only be removed by the Brander or someone in that brander's bloodline.

Reader: A Coesen who can sense the abilities in others.

Scanner: A Coesen who can reach into someone's mind to find intent or goals. They can also see past offenses and evil they are guilty of.
Snare: The ability to wipe another's memories
Saik: This ability is similar to that of a Protector. One has speed, advanced hearing, and has great strength.
Senser: A Coesen who can make their target feel pain or pleasure. This ability can kill.

Places

West Hills High School: A school in Arizona.
Ridgeview Park: Local park near Cianne's home where she usually run for exercise.
Valley Estates: Residential middle-class neighborhood
Kennecott University: Educational institution
Dorchester Psychiatric Hospital: Bianca received her treatment
Northridge Hospital: Hospital where Tristan was discovered during the Cycling
John Hopkins Hospital: Real Hospital in Baltimore Maryland
Wingate University Hospital: Hospital where the twins were born.
Ark Manor: Vivian's Canadian Home
Azazel's Gift Shop: New Orleans
Gering Academy: School for Coesen Three locations, Texas, Europe, and Canada with a small location on the Continent of Africa
Hammonds Drugstore: Local old style pharmacy. Where Tranae works.
The Broken Nail Tavern: Bill's establishment and front for Watkins

The Man Cave: The bar and grill where Tristan goes while on the run

Koves Glenn: California USA. Koves choice in Coesen. Kove Glenn is a community that Vivian set up for Coesen who fall in love with Middlings. The middling must sign a gag order in blood once they are welcomed into community. They know of the power the Coesens wield and must keep it secret. The Coesen is stripped of their abilities. Any offspring must be registered but it is assumed that they will not have any abilities.

Shoppers Row: Shopping district located in Koves Glenn

The Ice Cave: Bar located in Norway.

The Promise

In Lette words

"***Arkean**, you hold the bulk of my legacy.*" Arkean heard Lette's voice in his head. One look at his friends told him that they heard the newcomer too. "*You will be more powerful than the others because of your selflessness and eagerness to aid something as alien as me with no prejudice. Your bloodline with reign and yours alone will bear the Halo, the only one of your kind who will be able to contain all of my power.*

"***Bode**, you are strong and loyal. Your bloodline will produce the harbinger who will see the answers you all seek but will offer only what you need to know.*

"***Quende**, your bloodline will capture and command that which all Ilterian's hold dear. Life, birth and rebirth…change and growth. Nurture the cycle because without it we are all lost.*

"***Gedgi**, are the most innocent of the group. You have seen much and still you have not let the worries of your world or the influences of life's harsh nature wither your soul. It is of* *that innocence and your spirit that you will bear the essence of Ilteria.*

The Warning of a Protector & Ward Mating: The first union between a Protector and Coesen ended with the death of the Coesen and two others. That Protector was cursed. The second union resulted in the death of the Coesen and the mass murder of almost an entire tribe

9 781735 726755